FEATHERS OF DAWN

Jess Galaxie

feathersofdawn.com

The characters in this book are entirely fictional.
Any resemblance to actual persons living or dead is entirely coincidental.

ISBN 979-8-9889118-0-7 (eBook Edition)
ISBN 979-8-9889118-2-1 (Paperback Edition)
ISBN 979-8-9889118-1-4 (Hardcover Edition)

Cover Illustrator: Kaylie Leon
Editor: Nina Nicole
Graphic Designer: Rachel Nugent
Sensitivity Reader: Emeric Davis

I care far more about your safety than your reading this book. Please take the time to consider whether you are in the right headspace to read Feathers of Dawn.

Acid Burns
Adoption
Animal Trafficking
Being a Captive of the Government
Being Experimented On
Being Abandoned
Being Set on Fire
Blood
Blood Magic
Cliffs
Close Family Death
Conversations About Slavery and Prison Labor
Drinking (socially)
Emotional Abuse
Fire
Flashbacks
Gore
Grief
Heights and Falling from Heights
Homophobia
Human Trafficking
Hypervigilance
Imprisonment
Interactions with Police / Authorities
Kidnapping (an Adult)
Lost Time
Monarchy
People in Cages
PTSD
Remorse
Rituals
Separation Trauma
Starvation
Talk of Arranged Marriages
Threats of Death
Threats of Violence

For more detailed descriptions visit <u>feathersofdawn.com</u>.

This book is dedicated to a lot of people, which has made this difficult for me to write, so I guess you all are getting a stream-of-consciousness list of things I want to say.

Thank you to my incredibly supportive friends and partner. I couldn't have done this without you all. Especially Nina, Rachel, and Deanna. I appreciate you all so much.

Thank you to my college rhetorical grammar professor who told me I should just go for the MFA in Creative Writing instead of Medieval Literature. I didn't get the MFA, but I feel like this has the same energy.

And finally, to all the people who have shouted about wanting more dragons in their fantasy—I hope you're happy.

Year 570 with Vitiope
6th of Laha

Asith stood in the quiet street, watching the sky as he tried to use the houses for cover. Delri was near the village square; he just had to get there. That wasn't the fight they had been expecting. An unusually large group of Greens and a Blue that had decided to tag along threw off their entire plan. The villagers had claimed it was just four Greens, but they had clearly been wrong.

He stepped around a house, peering onto the next street to see a Blue, the eyes on the side of its head black and shining as it swung its head back and forth. The tongue lashed across its teeth, mouth open and ready to spit acid at any unfortunate soul it came across. Asith gauged the distance he had to run to get to the next row of houses. They had stationed the mage between the street he was on and the square, so if the dragon followed him, he'd have some sort of backup.

His foot dug into the ground, his axe in one hand and his shield facing the dragon in case it tried to hit him with its breath. Asith counted, slowing his breathing, and then ran as fast as he could.

The dragon dug its claws into the dirt street and launched toward him. Its chest swelled, and it hissed, signaling Asith to raise his shield against the acid shot to come. On cue, globs of acidic bile hit the front of his shield with an awful plop. But he didn't lose his speed. He was one of the fastest on his team, so he could evade the dragon—at least that's what he told himself. If he could get to Delri and Hamon and the others, Asith would be okay.

A searing pain crawled across Asith's forearm. His stomach flipped as he threw down his axe and unbuckled his shield. The shield hit the ground with an unceremonious clang as he staggered and tried to gather up his axe. His gauntlets made it hard to grab anything lying on the hard packed dirt of the street, but he knew he'd be in far more trouble if he couldn't recover his axe.

The dragon flew toward him, tongue hanging over razor-like teeth and its black mouth open and ready to swallow Asith whole. Its lips pulled back, and its head tilted to see Asith better. The scales and spiked horns around its face showed scars of fights won before then, hunts that were successful, that allowed it to grow to that size.

He grabbed his axe but not soon enough to avoid the dragon's claws piercing his shoulder. The pain was enough to make his ears ring and his teeth sink into his tongue. He breathed through his teeth, desperately trying to calm down as the dragon lifted him from the ground. Asith knew what would happen next: The dragon would fly as high as it could and drop him. If he let that ascent go on for too long, he'd certainly be dead.

He swung his axe upward hopelessly, trying to hit the bend in the dragon's leg. A good hit with a great axe could easily remove the dragon's whole claw at once. He opened a wound in the dragon's leg, but he didn't have the leverage to take it off. Instead, blood that steamed like it was hitting cold air even in the summer sun poured over Asith's head like thick raindrops.

Asith drove his axe upward again, that time entirely missing the dragon's leg. When he did, his axe went flying, leaving him dangling from a screeching dragon that was rising higher in the air, above the houses. Soon, they'd be up higher than the temple to Viteus in the center of the city. He unsheathed his sword and tried again to cut the dragon's leg away, but his sword didn't have the reach that his axe did. Asith flailed, his heart pounding in his ears as he tried again.

As they rose higher than the metal sun that sat on top of the temple spire, something exploded next to the dragon's face. It screamed as it tried to correct its flight. Just beyond the dragon's flailing wings, Eroan stood on the ground with his arm stretched out toward them, his hands moving as he mouthed another spell. The dragon let Asith go, and he plummeted.

Asith tightened his grip on his sword, readying himself to hit the ground because he might not survive otherwise. He shook with fear as he watched the clouds above him cover the sun for the first time since the fight had started. Closing his eyes, he waited for the inevitable.

Then a warmth spread over his body, starting in his head and shooting up his spine. The magic thrummed in his body like lightning traveling through a metal rod, which slowed Asith's fall and saved him from certain death. His eyes shot open and searched for Eroan, but he had already moved on. Asith slowly descended until he floated softly to the ground, covered in blood, both his own and the dragon's, his sword in his hand and his axe nearby.

Asith got up and scanned the area for Delri, or anyone, his hands gripping his sword tightly enough that his knuckles blanched. When he turned himself to look at the town square in front of him, the Blue dragon turned its head down to reveal its horns. It flew, dust and dirt kicking up and stinging Asith's eyes.

Hamon, his face covered in sweat and dirt, ran toward Asith, holding only his glaive. He couldn't see the dragon.

Asith shouted as loudly as he could and Hamon turned, but it was far too late.

Asith sat up with a wince and tried to stretch his back, but a sharp pain pinched his shoulder blade. Grimacing, he hunched his shoulders awkwardly so that the pain would stop and rubbed the bandages covering his wound. Asith craved sleep, but the second sun had risen, making it far too bright to get rest. His fingers trailed down his arm, the damp bandages a reminder of the injury that had trapped him in bed. The doctors said it would heal, but he wasn't sure he believed them.

"Don't move it." Delri rolled over to face him, her hand finding Asith's chest and gently encouraging him to lie back down. "That won't help."

"I know." Asith stopped moving his arm, instead setting his hand on Delri's. She sat up, her thin nightshirt pulling until her shoulder was bare, her hair tied in a braid that stuck to her neck. It was warm with the two of them in the same bed. Although the heat of the summer had crept up on them without either of them realizing, one of them still crawled into the other's bed every night.

"Did you have a bad dream?" Delri moved to set her cheek on Asith's shoulder. The sun lit up her dark skin, making the tops of her cheekbones glow. Her brown eyes, partially obscured by thick lashes, still hung heavy, like she wanted to go back to sleep. Asith couldn't blame her for that. Just two days before, their team had barely managed to push five dragons back.

"I did." Asith rubbed his head and leaned into Delri in return, her hand smoothing over his chest to his shoulder. "But it's hard to sleep because of this."

He gestured to his shoulder, and she sighed, nodding. Delri pulled away to look up at Asith, her eyes wide since she had woken up more. Her hand lingered on his chest, a fear settling into her face as her brow furrowed and she worried her lip.

"Are you thinking of leaving?" Delri asked.

There was no higher honor than becoming a dragon knight; they both knew that. Dragon knights were the protectors of the small, otherwise forgotten, towns at the far edges of Cairn where Blue and Green dragons frequently hunted. The townspeople would hold feasts and festivals, picking up what little was left of their town and inviting the people who saved it to drink from their stores of wine and ale. Towns saved by dragon knights came back stronger, rising from the ashes with a restored faith in Cairn's ability to protect them from dragons.

"You've already decided, haven't you?" Delri took a deep breath. "You're leaving."

"I am." Asith's voice cracked, tears coming to his eyes. He looked down at his left hand; it would be difficult to sew without it, and that was the only other way he had to make money. "I just can't stop thinking about Hamon, how his mother will look. How my mother would look."

The problem with the celebrations after a dragon attack was that not many dragon knights survived long enough to enjoy it. Even when Asith wasn't hurt, there was someone to mourn, and the knowledge that he would be doing that again in a few days weighed heavily on his shoulders. The villagers got to have a rebirth, but he only saw the loss of his friends in the smiling faces of the people he saved.

He and Delri were both at an age where leaving would be normal. They were both a year older than the age when most dragon knights retired.

Tears sprung to Delri's eyes, her mouth hanging open as a single sob rocked her shoulders. "I understand."

Asith wiped the tears from his face, letting himself cry for a few moments before he reached over to cup Delri's cheek. She didn't look at him directly, but she moved to wrap her arms around his shoulders, careful of the one that was bandaged. She settled between his legs, leaning on his chest. It hurt, probably for both of them, but it was better than not holding on to each other.

"Will you leave too? If I did?" He didn't want to leave her alone.

"I don't know." Delri draped an arm around his middle and set her head in the crook of Asith's neck, having to bend since they were about the same height. "Maybe I will go to Martivin for a while to heal, and then I will decide."

"If you come back," Asith said, "please at least ask that they don't assign you Kosor. He's the worst."

Delri's hardened expression slowly cracked into a smile, tears still streaming down her face. She laughed. "He is. He is the absolute worst."

Asith smiled, setting a hand on the back of Delri's head to smooth down her hair because he knew she liked the feeling. She wiped at her face, her smooth skin shimmering a little. He let her cry, cherishing that rare moment to breathe while injured, and that was as good a use of it as any other.

"I think I want to keep doing this." Delri looked up at Asith, the tears mostly gone, but sadness had settled itself into her skin. "I am not sure I can do it without you."

"I'm sorry." Asith held her tighter, settling his cheek on her head.

"It's okay." Delri swallowed audibly and moved to pick up a waterskin from the table next to the bed. "I think I will take some time away and think about it. Maybe I can train newbies and spend less time out in the field."

Asith smiled, thinking about the years they'd spent training together before they became dragon knights. Two of only sixteen that year, and the class had dwindled down to seven. After losing Hamon, they were at six, and with Asith leaving, that left them at five.

"We all knew it would happen eventually." Delri dropped the waterskin back on the table after taking a drink. "Thank you for being here."

"Of course," Asith said, "you're my best friend."

"You're such a sap." Delri smiled. "What will you do?"

"Go home to my mother." Asith looked at the window, settling a hand on his knee, still encircling Delri but not as tightly. "Maybe I will finally try to find my father."

"Your father is alive?" Delri sat back on her butt, moving her legs to either side of Asith's hips so that she could stretch them out while staying between Asith's legs.

Asith shrugged. "I don't know. My mother hasn't told me much, but from what I can tell, she seems to think he is."

Delri hummed and hunched her shoulders in to round her back and stretch it. It popped loudly, like snapping a stick that had dried during a drought.

"Do you think it's a bad idea?" Asith asked.

"No." Delri sighed again and stretched her arms above her head, her ribs visibly expanding under her shirt as she breathed into the movement. "I'm just surprised."

"Why?" Asith tilted his head. It made his shoulder hurt, but he tried to ignore it.

"I never thought you cared about who your dad was." Delri dropped her hands and leaned back on them, a smirk on her lips. "Because you're such a momma's boy."

Asith rolled his eyes. "If I wasn't such a sap, I'd kick you out of bed."

"I'm your best friend." Delri laughed.

"Unfortunately."

CHAPTER 1

Year 573 with Vitiope
7th of Penur

Asith had been sewing in the light of the small window in his home when it first appeared, sitting with a leather pauldron strap in his hands. He had made over a thousand since leaving the knights, and he would make thousands more in his life if he didn't find anything better to do. Asith paid the shape no mind as he finished the stitching. It looked to be a bird, so he tossed the finished strap to the side as he picked up the next piece of leather he'd cut. That was the sort of thing he did with his days, hammering careful holes in leather straps and bindings, which he then threaded a curved needle and waxed thread through, leather thimbles on his fingers so he didn't tear his skin while doing it.

When he had placed the first stitch and tied it off, the bird had grown to four times its size. He could make out the tail trailing behind it, broad wings shifting ever so slightly as it glided toward South Cairn. He set his needle down on his table without looking away from the window. Asith's eyes followed the dragon through the sky, taking in its four horns and broad bronze scales. It settled in the northwestern wheat field of South Cairn as the second sun rose to its peak in the sky. The dragon's teeth opened, with smoke streaming around its gums, the gray curls wrapping around its head and forehorns. It surveyed the town it threatened.

The farmers feared the worst, for their small and few worldly possessions could never live up to the expectations of a dragon. They were certain the fields would be scorched, and South Cairn would suffer for it, so they came to Asith. It had been over 850 days since Asith had last fought a dragon; he couldn't help counting even though it mattered to no one other than himself. He would still be asked to help fight.

South Cairn was humble and small. Asith had traveled to the Capitol and returned a dragon knight, but he had been the first in years to do so. His armor was made of the green scales of a beast he had slain during his training and mended with the scales of the dragons he fought with the legions of dragon knights. While it was his duty to protect the village from such dangerous pests, he wasn't sure how well he could do on his own.

He was used to working on a team with a mage to distract the dragons with explosives and other dragon knights to surround it. As he stood in his home, tying his grieves over his boots, his mind found many memories of friends being shredded by a dragon's claw or swallowed in two bites.

He shook those thoughts away; Asith didn't need to think about that right then. While he tied his second grieve, his mother entered his home without knocking. As she took one look at him, her shoulders sunk, but she picked up her skirt and readied his armor, wordlessly working alongside Asith.

Asith finished tying his second grieve before staring blankly at the journal on his desk. He'd only written a few pages, notes he'd made about his father based on what his mother had said. She hadn't told Asith much, but he'd started collecting what he could, trying to remember what she'd said in his childhood. In that moment, however, he was certain all of it would go to waste once the dragon killed him; he just hoped his mother wouldn't be upset with him for wanting to look for his father.

"Here." His mother set her hand on his shoulder and plucked her thimble from her pocket, the scissors hanging on her apron quivering as she did. "My lucky thimble. It's small, but it can still protect. Just like you."

"Thank you." Asith took the thimble and tucked it into his pocket. He watched her mouth wobble, her green eyes welling with tears as she turned her head down. "I'll come back, Mama. I promise."

"I know." His mother sobbed and wiped the tears from her face. "If you don't, I'll kill you again myself, like I always told you."

Asith's throat tightened, and she wrapped her arms around his shoulders, hugging him as tightly as she could with his scale shirt on. Her fingers trembled against his back. He tried to think of something better to say, a way to comfort her, but he couldn't.

When she pulled away, she sniffed and rubbed her eyes, trying to smile, but she failed. Her mouth pressed into a hard line for a moment, and then it went back to a frown. Asith averted his eyes to avoid seeing the tears because he couldn't handle them. She had spent years caring for Asith. With her two hands, she had held him through every sorrow and pain in his life, but when she was the one in pain, he couldn't even look at her.

His mother's hands continued to shake as she picked up Asith's breastplate so that he could fasten the leather belts at the shoulders. She then helped him with the back. His mother had completely pulled herself together by then.

Asith tied back his hair, then placed his helm on his head and took his axe, a sword sheathed at his side. He walked with the strength of the village that raised him and the confidence of the training he had brought back from the Capitol.

"Be careful," she said. "Don't do anything unnecessary."

"I'll be careful." Asith turned to face his mother, who stood in the doorway of his small house. Her face looked unusually pale, the smattering of freckles over her nose even looking lighter. As she set her hand on the doorframe, getting ready to close it as Asith had asked her to, her reddish hair fell over her shoulder, a little bit messy as it always was. It was funny, just how young she looked to Asith at that moment. Something about the fear made her seem just like every young mother he had seen in his years as a dragon knight, despite the fine lines at the corners and under her eyes.

Quiet voices chattered as he walked through the town. Most people had hidden in their homes or underground in the holds, but some opened the windows or doors a sliver to send Asith well-wishes. Others leaned out of their homes to throw dried yarrow flowers at his feet, something that was often done for teenagers as they left for the Capitol for the first time. It inspired confidence and reminded them of the security of returning home. All the citizens of South Cairn always had dried yarrow on hand, and they were giving much of it to Asith.

Asith had been alone in many towns, walking without a soul nearby, but never quite like that. Normally, he had the knowledge that Delri or Hamon would come to him if he needed help. Eroan, the squad mage, would hide amongst the houses, quiet, nodding at the dragon knights as they walked by before turning invisible again. That day, however, he was completely alone, on a road he had never seen empty. Usually, people were everywhere, holding armfuls of grains or fabric as they went about their day. South Cairn was a trade city, sitting at the southernmost tip of the country. People wound up there for all sorts of reasons and settled down. People that would smile at Asith, some with dark skin and some pale like his own, many of them with elven or gilliedhu or dwarf ancestry. They grew up with him, helped him with chores, taught him in school. Asith needed to protect them, because if he didn't, he wasn't sure he could live with himself.

Although, he likely wouldn't have to live with himself.

He kept his axe in hand, his head up as he confronted the dragon sitting patiently in the field, and while he could fight the beast, he feared the state of his village after the battle. Asith had a challenge in front of him he had not been trained for, per se, but at least he could find an outcome that would protect his mother and the villagers who raised him.

Sitting on its back legs, the dragon was still taller than many of the mature elm trees that surrounded the town. Its massive head followed Asith as he walked out among the wheat. Aside from its nostrils flaring and then soothing, it hardly moved otherwise. The colossal wings settled against its sides, and its claws pressed into the dirt. Asith made sure to stay out of reach of the dragon's tail, for it could do much harm in a split second.

"A dragon knight." The voice of the dragon was large and gnarled like an old tree. Its wings fluffed, and its long neck stretched a touch. "Are you going to slay me?"

Asith stopped just out of reach of the dragon, his head up and focused on the dragon's glimmering golden eyes. He set his jaw, ready to move if he needed. He had to appear in control.

"I am here to ask you to leave." Asith tightened his grip on his axe. "The village is small. These people are humble. We have nothing here that will match your hoard."

The dragon did something Asith could only call humming, its big head moving backward in a motion that looked like a nod. "You do not wish to slay me? You carry an axe long enough to reach me."

"My axe is for dragons who destroy towns and cities, killing everything in their sight. This village fears their crops being burnt." Asith let his eyes move to the dragon's horns. "And as I said, they have nothing of worth to add to your collection. I am here to ask you to leave without bloodshed."

"Ah, you are very clever, dragon knight." The dragon shifted its feet, wings stretching out like it might take off. Asith readied himself in case the dragon wanted a fight. "But I think you are wrong. There is something in this village worthy of my hoard."

Asith moved one foot back, his axe outstretched toward the dragon. "What do you see here of value? There is wheat, and there are wood homes."

The dragon let out a full-bellied laugh, its head tilting back as the wings flapped. Its voice held amusement as it said simply, "You."

"What?" Asith dropped his axe. For a moment, Hamon's face appeared in front of him, growing pale as a dragon's horn went clean through his middle.

The dragon's claw wrapped around Asith's arm and then tossed him just enough to grab Asith's around the middle. "Put me down! What are you doing?"

He kicked his legs, trying to force the dragon's claw open. It had to let him go, or it would drop him like the last one. His heartbeat kicked up, and he tried to slam his gauntlets into the fleshy part of the dragon's claw, to no avail. He was like a toddler who had been picked up by their parent to be taken home.

"You are going to be part of my hoard."

The dragon's wings propelled them upward at a speed that Asith wished he had never experienced in his life. It was nothing like being carried by a Blue, and as the dragon brought him higher and higher, Asith realized he could do nothing. Even if he had his axe, he could not risk attacking. Eroan was not there to back him up, Asith would fall to his death, and the dragon could rampage as it wished.

Defense was his best option, for he still had his sword. Therefore, he could likely fight in the dragon's lair. He had never done it, but he set his hand on the hilt of his sword, readying himself for when they touched the ground. As the dragon continued to climb, Asith's lungs burned, and his body shivered in the cold. He just hoped he didn't die before the dragon got him back to its hideout.

The dragon bent its neck to look at Asith with huge golden eyes. Once Asith had started to shake more violently, the dragon lowered, flying closer to the mountains. Asith could breathe better, but his armor wasn't warm. It was as though he had walked out of a hot spring naked and directly into the snow.

However, the dragon had to climb to fly over the mountaintop, the air leaving Asith's lungs. Asith lost his grip on his sword as he tried his hardest to stay awake, but his vision faded. The grip of the blackness took him, his body going limp with the dragon's claws pressing into him harder. Thankfully his armor could prevent them from sinking into his skin the way a Blue's claws had once before.

When he woke, he was still shivering, the stone floor beneath him cold to the touch, though walls surrounded him. The ceiling rose in a dome, peaking in the very center of the round room, where a golden chandelier swung gently. Asith could only guess, but the walls must have been twenty or thirty feet tall, the same stone as the floor. He couldn't tell if it was natural or not.

He didn't have time to survey the room just yet, for a young person approached him from behind with a heap of clothes in their arms.

"Good, you're alive," they said. "I was worried you were dead. Here, these clothes should fit you."

Asith blinked at the person. A headache had settled against the back of his eyes, blurring his vision, but they looked to be about Asith's age, having delicate brown skin with shimmering bronze undertones and a pair of honey-golden eyes. He couldn't immediately place their gender, so his guess was that they maybe did not ascribe to one. He would have to ask before addressing them. They held the clothes out to Asith, shaking them a bit.

"Are you also being held by the dragon?" Asith asked. He couldn't imagine what that person was doing up here otherwise. Unless they had allied with the dragon, which didn't seem likely, either. But he took the clothes, struggling to sit up as he did. They looked much warmer than his armor.

"You are easily fooled for a dragon knight. I didn't even try to hide my horns," they said, crossing their arms. Asith had only begun to take in the ink-black hair that hung over one of their shoulders in a thick braid. When he looked at their face again, Asith realized he hadn't even seen the brownish horns on their head. Hard and curved toward their back, they looked like the forehorns of the dragon who had picked him up.

"You can turn yourself into a human?" Asith had heard of it before, but it was a rare occurrence for a dragon to disguise itself as a human. Then again, a dragon taking a human to be a part of its hoard seemed a rather strange occurrence as well. Kidnapping never came up in any of the books he read about dragons at the Stonegarde. From what Asith knew, that dragon was certainly strange in its ways.

"Yes. I am a Bronze, after all. We have the strongest magic of any drag-on. Did you not learn that in training?" The dragon had a boyish grin on its face, its smile turned up on one side and its posture straight with its shoulders back. They puffed their chest like a smug young student.

What little they knew of Bronze dragons at the Stongarde was their curiosity. They were known for hoarding books and tools of science, any-thing they could use to learn. They were scholars, according to the books he'd read. When Asith looked at their human disguise, all that was there were unkempt bangs and a giddy grin.

"They did," Asith said quietly. "I do not understand, though. Why did you take me if you could just study humans when you look like that?"

Asith hadn't imagined a dragon could be like that. He had always pic-tured dragons of that nature being ethereal, wise, and uninterested in humans. Living up in hoards and only coming down when they wanted something new to add to their collection. Instead, the dragon before him crossed its arms like a teacher's pet who had just been told they were right by the teacher in front of a classroom.

The dragon laughed, still in its disguise as it crouched down to reach Asith's eye level. It set its head in its hand, leaned on one knee, and smirked at Asith. Despite its human-looking face, Asith noticed its teeth looked sharper than a human's, and its eyes might have been less unsettling if they at least shone blue-green like a cat's eyes in the dark. Instead, its eyes had a glass-like shine, glowing unnaturally in the low light.

"I have studied humans plenty. And as I told you, you were the only thing of value in that town. I took you to make you part of my hoard. You are still shivering. Change before you freeze to death."

Asith swallowed hard, trying to avoid looking at the dragon's teeth. He scanned the room and realized the unorganized pile of objects it stored consisted of golden items from all over the world. It was as if most of it had been tossed there because it was unwanted. There was, however, a golden partition, which was where the dragon must have wanted him to change.

He stood slowly because it was all he could muster. His feet seemed to have grown roots that he had to tear out of the ground with each step, and the headache behind his eyes only grew worse. The flight had taken more out of him than he had realized.

The dragon's eyes following his every move unnerved him, but Asith ultimately slipped behind the partition, then relaxed for a moment since the dragon's eyes weren't on him. His sword was gone, he noted, as he doffed his armor and carefully laid it out. He shivered in only his tunic and leggings, so he focused on getting the warm clothes on his body. The thick pair of pants had clearly come from somewhere near the Northern mountains, since they were lined with the soft down of snowbirds. Asith had a feeling they were currently in the Northern mountains. At the very least, it was his best guess. The doublet matched the pants, both patterned with small triangles along the hem, and while the body of the doublet was a warm maroon color, the sleeves shared the same tan color as the pants.

Those clothes looked nothing like what the dragon wore in its human disguise. Its clothes were light and reminded Asith of something the people from the Southern desert wore.

He walked back around, with a thick pair of leather boots and a scarf of some sort that didn't match the other clothes. Asith jumped back behind the partition upon realizing the dragon looked like a dragon again. Peering from behind the edge, Asith saw the dragon's eyes were following him, and its tongue was darting out of its mouth and licking its chops like a hungry dog. He forced himself to step out. Looking at the dragon's claws made his shoulder ache, so he tried to look at its wings instead.

"Those clothes suit you much better," the dragon said.

"Where is my sword?" Asith glowered at the dragon, who closed its mouth, its lips pressing into a hard line. For a moment, Asith could hear its teeth grind together. He managed not to turn and run, just barely. His legs and arms buzzed like that whenever he fought with the knights, ready to run at the sound of wings or hissing. Its tail lashed to the side and wrapped around its claws. Asith hadn't realized it was almost long enough to reach him where he stood; he would not be making that mistake again.

"I swallowed it." The dragon looked down at its claws, uncaring and cold, and moved its feet on top of its tail.

"What?" Asith's stomach boiled. To have dropped his axe was one thing, but for the dragon to swallow his sword was an insult. The sword was all he had of his lineage on his father's side. His mother had given it to him before he'd left for the Capitol to become a dragon knight. She said it should be passed from father to son, that his father had gotten it from Asith's grandfather, two people who Asith had never even had the chance to know. Two people he'd wanted to know so badly he'd spent the last several years researching everyone who lived in his mother's hometown behind her back. It was the only thing he had ever kept from her.

"Calm down, I am kidding." The dragon dropped its shoulders and tilted its head at Asith. "I disarmed you and hid the weapon. I wouldn't suggest trying to get it."

Relief washed over Asith, but he couldn't help the way he snarled. "You can't keep me here. You know that, right?"

The dragon slanted its head to the other side, its back horns nearly scraping the wall behind it. "Why is that?"

"I am a person. You can't collect people." Asith crossed his arms. If he could treat the dragon like a badly behaving child until it listened to him, maybe he could go home. It just seemed to annoy the dragon, though, for its neck extended a little and its snout turned up.

"The people beyond the Eastern mountains collect people," the dragon said with all the confidence of a scholar who had studied that topic for years. Asith gaped; he hadn't really thought of it that way. The dragon walked on its four claws toward an archway that led to another cavern. It somehow tucked its wings in and swept right through, despite the small entrance.

"In Wacot? That's prison labor. It's illegal, and they're both wrong. It's not something you should strive to replicate." Asith found himself following the dragon as it made its way into the other chamber. Despite Asith's gut telling him not to get closer, he didn't know what else he could do, so he followed at a distance that would keep him out of reach of the dragon's tail. A short, narrow tunnel led into an even larger room with an opening at the very top of the high ceiling. It looked just large enough for the dragon to slip through if it needed to escape that way. There was some sort of cover on it, though, because Asith could not see the sky through it.

"Well, I am not taking you as my prisoner." The dragon looked back at Asith before stopping near an enormous pile of soft pillows, all of which had various arrays of purples and reds in the fabric. "So, the country should have no issue."

Asith frowned. That room was clearly the dragon's actual hoard, books stacked in random piles alongside lots of strange items that didn't seem to fit together to make a collection. Clothes and blankets were folded and piled in one corner. Then various pieces of furniture, all of which looked expensive, were scattered around the room, with an occasional wooden table covered in scrolls and papers. A collection of ink and paper also sat on one table, along with some fine-looking feather pens, but there were significantly fewer of those than anything else.

The dragon stretched its wings out as it settled on the pile of pillows. It fit with quite a bit of room to spare.

"I have an issue," Asith said. "I don't want to stay here."

The dragon huffed angrily. "Why not? You have not even been here and conscious for very long."

"Because I have a home. Wouldn't you be upset if someone took you away from here against your will?" Asith wasn't sure the dragon was going to understand. It didn't seem interested in harming him immediately, which at least bought Asith time. At least he hoped. Every time the dragon opened its mouth to yawn or licked its lips, Asith quivered.

"My home is wherever my hoard is." The dragon stuck their nose in the air again, crossed its front legs, and shrugged. "If someone took me away, I would simply make a new hoard there."

"My home is where my people are, just like yours is where your hoard is. I can't just replace people." Asith walked around to look the dragon in the face better because it avoided making eye contact with him. "You have to understand that, at least."

"Would it make you feel better if I continued to pretend to be a human?" In a plume of smoke, it turned back into a human. Its eyes still glowing and glassy, the dragon was less threatening like that but not any less unnerving to Asith. He could not escape the unnatural sharpness of its teeth as it spoke or snarled at him.

Asith rubbed his temples. "No. It would not."

He didn't want to deal with the dragon further. Asith could scale down the mountains on his own, so he walked back into the cavern with the golden items and observed the two openings on either end of the stone walls. He checked to make sure the dragon hadn't followed him, and then Asith snuck over to look out.

To his dismay, both openings had a small rocky balcony that turned into a sheer cliff. It looked to be a few hundred feet down before he could reach another ledge. Asith staggered back, nearly falling over after he checked the second entrance. His legs had grown roots again, and the pain in his head had spread across his temples and up to the crown of his skull. There was no way he could climb down that night.

Asith also knew his limits; he was hurt, and he wasn't an experienced mountaineer. He needed rope, and a lot of it. The dragon probably didn't have any, or it wouldn't give Asith any. He poked around the golden items a bit, looking for anything of use, but the most useful thing in the pile was his own armor. The dragon strode into the room, still looking like a human with its arms crossed and its face in a pout.

"What is your name?" It swung its hand out like it was slapping the air, demanding Asith's attention. Asith couldn't turn toward it. Something about seeing it angry even in that form brought up images of a lashing tongue and the sound of hissing before acid shot from a Blue dragon's maw. It stared as Asith pulled an ugly golden pillow from the pile and settled himself down on the ground and laid his head on it. Just touching the floor made him shiver and curl up more to conserve heat.

"Asith, Asith Evrouin," he said. The dragon watched him for a moment, brushing its braid back over its shoulder and scoffing.

"Are you not going to ask mine?" The dragon looked at him like an obstinate child, and if Asith didn't know better, he thought it might start stamping its feet like one.

"I assumed like anything with such an ego, you would just tell me without my prompting." Asith shivered as soon as he said it, his stomach turning like he might throw up from the fear. Why was he antagonizing a dragon larger than any he had ever seen?

The dragon puffed up for a moment, the anger washing over it in a wave. Its presence loomed over him as though it were right next to him. Asith braced himself, squeezing his eyes shut and thinking of his mother. She would never know how stupid he had been, but Asith failed her entirely.

"Dradevai." The dragon unfolded its arms and squeezed its hands into fists. "If you sleep out here, you will freeze."

"Goodnight." Asith didn't open his eyes. He feared saying much else could push the dragon over the edge. It was not lost on him that Dradevai could easily throw him over one of the cliffs, and it wouldn't even need to get its hands dirty. He shivered there, on the ground, unsure if it was from the cold or the fear.

Eventually, he heard the dragon leave, and Asith finally let himself breathe. He moved a little, trying to warm himself up. As he shifted, something hard pressed against his thigh like a pebble on the floor, but when he checked, nothing was there. He checked his pocket and found his mother's lucky thimble. Asith ran his thumb over the pockmarks that had been carefully hammered into place, feeling the seam on the back where the blacksmith had sealed it. Elin's father, Roland, had given it to his mother. Roland had made it, along with a new pair of scissors for his mother, in exchange for a dress for his wife, Tiffany.

Asith had a lump in his throat, and he took a deep breath of cold air. It made his lungs burn as he cried on the stone floor, burying his face in the ugly pillow. He pressed the cold metal against the bridge of his nose, thinking of the way his mother would kiss him there every night before putting him to bed when he was just a child. Asith needed to live so he wouldn't break his promise and he could meet his father—he would find him. The tears froze on his eyelashes, making it hard for him to open them, and when he tried to rub them away, everything stung.

When he had left the dragon knights, Asith thought he could live out the rest of his life in South Cairn, where he could never think about drag-ons again. Maybe he would travel to meet his father or retire to the Zotia coast with Delri as they'd always joked. He didn't know what he did to deserve that treatment. Dying on the cold floor of the hoard of a dragon seemed like a cruel punishment.

Maybe that was Dradevai's goal. Revenge for each of the dragons Asith had killed, one hour of a freezing death for each.

He heard his mother's voice asking him to be careful over and over and over again, and Asith couldn't take it anymore. If he didn't move or get a fire going, he would likely die. If he stayed on the ground with only the pillow, which crunched and crinkled each time he moved, he would die. He weighed his options, but he didn't have time to come up with a solution because Dradevai came back.

Though, it was only Dradevai's head, its neck long enough to reach through the small cave that led to the other room. Asith stayed still, only to feel Dradevai's teeth on his back. His eyes shot open and he tried to jump away, but it had already caught him. He sobbed openly as the dragon held him. That was it. The dragon would eat him or gore him with its horns, and that would be the end of trying to keep his promise to his mother.

The dragon picked him up, the cold leaving Asith useless, and carried him back into the other room, where he was unceremoniously dropped on the pile of pillows. A pillow and three blankets fell on top of him, the dragon's eyes in a sneer as it settled its tail across the entrance to the other chamber.

"Don't be stubborn." The dragon hissed. Asith pushed himself away from it as well as he could, but his limbs were like hardened branches from the cold and the pillows were too soft. They would simply bend or flop under his flailing.

"Stop." The dragon pressed a claw onto Asith's chest. Paralyzed, Asith stopped moving entirely. As he did, he realized the pillows he had been set on were warm, as if they'd been enchanted to stay that way. And the blankets were heavy and delightfully soft.

To his surprise, there was no claw on him, though the dragon's foot was very much on his chest. It wasn't putting any weight on him, just held him still. He tried to breathe, but his lungs wouldn't take in air. His whole body froze, including his diaphragm. When the dragon moved its foot, Asith looked up at Dradevai. What he'd thought were leathery scales along the dragon's limbs were dense collections of feathers that shined slightly.

Asith lay there, silently, remembering his mother's face before leaving. He thought of Delri instead, but his mother would have to tell her of his death if he didn't survive. His gut sank into his feet. He had to survive; he didn't want his mother to tell Delri he confronted a Bronze on his own.

He looked toward Dradevai, only able to see their eyes in the cave's darkness. If he went back into the other room, he'd freeze to death. Staying there in the pillows with the dragon was his best chance to keep his promise to his mother. Asith pulled the blanket over his head so that he would not have to look at Dradevai's teeth and sank into the pillow. He was not sure he would sleep, but at least he would not freeze to death.

CHAPTER 2

8th of Penur

He still had his mother's thimble on his thumb, small dots in his palm from where it had been resting in his sleep. Asith ran his fingers over the indentations and then the thimble. When he took the blanket off his head, he saw that he was alone in the pillows. Keeping his promise seemed easy in that moment alone, no dragon with horribly sharp teeth or heavy claws to stop him.

Asith had passed out from exhaustion—he was familiar with the feeling. However, his headache was gone and so was the heaviness in his legs, which had persisted after he'd passed out while airborne. To his surprise, his armor had been settled on a clear table not far from him, and next to it sat two more sets of clothing that looked as warm as the ones he was wearing. The pile of clothes, blankets, and fabric was folded neatly, rather than being in slightly disheveled piles, which meant that the dragon must have gotten the clothes out from there.

Seeing his armor reminded him that the dragon had taken his father's sword. He gritted his teeth and told himself not to think about it further.

Eventually, Asith stood to get a closer look at the clothes set out for him. Something could be useful. Mostly, they seemed like they would keep him warm. A thick doublet, a knitted wool sweater, and heavy pants made of what looked to be a bison pelt. Asith stared intently at each item of clothing as if he were trying to turn them into rope with his mind.

"You're finally awake."

Asith jumped and dropped the wool sweater before backing into the table. He couldn't see the dragon, so he scanned the room frantically to make sure he saw it before it saw him.

Dradevai appeared in human form from behind a bookshelf near the back of the chamber. With a basket in its arms, it continued toward him. It almost looked like a normal person, with its mouth closed and the sunlight hiding the glow of its eyes. However, the horns on the top of their head ruined the illusion. Even though they held an entirely different shape from the previous Blue he'd faced, the sharp ends reminded Asith of the color draining from Hamon's face as the dragon's horns drove through his chest. Asith squeezed his eyes shut, biting his lip to distract himself from the memory.

"Are you all right?" the dragon asked as Asith heard the thump of the basket hitting the table. The hollow sound of the wood made Asith cringe.

"I'm fine." Asith opened his eyes, first looking down at the basket, which was full of eggs, then back up at Dradevai.

The dragon's eyes lingered on him for a moment, its lips pursed and brow furrowed. He didn't particularly like the way it looked at him, so he picked up the cable-knit sweater. It was the kind wives would make for sailors. His mother once had to explain to a woman who wanted one she was a seamstress and not a knitter, so she could not make one. No matter how many times the woman asked.

"Where did you get all these clothes?" Asith pointed at the eggs. "And those."

"I was curious about human clothing, so I asked the humans for some. It took a few tries to get something that fit me in this form." Dradevai took an egg from the basket and ate it whole, shell and all. "The eggs I gathered in the forest."

"You asked humans for them?" Asith's mouth dropped open as he watched in horror, and then what it had said caught up with him. "Wait, you asked for them. Meaning you sat in villages and asked them to give it to you in exchange for leaving?"

Dradevai paused, biting its lip and revealing a few sharp teeth. "Well, I never told any of them I would leave if they gave me some clothing. I asked, and they brought them to me without question."

"Well, of course, they thought you were going to destroy their town if they didn't give you what you asked for." Asith watched Dradevai crunch into another egg. The dragon's eyes turned up toward the ceiling thoughtfully, and it rubbed its jaw slowly.

"Why would I waste my time destroying their town?" Dradevai looked down, squinting at the basket for a moment, and gestured to the eggs. "You are welcome to these."

"I feel that is a question better asked to a dragon that enjoys destroying towns than me," Asith said. "Also, humans need to cook eggs before we eat them."

"I guess that is fair. Is that common? Dragons destroying towns?" Dradevai looked at the eggs. "That is inconvenient."

Asith furrowed his brow, instantly frustrated. "Yes, it is very common. That is why we have dragon knights. If a dragon attacks, we kill it."

Dradevai bared their teeth, their lip curling into a sneer. "It? You make us sound like livestock that has gotten out of line."

"Well, I…" Asith stopped himself. He didn't want to make the dragon angry. "It is only killed if it attacks."

"You just said 'it' again. Do you think I am an 'it?' I am not 'it'; I am a 'they.' Please do not call me 'it,'" Dradevai snapped. Asith cringed again, but he couldn't look away from the dragon that time. He stared, blankly realizing what he had been doing.

"We were not aware that dragons could be like you." Asith searched for a better way to explain it, but he struggled to find the words.

Dradevai narrowed their eyes at Asith. "You were, weren't you? You've been thinking of me as an 'it' this whole time."

Asith's skin grew hot, something he hadn't felt since Dradevai had taken him. His eyes darted to the ground, his hands curling into fists. He didn't even want to entertain Dradevai's point, but somewhere in the back of his mind, he could hear his mother's voice telling him not to be stubborn.

"I'm sorry, I will call you 'they' and not 'it.'" Asith gritted his teeth.

"And which do you use?" Dradevai asked.

"He, please." Asith hated that Dradevai was right, because they had done so many awful things to him, seemingly for their own pleasure. He was small and burdensome, but in some way, he knew it was irrational. Asith could not be a burden to Dradevai, for they had kidnapped him.

Dradevai's stare made Asith's stomach turn in ways he didn't like. His hand found the side of his neck, rubbing it gently. If he'd stood his ground, Dradevai might have kicked him out of their hoard. Asith couldn't bring himself to wish he had. Something about the way he'd been thinking of Dradevai and treating them made bile rise in his throat. And, of course, Dradevai could still just throw him off the cliff face if he did anything they didn't like. So he just stood there.

"I guess it is fair that you would not have a favorable opinion of people that regularly try to kill you," Dradevai argued, "but I am sure that you would not like being referred to as 'it' either."

"I wouldn't want to be referred to as an 'it,' no," Asith said. "But I'm sure you wouldn't want to be kept like a pet—"

"But I am not trying to keep you like a pet. Being a part of a hoard is more prized than that. You should eat. How do you cook eggs?"

Asith wanted to continue the conversation, but Dradevai spun on their heels and headed into their hoard, searching various piles and pulling out mostly useless cooking utensils. He had to admit, he was running out of fight with Dradevai's whims. Following them almost seemed easier than trying to stop them. That, and Asith's stomach was growling. He would have liked to eat the eggs if he could.

They had an arm full of various spoons, ladles, and pans they'd collected. "That will work." Asith took a metal pot from Dradevai's hand. "I just need water and fire now."

"There is snowmelt in that barrel." Dradevai pointed at the corner of the chamber. "I can make a fire in the stove."

Asith followed Dradevai's instruction, looking for the stove as he filled the pan. He hadn't seen a chimney, so he didn't quite understand where it could be. Once he had the water, he carried the pot over to Dradevai. To his surprise, the stove was low to the ground and the chimney on it only rose a bit taller than Dradevai's head. The smoke that billowed out of the top easily rose toward the opening in the ceiling, floating out in the gap between the stone and whatever Dradevai had used to cover the hole.

"How do you cook the eggs, then?" Dradevai looked up at him from where they'd settled on the floor in front of the stove. Before closing the door to the stove, Dradevai took a deep breath and blew a billow of flames into it. Asith had to look away, but at least Dradevai did not hiss before they breathed flames.

"You put the eggs in the water and then boil them." Asith took three eggs and set them in the pot carefully, then placed the pot on top of the little stove. It was already rather hot, though the water was so cold it might still take time to boil. "Do you only eat eggs?"

"No, I mostly eat deer. I eat the eggs between hunting, so I don't have to hunt so often." Dradevai looked up at Asith before they stood. They picked up another egg and added it to the pot. "I want to try one like this."

Dradevai did not like the hard-boiled egg. It did not agree with their teeth and tongue. Of course, they had tried to eat it with the shell on despite Asith's advising against it. Watching them gnash their teeth and stick out their tongue made Asith's skin crawl. It was like watching a wolf eat raw meat, something he knew happened but didn't want to see. He had the urge to run away from Dradevai again but he didn't have anywhere to go, so he averted his eyes instead.

After they had eaten, Dradevai left Asith be, turning back into their hulking dragon form and perching on the pillows as they nudged and licked at their feathers. When they weren't preening, their eyes followed Asith around. Large glass-like orbs just leering at Asith. He did his best not to move around too much. The less he moved, the easier it was to not think about Dradevai watching him.

The temperature dropped again, snow falling outside as Asith shivered and pulled on the cable-knit sweater and the doublet over that. Dradevai's head followed Asith closely as he added a blanket to his many layers and sat at a table to read. Dradevai had a lot of books that caught Asith's interest, and since he had the time, he didn't mind reading.

At some point, Dradevai had gotten up and left. Their tail had lashed back and forth as they slipped through the passage to the other cavern. Asith stood up immediately, looking around for any sort of rope or something he could use to climb down. He pulled some finely made rope from a box and tucked it right back into its place. He knew where it was and didn't want Dradevai to know that. It was far too cold for him to make the climb that day. Even as he walked around the hoard, he had to keep the blanket around him to stay warm.

If he wasn't careful, Dradevai would take the rope from him. Dradevai had shown no sign of wanting to kill him, so Asith could wait for the right moment to get away. He went back to reading, taking careful note of how long Dradevai was out.

Eventually, Dradevai returned, and to Asith's surprise, they had a package in their arms. Asith recognized it right away—the butcher's twine wrapped around the brown paper. He got up and followed Dradevai to the back of their hoard, trying to see what they had.

"Is that butchered meat?" Asith asked. Dradevai paused near the basket of eggs, and Asith took in the small area behind the bookshelf. A decent amount of food was back there, probably because it was cold enough in the hoard that they could just keep it all out on shelves. There was hard cheese, a little bread, something that appeared to be dried sausage, and a carafe full of cream or milk—he couldn't tell. "Where did all of this come from?"

"From a village at the base of the mountains. This is jerky. You are free to eat any of it. I wasn't sure what you could have, so I went to get something I knew you could eat." Dradevai settled the jerky on a shelf near the eggs, and Asith's stomach dropped.

"You didn't threaten the village to get me food, did you?" Asith watched Dradevai's face carefully, looking for any sort of lie.

They tilted their head to one side, their eyes wide and a single eyebrow raised at Asith. "No, I know humans need food. I try not to take it from them. To get this, I took a gold goblet from the other room and dropped in someone's hand and asked them to bring me the jerky in exchange."

"Oh." Asith shouldn't have assumed. Though, that didn't really explain the cheese and other items, but maybe Dradevai liked to eat them and they'd done the same to get it. "You know, if you went to a butcher in this form with a golden goblet, you could have gotten it yourself."

Dradevai frowned. "When they see my horns, they call me a demon and run."

Asith looked at Dradevai's horns, and really, he could understand it. If Dradevai walked into South Cairn, Asith's hackles would be raised, and he likely would try to interfere with them. After all, he'd gotten himself in that position by willingly putting himself between Dradevai and South Cairn in the first place. Someone like Dradevai, with their glassy eyes, horns, and uncomfortably sharp teeth, couldn't get away with wandering into a town.

"Couldn't you just hide them with your magic? You mentioned it when I first woke up yesterday." Asith watched as Dradevai touched one of their horns. They swayed like they had been shoved when they didn't expect it.

"I-I could. Probably." Dradevai's looked rattled, their shoulders slumping and their hand wrapping around their horn. "I think."

"You have no idea how, do you?"

Dradevai frowned, their lips pressing into a hard line and their brow lowering. They turned to Asith to glower at him, and if Asith was candid, he'd have to admit that something about it disarmed them. They didn't seem so intimidating like that, and if he hadn't known better or if he couldn't see their horns, Dradevai would look like any other person around his age. Asith couldn't fathom that a dragon could act so very human.

"I don't exactly have a guide on how my magic works." Dradevai puffed up a bit and stomped past Asith. The movement made him jump and press against the bookshelf. He stood still, waiting for Dradevai to hurt him or grab him. His shoulder burned with white hot pain like it had when the Blue dragon had sunk its claws into it, and Asith smoothed a hand over the spot to rid himself of the phantom ache. After a few moments of waiting, Asith slowly relaxed, his muscles feeling weak from the cold and getting stiff. He had to leave tomorrow. Even if the weather wasn't perfect, he needed to escape.

Asith didn't follow Dradevai for a few minutes, for he didn't want to be thrown off the cliff. Asith's chest heaved for a while longer, and he waited until he could unclench his jaw before he moved to open the package from Dradevai. As he took one piece of jerky because, his mouth watered. While he was hidden behind the bookshelf with the food, Asith pulled the thimble from his pocket and rubbed it with his thumb.

"I'm sorry," he whispered. "I promise I will come home."

He then walked back to the table, wrapped the blanket around himself tighter, and sat with the book laid out in front of him. Dradevai, still in their human form, had rested on the pile of pillows, a book in front of them. They had settled their head in their hand, flipping pages quickly as they read. He didn't want to risk bothering them, but he couldn't help thinking of his mother again. His mind wandered away from her to the journal he had left on his desk, all his notes about his father. He wondered if his mother had found it yet.

Asith watched the swift movements of Dradevai's hands and the way they occasionally rolled into a new position without their eyes ever leaving the book. He had thought about trying to convince Dradevai to either take him home or tell him he was allowed to leave, but with their temper, that might be difficult. Perhaps trying to determine their intent with Asith would work better. If Asith could understand why they took him, he might find an opening of some sort. He would take any information at that point even if Asith had to work with Dradevai's intentions to create an opportunity to escape.

Dradevai looked calm, chewing absently on the edge of a pillow. The act hid their teeth enough that it didn't bother Asith in the same way their teeth normally did. Their face had softened as well, eyes wide as they read their book intently. Asith didn't want to risk asking a question that could make them angry again right away, so he tested their mood first.

"Do you know what kind of jerky this is?" Asith asked.

"Goat or bison, they raise both in that village." Dradevai looked up at Asith, their hands still curled around the book. "What are you reading?"

Asith nodded. Based on the size of some pieces, it must be bison. "It is a book from the country to our south about making clothing."

"Making clothing?" Dradevai gave Asith a look of disbelief. "What would a knight need with that?"

"My mother is a tailor. I have been sewing since I was small." Asith flipped the page he was reading. "There was a time before I was a knight, you know, and after."

Dradevai hummed, turning back to their book. "I guess."

Asith kept his gaze on Dradevai, wondering about the way his instructors had spoken about the Sterling dragons. They rarely spoke about Sterlings, but when they did, it was always implied they were just as quick to violence as the Blues and Greens. Dradevai wasn't like that all, though, even if Asith didn't trust them fully to not hurt him. Dradevai was nothing like a Blue or Green.

"Why did you want me to be part of your hoard?" Asith hoped the question seemed innocent.

"Because you're pretty." Dradevai's voice sounded bored, their eyes not even leaving their book. Asith made a noise he had not intended on making. Not much caught him completely off-guard and it wasn't like he hadn't heard the compliment before, but the way Dradevai said it somehow made it frustratingly more impactful. "That made you blush, didn't it?"

"Forget that I asked." Asith picked up the book he'd been reading and hid behind it. They laughed, full-bellied and when Asith glanced at them over the book, their glowing, golden eyes were still watching him.

"Plus, you are the only human to not look afraid at the sight of me." Dradevai closed their book, settling their head in their hand as they looked up at Asith with shining eyes and a smile that looked far too soft. "Why do you ask?"

Asith kept the book standing up but let it go so that he could pull the blanket up. Looking over the top of the book at Dradevai, he tilted his head. He couldn't imagine that he did not look scared when he first spoke with Dradevai.

"I do not understand why you want me around. That is all," Asith said.

"I told you. You were the most valuable thing in that village." Dradevai flopped down on their back, holding their book above their head. Since Asith considered it, he realized the book did not look dragon sized and that Dradevai might be in human form so that they could hold the book.

"That doesn't explain exactly why a dragon would want to have a human in their hoard." Asith set his book back down. "I am more of a burden to have around than a book or a piece of gold."

"But you are far more entertaining than a book or a piece of gold." Dradevai turned their head to look at Asith again, their shoulders slumping. "You haven't tried to escape. Is this your new plan? Trying to convince me that you are a burden?"

"No, that was not my plan." A chill ran down Asith's back. He stood, taking his book so he could climb into the pile of pillows, and found the group of magical heated pillows.

Dradevai's eyes followed Asith, and they closed their book again. "Are you cold?"

"Yes, very." Asith flipped his book open, trying to sink into the pillows more and then pulling the blankets over himself. Dradevai chewed on their lip and then turned back into a dragon. Asith only jumped a little that time, too frozen from the cold to do much more. It was late in the day, the suns had long set, and the room was lit by the chandelier and some torches on the walls that put off too much light to not be magic.

"I can keep you warm." Dradevai spoke quietly, their body curling in on itself like a dog would curl into a ball. Asith looked up at Dradevai's head, unable to see their horns in the low light, but their eyes glowed enough to illuminate their lips and teeth slightly. He didn't like that idea.

"How?" He looked over his book at Dradevai a moment too late. He hadn't noticed them moving, and they already had Asith by the back of his shirt again, picking him up like a kitten. Asith's legs flailed, and he reached to hit Dradevai with the book. But it slipped right out of his hands. He forced himself to stop moving, for Dradevai would probably get angry if he'd hit them, and the thought of them already having a hold on him while angry made his stomach rise into his throat.

After they settled him down on their claws, Asith tried desperately to escape, but a pillow and a few blankets landed on top of him so that he could not roll away. It seemed like their claws had been retracted in some way, leaving behind more paw-like feet. That didn't make Asith feel much better.

Asith's mind raced as he tried to move the blankets and pillows away. He pushed them toward Dradevai's head, figuring a soft barrier couldn't be offensive enough to incite their rage, but Dradevai wrapped their tail and head around him. His breathing quickening, he tried to sit himself up to crawl out of the opening at the top. They were not touching him, just creating a small barrier between him and the outside. Asith didn't understand why exactly, and he didn't care; he needed to get out.

His hands trying to find a position to climb up Dradevai's body. Then, Dradevai covered the opening with their wings. Asith blinked in the dark for a moment, finding one of Dradevai's golden eyes looking at him, their nose settled not far from his feet. It was much warmer than being out on the pillows. Despite how cold it was outside, the air was like being inside of a house with a fire.

"Better?" Dradevai turned their head enough to look at Asith.

"Yes, but please stop picking me up like that," Asith said.

Dradevai rolled their large glowing eyes. "You would have insisted on staying on the pillows if I'd told you what I was going to do."

"Still, you shouldn't just be picking people up like that. I am not your defiant pet." Asith frowned, watching Dradevai settle their head back down and huff at him.

"I didn't want you to freeze to death." Dradevai's voice was unusually soft and worried, no bravado or snark, no tilting their nose up or rolling their eyes. Asith gaped at Dradevai, his words lost to the realization that the dragon cared about whether he lived or died. Dradevai closed their eyes. Asith couldn't see Dradevai anymore, but he could feel their warm breath on his legs.

Dradevai had been so carelessly cruel to Asith, but it did seem at times like they were genuinely trying to be kind. It bothered Asith; how could Dradevai not understand they were terrifying? That every movement of their jaw and lick of their lips made Asith fear being between their teeth? The only reason he could remotely exist in the same space as them was because they sometimes looked human enough, but even then, they unnerved him.

Even as Asith had a sneaking feeling what Dradevai's real motive was, he couldn't fathom that he was correct. It didn't ultimately matter, though. If he wanted to keep his promise to his mother, to make it home, he needed to find a chance to escape. Maybe if he unnerved Dradevai enough, they would fly away for some time alone. He had to do it without making them angry.

"Are you lonely?" Asith asked.

"What do you mean?" Dradevai's eyes opened again, and they turned their head toward Asith.

"Is that why you want me to stay?" Asith moved the blanket, shifting the pillow behind his head. He had a feeling that if dragons could blush, Dradevai might be blushing.

"That's absurd. Dragons always live on their own." Dradevai shut their eyes, turning their head away from Asith.

Asith paused, hoping Dradevai would open their eyes again, but they started snoring, well, pretending to snore. It sounded rather exaggerated and fake. Asith sighed softly. They didn't seem to be incredibly old, and while powerful, they showed gaps in their knowledge that likely came from lack of experience. Asith pulled the thimble from his pocket again, trying to see it in the dark, but he could only feel the cold metal on his fingers. He rubbed it until the thimble was warm, trying to pretend he was in his mother's home instead of in the hoard of a dragon.

He ran his fingers through his hair and closed his eyes in order to still himself enough to sleep, but his entire body buzzed. Asith shifted his position and did his best to settle down on Dradevai's claws, but he couldn't. While he wouldn't die from the cold lying in there, that didn't mean he could sleep like that. Asith shifted in one last vain attempt to be comfortable, avoiding thoughts about the claws that held him so tightly and had carried him off into the mountains.

Dradevai groaned, picking their head up and shifting their claws. The movement knocked Asith off balance, and he fell into an outstretched claw, feeling the hard nail against his left shoulder. Asith shot up straight and stood on Dradevai's legs

"I can't do this." Asith pushed his way past Dradevai's wings but fell to his knees as he tried to step over Dradevai's back. Dradevai made small noises of pain, like someone would when their cat stepped on the wrong spot while walking over them in bed. Asith fell into the pillows and found one of the warmed ones in the dark. His blood throbbed in his temples, the feeling almost as difficult to bear as the phantom pain in his shoulder.

"Where are you going?" Dradevai's neck was craned to look at Asith and then reached toward him like they might try to pick him up again.

Asith pointed straight at Dradevai's face. "No. Don't pick me up."

Dradevai stopped moving, their eyes the only source of light. They must have used magic to snuff the torches and chandeliers.

"I am fine over here." Asith got on his hands and knees and felt around for the rest of the warm pillows. When he found them, he sunk himself deep enough that he was under several of them and grasped at the pillows until he had found three blankets to pull over him. "I don't want to sleep on you like that."

The quiet made him nervous, especially with Dradevai's glowing eyes staring at him. Their mouth opened, and Asith was thankful that he could barely see their teeth with just their eyes for light. Dradevai's eyes then disappeared behind their wing, and Asith braced for some sort of impact, or even for them to yell or snap at him.

Instead, the blanket and several pillows that Dradevai had picked up fell on top of him.

"Goodnight." Dradevai's eyes closed, and he could feel them shifting on the pillows. When they finished adjusting, the room grew quiet.

Asith swallowed, relaxing into the pillows, and pulled a blanket over his head so he wouldn't have to look at them in the morning. He lay still. Dradevai wasn't scaring him intentionally, at least he didn't think they were, but he was scared, nonetheless. Asith still wanted to leave and he wanted to sleep in a bed and he wanted more than anything to see his mother. He started to cry again, the tears dripping down his nose, but they didn't freeze. At least that meant he would survive the cold that night.

CHAPTER 3

9th of Penur

Asith woke to the light of the sun as Dradevai stretched their wings, their front legs extended out in front of them. He tried to remember what made him fall asleep the night before, but he mostly remembered Dradevai's snoring. The cool rush of air hit him, so he curled in on himself more, though the temperature wasn't nearly as cold as the day before. Because the day seemed to be warmer, he could perhaps use the rope he'd found when Dradevai wasn't looking.

"Are you still too cold?" Dradevai asked, nudging Asith with their nose, nearly knocking him over. His vision was still bleary from sleep, and it sent a spike of fear directly into his stomach. Asith jumped away from them, reaching for his sword on instinct, and panicked for a moment when there wasn't a sword to grab.

Dradevai stared blankly, their mouth open and their sharp teeth glinting in the sunlight. Then they repeated, "Are you still too cold?"

Asith heard one of Eroan's explosions go off in his head. It was the queue for him to attack, providing him a moment of opportunity to sink his axe into the meaty part of a dragon's leg.

"I would be much warmer with a proper cloak," Asith said. Dradevai turned into a human, their eyes shining a bit as they stood at Asith's side. They stretched their arms above their head, their exposed stomach pulling taught while Asith shivered at the thought of wearing a cropped shirt in the cold.

"A proper cloak?" Dradevai started toward the food storage, so Asith followed. He had planned while falling asleep to eat some of the bread Dradevai had with melted cheese on it, like his mother used to make him as a child. So, he found what he needed and started to cook. Meanwhile, Dradevai leered at him from a table nearby and ate jerky.

"Yes," Asith said, "a heavy wool cloak would be much better than just a doublet."

He was hoping he could convince Dradevai to leave for a while again, which would give him a chance to climb down. Though, Dradevai had so many unusual things stacked up in their hoard that Asith was certain he could find something to make the climb easier. But that would mean he had less time to climb. He would sort that out once Dradevai had left.

"I don't think I have any wool." Dradevai walked over to the large pile of fabric they had sitting near a table off to one side of their pile of pillows. They poked through the bolts of folded fabric, carefully looking them over and smelling them. "Wool is from a sheep, yes?"

Asith furrowed his brow. "Yes?"

"Why do you sound unsure about that?" Dradevai looked up at him.

"Because it's a mildly unusual question. Why are you sniffing the fabric?"

"To see if any of them smell like sheep." Dradevai turned back to the pile, pulling one out and holding it up. "This is rather thick, and you said you know how to make clothing."

Asith did not anticipate that at all, that was a serious hole in his plan, but he walked over to look at the fabric. He promptly shook his head; while it was rather thick and he could make a fine cloak out of it, he needed Dradevai out of the hoard more than he needed a cloak.

"This won't keep me warm enough up here," he said. "I need real wool."

Dradevai huffed, their shoulders dropping. "I don't understand how humans are alive if they succumb to the slightest cold weather."

"That is just how we are. We don't have feathers to keep us warm, nor can we breathe fire."

Dradevai put the fabric back and frowned at it. They narrowed their eyes at Asith, their arms stiff at their sides, but didn't say anything further on it.

"Then I'll go get you a proper cloak," they snapped, "or some wool so you can make one."

"Thank you." Asith shivered as he watched them stomp toward the tunnel that led into the other chamber. He hadn't expected them to leave immediately, but he wasn't complaining. Though, it still made his skin crawl to think that Dradevai might be angry with him, a strange churn returning to his stomach. Something about the way Dradevai's lips turned down and their eyebrows knitted together made them look confused and maybe hurt rather than annoyed. Asith looked down at his feet.

Thankfully, Dradevai didn't give him much time to think about it. He heard them tug something out of the pile of gold, causing a loud clatter as other items fell, and then promptly left Asith there alone. The flap of their wings was the only sound left in the quiet of the mountains, and soon, it was too far to be heard.

He flew into action, forgoing breakfast in favor of finding anything he could use to escape. He pulled out the rope he had found first, setting that on the table before continuing. There were magic items around, but Asith didn't really know how to use them. And really, he only thought they were magic because they had runes on them. He had seen that sort of thing in the Capitol, though these didn't look exactly the same.

Asith rifled through anything and everything in the hoard. It took longer than he wanted, and each passing moment made his hands shake a bit more. He wasn't sure if Dradevai would be angry with him if they caught him going through their things, and he never wanted to see Dradevai truly angry, especially not in their dragon form. Their teeth looked even sharper than a Blue dragon's, and they had teeth that could sink straight through metal armor.

He was counting the minutes in his head, and the more he looked, the more he realized there was no rhyme or reason to what was stacked where. It didn't help that his hands were tight and clunky in the cold, making it difficult for him to move things around, and occasionally, he'd touch something metal that was so cold it almost burnt his hand. The only things that seemed purposefully together were the books, and sometimes he'd find a stray book buried under a pile of other things. Asith didn't know how much time he had left, but there had to be something more than the rope.

Eventually, he found what looked to be spiked cages. He was fairly certain he could attach them to his boot and hold on to the cliff face. Asith came across a pick and some hooks most likely meant for climbing rocks.

The more he looked at his odd collection of weatherworn tools, the more Asith wondered if falling to his death was worth it, but he didn't really have another choice. He wrapped the rope around his legs before tying it around his waist. It felt as if he had tied sewing thread around him. Hopefully, it would hold his weight.

Asith pushed down the fear and walked out of Dradevai's hoard to check each cliff. He edged himself close to each drop-off, determining which one looked like the shortest climb. Once he'd made his choice, he secured the rope to a large narrow rock in the cavern and sat a few feet from the edge. He attached the metal cages to his boots as quickly and as well as he could.

Just as he got the cages on, he looked out to see the shape of Dradevai, their wings carrying them lightly over the tops of the smaller mountains. Asith reached for his mother's thimble in his pocket, finding that it was no longer there, and his throat tightened. He didn't have time to look for it, so he swallowed his fear and scooted to the very edge of the cliff. Asith turned himself around and kicked the spikes on his boots into the wall of rock. Trying not to look down, he carefully lowered himself. He wasn't sure what he was going to do once he got to the end of the rope, but he had the hook and pick on his belt. He'd crossed that bridge when he got to it.

There was no way to hide on the cliff face; in fact, he wasn't even sure why he thought he had enough time to get down all two hundred feet or so in the time he had before Dradevai got back. He thought he had only made it a few feet down, but when his eyes shot up, he shuddered. He had made it quite a way down. Asith's stomach plunged as his eyes focused on the rock face in front of him. His arms were already trembling from effort, and his fingers had gone completely numb. There was no way he could climb back up if he couldn't make it down.

One of the leather belts holding the spiked cage onto his left boot snapped, and in his surprise, he lost his grip. Asith plummeted like a stone tossed into water, a scream coming out of him, but he didn't really process it. He did, however, feel the rope catch, and he bounced for a moment before hanging there, upside down.

Asith sucked air through his teeth, trying to calm himself as he stared down at the rocky ground below. His hands shook uncontrollably when he reached for the rope to right himself. He prayed to the gods that he wouldn't die in that very moment. Unable to reach the wall with his legs, he had to rely entirely on his arms, and they jiggled like cooked oats.

It didn't really matter, though, because he heard a horrifying noise that was followed by a slight drop. The rope caught again for a moment, and then, as if the rope had been cut, Asith fell again. In an instant, he was spinning, watching the horizon go around in circles, the second sun barely peeking over the line of mountains as it rose for the day. That had to be it. He was too startled to react and too scared to do more than pass out, Everything faded to blackness in a moment as the wind rushed past him

He woke when his shoulder hit something hard. He wasn't dead. In fact, a very familiar sensation washed over him, like he was floating through the horribly cold air with four claws wrapped around him like a cage. Asith's thoughts caught up with him as Dradevai laid him out on the stone floor next to the pile of gold where he had woken up when he first arrived. The room spun around him, and he wondered if maybe he had been rotating as he fell. So he closed his eyes.

"Please be okay." Dradevai had dropped their dragon form and was kneeling beside him. He felt their hands on him but couldn't tell what they were trying to do.

Asith's head continued spinning, and he wondered why they even cared. They had been treating Asith like a prize or another random gold object in their hoard, so he certainly expected them to care far less than that. Then again, they had also gone out of their way to make sure Asith didn't freeze to death.

"Hey." Dradevai's warm hands found Asith's face, holding his neck gently as if checking for a pulse. "Hey, Asith, it's okay."

The warmth that washed over him was oddly bright, like the sun shining down on him in midsummer. The rope burn and his dizziness faded. He opened his eyes slowly, looking up at Dradevai's knitted brow and the indentations their teeth had left on their lower lip. As soon as they noticed he was looking, they frowned at him.

"What were you thinking?" Dradevai's voice cracked, and as Asith gathered himself, their hands shook. "I knew you were going to escape, but you're lucky I decided to turn around last minute to make sure you didn't actually try to climb down."

"You knew?" Asith asked.

"Of course I knew! I'm not stupid!" Dradevai rubbed their temples, their jaw locking as they ground their teeth together. They pulled away from Asith as tears slid down their cheeks and trudged toward the rest of their hoard.

"Wait, then why did you leave?" Asith took longer than he expected to sit up, his arms aching and his right foot still stuck in a spiked cage while the other dangled off his left leg by a single strap.

"I could tell you wanted me gone, so I went." Dradevai didn't wait for him, heading through the tunnel into the rest of their hoard.

Asith rubbed his head and neck, taking stock of how he felt. Dradevai's reaction didn't feel entirely justified; it was unfair for them to get so upset with him for trying to escape. Even if he wanted to convince himself Dradevai was upset because he tried to escape, Asith knew they were actually upset because he'd nearly killed himself.

He sighed and got the climbing cage off his boot and easily slipped what remained of the other off his leg. Dradevai had so much in their life, but the more that Asith thought about it, Dradevai hadn't mentioned a single other person or dragon. They didn't seem to have anyone in their life at all.

Asith stood, looking around on the ground to see if he had dropped the thimble in his rush to climb down. He walked into Dradevai's hoard without looking at them and climbed into the pile of pillows. His best guess was that the thimble had fallen out of his pocket in his sleep. A thimble in a pile of large pillows was like a needle in a haystack. He sat on his knees, letting his mind wander to keep from crying over losing the thimble.

As far as his mother knew, she was all alone in the world. Just the thought of his mother not being a part of his life anymore made his ribs ache so badly that he had to stop thinking about it, which left him thinking about Dradevai.

When he spared a glance at Dradevai, they were sitting at a table, a book in hand and their jaw set hard. They had their brow furrowed; their shoulders hunched up awkwardly as they chewed on their lower lip. Their posture made them look like a little old man. They didn't seem to notice Asith, so he had a moment to watch them in the dim, late-morning light of the cavern. Dradevai had tears in their eyes and looked like they were desperately trying to swallow them down. He looked back at the pillows, unable to watch Dradevai cry, and dug for the thimble again.

Asith tried to picture home, finding himself lost in memories of him and his mother in South Cairn. One thought caught him, maybe because Dradevai had looked as hunched as Mr. Avron.

> *"I don't understand why we help Mr. Avron with his chores every week." Asith held his mother's hand as they walked to the old man's house. "He's mean to me. All the time. Even when he doesn't mean to be."*
>
> *"Because it is the right thing to do." His mother smiled down at him, then stopped him in the middle of the street. She knelt to his level, her hands squeezing his shoulders gently. "Sometimes the people who are the most carelessly cruel are the ones who know kindness the least. Does that make sense?"*
>
> *Asith pouted, but he looked at his mother and nodded. "Yes."*
>
> *"Good." His mother chuckled and kissed the top of his head as she stood. "Come on, he's expecting us."*

Asith rubbed the top of his head, feeling the tingle of his mother's kiss on his hair. He couldn't imagine not knowing her warmth and love.

He looked at Dradevai again, considering everything he knew about them. He couldn't imagine what it was like to never have anyone around to help them. As he got himself up off the pillows, he wondered about the way Dradevai acted. They frequently seemed to have good intentions; they were just going about it strangely. In fact, nearly everything about Dradevai and their hoard seemed abnormal to him. Asith might only know the very basics about Sterling dragons, but Dradevai seemed to know hardly anything at all beyond what they knew of themself.

Dradevai had tears running down their cheeks that they were desperately trying to wipe away. Abandoning his search for the thimble, Asith took a deep breath and stepped off the pillows. They blinked and shook the tears away when he approached.

"I don't want to talk," Dradevai said without looking up from their book.

"I'm sorry," Asith said, "for scaring you. I won't do it again."

Dradevai looked him over intently, their eyes sliding over Asith's face, and nodded. They didn't say anything else, probably because they kept swallowing their tears back. He shouldn't feel guilty for wanting to leave; he just hadn't expected his attempted escape to affect Dradevai in that way. The whole situation had given Dradevai some sort of panic attack. Even if they had pushed Asith into panic as well, he didn't really want to do the same to Dradevai.

Asith said nothing else to them for a bit, finding that heavy fabric he'd rejected earlier so he could make a cloak out of it. Once he found a sewing kit and a pair of old scissors that still had a decent blade on them, he cut the fabric out. He'd made cloaks before, a basic one wouldn't be difficult, and he could use the leather from the spiked cages to make a closure.

As he cut and sewed the hood onto the cloak, Asith found a weird sense of calm in such an odd place for him. He thought about his mother a lot, the way she used to tell him to always watch other people and that she'd once told him the loneliest were usually the ones who struggled the most to reach out. They didn't always know how, and sometimes, when they did try to connect with others, they did it wrong. She had told him that once about himself, after he'd come home crying because everyone at school ignored him when he tried to talk to them, and anytime they were told to get into groups, he was left out. But his mother had smoothed his hair down and explained he'd figure it out soon enough, or someone would come along and teach him the right way to do it.

Asith could be that person for Dradevai, teach them how to navigate the world on their own. He had to stay, not just so that they would release him but because Asith was the only one who could provide them help. Even if he didn't like it.

He hoped his mother wouldn't be too angry with him for what he needed to do in that situation. Though, she would probably tell him he was doing the right thing if he could explain it to her.

Dradevai didn't move for a few hours, their hands on their book and their shoulders still tight, but eventually, they straightened up and stood. They stretched out a bit, like they were still trying to shake off the last bits of their argument, and then they stepped away from the table and started toward the food storage.

Asith kept sewing, keeping his head down so that Dradevai would have the space they needed to deal with their feelings on their own. To his surprise, they came back with a plate of finger food that didn't seem to be for them. They walked over to Asith's table and set the food down.

"I'm sorry," they said. "I shouldn't have made you feel bad for trying to leave."

Asith opened his mouth, but Dradevai turned on their heels and went back toward the food storage. Left with the plate of food in front of him, Asith pursed his lips at the bit of bread on one side. They must have melted the cheese with their fire breath; he hadn't even noticed them do it. That also meant they had been paying more attention to what he was eating than he thought.

Eventually, Asith finished sewing the hood onto the cloak and decided that he didn't want to tackle the hem that night. It was going to take a while to sew all the way around the bottom, so he sat and ate the food Dradevai brought him while watching them read. He realized Dradevai was sort of small; in fact, in their disguise, they were about a head shorter than Asith. Their hair was silky and long. Though their bangs appeared haphazardly cut so they would be out of their face, they still looked nice. With big, rounded eyes and a flat nose, Dradevai looked like any other person Asith might meet as they traveled through South Cairn. And their teeth were not that unnaturally sharp, and their eyes, while bright, didn't really glow so much as reflect a lot of light. If he had seen them in any other place and time, Asith would have probably had a very different first impression of them, a rather positive one, if he were being honest with himself.

Seeing they held a book about magic, Asith realized helping Dradevai was the best option. He certainly didn't want to risk climbing down again, and really, Dradevai didn't seem to want to hurt him.

After getting up, Asith got a small bucket of water out to clean his plate and then set it back where Dradevai kept it. It was the only plate they seemed to own, after all. Then he sat across from Dradevai, who became a bit startled.

"Dradevai, I want to make a deal with you." Asith folded his hands to keep them warm after touching the cold water. Dradevai set their book down slowly, their brow furrowed.

"A deal?" They narrowed their eyes and crossed their arms.

"Yes, a deal. I know that you're second-guessing yourself keeping me here; I can tell." Asith watched their hands twitch as they moved them under the table.

Dradevai frowned but didn't deny it. "And how do you know that?"

"Because you seem worried I would die from the cold and skeptical that I won't try to climb down again."

Dradevai looked a bit like they had been caught with their hand in the cookie jar, promptly trying to cover it up with their usual bravado. "Also," Asith added, "you don't really know what I can and can't eat.

"I knew what to feed you," Dradevai argued confidently.

"You thought I could eat raw eggs."

Dradevai frowned as if they didn't know how to respond to that. Asith had already worked that out in his head and he was confident about his plan, so he continued, "But I will stay here if you're willing to teach me magic."

Dradevai tilted their head to the side, their hair falling off their shoulder, then glanced at the book in front of them. "I could teach you, but you looked like you were going to freeze to death all day yesterday and I barely caught you…"

"I'll be fine, and I promise I will not try to leave on my own again," Asith said, holding out his hand to Dradevai. "If you can teach me magic to help me find someone who's missing, I think this would really help me. So, do we have a deal?"

Dradevai's eyebrows raised as they leaned toward Asith for a moment. It didn't last, though, their lips pressing into a hard line and their eyes darting between Asith's hand and face. "Do you promise you won't try to climb down again?"

"I promise." Asith kept his hand outstretched to Dradevai, and after a moment, they reached out and shook it.

"Also, can you give me my sword back?" Asith added as Dradevai grew suspicious of him.

"This whole thing hasn't been a ploy to attack me, has it?" Dradevai watched him carefully, but something in their posture and the slight pout of their lips gave away that they were kidding.

"No, it has not been a ploy to attack you." Asith rolled his eyes. "But it was my father's, and I would like it back."

Dradevai stood. "Yes, one moment."

They went to their bed and dug under the pillows until they disappeared entirely. Asith hadn't realized how many pillows there actually were. As they did, Asith watched something small and silver go flying, so he ran after it and retrieved his mother's thimble quickly. He rubbed his thumb over it before tucking it back into his pocket. When Dradevai pulled themself out of the pile, they had Asith's sword in hand, still in the sheath.

"You just stuck it under all the pillows?" Asith couldn't believe he had been lying atop his sword the entire time and couldn't even tell it had been there.

"There's a room underneath. It only fits one and a couple of items." Dradevai set the sword on the table.

Asith picked up his sword, smiling at it as he rubbed the decorative carving of a running rabbit on the hilt with his thumb. It was something he'd asked his mother about several times over the years, but she had told him she honestly didn't know why there was a rabbit on it. The blacksmith at the Stonegarde had offered to replace it with a dragon for him once, but Asith had gotten so offended by it, they wound up having a long argument about it. Delri had to pull him away before the fight became physical. It still bothered him to that day.

His stomach clenched. Of course, he had asked Dradevai to teach him magic to aid him in the journey of finding his father, but he didn't know how long that would take. The prospect of being up in Dradevai's hoard for years overtook him, his hands quivering around the sword. Asith's eyes burned as tears gathered in them. He tried to remind himself that he only had to fulfill his end of the deal to go home. He could tell Dradevai they'd taught him enough magic and then he'd be free, so he was only there if he wanted to be.

"Can I ask why you want to learn magic to find a lost person?" Dradevai asked.

Their voice drew Asith out of his thoughts, and he saw a thick tome in their hands. Asith had seen them with it before, sometimes reading it and sometimes writing in it. It must be their spell book. He swallowed roughly, trying to push down the feelings about putting his search for his father on pause.

"I never knew my father." Asith walked to his armor and set the sword down on the same table. "I've always wanted to know him, and my mother says he's still alive somewhere. I want to find him."

Dradevai's head raised, their eyes wide and their mouth open just a bit. They closed the book and turned to face Asith head-on. Asith hadn't seen them like that before, their gaze soft and their eyebrows pulling together. They grabbed his attention fully, watching their eyes, lips, and neck. He had never seen them so serious.

"That sort of magic is rather complex and dangerous," Dradevai explained. "I can try my best to teach you, but you may never be able to cast a spell like that."

Asith's breathing stalled. But he took a step toward Dradevai and tilted his head. "Could you?"

Dradevai let out an unusual, self-deprecating laugh. "Maybe?"

Asith had never seen their confidence falter like that.

"Well," Asith said, "maybe if you start teaching me, it will help you get to a point where you feel like you could?"

Dradevai gently chewed on their lip, their eyes on the ground. A little smile crept across their face, and they nodded.

"Maybe. It's worth trying."

CHAPTER 4

14th of Baltha

Dradevai had turned out to be a surprisingly good teacher. Asith learned more than he had expected in just a few weeks, the runes and chants coming easily with Dradevai diligently helping him study. They forced him to read quite a bit, something that Asith didn't particularly like. Though, it was easier reading about magic than it had been reading about historical battles at the Stonegarde. Unlike Asith, Dradevai could read endlessly, and Asith sort of liked watching them make faces at books as they concentrated. If he was tired of reading, he'd peek over his book at them, and they never seemed to notice, too focused on their reading.

Asith's mother was on his mind constantly, though, even as he tried to read or watch Dradevai demonstrate drawing runes. His mother must have certainly thought Asith had died by then, and the journal he'd left behind about his father could only make her feel worse. He would make it back eventually, and when he did, keeping his promise would hopefully be enough to get her to forgive him, especially if he accompanied it with several apologies.

"Asith." Dradevai waved their hand in front of his face, leaning over the table toward him.

"What? Sorry." Asith shook his head, setting his pen down and rubbing his eyes. He had forgotten what they were trying to teach him, something about runes for fire or warmth, but he couldn't bring the information to the front of his mind.

Dradevai's shoulders dropped, and they picked up the pen Asith had been using before setting it in the holder so that it didn't get ink every-where. Once they had, Dradevai moved the papers in front of them aside.

"Let's take a break." Dradevai stood up and started toward the back of the cave. They reached up high toward one shelf of food before taking their carafe of cream from where it was next to the cheese.

Asith rubbed his forehead for a moment, then gathered up the pa-pers he'd been using for practice. They had discovered quickly that even Dradevai was not advanced enough to cast a spell to find someone neither of them had met. Dradevai said they could try to create a spell but they wouldn't know where to begin, and doing it wrong could cause serious injury to them both.

When Dradevai came back, they were holding a copper saucepan, two cups, and a wooden spoon. They poured the cream into the saucepan and set that on the stove before unwrapping a large block of chocolate. With a dull knife, they shaved small curls off it.

"Sorry." Asith stood and approached Dradevai. "I'm having trouble focusing."

"It's okay." Dradevai smiled at him. They carefully spooned two heaps of the shaved chocolate into one cup, then shook it gently to even out the flakes. "Do you like sweets?"

"Where did you get chocolate?" Asith looked over Dradevai's shoulder as they gathered another spoonful of the slightly curled flakes. "I've only ever seen it in dessert shops in the Capitol."

Dradevai hummed. "Is that what this is, then? I had a suspicion, but no books I have that talk about chocolate describe what it looks like."

"That would be my guess," Asith said, "but to be honest, I've never had it. It was always outside of my family's means."

"Would you like to try it?" Dradevai asked. "I figured out I could mix it with warm milk or cream. It might help with the cold, and some food in your stomach might help with the focus."

A bit surprised by Dradevai's consideration, Asith nodded quickly. He had seen the sweets shops with his mother when he was a child, and he had to admit to being curious. Even though it was the type of thing only politicians and rich merchants really had the chance to buy.

"Where did you say it was from?" Asith asked again. Dradevai dropped spoonfuls of chocolate into the second cup.

"It was given to me in a town near the jungle." Dradevai made a face that Asith could only assume was shame. "I had only been asking where I could find water, but they didn't speak the language we speak here, and I didn't know theirs."

Asith chuckled. "How many things do you have here that you received accidentally?"

Dradevai looked up at him, a giddy smile coming to their lips, and they straightened their shoulders. Asith hadn't seen them like that, a warmth in their face as they picked up the carafe of cream and poured some of it into the saucepan.

"Well, all of the gold." Dradevai looked up from the mixture they were stirring. "Some of the cookware and a lot of the furniture…"

"All of the gold?" Asith glanced at the door to the other cavern. "You didn't ask for any of that?"

Dradevai shook their head. "No, what would I do with gold? I only figured out that I could exchange it for other things a few years ago."

"Well, a lot, but Greens and Blues tend to hoard it because it's pretty, from what humans can tell." There were still many mysteries about dragons, but it shocked him that a Bronze dragon wouldn't have any interest in keeping gold. He'd thought most dragons liked to pile their wealth and sleep upon it; that's how the teachers at the Stonegarde had made it sound.

"I do not know much about the habits of Blues and Greens." Dradevai stirred the contents of their saucepan and sighed. "Most of what I know comes from books, which are written by humans, after all."

Asith furrowed his brow. "How much do you know about other dragons?"

Dradevai narrowed their eyes at Asith and crossed their arms. "Plenty."

"So," Asith said, "nothing?"

Their confidence faltered, transforming into an annoyed pout. "That is not what I said."

"Yes, but you were lying." Asith crossed his arms, and Dradevai grumbled softly. "Why don't you know much?"

Dradevai frowned. "It is not like I have someone around to tell me about others. I only know what I have figured out about myself."

Asith thought that over for a moment. It might not be normal, and Dradevai seemed touchy about being alone. In that moment, they sounded exasperated, throwing their arms around to emphasize their point.

Greens and Blue dragons lived in pods, clusters of twos and threes, but Asith had to admit, even the archives the dragon knights kept in the Capitol had little information about Bronze dragons, or Silvers or Copper dragons, for that matter. Part of it was that they rarely attacked humans, so the knights didn't need to keep information about them. The research library owned by the Southern archivists likely had more, but Asith hadn't exactly been one for studying during his training.

"How much do you know?" Dradevai's voice was small. They'd turned back to the cream, stirring it slowly.

"I know more about weaknesses: where to sink my axe, how many there might be if a town is under siege, how to stun them temporarily." Asith stared off into Dradevai's hoard. He could still hear his axe hitting the ribs to drive the bone into the heart. It was a sound he usually wanted to hear, a sign of relief that the battle might be over soon, but the thought left his mind feeling like it was full of wool. Asith shook his head, turned to Dradevai, and examined the way their lips had turned into a hardened frown.

"I probably should have known." Dradevai turned away from him, their bangs obscuring their face as they checked the temperature of the cream. "How many?"

"Have I killed?" Asith asked. Dradevai nodded, their posture rigid.

"Nine." Asith rubbed the back of his neck, trying not to look directly at Dradevai. "Two Blues and seven Greens."

Dradevai fiddled with the necklace they always wore, a single pendant made of amber. "Attacks are that common?"

"When I was in the Capitol, we would be sent out to areas being plagued. Greens attack in groups usually, so sometimes we'd be dealing with two or three at a time." Asith crossed his arms, pulling his shoulders in on himself as he looked down at the floor.

"I have only ever met a Copper, but they were very old and lived deep in the mountains." Dradevai sighed. "They told me I should be afraid of humans and that if I went to their villages, I might encounter a dragon knight in scaled armor. And if I did, I should run. I never knew why they said that, but I guess this must have been the reason."

"But you didn't stay with them?" Asith realized then that must have been why Dradevai knew he was a dragon knight; his armor was clearly made of hardened scales he'd cut from several larger ones. That thought made his stomach clench strangely. He couldn't really fault a dragon for saying so, though he didn't entirely understand. From what Asith understood, a Copper dragon could take out a legion of dragon knights if one surprised them. Dradevai shook their head, then looked at Asith over their shoulder.

"They had already started to root. They couldn't talk much and told me they would be fine alone." Dradevai looked sad for a moment, turning back to their pot of cream and gently stirring it.

"Started to root?" Asith blinked at Dradevai, who blinked back at him.

"Dragons root and turn into trees when they die." Dradevai clicked their teeth, sneaking a look at Asith's armor, which still sat out on a table nearby. "I guess it might not happen if you cut them up shortly after they do."

Asith felt sick to his stomach. "I was not aware they returned to the land in that manner."

"We are born knowing we will die that way." Dradevai grabbed a metal funnel and picked up the saucepan with their bare hand, unfazed by the heat that certainly would have left Asith with a severe burn. Dradevai poured the cream into two cups, not even flinching when the cream splashed onto their hands and the table. They stirred each briefly with the handle of the wooden spoon before they set one in front of Asith.

"Thank you." Asith took the cup and picked up a towel before wiping up the cream that had spilled. As Dradevai set the saucepan aside, he frowned, looking at the stiff way they moved. They didn't have the bounce in their movements they'd had over the past few weeks. Asith sat across from Dradevai when they returned to their spot at the table. He looked over his sword briefly, thinking about the running rabbit design on it.

"Did you still want to enchant fabric as we'd talked about a few days ago?" Dradevai asked, thankfully changing the subject. Asith did not want to speak about his time as a dragon knight much further. "What kind of enchantment were you interested in?"

Asith nodded. "Enchanting fabric, yes. Maybe something like those pillows that stay warm. I think that could be useful for people. And these torches, actually, how do you make those?"

"Oh." Dradevai leaned over in their seat, scooping up a piece of nearby wood. With a small puff, they set the end ablaze with the same blue flame that lit the torches. "That is not something I can teach, unfortunately."

Asith drew back, nearly dropping the mug he was holding. "Careful, I'm not fireproof."

"You're not?" Dradevai moved the flame away from Asith, a smile on their face that led Asith to believe they were teasing him. "This will not burn you. It doesn't even put off heat, see?"

"This is not just a ploy to attack me, is it?" Asith asked. He shot Dradevai a look and carefully reached out for the flame while they chuckled. It was not throwing any heat as Dradevai had said, instead only creating light. "How many kinds of fire can you make?"

Asith sat back and cradled the chocolate drink as Dradevai waved the piece of wood. Once the flame was out, Dradevai gently threw it back into a pile of small pieces they kept for the stove. They seemed to contemplate Asith's question and then picked up their cup again.

"Three. A normal flame that I use to start the stove, the flame that only emits light that I used on the torches, and then something I wouldn't really consider fire." Dradevai sipped at their chocolate, seeming to get lost in thought.

"Oh?" Asith commented. Hoping to get more information, he leaned over a bit, trying to look at the book Dradevai had been reading.

"It is more like the heat you would find in an oven. There is no open flame, but it's hot on your skin."

"I think I understand what you mean. It's as if you can warm just the air?" Asith could imagine something like that being rather useful. It could keep a house warm without the risk of a fire, and considering how often his mother used to wake up on the coldest nights of winter to add logs to the fire, Asith realized it might provide a lot of convenience for people too. Not only his mother but also his elderly neighbors would probably love to have something like that in their homes.

"Yes," they said, "so I cannot teach that to you, but I know an enchantment that might create something similar."

Asith perked up. "Really? Like an oven without a flame?"

Dradevai nodded and stood up, gesturing at Asith to stay seated when he started to move. Dradevai wandered over to their bookshelf, and with a flick of their wrist, a book floated down from the very top and settled itself in their hands. They flipped through it briefly and set it on the table beside them before flicking their wrist again, another book settling in their hands.

Asith kept his eyes on them, trying to remember why he had been so afraid of Dradevai's slight frame and gentle movements. Even their horns, while tall, were no sharper than a goat's. When Dradevai was a dragon, they were large with sharp teeth and talon-like claws if they were out, so it made sense. Dradevai was so different as a human, though, their eyes expressive and bright and their disposition inquisitive and happy.

"Ah here." Dradevai spun on their heels, holding the fourth book they'd pulled down from the bookshelf. Asith had to cast his eyes down, picking up the cup of cream and chocolate to hide the movement. He didn't want them to know he'd been staring, and when Dradevai slid back into their chair excitedly, Asith was sure they hadn't noticed.

"This book has a lot of information about enchanting metals. The only issue is, we might need to forge things ourselves to do it," Dradevai said.

"I don't know how to do that, do you?" Asith asked, finally sipping on the warm chocolate. It was surprisingly bitter, considering Dradevai had asked if he'd liked sweets, but there was an underlying sweetness that might be from the cream. It was very good, though; he could understand why it was in expensive sweet shops in the Capitol, for it certainly tasted decadent and like it was meant only for people with money.

"No, but I'm sure we can figure it out with some reading." Dradevai set the book in front of them so that Asith could see the pages. Asith finished his chocolate as Dradevai pointed out and explained different runes that made enchantments. They seemed to think heating was a good enchantment for Asith to start with. Even though they lacked blacksmithing equipment, the runes for creating heat were apparently simpler than the ones used for other things like flight or making ice.

Asith followed the runes easily, finding their meaning and translating them over to the common language, Matsic, without much trouble. So much so, Dradevai seemed a bit jealous of his skill at it when they'd first started teaching him magic. It wasn't much different from learning the alphabet to Asith, and he pointed out to them that someone was teaching the subject to him; Dradevai probably learned it alone, which seemed to make them feel better.

They spent the next few days working on Asith's ability to draw the runes for the enchantment. Dradevai carefully coached him through the order in which the strokes needed to be laid down and how some symbols contained others within them. While the runes came to Asith easily, his penmanship had never been good, so his hand ached from holding the pen in just the right position or writing with his wrist instead of his arm. When they climbed into the pillows after days of sessions, he rubbed his wrist, trying to soothe it as Dradevai looked at him in their dragon form. It made Asith quiver for just a moment, but he reminded himself that the dragon would not hurt him.

"Will you be all right?" Dradevai asked. "With just the pillows?"

Dradevai had taken to asking him every night if he would be warm enough. Even if he always gave them the same answer, they still asked.

Asith thought about Dradevai's claw pressing against his shoulder, and he nodded. "Yes, I'll be okay."

"Just let me know if you're too cold." Dradevai settled their head near Asith, their eyes closing slowly as they stuck their tongue out and licked their lips. He almost wished he hadn't seen that movement. While Asith rarely found Dradevai unnerving when they were in their human form, their dragon form made him tremble at times.

"I will." Asith closed his eyes, trying not to think about Dradevai's teeth. He couldn't sleep, still rubbing his wrist while he listened to Dradevai snore lightly. The sound mixed with his exhaustion, the rumble shaking his limbs the way the roar of a Blue would. Asith tried to put it out of his mind, with sleep overtaking him.

Asith's eyes shot open as he lay on the ground, his sword still in hand as he turned over, trying to shake the dizziness from falling. His eyes swam over the town square and landed on Hamon running toward him in a desperate sprint.

Tears shined brightly on his cheeks; his teeth were bared in a desperate yell as he ran toward Asith. He couldn't see the dragon behind him, the blue scales and black horns on the top of its head revealed as it flew toward him. It batted its wings, kicking up dust and rocks as Asith yelled a warning.

But it was far too late. Asith watched the horns drive through Hamon's chest, his voice cracking and the scream of pain coming out higher in pitch. Hamon's lifeless body was hurled away. Asith scrambled for his sword, the world around him going dark as Hamon's body made a horrible thud on the ground somewhere out of his sight.

Covered in blood, Asith ran down an alleyway, his eyes out for one of the mages or another knight. He heard the dragon cracking wooden buildings and beams as it tried to force its way down the alley after Asith. In order to widen the path, the dragon snapped its teeth and drove its horns into wooden walls.

"You're next!" The dragon's voice came out loud, and it shook the ground under Asith's feet. His shock knocked him flat on his face and sent his sword clattering across the cobblestone. He panted, shooting a look back at the dragon. He had never heard one speak. "This is your fault."

Its black tongue lashed out, and it hissed.

Asith woke with a start, tears in his eyes as the low light of the first sun appeared. He wrapped his arms around himself, and while his body was warm, he couldn't stop shivering. Picking up three pillows, he laid them out on himself, trying to weigh down the blankets on him so that he could pretend Delri was there. He wished he could lie with her like they always had after a fight, sharing each other's weight.

The tears fell down his face as the panic faded. Asith took long, shaky breaths, closing his eyes only to see the Blue dragon's face again. He opened them quickly and jumped at the sight of Dradevai sleeping there. Asith put two more pillows onto his pile and tried to breathe. If he could breathe, he could put the memory out of his mind.

Eventually, he wiped the tears away from his face and examined Dradevai. They were fast asleep, a sliver of their pink tongue sticking out at the front of their long snout. For a moment, in the low light of the first sun, Asith noticed the spikes on the top of Dradevai's head were actually just feathers. And when the sunlight hit them right, he could see through the delicate fibers and find the top of the shaft. The feathers quivered slightly as Dradevai breathed, long and almost golden in the lighting, with a slight point at the end.

Blue and Green dragons had looked nothing like them. The way their cone-shaped tongues lashed whenever they opened their mouths, and how they swung their heads back and forth to see with the eyes on the sides of their heads, didn't compare to Dradevai's graceful movements. Their tails had spines, and their teeth jutted out in strange directions, sometimes sticking out of their lips.

Dradevai had feathers and a sleek tail. Their teeth weren't perfectly straight, but they stayed within their lips. Their tongue was pink and rounded like a dog's, especially in that moment as it peeked from their mouth. Their teeth didn't look that much different from a dog's either, and something about that realization brought Asith some comfort.

As Dradevai shifted in their sleep, rolling over onto their back with their wings tucked around them and their legs sticking up in strange positions, it was hard for Asith to think they were a dragon at all. Of course, they were, but as the second sun began to rise for the day, Asith realized Dradevai's dragon form was sort of cute.

CHAPTER 5

10th of Kasdiel

It was clear in the weeks following that Dradevai took to spell work far more naturally than Asith did. While he could read the runes faster, and Asith connected them like writing poetry, he had a hard time controlling the results of his spells. Although Asith wrote rings of runes in hopes of creating enchantments, he was often unsuccessful.

It bothered him like doing poorly in school used to. Asith had never particularly liked the feeling of being bad at things, but he had been terrible at arithmetic and mediocre at reading. He remembered plenty of days when he cried over bad grades; it's why he always preferred sewing or fighting with the dragon knights. Asith was hoping that if he took to the runes so quickly, he'd take to spells the same way. He wished he weren't wrong.

When he did find success, Asith carefully worked through enchantments, taking his time to learn the ones most useful to him before moving on. That included enchantments he could put onto fabrics, since his mother might like them, but he found he would also have to make the garment or pillowcase himself to keep the enchantment from fading quickly. Cutting into the fabric and changing its shape often ruined the enchantment even when he didn't cut the actual spell circle. He could maybe embroider the spell into the fabric, hoping more stable enchantments wouldn't dissipate when the fabric was cut or sewn together. Dradevai pointed out over and over that Asith could always enchant garments after they'd been made, but something about that felt like admitting to defeat. They eventually gave up trying to convince him otherwise.

They were surprisingly reasonable when they disagreed with Asith, which was one of the reasons Asith found living with Dradevai rather comfortable. They would try to come to an understanding rather than argue with him. It shocked Asith; normally, he didn't get along with people as overconfident as Dradevai, but something about the way they acted didn't bother him. He had a feeling it was because Dradevai was overcompensating for things they didn't want to admit. They were ultimately good-hearted.

He started getting up with the light of the sun, since Dradevai woke around then, anyway. They rivaled each other for who woke up the earliest, which Asith wasn't used to. As a child, he remembered his frustrated mother begging him to go back to bed when he'd woken at the first light of morning. Dradevai, on the other hand, took Asith getting up as early as he did as a challenge.

When Asith woke up early to stretch and practice with his sword to keep fit, Dradevai tried to wake before him. It didn't always work; Asith had gotten good at slipping off the pillows without waking them.

He remembered the forms he learned in training well, though the sword work he'd learned was rudimentary. Swords didn't have the reach to fight Blues and Greens, so he only used them as backup. It somewhat substituted for exercise. While Asith was not confident he could keep up in a sword fight, it warmed him up in the morning.

Asith started with the basic drills, swinging the sword in careful motions as he moved about the small space he made for himself. He slipped his doublet off after a bit, then moved on to the more complicated forms. Mindful of the furniture around, he didn't want to break anything of Dradevai's, so he moved toward the table where they practiced magic until he was too close and turned around.

Dradevai was watching him intently. They had turned back into a human already, their gaze soft and their eyes lidded. The back of Asith's neck tingled, the feeling sweeping over his cheeks as he looked at them. He hadn't even heard them move, but the moment they realized Asith was looking, their eyes grew wide and they dipped their chin down.

"Tired still?" Asith moved through the form he'd been working on, though he couldn't stop thinking about how Dradevai had been staring at him.

Dradevai shifted, slower than usual, and stretched their arms above their head. They rolled over, turning away from him, and curled up into a ball on the pillows. Asith stopped moving, his brows pulling together.

"Yes, I need some more food," Dradevai said. "I usually have three or four deer, but yesterday I could only find a handful. Even then, I was only able to grab two. Maybe I will find a boar today."

"Boar like to eat farm crops," Asith said. "If you are down in the village, they might be able to tell you where to find one."

Dradevai turned over to face him again and rubbed their cheek. "Really?"

Asith nodded. "It's a constant problem where I'm from. Deer, too, they eat our corn."

"Well…" Dradevai considered Asith for a moment. "Would you like to go down to the village with me? They might talk to you more easily."

Asith blinked at them, lowering his sword since he was at a loss for words. He hadn't been around other people in quite a while, and if he went to town, he could send a letter to his mother. It wouldn't be a great way to tell her what had happened, but at least she would know he was alive. The thought made him light up, his heart fluttering as he put his sword back into its sheath.

"I could," Asith said, but then the way Dradevai had first carried him in his claw came to his mind. "How would you take me?"

Dradevai popped up, landing on their feet with a light tap as they hit the stone and walked toward the far end of their hoard. "You can ride on my shoulders. If you're tied on, it should be safe."

They pulled a sturdy rope from a box, but the end was frayed.

"Is that the rope that broke when I was trying to climb down?" Asith scrunched his nose up.

"It is." Dradevai walked over to Asith. "But I've enchanted it to make it stronger, see?"

They held up the rope so Asith could get a better look. It had a small circle of runes on it. The ink was long dry, which meant Dradevai had been thinking about that for a while.

"Okay, we can try it." Asith took the rope, triple-checking it for weaknesses. He didn't want it breaking on him like when he'd tried to climb down the cliff. Dradevai stood near him, leaning over his shoulder and watching his hands intently.

Once he had thoroughly looked it over, Dradevai turned back into a dragon. They settled their head on the ground and lowered one of their wings so that Asith could better see what he needed to do. He looped the rope around Dradevai and tied it off before Asith wrapped it around his waist. "Is this bothering you?"

Dradevai shook their head and craned their long neck to look back at Asith. "Is that enough to make you feel safe?"

"I think." Asith carefully settled onto Dradevai's shoulders, his legs dangling slightly as Dradevai slowly stood. "You promise to catch me if I fall?"

"Of course." Dradevai laughed softly, and Asith nodded. He got off Dradevai to get his leather gloves and thick scarf, then pulled on the heavy cloak he had made. In the pile of gold items, he found a purse full of gold and platinum coins. After pocketing a few gold coins, he left the purse on a table so that they could find it again later.

"Okay." Asith finished tightening the rope, his normal belt swapped for one wider and heavier at Dradevai's last-minute suggestion. Hands shaking slightly, he grasped the rope as tightly as he could, his knuckles quickly turning white. Asith tried to relax them, for if he held on too tightly, his hands would just get tired. Once he had said the word, Dradevai would take off, and Asith suddenly wished he had suggested waiting until he had learned a spell for falling slowly.

"I'm ready. Go ahead," Asith mustered.

"Yell loud if you need something," Dradevai said, and with a leap, they carried Asith off the ground. His lungs burned; they probably wouldn't be able to hear him even if he yelled. Dradevai turned their wings once they were past the rocky hills next to their hoard, lowering them closer to the treetops where there was more air. Despite his best efforts, Asith's hands hurt already from clinging to the rope, but even as Dradevai sped over the forest, he didn't feel like he'd moved much.

Asith only appreciated the feeling once Dradevai was gliding down the mountains, their wings spread out wide and barely moving as they directed them toward their destination. His eyes watered and he struggled to keep them open, but the valley grew around them, giving way to soft, rolling farmland that only had a small dusting of frost, unlike farther up the mountains where Dradevai lived. It made everything shimmer in the sunlight, the grass peeking out from under the sparkling ice crystals.

They descended toward a collection of little buildings with people bustling between them. Asith leaned down and yelled to Dradevai, "Vai, is there a place we can touch down where we'll stay hidden?"

"What?" Dradevai craned their neck to look at Asith, turning it in a way that looked horribly uncomfortable.

Asith took a deep breath and shouted as loud as he could, "Is there a place we can land where we'll stay hidden?"

"I can try," they said.

Dradevai changed directions, their colossal wings folding over as they slid into the tree line with surprising ease. They carried them up along a wooded foothill that touched the very edge of town, and Asith spotted a small walking trail that probably went up into the mountains. He directed Dradevai near the edge, and they settled within the trees even though few people were around.

It was much warmer in the valley, which didn't surprise Asith, but it gave him a rather good idea. He slipped the cloak from his shoulders and removed the coat he'd been wearing over his doublet.

"Here, put this on." Asith held up the coat to Dradevai. They raised an eyebrow at Asith, but they took it, slipping it over their shoulders. Dradevai looked like they were swimming in the coat since it was even big on Asith. He rolled up their sleeves, his fingers brushing their skin and an unexpected rush of warmth spreading over Asith's stomach. Dradevai's skin was soft and pleasant under his fingers, something that was hard for him to ignore. Asith did his best to focus on disguising Dradevai, slipping the hood over Dradevai's head to hide their horns, which Dradevai frowned at. But it worked, so they kept it on.

"What is the point of this?" Dradevai's form was not suited to such bulky clothes, but with the coat and hood, they at least looked like they could pass as human.

"These people are usually afraid of you because of your horns, yes?" Asith asked, and Dradevai nodded. "Well, now they won't know you're a dragon at all. We are going to tell them we're hunters."

"We don't have any weapons." Dradevai frowned, and Asith smiled at them, rolling up the rope and tying it to his belt.

"We have set up all our traps already." Asith had become a confident liar when he was in training, entirely because he had a busy-body room-mate in the Capitol. He didn't particularly enjoy lying, but he didn't mind doing it to keep Dradevai safe. "I promise, it will work."

"Okay, I trust you." Dradevai adjusted their hood, then paused to take their braid and wrap it around the very base of their horns. It was enough to further conceal them within the hood.

The busy village was alive and working already. Dradevai kept close to Asith, watching women scoop up their children and hold them on their hips as they walked past them. Asith hoped showing Dradevai the little village might make them more comfortable being in a town. Maybe if they liked it, Asith could convince them to return to South Cairn with him. His mother would probably like Dradevai, and he wanted nothing more than to see her again.

As they made their way toward the general store, he looked at a booth selling fine fabrics from Syuty. The rich purple and deep navy wool made him want to buy a bolt for her, but he had no way of getting it home, though. Even if he asked Dradevai to return home with him, they'd have to go back to the hoard to get Dradevai's things, and they wouldn't have the space for an extra bolt of fabric.

Asith pushed himself away from the fabric and led Dradevai to the general store. A handsome man with no hair and a flamboyant mustache greeted them from behind the counter, his doublet similar to the one that Asith wore. Dradevai must have gotten the doublet from around there, and while the man eyed them strangely, he bought every lie Asith told him. He sold them eggs and bread, and while Dradevai talked little, they seemed interested in absolutely everything about the store, closely examining Asith's interactions with the owner.

Once they had the food, Asith decided the easiest way to find out where a boar problem might be was at the small inn the general store owner had mentioned. Dradevai didn't understand stopping to eat if they had just purchased food to consume, but they seemed far more interested once they smelled the bacon. Asith ordered for them both, including water and a local ale.

"You're rather good at lying." Dradevai studied the wood on the table in front of them.

"I guess," Asith said. "I had to lie a lot when I was training to be a dragon knight."

"Why would you need to lie to fight dragons?" Dradevai's face pinched, their lip curling up.

"I didn't. I had a roommate who liked to gossip, and I was just trying to keep him out of my business." Asith looked at Dradevai over his cup. "Is something wrong?"

They fidgeted with the handle of their cup of water and chewed on their lower lip. Then they straightened up, looking at Asith with their jaw clenched.

"I just," they said, "it's strange to hide my true self and for you to be lying so naturally."

"Hide yourself?" Asith tilted his head. "Like hide that you're—"

He stopped himself and set his cup down, his shoulders dropping. Asith had told Dradevai to hide their horns to keep them safe, not to make them feel like they were lying, and he had only lied to keep them safe.

"I'm sorry. I didn't think it would bother you," Asith said. "I promise, I don't lie to you. I'm only lying because it will keep you from being noticed."

Dradevai's face softened, their jaw relaxing as they raised their eyebrows. "No, I didn't think you'd lied to me. This is all just, strange."

They wrapped their arms around their middle and pressed their lips together as they looked at the table again. Asith looked down at his cup, for he was having trouble looking at Dradevai. Then, seeing a woman in the corner of the tavern clutching an embroidery hoop in hand, Asith remembered something his mother had said to him many times when he was little.

"It's new. Of course it feels strange." Asith repeated his mother's words and rubbed the handle of his cup. "Flying with you felt strange earlier, but it was also nice to see the valley like that."

"So, it will start to feel less weird?" Dradevai asked.

Asith looked up at them. "Probably."

Their eyes wandered away from his face, their expression growing gentle as they pursed their lips.

"I guess I will just have to give it time," Dradevai said.

Asith smiled, and he changed the subject. He hoped talking to them about the most recent enchantment they'd tried would distract them. It seemed to work, their excitement for magic overtaking them.

When their food came, Dradevai gladly ate the indiscriminate chunk of freshly cooked bison and bacon that Asith had ordered for them. He got himself fried eggs and roughly cut potatoes, which he let Dradevai have a bite of, their curiosity sweet. While they hadn't liked the hard-boiled eggs, they rather liked the warm, runny yolks. They gave Asith some bison in exchange, which, Asith had to admit, he liked better than beef.

Dradevai snuck an egg from their basket, too, crunching into it as they always did at the hoard. Asith's sighed as his shoulders dropped. He was about to inform them not to do that in public but stopped upon noticing a man in the corner staring at them. He had his hood up, pale skin peeking out from under the fabric as his dark eyes bore holes into Dradevai's side. Asith swallowed and looked back at Dradevai, trying to convince himself the man couldn't have seen. Besides, Dradevai had eaten the egg whole, so he couldn't confirm what they'd done.

"Vai, please don't do that again." Asith set his jaw, trying to avoid the man's gaze.

Dradevai's lips parted, their brows pulling together. "Okay, I won't."

Asith nodded, keeping the man on the edge of his vision. He was still staring, but eventually, he set money down on his table and got up. Dradevai seemed unaware, chattering about various things they'd noticed in town. After about fifteen minutes, Asith just hoped the man was long gone, and it was nothing. There wasn't anything he could do, anyway, and they needed to find a place for Dradevai to hunt.

The man serving them knew enough about the local farms to point them toward one that had been struggling with wild boar digging up seeds. Asith gave him a few silver for the information, which caught Dradevai's attention.

"Did you pay him for that?" Dradevai asked when the server walked away.

Asith nodded, sipping on his ale. The drink was rather good. He hadn't had it in so long, he had almost forgotten how much he liked it. Dradevai considered his answer for a moment, though, drinking their water. They hadn't tried the ale yet; they had sniffed it and scrunched up their face as if they found the smell dubious.

"Why?" they finally asked.

"The information was useful," Asith said. "Humans pay each other for more than just goods. He did me a service giving me that information, and I paid him for that service."

Dradevai reflected on that. "Did you pay for your training to become a knight?"

"My mother paid for my schooling, but yes." Asith nodded. "She saved for a very long time to pay for my education."

"I know that you said you're looking for your father, but I'm sort of wondering why." Dradevai paused, their eyes on the table as they thought about their words. "You have a mother, after all, and you only ever speak highly of her."

Asith froze, the tankard in his hand halfway to his mouth as he tried to process that question. Dradevai wasn't trying to be rude, but it still made his chest cave in to hear it said out loud.

"I've just…" Asith swallowed and set his tankard down. "I've always wanted to know him. My mother never spoke poorly of him."

"Your mother still thinks well of him even though he's never around?" Dradevai paused. "I mean, I'm sorry, you don't have to answer that."

Asith sighed and shook his head. "No, it's okay. I've always thought that was strange too. That's part of why I'd like to meet him."

"That makes sense." Dradevai picked up their drink, looking away from Asith. Their eyes held a distant look, and their fingers tapped on the table. He had never heard them say anything like that before. Something Asith had learned in their time together was that Dradevai moved through conversations with little regard for Asith's feelings. It never seemed on purpose, so he had always tried to make it clear when they upset him during the past few weeks, and they would apologize quickly. But that was the first time they'd offered an apology on their own.

"You've always been alone, yes?" Asith asked. Dradevai's shoulders pulled in, hiding behind the tankard in their hands.

"I hatched alone," Dradevai said, "and I knew I had parents, but they weren't around."

"And you think that is normal for dragons?" Asith thought about the times he asked his mother why his friends had two parents and he only had his mother.

"I think it is." Dradevai didn't sound sure of themself. Asith resisted the urge to sigh, for he didn't think it was normal, but he didn't need to tell Dradevai that. Asith just wanted Dradevai to feel better.

"Maybe we can find them, or more dragons, somehow?"

"Maybe." Dradevai took a long sip of their mead and then turned their attention back to their food.

Dradevai eventually tried the ale and decided they did not hate it, although they complained of its bitterness. Asith promised to get them a sweeter one next time they had it. Once they finished their food, Asith led Dradevai to the farm the server had suggested. They perked up again after that, though they were not quite their usual self yet.

There, they found a young man and his mother, both wearing heavy clothes so they could work in the cold for hours at a time. Asith couldn't help but miss his own mother as he and Dradevai spoke to the farmers, explaining they could help with the boar so long as they could keep what they caught. The farmers thought it a very fair deal, and while the woman considered Dradevai longer than many other people in town had, she also didn't seem to figure out they were a dragon. Asith tried to speed the conversation along, clutching the basket of food they bought tightly in one hand as he spoke.

Dradevai made quick work of stalking and capturing a large boar, one that Asith wasn't sure could be brought down with just a bow and arrow, maybe a crossbow, but even then, it seemed far too big. It was no trouble for Dradevai, who sunk their teeth in and swallowed the boar in large chunks, while Asith made his way back to the farm. He didn't want to put Dradevai in front of that woman again if he could avoid it, for something about her narrowed eyes and raised chin worried him. So, he explained they'd caught a boar so large, they likely wouldn't be able to carry a second.

"That's all right," the older woman said, her foot up on a shovel, and despite the chill in the air, her sleeves were rolled up to her elbows. "We had only been seeing one, so the two of you must have gotten it."

"I'm glad to hear it." Asith fidgeted with the handle of the basket. "We might pass through here again, so do you want us to stop to see if you need our services again?"

The woman had already picked up her shovel again, but she stopped and turned back to Asith. Her eyes landed on him, scanning his face as she chewed on her lip. They bore a hole directly in his chest, opening him up like his mother always used to. As she set her hand on her hip, he feared she would call him out for bringing a dragon to her farm. He wondered how quickly he could run back to Dradevai; he was fast enough to run from dragons when he was a knight, so he was pretty sure he could get to them before that woman found a pitchfork.

"Sounds mighty good to me." The woman smiled, her thin lips curving in a way that was knowing and wise. "I hope it was a good meal for that peaceful one. They never do hurt anyone when they come down here."

"Dradevai?" Asith's jaw dropped open, and the woman nodded. The peaceful one was probably a good name for them compared to other dragons. A smile spread across his face, one that matched the woman's. It didn't need to be said they both knew what was going on. "So, you're not afraid?"

She shook her head. "Not much scares someone my age. I believe that they are a good omen when they appear. I assume you are the one they have been buying food for?"

"Yes. I hope that they have never crushed your fields by mistake." Asith chuckled when the old farmer laughed, her head falling back. That woman might be someone good to talk to if they ever needed anything.

"A child's mistake, no different from the ones my son has made and I am sure you have made yourself, right?" Her smile grew warmer at the mention of her son, and the pang of guilt hit Asith's stomach like a sucker punch. His mother probably didn't even know he was alive.

"Ma'am, can I ask one last thing of you?" Asith crossed his arms. Dradevai was walking toward them, looking like a human again. The farmer nodded, her eyes studying Asith curiously. "Is there a post here? Somewhere I can send a letter?"

"Of course." She gave him directions, and he gave her a gold coin, which she tried to refuse. Asith convinced her by saying it was to keep Dradevai's secret as well, and when she realized he was not going to back down, she took the money.

When they left the farm, Asith brought Dradevai to the post, bought some paper, and borrowed a pen to write his mother a quick letter. At least she would know he was alive. Dradevai watched with quite a bit of interest; they had pens and paper back at their hoard, but they largely got used for magic. They seemed to understand that was different.

He didn't really know what to say, so he went simple and decided he could hopefully explain the rest in person, writing:

Dear Mama,

I'm sorry that I haven't written to you sooner. I have a lot I owe you an explanation for, but I wanted to let you know that I am alive and well. I am working on returning, and when I do, I promise to explain everything to you.

Love,
Asith

He read the letter over and knew it was going to get him into trouble, but at the very least, his mother would know that he's safe. Asith drew a small needle and thread to one corner of the page, something she used to draw in the letters when he lived in the Capitol. Only Asith would think to add it, so she would know the letter was real. He folded the letter slowly, thinking about whether Dradevai could just take him home. If he asked, Dradevai would probably take him, but that would break their deal. Even if he said it was just for a visit, Dradevai had acted so strangely about his lying that he worried they'd misunderstand why he was asking.

He didn't want to hurt Dradevai's feelings, but his mother had raised him on her own and didn't deserve to think he was dead only to get a letter from him with little explanation. His disappearance was worse than the years he put her through when he was a dragon knight. He paid to seal the letter with wax, pressing his thumb into it since he had nothing better, and had the letter sent home. At least he had paid so that she wouldn't need to pay to receive the letter.

Finally, he and Dradevai walked back out into the woods where they could leave under the cover of trees. He was quiet along the way, telling Dradevai he was only tired because he didn't want to talk about it.

"Who did you send that note to?" Dradevai asked.

Asith settled the basket of food on the ground as they turned back into a dragon. They had agreed Dradevai would carry it in their paw so that Asith could hold on to the rope with both hands.

"My mother." Asith carefully tied the rope to his belt. He contemplated asking Dradevai to go back to South Cairn right then and there but feared they'd think he was lying about his reasoning. Asith could probably explain if there was some distance between all the lying he had done in town and asking Dradevai to take him home.

Dradevai watched him quietly, their eyes narrow like they had gotten lost in thought as they so often did. Once Asith finished readying himself, he settled on Dradevai's shoulders again and gripped the rope. But he caught movement at the edge of his vision. Asith followed it, the shadow of a hood and dark eyes looking back at him. His breath caught, his knuckles turning white as the figure shifted.

"Dradevai, we should leave, now," Asith said, his lips barely moving.

"All right." Dradevai took off without questions, their wings beating rapidly as they lifted off the ground. Asith looked back at the figure, a shimmer at his fingertips and his eyes glowing blue. He looked like the man from the tavern, but Asith couldn't be sure because Dradevai flew away too quickly.

The flight was just as quick, but climbing up the mountains made Asith's lungs burn no matter how close to the trees Dradevai flew. When they finally arrived, his eyes were watering so much that tears were streaking down his face, and parts of his hair were frozen.

Dradevai looked guilty as Asith rubbed at his eyes and face. "I'm sorry, did I fly too fast?"

"No, no." Asith shook his head, finding one of the warm towels to wipe his face down. "My eyes are just not meant for flying like yours are. I might need to get something to protect them if we fly like that again."

Asith sneezed and took a shivering breath, which only made Dradevai more worried. They promptly wrapped him in a warm blanket and forced him to sit near the stove while they made him one of those warm chocolate and cream drinks.

"Here." Dradevai set the cup next to Asith on the table. They had already put away the eggs and bread. "Warm up before we do anything else."

"Yes, yes." Asith sipped on the chocolatey cream, which felt nice, and his face warmed up quickly.

"Why'd you tell me to leave like that?" Dradevai asked.

"I thought I saw someone in the woods." Asith pressed his fingers to the sides of the mug.

"When I was a dragon?" Dradevai tilted their head at him, and Asith nodded.

"Something about it gave me a bad feeling." Asith looked at his drink, his stomach rolling. He didn't want to scare them by telling Dradevai about the magic the man had been using, but it felt like a lie to not mention it.

Dradevai hummed and looked at the ceiling as they wrapped their hands around a mug of their own.

"Did you like being in town today?" Asith asked. He didn't want to worry Dradevai, and there was no way that man could have followed them while they were flying. It was probably nothing, anyway, and maybe Asith hadn't even seen the man doing magic.

Dradevai's shoulders pulled in a bit, their whole being becoming sheepish, but underneath that, Asith could see the excitement in their honey-colored eyes. "Yes, I never knew that it might be that easy. Of course, it helped that I had someone who knew what they were doing."

Asith smiled. "Good, I am glad. I can teach more of how to handle being in town and using money."

"I would like that." Dradevai rested their head in their hands for a moment, looking over their collection of books. "Maybe I can start hunting for humans, get rid of their pests."

"That is a good idea. You could also sell the enchantments you make." Asith sipped at his cream, and Dradevai's eyes grew wide.

"People would pay money for that?" Dradevai asked, and Asith nodded quickly.

"Magic isn't easy to come by." Asith sat up more, meeting Dradevai's excited gaze. "To be honest, when I asked you to teach me, I wasn't even sure if it was something I would be able to learn, but my mother told me that my father knew some magic."

"I came out of the shell knowing I could do magic," Dradevai said, "and you learned so easily. I thought it was something humans could do as well."

Asith shook his head. "There are people who think dragons might have taught humans magic at some point and it was only through teaching that one could have magic abilities."

"Do people still believe that?" Dradevai asked.

Asith shook his head again. "Not really, from what I understand." He couldn't remember it all clearly, for he hadn't liked the history classes he'd taken during his training or in basic schooling, and the scholars who thought dragons taught humans magic were largely regarded as being incorrect. "Now it seems that while it is more common in people in certain areas or families, it is not necessarily a requirement for magical ability."

Dradevai seemed to consider that again, and then they nibbled on their cheek. "I wish I could go to school somewhere."

Surprised, Asith's eyes darted to the purse full of coins on the table and then to Dradevai's horns. "Vai," he started gently, "you could easily pay to go to school. Though, you might need to change your human appearance to hide your horns."

"I have enough for that?" Their hand drifted to their horn, carefully running a finger over the ridges. An ache spread from Asith's stomach into his sternum, running up the middle of his chest and spreading as he imagined Dradevai moving to the Capitol to attend the Maeria Spire. The purple student robes would look nice on them, and he could imagine the bright smile on their face at the sight of the library or floating spires where the students lived. Encouraging Dradevai to go to school might mean the end of his time in their hoard, but that didn't mean Asith shouldn't suggest it. He knew better than that.

Then it hit him he didn't want Dradevai to leave, and he didn't want to leave Dradevai. Asith's arms hung loose at his sides, everything around him going blurry as his eyes unfocused. He couldn't keep thinking about it; he needed to answer Dradevai's question.

"Yes, easily in that purse is enough for a few years' tuition, and if you sold all the gold in that other chamber, it would be enough for a few years' living expenses," Asith said. Dradevai's eyes drifted to the purse and then toward the hallway that led into the other chamber. They furrowed their brow and then looked back at Asith.

"I would need to leave here, though, wouldn't I? And go to the Capitol like you did?" Dradevai shrunk back, their shoulders pulling in toward their chest, making them look even smaller than normal. Asith nodded, smiling at them.

"Yes, to get the education you deserve, you probably would." Asith picked up his cup of cream, hiding in it in hopes that Dradevai wouldn't be able to read his emotions too easily. The conversation made his limbs feel heavy and his shoulders droop even if it also meant returning to South Cairn. He wanted to see his mother, to explain the journal about his father, and apologize for only sending a letter.

"It is something to consider," Dradevai said, "but for now, I have a deal with you I have to fulfill."

Asith smiled slightly and nodded. After he finished the warm chocolate and cream, Dradevai left him to his own devices while they stewed over an enchantment of some sort they'd been working on. Asith found a book he had been reading on and off about runes next to a crystal Dradevai had given him. The crystal lit up when he shook it, so he settled across the table from them as they studiously took notes about whatever spell they were working on.

Dradevai eventually picked up a book and climbed onto the pillows. They lay out on their stomach and propped the book up in front of them, with their head in their hand and their ankles crossed. They weren't very far apart; Asith could probably reach out and rub the warm skin on their arm, like he used to with Delri when they'd face each other and talk about their day because neither of them could sleep. Delri would love Dradevai. Asith couldn't help thinking about the two of them meeting, his best friend and that wayward dragon. Once Delri got past the shock of Dradevai being a dragon, they could be good friends.

He shifted his book in his hands, toying absently with one page. Asith didn't want to leave Dradevai, and he wanted to reach out and touch them like he would with Delri. But it wouldn't feel the same. Delri was his best friend, and while they were physical with each other, nothing more had happened between them. Dradevai's attention, the feeling of them being nearby, wasn't like what he had with Delri at all. His limbs became light as he thought about it and a sudden heat came over his body, so he decided to focus on his book. He moved the crystal closer as he tried to fill his brain with rune circles that could cool stone.

CHAPTER 6

11th of Kasdiel

Asith was swinging his sword when Dradevai settled their front paws on the stone floor and stretched their back out, their feathers puffing up like a cat's fur would. He sort of enjoyed imagining them that way, like a large winged cat that could breathe fire. Dradevai was, after all, about as dangerous as a cat when it came down to it. They didn't seem likely to hurt anyone, save for deer and boar and eggs.

He finished his stretching and sword swinging, and they both ate breakfast. Then they returned to magic lessons since they had run their errands the day before. Dradevai seemed to be doing much better with higher quality food in their stomach, their fatigue waning and the number of naps they took going down significantly.

Days went by much faster since Asith had at least tried to inform his mother that he was alive. He could focus on learning the magic Dradevai wanted to teach them without guilt. As they fell into a rhythm, they also got closer, Dradevai asking Asith questions about the Capitol and South Cairn, and he shared a lot with them. They opened up a little bit, but certain things still seemed to be too much for them to talk about. Asith always let the subject drop if Dradevai looked too upset over it.

Dradevai took to teaching, encouraging Asith regardless of how difficult he was being about performing the enchantment. Their understanding of their own magic seemed to expand each time they explained a concept to Asith a second time, and as they worked together, they found the enchantments they made rather powerful.

They focused on warming pillows at Dradevai's suggestion, both because Asith was interested in it and because they thought it was simpler than other enchantments. Asith liked having more warmed blankets and pillows to sleep with as well, so he went along with Dradevai's lesson plans.

One afternoon, after they had eaten lunch, they spread a blanket across the floor and drew a ritual circle on it with chalk. Dradevai then instructed Asith to place some magnesium powder, several torches, and a bundle of kindling along the edges of it. That would imbue the blanket with what it needed to stay warm.

"Do you remember the chant?" Dradevai knelt across from Asith, pressing their hands directly under the kindling and one torch on the edge of the circle. Their eyes traced the chalk lines Asith had drawn. Although the blanket was only a few feet long, they looked far away from Asith.

"Yes." Asith watched Dradevai for another moment, his eyes on their lips as they counted the components on the blanket. He shook his head a little. "Are you ready?"

Dradevai looked up at Asith and smirked. "When am I not?"

Asith chuckled, having to peel his eyes away from Dradevai's lips again. He didn't know what it was, but he struggled not to stare. Sometimes, it appeared they were doing things to achieve that result, but Asith tried his hardest not to think about that. His ears were already warm; he didn't need to make it worse.

"I'm going to start." Asith started chanting, Dradevai still smiling at him.

The chant didn't feel right from the moment he started, his eyes darting around the circle as he tried to figure out if he was overthinking or if something was actually wrong. The magnesium burst into a bright flame, flaring white hot and igniting the entire chalk circle. Asith didn't feel the heat right away, the wood and kindling bursting into flames as Dradevai's hands pulled away from the circle. The light was so bright that Asith couldn't see anything else. Even as the flames consumed the blanket, his body didn't move, and he didn't stop chanting, fearing what a half-finished spell would be like.

He shrieked when the heat reached his hands, jumping backward and completely forgetting the chant. The flames extinguished, Asith panting as he tried to process what had happened, but large black spots from the bright light of the magnesium were still in his vision.

Dradevai's hands caught his shoulders before he completely lost his balance. Not being able to see threw him off more than he expected; although he was used to fighting from behind a shield, it differed from having no vision. He fell back onto his butt, then closed his eyes. When he tried to close his hands into fists, he twinged in pain. It was like the first time he'd put his hand on the wrong piece of metal at the blacksmith's. He'd only made that mistake once.

"Hey, come on." Dradevai lifted Asith to his feet like he weighed nothing. He had never noticed how strong they were in that form, though it made sense that their strength would not leave them. They were still a dragon, even if they looked like a human. It startled Asith slightly, especially since Asith couldn't really see Dradevai. The black spots were fading as Dradevai walked him a few feet through the hoard to a water barrel. Dradevai's soft hands found Asith's, not touching his palms, and deftly rolled up his sleeves to his elbows before guiding his hands into the water.

As their fingers held his wrists, their body was pressed up against Asith's side to hold him there. Their chest moved as they breathed; it was fast and a little panicked, but it was all Asith could concentrate on. His vision returned, and he focused on their long lashes fluttering. He considered their face, which was soft and round, with dark feathery brows that sat low across round eyes. Dradevai's eyes were set deep in their face, a soft puff of skin underneath their waterline creating a small shadow just underneath it. Their upper lip had a subtle bow, the skin there a lighter brown with the slightest pink undertones. Lips he had seen purse to point at something when their hands were busy, or curl over their teeth as they laughed many times over. They had their hair braided or tied back most of the time, and their bangs had been growing out since Asith had first met them, which Asith found pretty. Asith thought Dradevai was pretty.

"I'm going to go get bandages and something for the burns. Stay here," they said.

Dradevai's stare snapped him out of his line of thought. He nodded, speechless, figuring they would attribute it to the shock of being burnt. Asith could feel the heat in his cheeks, though, which were most definitely flushed, but Dradevai didn't seem to notice. They simply told him they'd be back and left to dig through their hoard.

After a while, he slipped his hands out of the barrel, examining them. They weren't even blistered, honestly, so perhaps both he and Dradevai had overreacted.

"I think I'm okay." Asith wiggled his fingers and decided they'd be fine.

Dradevai's head popped up from behind a lumpy pile of small tools, random furs, and a few boxes. "Are you sure?"

"I'm sure," he said.

Dradevai walked back to Asith, with a downy feather stuck to the top of their head and a small box in their hands.

He dried his hands and approached the circle. Steam still spewed from the blanket, so Asith used his boot to move it, basically mopping the floor with the hot, sopping-wet fabric. In the panic of his yelling and pulling away from it, he hadn't noticed Dradevai dump water on it.

"Okay, but I still think we should put a salve on them." Dradevai set the box down on the table and popped it open. They rummaged through it, then pulled out a little jar of flakey dried balm.

"That doesn't look like a salve," Asith said. Dradevai pursed their lips, and their shoulders dropped, a scowl on their face.

"I'll have to make more, but I need to go find the herbs." Dradevai dumped the crusty greenish salve out into a bowl and cleaned out the jar.

"If you really think it's necessary." Asith rubbed the back of his head as they collected a pair of sheers and a basket as well. He had a feeling Dradevai wouldn't drop it, so he let them go. Asith waved as they turned into a dragon and slipped out of their hoard.

Asith didn't really want to attempt another enchantment without Dradevai around, so he got something to eat. After he had eaten a snack, Asith reorganized the various pens, inks, and papers they used for spell work and enchantments. He was surprised to find a thick journal written entirely in Dradevai's careful looping script, but he promptly closed it and set it back where he found it.

When he no longer had anything to clean, Asith bathed and trimmed his hair, which he realized he was not very good at. Delri used to do it, or his mother would. He forced himself to stop fussing with it once it was even; otherwise, he'd accidentally end up with no hair at all.

Dradevai reappeared as Asith was drying his hair, rubbing the warm towel into his head and then letting it drape over his shoulders. Their eyes lingered on Asith, lips parted as they set the basket on the table.

"Did you find everything you needed?" Asith picked up a little cup and lathered some shaving soap on the brush.

"Yes." Dradevai nodded and removed some supplies from the basket. Their eyes darted toward Asith again, and after a moment of hesitation, they asked, "Where did you get that scar on your shoulder?"

Asith touched the pinkish mark Dradevai was referring to on his left side, realizing he hadn't looked at it in a while. "A Blue dragon picked me up once in a fight. It's from their claws."

"What was it trying to do?" Dradevai watched Asith with an intensity that made his heart speed up. Their diligence in caring for him was a reminder of how fond they'd grown of each other. Though they hadn't talked about it, Dradevai was very much the object of his own solicitude, and if he was reading Dradevai correctly, he had a feeling they felt the same about him.

"It was trying to carry me to a height it could drop me from and kill me." Asith rubbed his shoulder briefly, feeling the phantom pain bubble under his skin. "It is an old injury, though, not something I need to worry about now."

Dradevai considered the scar for a moment and nodded. "You should hurry and put your clothes back on before you freeze."

"Yes, yes." Asith returned to shaving his face. "I just didn't want to get my shirt wet."

Dradevai held out his tunic when he finished, their eyes lingering on his chest as Asith thanked them quietly. They picked up the salve they'd finished making and took each of Asith's hands in theirs before spreading the medicine across his palms. It soothed the mild pain.

"I'm glad your hands are all right," Dradevai said. "I was worried you wouldn't be able to sew again."

Asith stiffened, then glanced at Dradevai. "I hadn't even considered that."

Dradevai frowned. "You should really be more careful."

"Maybe I should." Asith picked up a book on runes they'd laid out on the table. "But doing magic is hardly more dangerous for my hands than fighting dragons was."

"That doesn't mean you shouldn't be careful." Dradevai had a look on their face like they would keep scolding Asith, but the expression faded quickly. Their eyes narrowed, and a sly smile grew on their lips. "After all, you are the most valuable possession in my hoard."

"Don't start that again." Heat rose to Asith's face, and he turned to the bookshelf. They hadn't brought their kidnapping up in a while, but honestly, whenever they teased him about it, Asith burned up inside. "You know I am not part of your hoard."

Dradevai chuckled, and to Asith's surprise, Dradevai pressed into his back, their arms securing around his middle.

"But you are part of my hoard, Asith." They hugged him close for a moment, their face pressed between his shoulder blades. His entire body buzzed with an excitement he hadn't experienced in a long time. Then they let go as fast as they'd snuck up on him. "I am glad you are okay."

When he turned around, Dradevai was already bottling up the rest of the salve. They were focused enough that Asith thought it was safe to get out the clothing he'd been sewing for them, gather a few books, and settle at the table that he'd turned into his sewing area across the room. He carefully stitched the tunic's sleeves before taking some of the leftover red fabric and adding piping to the vest, which would carry the color through the full outfit.

He then cut a sash to go over the vest. Since it would fall just beyond Dradevai's waistline, it needed something to keep the vest from falling forward, but the laces near the chest wouldn't be enough. Luckily, he found a piece of silk with an intricate pattern on it just a few shades lighter than the tunic that would work well. The embroidery was completed with a shimmering gold thread, each small flower or line catching in the light in the most beautiful way. It was befitting for someone like Dradevai.

Dradevai had also mentioned rather liking the fabric; they had explained it had been there when they first hatched from their shell. Making the sash didn't take him long at all, either, cutting the shape and carefully basting the edges so that it wouldn't fray.

Once he had finished, he chewed on his lip as he tried to find a good reason to measure Dradevai again. He hid the rest of the clothes he'd been working on, leaving out only the black suede he decided to use on the trousers, and then thumbed through the book of enchantments they'd been working on.

He found one that made water roll right off cloth, and while he probably wouldn't put it on the leggings he was going to make Dradevai, it was a good excuse. He picked up the book and read it over, then gathered the materials as if he were about to attempt to make the black suede waterproof.

"Can I measure you for something?" Asith called. "I am going to try a new enchantment." He held a leather measuring tape, hooked his foot around a stool, and pulled it out from under the table.

"What is this one?" Dradevai asked and stepped up carefully. They didn't seem to question the fact that Asith always wanted to measure them instead of making things that would fit himself, but Asith had told him after the first time it was hard to measure his own body and that had been enough. Asith could probably measure himself if he really wanted to, though. He felt a little bad about that lie, but he reminded himself it wasn't really a lie to conceal a gift.

"It will make the fabric water-resistant. I am going to try to do it with a pair of leggings rather than the whole bolt of fabric."

Dradevai nodded, their eyes following Asith's hands as he started to measure and write their size. His fingers tingled when he ran his knuckles down the side of their leg, the silky fabric of their pants smoothing down against their skin easily. He tried not to look up, horribly aware of Dradevai's eyes still on Asith as he pressed the measuring tape against their ankle. When he risked a glance, they straightened up just a bit, shifting to play with the amber pendant on their necklace.

"Done?" Dradevai asked. Asith shook his head and wrapped his arms around Dradevai's waist. Their grip on the necklace tightened.

"One more thing." Asith set the measuring tape against the small of Dradevai's back, his hand brushing their skin and feeling the fine hair that gathered there. He barely resisted the urge to smooth the pads of his fingers against their spine and instead wrapped the tape around their waist. Asith looked up at Dradevai, his eyes falling on their parted lips. "There, done."

"Right." Dradevai blinked quickly and shook their head. They ran their hands over their clothes and stepped off the stool so that they could return to what they'd been doing. Asith called a thank you after them and went back to his table, making quick work of drawing the pattern and cutting it out. The leggings would take much longer to create than the tunic and sash had, so he settled into sewing for the rest of the day. He took care to make deep pockets and make space for laces to keep the leggings from falling.

Asith was correct in thinking it would take a few days to finish, between making the leggings themselves and sewing a second seam into the pockets so that they wouldn't get holes. It didn't help that he needed to be sneaky. He had to switch between projects when they were paying too much attention to Asith.

Eventually, Dradevai left to hunt, but when they returned, they had something in a bag they were trying to hide behind their body. They quickly tucked it under the table and jumped a bit when they realized Asith was smiling at them. They went right back to whatever enchantment they'd been working on. It must have been complex, from what Asith could gather, for it had taken them quite a bit of time. They were even careful to hide whatever they were enchanting.

Asith assumed they would tell him what they were doing soon enough. So, he focused on learning the new spell Dradevai had shown him. It would allow him to fall slowly like a sheet of paper so that he wouldn't be hurt. He had a feeling it would be useful.

He lost track of time as he read and gathered materials for the spell. Asith had come to rather enjoy studying magic on his own. Something about it was relaxing, spending his time reading and writing out spells. It was just nice.

"Can I show you something?" Dradevai rubbed their hands together as they wandered over to Asith. They'd been working for a few hours without saying a word, but in that moment, they fidgeted with their hair.

"Is it whatever you've been sneaking around to do?" Asith asked. Dradevai pouted and started back toward the table they'd been working at.

"Yes. Was it really that obvious?"

"Only a little," Asith said.

Dradevai grumbled, picking up a pair of goggles. "These are for you, for flying." Dradevai flipped them over quickly, pointing out an etching in the lens, careful to not touch the front of the glass too much. "I found an enchantment to make the thin glass shatterproof, so you'll actually be able to see through them."

Dradevai offered the goggles for Asith to take. The soft leather padding that held the lens also had a sturdy leather tie attached to it. He looked over the simple warming spell in the leather, feeling the soft heat it gave off.

"Thank you." He knew his words weren't enough, but Dradevai was beaming, their grin only growing wider. "How did you even get the goggles?"

"I went into town like you showed me. I had to go to a few different towns until I found one that had what I was looking for, though."

"That's good. I'm proud of you, Dradevai," Asith said. Dradevai immediately grew sheepish, and they held their elbows in their hands, smiling without looking directly at Asith.

Something settled in the back of Asith's throat. If Dradevai could handle going down to the village on their own, that meant they were closer to their deal being finished and they would take Asith home. He rubbed the leather on the goggles, thinking about Dradevai being alone in their hoard again.

Asith tried to find the words. "Dradevai—"

"Wait." Dradevai held their hand up, their eyes hitting the hallway to the other chamber and their whole face growing hard. "Someone is coming."

"What?" Asith furrowed his brow, and then he heard it too. It was soft at first, but then it sounded like voices. He couldn't tell how many there were. "How are there possibly people here?"

Dradevai shook their head and approached the hallway, with Asith close on their tail. "I don't know, but you should hide."

"I am not going to hide." Asith kept his voice low as Dradevai peered over their shoulder. Dradevai turned around and set their hands on Asith's chest.

"Yes, you are." Dradevai pushed Asith back a few steps easily. Their strength didn't leave them even in their human form. "Whoever they are, they pose much more of a risk to you than they do to me."

"I am not going to let you go out there alone." Asith frowned, not resisting Dradevai's touch since he knew better than to fight them on it.

"Asith." Dradevai's voice grew sharp despite its quietness. "You are worth more to me than anything else in my hoard. Now, stay here."

Heat crept over Asith's face, and before he could say anything more, Dradevai spun around and turned down the hallway to the other chamber. All the words caught in Asith's throat, and while he wanted to scream to let out a myriad of emotions, he didn't want the other people to hear it. So, he pressed his hand over his mouth and did exactly what he thought he should: He turned and pulled on his armor.

The voices grew loud quickly, and as he heard Dradevai returning to their dragon form, and beginning to gather fire in their throat, Asith sped up his movements, leaving his helmet behind in favor of taking his sword. He pressed his hand over his mouth when he heard Dradevai let out a horrible shriek. Asith pulled his sword from its sheath and listened to what sounded like Dradevai being tortured.

When he peered around the stone wall of the doorway, Dradevai was crumpled underneath what looked to be a metal net. Even as large as they were, Dradevai looked so small lying on their side. Asith ground his teeth together, trying to figure out what could have possibly taken Dradevai down so easily. Only two men were in the chamber, and they didn't bear the mark of dragon knights. He couldn't imagine two people taking out a Bronze dragon even if they had been trained.

One man held a long staff with some kind of blue light at the end, heavy gloves on his hands. As Dradevai fussed underneath the net, the man touched the light to it. The metal lit up with what looked like lightning, and electricity coursed through the net and then through Dradevai's body. Asith had seen a wizard harness electricity like that once in the Capitol, but they had used it to light the lamps in the streets.

Asith had leaned just too far out, and the man with the staff caught sight of him when he met the man's eyes, Asith's heart skipped. He recognized him from the tavern, the man who had followed them into the woods the first time he'd gone to town with Dradevai. And that was the first time they had gone to town on their own. Asith had never warned them about it, and the man had found them. He pressed his back against the wall behind him again, hoping they wouldn't think anything of it. That, or to give him the advantage when one of them came around the corner.

"Go take care of that before the boss gets up here," one man said. Asith clenched his jaw and then let it go slack. Clearly, they knew he was there, but he had a feeling they didn't realize he was armed. He readied his sword, hearing the man slowly approach the opening to the hallway, and Asith decided patience was his best bet. Waiting felt like an eternity, but eventually, the man tried to jump around the corner and that was when Asith struck.

His sword caught the man's arm first, armed only with a dagger, and he quickly realized his error, stumbling back and away from Asith. Asith's lunge was quick, and a glancing blow to the dagger sent it flying. As the man tripped backward, Asith set his sword on his opponent's neck, only to get hit with a dagger that the other had thrown at him.

It seared; the blade sunk into his arm just where the bracer didn't cover. Asith staggered, his grip on his sword tightening as he tried not to drop it. The second dagger didn't hit him, clanking on the stone wall. He decided to close the distance on the man with the staff. He pulled the dagger from his arm and ran full speed at him, watching his face as he stepped back to get away.

The man seemed to gather himself, holding out the staff, but his grip wasn't strong; Asith could see he relied too much on his weapons. He took advantage of it, side-stepping the staff when the man tried to stab Asith with it and bringing his sword down on the wooden handle. Asith watched the piece that created the electricity roll away, and the man stumbled backward, a piece of wood in his hands.

"You have made a mistake coming here." Asith hoped he could scare the men into leaving, but that didn't seem to be the case. The man in front of him growled, his dark eyes glowing again as he grabbed a dagger at his side. He flew at Asith and tried to stab him again. Asith didn't hesitate to glance the dagger away with the guard of his sword and slashed the man's throat. The blood smelled stronger than Asith expected, for his experience was certainly not in killing other humans, he had to admit. Bile rose in the back of his throat, his body tensing as he tried not to heave. He needed to defend Dradevai.

The man he'd knocked over was trying to grab his dagger again, but Asith kicked it away. As he stepped forward, the man scrambled backward on the ground, his eyes wide. "B-but that armor, dragon knights are supposed to kill dragons, aren't they?"

Asith stomped on the enchanted gem on the top of the staff, which was enough to scare the man into cowering with his hands in front of his face. When Asith leaned down, he looked the man over and took stock to make sure he had no more weapons.

"Only when they are attacking villages." Asith kept his stare icy. "Tell me how to get the net open."

"You, you can just pull it off. The staff is what makes the lightning." The man kept himself hidden behind his hands.

"And before, you said there was someone else coming. What are their intentions here?" Asith tapped his sword on the man's arm, watching him try to desperately move away.

"Hunters, we hunt dragons. We're just scouts. Usually, we wait for everyone, but the dragon, it walked right into the trap."

Asith frowned, his throat thick as he realized how stupid he'd been. "You better head off and tell them not to come. Otherwise, they will have a dragon, no trap, and two powerful casters on their hands."

The man froze, then he nodded once he realized Asith was letting him go with his life. After the way he'd been hurting Dradevai with no remorse in his face, Asith didn't particularly want to. But if there were more coming, and if he could keep them from coming, that would be for the better. He backed away, and the man got up. In a rush, he grabbed some sort of climbing gear on his person and descended the sheer face of the cliff.

As soon as he was out of sight and Asith had confirmed that the other man was, in fact, dead, he rushed to Dradevai's side, setting his sword on the ground. He pulled the net off Dradevai, and Asith dropped to his knees and stroked Dradevai's head.

"Dradevai, please be okay." Asith ran a hand over the feathers on their nose. "Please wake up."

Dradevai's eyes opened just a slit, their tail moving slightly. They picked up their head and stretched out their wings as far as they could in the cavern. Then they transformed back into a human, wobbling slightly as Asith stood to support them.

"They hurt you," Dradevai said with a frown, leaning into Asith a bit as they got their bearings. Asith had forgotten about his injury almost entirely, but since Dradevai pointed it out, it hurt again. "Here."

Dradevai set their hand over the wound and said a few words, and the warmth of the spell spilled over Asith's skin. He cringed, the pain intensifying for a moment before going away completely, and to his surprise, the wound had closed when Dradevai pulled their hand away. All it left behind was an angry red mark and some bruising.

"Thank you," Asith said. Dradevai pulled away from him, moving to assess the man on the floor. They seemed upset for a moment and then looked back at Asith.

"I am sorry you had to go through this," Dradevai said. Asith shook his head. "I should have listened to you. Maybe if I hadn't gone alone, we could have talked to them."

Asith shook his head. "They were dragon hunters, Dradevai. I would have been caught with you, and I doubt they would have paid my life any thought."

"I guess that is true." Dradevai frowned and took a deep breath. "They said more were coming. You should leave before they arrive."

"Dradevai." Asith drew back slightly. "I am not leaving you here."

"I will be fine. I can seal off my hoard and start preparing to move—"

"Dradevai, you don't even know how long it will be before they get here." Asith took a step forward. "I can't just leave you here alone."

"You have to go. You shouldn't stay here and risk your life for me." Dradevai's face screwed up, their figure seeming taller than Asith ever remembered them being. They stepped into Asith's space. "Taking on two of them is one thing, but a whole group of hunters? I will come find you after I move the hoard."

Something burned in the pit of Asith's stomach as he studied their protective eyes. Something about the way they looked up at him made him snap. He wasn't going to get through to Dradevai if he kept using words, so he stepped toward Dradevai, leaned down, and pressed a kiss on their lips. They jolted in surprise, almost recoiling, but they stopped themself. Instead, they pressed into the kiss like Asith had wanted them to.

He couldn't leave Dradevai here, but they wouldn't be safe in just any town, either. In South Cairn, at least Asith and his mother could protect them from the people, and eventually, they would grow to trust Dradevai. They could fly deeper into the mountains but then they'd be alone, and Asith couldn't bear the thought of leaving them lonely all over again.

"Come with me." Asith pulled away, taking in the look on Dradevai's face. For the first time since Asith had met them, they looked completely flustered, their face red and their eyes swimming as they tried to rebalance themself.

"What?" Dradevai shook their head slightly, confused.

"We can move everything into the other cavern, seal off your hoard, and go back to the village where you found me. We will be safe there. Please, don't make me leave you here alone."

"But this is where my parents left me." Dradevai wrapped their hands around their amber pendant. "What if they come back looking for me here?"

Asith's arms stiffened. They weren't looking directly at Asith, and their lips quivered, a tremble starting across their entire body.

"Vai, I'm sure your parents would want you safe more than they'd want you here." Asith squeezed their shoulder.

Dradevai looked up at Asith, tears gathered in their eyes. Their mouth fell open like they might say something, but nothing came out. Dradevai's teeth clicked audibly when they shut their mouth as if they had forgotten they'd left it open.

"You're right." Dradevai's eyes scanned the pile of various gold items, and they looked back at Asith. "We'll have to be quick."

Asith nodded back, and they immediately set about getting ready. He started by taking his sword off the ground, sliding it back into its sheath, and then heading into the other room to pack some books. Dradevai moved all the gold items with a spell and, at Asith's suggestion, used a spell to gather any remaining coins from the pile. They tossed them into the purse they'd found previously, and Dradevai moved on to sealing off the hallway.

They found the chalk, drawing the symbol they needed for the incantation, and moved the stone as if it were soft earth to close off the door easily. It must have been how Dradevai had dug out the two caverns in the first place, though he didn't have time to consider that thought further.

Asith took the chunk of chocolate Dradevai hadn't shredded, then packed the clothes he'd been making for Dradevai and the book of spells he'd been working with. Dradevai came over with Asith's helmet in hand and set it down near him. Asith only glanced at it before picking up the goggles Dradevai had made him and tying them around his head tightly. They couldn't take much, and Asith cared less about his armor than he ever had.

Dradevai turned into a dragon, their colossal form elegant as they bent their head for him. He repeated what he'd done before, tying himself to Dradevai and adjusting the backpack.

"I have to go up, so be ready." Dradevai bent their neck toward Asith as he adjusted the goggles on his face. He nodded, smiling at Dradevai.

"I trust you." Asith tightened his grip on the ropes and held his breath, then nodded at Dradevai to go. They took off with a jump, flapping their wings and sending most of the items in the chamber flying, but they couldn't worry about them. As Asith looked back on the home he had shared with Dradevai, he suddenly wanted to defend it. They could come back; they would be okay.

His lungs didn't burn quite as much when he started breathing again, Dradevai gliding down the mountainside until they were nice and low. They stayed somewhere that Asith could breathe easily, and as they flew out toward the dark horizon, Asith smiled. Dradevai would carry him home.

CHAPTER 7

15th of Kasdiel

Asith fell off Dradevai's back and hit the ground with a heavy thud, with a sky he recognized above him. He stripped the pack he was wearing and dropped it next to him. For the first time in a long while, he wasn't terribly cold; in fact, he was warm, too warm, but far too tired to take off his heavy cloak. His breathing sputtered as he tried to slow it down, which prompted Dradevai to scramble to his side the moment they'd turned back into a human.

"Are you okay? What's wrong?" Dradevai knelt next to him.

"Everything hurts." Asith took a deep breath, trying to straighten out his legs for the first time in hours. "No wonder I passed out when you carried me there."

Dradevai's shoulders dropped, and they poked Asith's chest. "So you're just being dramatic?"

"Only a little!" Asith dragged himself to sit up. "Everything does hurt."

Dradevai rolled their eyes and leaned back on their knees, looking over the small field as people wandered out of their houses. The sound of Dradevai's wings must have woken the farmers who lived close to the fields.

"Yes." Asith nodded and carefully pushed the goggles onto his head. "Thank you."

"There are people coming." Dradevai stood and shuffled behind Asith the moment he was standing. "Should I hide my horns?"

Asith slipped his cloak from his shoulders and offered it to Dradevai. It would be enough in the dark to get them back to his house or his mother's safely.

"Here, if you feel safer with your horns covered, you can use this, but I don't think anyone would attack you if I told them not to." They would listen to him, and if they didn't, they'd listen to his mother. "It will be fine. The people here know me, and I will protect you, I promise."

Dradevai looked up at him nervously for a moment and simply nodded before they put the cloak on and pulled the hood up. Asith let Dradevai stay behind him, figuring it wasn't worth it to force them to face a large number of new people right away. Asith led Dradevai down the small dirt path so they wouldn't mess up much more of the wheat. The two people closest to them were Lash and Colia, who owned the field they were in.

"Who's there? We have dogs." Lash held a pitchfork, but his dog, Patch, ran straight up to Asith, tail wagging and paws beating on the ground with excitement.

"It's Asith." He set his hands on Patch's head and scratched his ears as Colia caught up with Lash. "I have someone with me."

Lash stared at him, his pitchfork still raised. "How do I know it's you? Asith got carried off by a dragon."

"Your dog's name is Patch. Look how he's acting with me." Asith had known Lash since they were children and Patch since he was a puppy. Patch loved Asith and his mother for whatever reason. He stood still, keeping between Dradevai and the pitchfork even though Lash probably wouldn't use it.

"You're not a dragon?" Lash asked, to which Asith frowned.

"Lash, please." Asith held up his hands and glanced at Dradevai, who looked ready to cast a spell. He needed to prevent that from happening, for that certainly wouldn't help their case.

Colia took a few steps closer to him, looking at Patch and then Asith again. He met their eyes, trying to clarify it was really him as best he could. He didn't really know what else to do besides plead softly at them.

"You're alive! I can't believe it! They all said you were carried off by a dragon and you were certainly dead." Colia's face lit up in the low light of the moon. They took another step closer with their lantern to see Asith. Once they confirmed it was him, their face paled. "I need to go tell your mother. She would kill me if I didn't get her right away."

Lash relaxed as Colia turned to scramble into town. Their neighbors, the Rossitters, were checking out the commotion and torchlight. Patch sniffed Dradevai's legs curiously, so Asith gently nudged Patch to get him to return to Lash.

"Are you okay? What happened to the dragon?" Lash set down the pitchfork, looking at Dradevai more carefully. "Who is this?"

"This is the dragon." Asith gestured at Dradevai, and Lash's eyes grew wider than dinner plates.

"That isn't a good joke, Asith." Lash took three steps back, his grip on his pitchfork tightening.

"I thought it was sort of funny," Asith said.

Asith took Dradevai's hand and pulled them past Lash. Patch was sniffing at their feet, interested in and unafraid of Dradevai. Dogs usually had good judgment, so Asith wasn't surprised.

Asith wanted to get to his mother first because he needed someone that would assuredly be on their side despite her anger. She had a reputation in the town that would protect Dradevai long enough to prove they weren't a threat to anyone.

People stared at them from their windows, some calling out to Asith excitedly and waving, while others eyed Dradevai strangely. It didn't take long for a small crowd to form around them, a few people trying to speak to Asith about where he had been and who Dradevai was. He did his best to put off their questions, saying he needed to find his mother, though the crowd made that difficult.

Of course, Asith should have known his mother would find him before he found her. She barreled down the road at them, her eyes wide and glittering in the light of the half-moon. He expected her to look angry, but the soft, excited look on her face made him feel a form of guilt that made his body shiver. She threw herself into his arms so hard that he let go of Dradevai and nearly fell over, and he wrapped his arms around her.

"Asith Evrouin, you have been missing for months!" His mother, with a tight grip on his shoulders, pulled back as she bore down on him. Tears were streaming down her face, and her red hair was pulled off to the side, with a coat over her nightgown. She looked cold and small and sad, while, at the same time, anger bubbled below her skin. He could see in her hardened eyes and the way her forehead wrinkled that she was fuming. Asith recoiled, his anxiety spiking as his mother turned into the woman he feared as a child when he'd done something wrong. "You didn't think to let me know that you were alive?"

"You didn't get my letter?" Asith asked. He knew a letter sent more than a month after a dragon carried him away really wasn't enough. She had every right to be angry with him.

"Um, sorry, Asith being gone for so long is my fault." Dradevai stepped to Asith's side and waved slightly at his mother.

She turned on Dradevai, her brow still furrowed and her hands balled up into fists. Dradevai's eyes grew wide, and they took a step back. Some of the people who had gathered to watch them were pointing at Dradevai, while others whispered to each other nervously.

His mother's eyes snapped back to Asith. "Is this the dragon?"

"Yes, ma'am." Asith's legs trembled. "I'm sorry, but maybe we should go inside before more people see us."

His mother looked from Dradevai to Asith, taking him in for a moment. She sniffed, rubbing the wedding ring on her finger. Finally, she took them both into a hug. Dradevai shifted their weight and stole a glance at the crowd. She softened slightly and set a hand on their shoulder.

"I am angry with you for taking him," his mother said, "but he is still in trouble for not telling me sooner. He is an adult who should know better, after all."

She shot Asith a look that, truly, he deserved. He nodded, then glanced at Dradevai to check on them. They crossed their arms, crumbling under his mother's words. Asith tried to smile at them, but they weren't looking. His mother straightened herself up and scowled at the people gawking at them.

"Come on, we should get the two of you inside." She turned, gently nudging them along. Once they were moving, his mother spun on her heels and stomped toward the crowd. Several people twitched or took a step back. Asith couldn't blame them.

"Also, all of you busybodies can go back to sleep." She pointed at the group, stamping her foot. "If you don't, you're going to regret it."

Asith quickly led Dradevai to his mother's house, noticing that, once she was done yelling, she naturally flanked them—a protective instinct. When he stepped up into his childhood home, Asith's knees buckled, and he barely carried himself to the table. He settled in a chair at his mother's command and dropped the pack of books and various food items. As Dradevai sat near him, his mother put a kettle on the small stove and threw a few logs into it so that the flames would grow.

"I'm sorry," Asith said. "I should have found a way to contact you sooner. I'm sure I could have found a spell."

"You should have," his mother snapped.

"Oh, I know of one." Dradevai perked up as they always did when they were trying to be helpful. "You should have asked. I would have taught you."

Asith's shoulders dropped as he looked at Dradevai with a level of frustration he couldn't convey to them. Dradevai stared back blankly and tilted their head. He resisted snapping at them, they were having a rough night already, and they obviously hadn't done it on purpose.

However, his mother laughed, and she walked over and ran her hand over Asith's hair. She even kissed the top of his head like she always did when he was a child and wrapped an arm around his shoulders.

"It's all right. My uncle always told me my children would disappoint me somehow." She tousled his hair and moved to find tea for them.

"Besides, you are home safe. That is all that matters." She turned toward Dradevai. "I'm glad that you didn't eat him."

Dradevai's jaw dropped open, and they glanced at Asith. "That's a thing a dragon would normally do?"

"A Blue or a Green might. I don't know about the others." Asith nodded as he spoke, but most of all, he noticed how his mother looked at Dradevai. Her confusion rapidly turned to worry.

"What is your name?" His mother returned to the table with three mugs and the heated kettle.

"My name is Dradevai. It's nice to meet you." They smiled as they sat up slightly, trying to look polite, which struck Asith as unusual. Normally, Dradevai was so haughty that he could hardly imagine them trying to make a good impression.

"You can call me Maryan. It's nice to meet you, Dradevai." Her smile wavered, but Asith was just happy that she seemed more focused on Dradevai. "Are you planning on staying here?"

Dradevai nodded, and so did Asith when his mother looked at him. She rubbed her wedding ring again, watching the two of them with a furrowed brow. Asith shifted in his seat slightly as his mother added the tea leaves to the kettle.

"Actually, Mama, we're here because they were attacked by dragon hunters." Asith gestured at Dradevai. Despite how brave they'd been acting, they shivered, their fear taking over for a moment. "So, we're planning on staying here a while."

His mother seemed to see his fear, too, settling a mug in front of Dradevai first. She then set one in front of Asith before she finally sat down with them. A troubled look spread on her face as she processed what Asith had said. She had always been empathetic, she was the one who had taught him to pay attention to people, and that was how he'd figured out Dradevai was so desperately lonely. He could see it in her as she studied Dradevai like they were her own child, and then she looked down at her tea. She opened and closed her mouth once, taking another moment to think before she spoke.

"Well…" She took a deep breath. "Since Dradevai came here with you, people will learn to trust them. But I can't promise they'll be safe."

"Do you think people will try to hurt them?" Asith touched his fingertips to the hot mug.

"No, because if anyone here hurt them, they'd feel my wrath, and they know it." His mother smiled at Dradevai. "But please, it's late. Sip your tea and relax a bit. The two of you are welcome to stay here tonight."

"Thank you, Mama, but is my house still mine?" Asith picked up his tea, sipping on it and feeling so wonderfully at home. It was his mother's favorite blend. When she nodded, Asith smiled and set his mug on the table. "I'm so glad. I miss my bed."

His mother laughed, then set her head in her hand and yawned. It was quite late, and even Dradevai started to look tired, sipping their tea and wilting in their chair. They finished their tea, and by the time they left his mother's house, most people had returned to their homes. Asith could lead Dradevai to his house in peace.

He didn't live far from his mother. His small, round house matched the others, save for the green awning he had placed over his front door just before he'd been taken by Dradevai. He'd reused the fabric from making himself a heavy cloak for the rain, so it looked newer than everyone else's. His front door was a step up, and his mother had a copy of the key.

"The houses here are all round," Dradevai said.

They strayed from Asith to examine the houses and inspect the rain barrels. Dradevai was particularly interested in the showers, asking Asith questions about them until they were inside his house, which, at that point, Dradevai was far more interested in.

The room had a short staircase on one side as his mother's home did, though his home was smaller. But like every house in South Cairn, the stairs led to a low loft only a bit taller than Asith. That separated where he slept from an area with a small table and his unlit stove. A comfortable chair was pressed in one corner with a bookcase next to it, and it looked like his mother had cleared out some of the food, which wouldn't have lasted.

His loft had his bed and the mannequin where he kept his armor, as well as a small trunk that stored clothes. Dradevai was interested in everything, wandering around and going up the stairs to look at the bed, while Asith set a few logs in the stove and naturally picked up the flint lighter next to his spices.

"Would you like me to light that?" Dradevai was leaning over the small rail that ran along the loft so that Asith wouldn't walk off it in the dark. Asith paused and chuckled. He had forgotten Dradevai could just light it.

"That would be helpful, actually." Asith set the flint back, and Dradevai hopped off the railing and landed gently next to Asith's small table. The sudden movement startled Asith, and they apologized quickly before they walked over and carefully blew fire into the stove. The room warmed up immediately, and Asith unloaded the pack of supplies from Dradevai's home.

"Is that the chocolate?" Dradevai asked, getting on their toes to look over Asith's shoulder.

"Yes, I'm not sure what made me grab it, but it seemed important." Asith set the books in a pile and put the chocolate on the shelf as far away from the stove as possible so that it wouldn't melt.

Dradevai chuckled. "Well, you weren't wrong. It was important."

Asith stopped to laugh, setting the jerky on the shelf before he peeled away his armor. He positioned it on the mannequin, then carefully placed his grieves down behind the tunic and scale mail that was starting to make him uncomfortable. His bracers went on the ground near the grieves out of pure exhaustion that started to take him.

Dradevai poked through the books on his shelf and claimed one despite how dark it was. It would probably help them sleep if they read for a bit first, so Asith said nothing about it.

However, when Dradevai walked up the small set of stairs, they asked, "Where should I sleep?"Their eyes glowed in the light of the single lantern on the bedside table.

"We're going to have to share." Asith looked at his bed. "And I guess you'll need to sleep in your human form. Is that okay?"

Asith slipped his undershirt over his head, thinking about the clothes his mother made him that he had left at Dradevai's hoard. He picked up an old tunic, then glanced at Dradevai to ask if they wanted one as well, but their eyes were locked on Asith's chest. Sleeping in the same bed might not have been the best option.

"I have a bed roll. You can sleep in the bed," Asith said. Dradevai shook their head and looked at Asith directly.

"We can share." Dradevai stood to the side of the bed, waiting for Asith's response as they toyed with the hem of their short blouse. "I don't mind."

Asith stared at his bed. He wanted to sleep in it so badly. It had been weeks, and while the pillows had been soft, they weren't always the most comfortable. To his surprise, when he looked back at Dradevai, they weren't looking at Asith. They gazed at nothing, still waiting for his response. It was cute, actually; Asith liked that side of Dradevai. There was less trying to figure out who they really were under the sharp tongue and overly confident smile.

Asith took a step closer to Dradevai, setting a hand on their shoulder. "We're used to sleeping in the same bed. You're right, let's just share."

"Yes, please." Dradevai leaned toward Asith, but they didn't press into him. Instead, they looked up at him carefully before they stepped around him, and Asith wasn't about to question it. The night had been long for them both; they might just be tired.

"Do you want something else to sleep in?" Asith asked. "I could give you a tunic or something."

Dradevai nodded and followed Asith back to the wardrobe. He took a navy tunic out for them; it was old but soft and long enough for Dradevai to be completely covered. Asith turned around so that they could change.

"Is it okay if I sleep on the side that's not on the wall?" Dradevai rolled the sleeves of the tunic up to their elbows.

Asith sat on the edge of the bed. "Sure, that's fine, why?"

"In case I wake up before you."

Asith crawled into the bed and settled into the pillows. He had to admit, he already missed the self-warmed ones.

"I would normally argue with you about that," Asith said, "but I am so tired that you probably will wake up before me."

Dradevai got under the blankets next to him, and they pressed close. They looked at Asith with their head on the pillow.

"Are you really that tired?" Dradevai had lain out on their side, almost awkwardly, as if they didn't know quite how to sleep in that form, which wasn't entirely shocking. Asith had only ever seen them asleep in their dragon form, so they probably needed to get used to that. Though, he rather enjoyed lying next to Dradevai and looking them in the eyes, especially when they were so wide and curious.

"Yes." Asith turned to Dradevai. "Are you going to be able to sleep?"

"I think so." Dradevai shifted. "I just have to get used to it."

Asith shook his head. "We can always find a way to make you more comfortable tomorrow. You need to be able to sleep while you're here."

"I don't want to be a bother." They avoided looking directly at Asith. "I don't know how long I'll be here."

"You're not a bother, Vai." Asith reached for Dradevai's hand and stopped himself, setting it flat between them instead. "You can stay here for as long as it takes for you to feel safe again."

Dradevai was quiet for long enough that Asith was struggling to keep his eyes open.

"Thank you for bringing me here. For wanting me to feel safe," Dradevai said.

"Of course, Vai." Asith softened, worried for Dradevai's state of mind for a moment. They smiled at him, big and sweet, before they rolled over and tried to settle into the bed. He watched them for just a while longer, his eyes sliding down their neck and back. Asith smiled; something about Dradevai wearing his clothes had his attention, but he was far too tired for his body to react. Instead, he settled into the pillows and listened to them until their breathing slowed.

CHAPTER 8

16th of Kasdiel

He woke to the smell of toasted bread and eggs frying in a cast-iron. It was familiar in a way, like when Delri would visit, and he'd wake to his mother cooking them breakfast. They'd talk until Delri woke up, taking the time to cook together. Asith heard his mother and Dradevai talking in low tones. At least, he assumed it must be his mother, for he doubted Dradevai had suddenly learned to cook while Asith wasn't paying attention.

"Ah, you're finally awake," his mother said. She was smiling as he sat up and looked over the railing at the two of them. A pot of something was simmering on the stove, and a plate full of bacon and eggs sat in front of Dradevai already. "Come down, I have breakfast for you. And there's chicken stew for later."

Asith found a pair of leggings, leaving on the tunic he'd slept in. As he looked for his clothes, he realized the journal about his father was gone completely. His mother must have taken it, which didn't entirely surprise Asith. But for that moment, he would focus on breakfast, since he certainly would not turn away a meal he didn't have to cook for himself.

"How long was I asleep?" Asith settled in the chair next to Dradevai and pushed his hair out of his face. His mother set a plate of food in front of him quickly, which, if he were being honest, nearly made him cry. Eating something other than boiled eggs or chewy jerky nearly brought tears to his eyes.

"I woke up a few hours ago," Dradevai said. "Maryan has only been here for an hour or so."

"You could have woken me." Asith realized he'd left Dradevai sitting around. It was well into the afternoon. But Dradevai shook their head.

"I tried. For a moment, I thought you were dead, but you started to snore."

His mother burst out laughing before setting a teapot on the table and settling into a chair. They added, "So, I left you there and started to read."

"The two of you were up rather late, so it's not surprising," his mother said. "I didn't bother to come by until past noon." His mother poured them each tea and nudged the cream toward Dradevai when they reached for it. "I was surprised to find Dradevai awake."

"They're usually awake before I am." After adding honey to his tea, Asith ate, while Dradevai was finishing their plate. His mother smiled warmly at both of them. Her lips had a knowing curve to them, and her eyes gently narrowed as she wrapped her hands around her teacup. She was sizing them up as she rubbed her wedding ring with her thumb. He turned his eyes to his food, trying to avoid her gaze.

"That's impressive. Asith has always been an early riser, much to my chagrin." His mother sipped at her tea and let the conversation quiet for a moment before she looked at Dradevai more carefully. "The two of you seem to live together well."

Dradevai nodded and rubbed the back of their neck. "We do. Also, I really am sorry about taking Asith. I didn't understand what I was doing."

Asith looked between Dradevai and his mother, unsure of how she was going to react. He knew his mother well, but honestly, he had never seen her that troubled. Her face scrunched up, and she pressed her lips together, her forehead wrinkled. She stared at her hands, still rubbing the ring on her finger.

"It's, it's not okay," his mother said.

Dradevai's eyes grew wide, their jaw falling open as his mother looked up at them. She still had a scrunch on her face, but she smiled.

"It's not okay," she repeated. "But I will forgive you. In time."

"Oh." The tension in Dradevai's body released as their shoulders dropped. "I can be patient."

His mother nodded at them, blinking back tears as she stirred her tea. Asith reached out and took her hand, stopping her from rubbing the wedding ring.

"I'm really sorry, too, Mama." Asith squeezed her hand like he would when he was little and didn't know what else to do. "But Dradevai did teach me some magic while I was there. I learned some things that could make us more money."

"I was not aware that you could do any magic at all," his mother said. Her hand went slack in his, the other moving to her collar to adjust it.

"I didn't know I could," Asith said, "but Dradevai was able to teach me. I suppose, as the stories go, that means I could have always done it."

His mother hummed softly, then smiled. "I suppose it does."

She stared at them, not saying anything. Asith shifted in his seat and squeezed her hand again to gain her attention.

"He's rather good at it too," Dradevai said slowly, looking at Asith. "He's a fast learner."

"That's wonderful." His mother laughed awkwardly. "Well, why don't you reorganize yourselves? Watch the pot; I'm going to go buy you both more food."

She stood quickly, letting go of Asith's hand. Dradevai looked sidelong at Asith, nervously tapping their nails on the table as his mother bustled through the kitchen. She picked up her basket, smiling at Asith. Her eyes didn't sparkle like they usually did.

"Okay, Mama." Unsure what else he could say, he added, "We'll watch the stew."

"Thank you." His mother bent down and kissed the top of his head before she left.

Dradevai stopped tapping their nails, looking at Asith. "Is she okay?"

"I think she'll be okay." Asith sighed, turning back to his food. "I left something behind here that I think hurt her feelings. And not telling her I was okay sooner made it worse."

"Okay," Dradevai said. They watched Asith eat for a few moments, their lips pursed like they had more questions, but eventually, they picked up their book. They sat in the soft chair next to the window.

Asith finished his food, cleaned the plate, and stirred the stew. Then Asith slipped upstairs and retrieved the leggings he'd been working on for Dradevai. They were focused enough on their book that they probably wouldn't notice what he was doing, and he wanted to give them their gift, since they had given him one.

After finding his thimble on the bookshelf where he had left it. Asith threaded a needle. He sat at the table and carefully stitched them with just enough seam allowance that they'd be snug but not too tight. It was peaceful, sewing in his home again, but something about having Dradevai reading nearby made it better than when he'd be making hundreds of armor fittings on his own. He made quick work of the hem and glanced at Dradevai to make sure they weren't looking before he walked back up to the loft. He added the leggings to the paper he'd wrapped the rest of Dradevai's present in, then tied it off with twine.

"Dradevai?" Asith walked down the stairs to the table, holding the present. "I have something for you."

Dradevai peered over their book and straightened when they saw the gift. With eyes wide, they stood, dog-earing the page, and set the book down on the chair. Their head cocked to one side, and Asith had a feeling they had never gotten a wrapped gift before.

"What is it?" they asked.

Asith chuckled, handing it over to them. "Open it."

They turned the package over in their hands, glancing at Asith briefly before they pulled the bow loose and unwrapped the paper. Their eyes lit up as they pulled out the vest first and then the sash. They seemed to understand quickly what they had been given, so, after a quick glance at Asith, they scooped up everything and scurried away to the loft to change.

"There is an enchantment in the vest." Asith followed Dradevai but stayed at the bottom of the steps to give them privacy.

"What does it do?" Dradevai threw the clothes they'd been wearing over the door of the armoire they were changing behind.

"It's a homing enchantment," Asith said. "No matter where you are, if you're wearing the vest, you will know which direction your home is."

Dradevai moved around the door while slipping the vest on. They had changed rather quickly, and to Asith's delight, the clothing fit them well. The tunic didn't need to be hemmed more than it was already, especially once Dradevai laced the vest and tied the sash around their waist. Their eyes glinted in the sunlight as they stepped in front of the mirror hanging on the side of the armoire. As Asith had expected, the rich red and orange suited them rather well.

Dradevai paused by the mirror and removed all the jewelry they had been wearing as well. The red earrings and gold bracelets were set aside, including the bracelet they kept on their upper arm. They left one on, though: the hand-carved amber pendant on a black leather cord that Asith had never seen them take off.

"The enchantment works." Dradevai smoothed down the vest and rubbed the suede at the hem, their face becoming soft and fond for a moment. Then an uncertain sadness settled on them. But they forced a smile at Asith, and he wanted nothing but to comfort them. "You really have learned magic quickly. I feel like our deal is complete."

Asith's throat tied into a knot, and he carefully edged closer to Dradevai as they turned back to the mirror. They smiled at themself, touching each of the embroidered flowers on the vest and running their fingers over the sash.

"Dradevai, I—" Asith jumped when his front door opened. His mother had a basket full of food, her hair tousled from the wind as she tried to blow her bangs out of her face.

"I'm back!" She set the basket on the table and talked all about the marketplace. Dradevai stepped down from the loft, offering to help un-load the groceries. Asith put away his sewing materials before he returned to tend the stew. Once the food had been put away, his mother joined Asith's side, looking up at him while he stirred the pot.

"I think that you should take Dradevai to get registered." His mother picked up his little bowl of salt and added some to the stew. "I spoke to a few people in town, and I think if you have Corym on your side, no one will be able to argue with Dradevai being here."

Asith stopped stirring. "Do you think that will help?"

"If they have a job and help the town, people will be more accepting." His mother nodded and took the spoon from him, nudging him from his place. She smiled as Dradevai walked up to her side.

"Registered?" Dradevai asked. "Could I get a hunting job like I did in that other village?"

"Yes, I can explain on the way."

Asith wiped his hands off on a towel and went upstairs to change his clothes. He wanted to discuss the matter further outside. He led Dradevai down the street before he explained, "Did you want to stay here in town? You are welcome to stay with me, but I would understand if you wanted to have a place that is your own."

"Well..." Dradevai looked around nervously. Some people were al-ready observing them, but mostly, they seemed curious and not threaten-ing. At least to Asith, they did. "I don't think I would like being alone here. You wouldn't mind my staying with you?"

Asith smiled at them, shaking his head. "No, I don't mind. I just want-ed to make sure you'd want to stay with me."

"I do." Dradevai nodded. "So then, what is getting registered?"

"We just have to go down to the village representative and let them know you live here now." Asith turned a corner, making sure Dradevai followed. "It will get you a bit of money monthly and some food."

"They give everyone food? But I really only eat eggs and fresh game, and I don't think I really need money." Dradevai tilted their head, befud-dled in a way Asith had never really seen them before. It made him laugh softly, and Dradevai glowered at him.

"I'm sorry, but you are right. You don't really need money or food." Asith smiled at Dradevai, and their pout faded. "It would be useful to have an income if your money were ever stolen, and you can use your food stipend for eggs."

Dradevai looked as if they might protest but stopped themself.

"Actually, that is a good point."

"The food is also helpful," Asith said. "It includes things that are grown or raised near here, so it's fresh and good."

"Will I be able to get fresh game somewhere?" Dradevai kept on Asith's heels as he turned another corner and headed toward the center of town.

"I think we should make an agreement with the farmers as we did in that village near your hoard." Asith took a deep breath and tried to think for a moment. "The Casts were having a problem keeping deer out of their corn before I left."

"You know a lot about the people here." Their eyes were inquisitive as they looked up at Asith. He wasn't sure if it was because they were getting used to the new environment or if Asith genuinely surprised them. He smiled at them, though; he had known bringing Dradevai here meant he'd be spending a lot of time answering questions.

"I've lived here most of my life," Asith said, "save for the few years I lived in the Capitol and the time I was with you."

Dradevai considered that. "I guess I have only lived in one place."

"I'm sure you know just about every book in your hoard. This is not much different." Asith paused, looking at the small bookstore and then back at Dradevai, who appeared confused. "This is a bookstore, if you ever want to buy more. We can stop here on the way back if you'd like."

"Bookstore?" Dradevai's eyes grew huge. "I can trade gold for books? Yes? They'll just give me a book for gold?"

Asith laughed. "Yes, but you get to pick the book out."

Dradevai looked like they were struggling to not go running into the store. "W-we can come back, please? I don't have any money with me."

"We will come back, I promise." Asith nudged Dradevai's arm, encouraging them to walk again. He glanced at the suns briefly; they would have time to stop on the way back, and Asith had money with him.

"Thank you." Dradevai continued to look back at the bookstore as they walked away, and Asith could honestly say he was excited to take Dradevai to a library.

The office was one of the oldest buildings in South Cairn, humble and piled with books and papers that held records for everyone who had been registered to South Cairn over the years. Asith mostly remembered his mother bringing him there after the woman he knew as his grandmother passed away so that she could be buried in the local graveyard. Therefore, Asith's memories of the place were mixed and rather boring.

Corym was waiting for them as if his mother had already spoken to her. She had the papers ready on her desk, and she launched immediately into asking Dradevai basic identification questions. She recorded Dradevai's answers. Dradevai was perplexed by the whole thing, answering slowly or asking for clarifications, but Corym was patient with them.

"Well…" Corym clicked her tongue, writing that Dradevai was born during Laha in 550. "I guess you get to choose a surname for yourself."

That seemed to stress Dradevai out, for they turned to Asith desperately for some kind of direction. Asith thought it over for a moment and ran his hand over the back of his head.

"You could use Bronze," Asith suggested and then quickly added, "Or you could take mine and my mother's."

"I was born knowing myself as Dradevai, Freer of Wings. Will that work?" Dradevai asked.

Corym considered it. "I could use Freewing for the papers? And register you as from South Cairn?" Dradevai nodded. Corym smiled at them sweetly. "Then welcome to South Cairn, Dradevai Freewing. It is a delight to have you here."

"Thank you." Dradevai grinned back at Corym. Before they left, Asith asked which farms needed large pests removed, and Corym rather liked the idea of Dradevai eating the deer and boar to keep them out of the fields. It didn't take long for her to enlist their help to remove trees, for she discovered Dradevai had pulled trees from the ground before.

Once they had finished chatting, Dradevai bounced out of Corym's office with a renewed excitement. They looked less nervous as they peered into the market, which was situated on the other side of the representative's office. Their nerves only seemed to come and go, which hopefully meant they would only last as long as it took for Dradevai to settle in.

"Did you want to stop at the bookstore on the way home?" Asith followed them into the road.

Dradevai stopped, still looking around the town slowly. "Maybe we should go tomorrow. Maryan is waiting for us, after all."

"We can go first thing in the morning, then." Asith really thought Dradevai would still want to go to the bookstore since they usually put their interests above others, but Dradevai was changing. "Do you want to try to lead us home?"

"I think we will get lost, but I will try."

Asith laughed, reminded of something Delri had said to him when she visited South Cairn. They started out ahead of Asith for the first time that day, leading him back to the bookstore first. The sun was setting as they got there. They needed a little nudging in the correct direction, but otherwise, they managed well on their own.

His mother was waiting for them with chicken stew and a nice fire, which warmed his house considerably. A shiver ran through him as the suns dipped under the horizon. Dradevai looked at him worriedly, but Asith pulled on a doublet, which seemed to calm their nerves.

"I've been wondering…" His mother picked up the lid of the pot, checking the stew. "Where did you get those clothes, Dradevai?"

Dradevai perked up and Asith could already feel their response coming, so he shoved a large piece of bread into his mouth so that he wouldn't have to respond to whatever his mother would say. And of course, Dradevai beamed with pride the way they always did; however, they didn't look pompous, simply excited.

"Asith made them for me." Dradevai's smile made Asith want to hide. The look on his mother's face would only make that feeling worse. "The vest even has an enchantment sewn in it."

"Did he really?" The sound of his mother's voice was enough to make him want to hide under the table, the high-pitched emphasis on every-thing she said and the rather knowing way she turned to him. Worse, his hunched posture probably only made his feelings more obvious to his mother. "I'm surprised. He normally only makes armor fittings."

Dradevai didn't seem aware, at least not yet, but they smiled sweet-ly at him and held out their arms to show off the billowing sleeves on their tunic.

"Yes, they fit me well too. I've never had clothes that fit before," Dradevai said with a nod.

"Well, they look rather nice on you. What does the enchantment do?" She looked back at Dradevai, a quiet coming over her as she chewed on her lip. Dradevai looked flustered for a moment, and they cleared their throat.

"Uh, it points me home."

If Asith didn't know any better, he'd say Dradevai was trying to hide that the question had embarrassed them. His mother seemed to catch on, smiling kindly at Dradevai and leaving it be.

"That must be useful." She set the lid back on the pot. "This needs a few more minutes."

Asith braved a direct glance at his mother, nearly dropping the knife in his hand. Her expression was pinched and tight, her brow low as she looked at her wedding ring. Dradevai wasn't looking, and he was thankful because he feared how they would have reacted to that look. Her eyes swam over the room and found Asith's, then she shook the expression away, her curls bouncing. With a smile, she went right back to tending the stew, acting as if nothing had happened.

He did his best to move on as well, but when they sat down to eat, the anxiety that had plagued his mother earlier hadn't left completely. Her eyes lingered on Dradevai for long spells, her fingers absently touching and tapping the ring on her left hand. She didn't look at them like she was afraid, though. Her expression reminded him of the one she got whenever she watched him do something dangerous as a child. She always said she didn't have the heart to watch Asith train with weapons, so he wondered what was causing her to look that way at Dradevai.

"Is everything all right, Maryan?" Dradevai looked considerably worried. His mother shook her head, sitting up a bit, and took a drink of her tea.

"Yes," she said. "Well, no."

Asith's mind filled with thoughts of what could be wrong. His mother was his best friend, and he couldn't really bear the thought of her hurting. He had realized that during the time he had spent in Dradevai's hoard. Setting a gentle hand on her arm, he let her take his hand in her own, which made her smile in a way that was so, so sad.

"I have a confession to make to you, Asith, and I am sorry I did not tell you about this sooner."

Her eyes were soft on him, the worry bubbling over as tears pricked her eyes. That terrified Asith, he had rarely seen his mother cry, and it had always been reserved for death.

"I had always thought that your lineage did not matter, that you were my boy and that was that, but I think it is time for me to tell the story of how I met your father."

He nodded slightly, still worried, but less so than before, and she started her story.

CHAPTER 9

Year 544 with Vitiope
13th of Asdel

The wildflowers grew like weeds in the spring, making my long walks into the woods to find clearings full of yarrow and cornflowers worth every step. Before I brought home flowers to place in my uncle's clinic, I wanted to lie among the tulips and read. I used to do that walk with my mother weekly, but an accident in the silver mines took both my parents from me, leaving me to the village. Onas, the town's doctor who had lost his wife several years before, took care of me. He raised me like his own daughter, teaching me the basics of medicine and caring for the people who worked in the mines, but sometimes, I still followed my mother's or father's old habits when I wanted to feel closer to them.

No day in the woods ever felt the same, especially not in the foothills of the Barren Rise mountains. I carried my scissors to trim flowers but also for protection. The days were starting to get longer, early spring taking the valley and making it easier for me to find tulips to leave on my mother and father's grave. I lined my basket with a handkerchief and tucked a book into it, expecting to spend my day out in the wildflowers.

The second sun rose slowly over the mountains as I followed a small foraging trail into the woods, the trees rising around me like a blanket, making the world around me quieter. I walked until I was deep in the hills, the rustling of new leaves becoming like accompaniment to birdsong.

When the birdsong stopped, I hadn't noticed at first. As I approached a clearing I had spent many days in since I was a child, I realized something was in it. I grabbed my scissors and watched as a long, slim body shifted slowly. My knuckles went white around the scissors as the form shivered in the wind. It was covered in feathers, which shimmered all different colors in the sunlight. The tail lay limp among the wildflowers, and at first, I didn't see the head, but then I saw it on the ground rocking strangely like it wasn't fully conscious. I didn't move or blink, trying to be sure that it wasn't a hallucination.

When it made a noise of pain, I edged closer. My footsteps were careful to avoid startling it. The more I looked, the more I was certain a dragon was in front of me, but I had never heard of a dragon being any color other than green or blue. People told children all the time dragons were dangerous, to never get near them, but I couldn't stop myself. The way it shifted and moved made me worry it was hurt, that it might need my help.

The dragon writhed and peeled its eyes open. Then it tried to stretch its wings but was only successful with moving one. I pressed against a tree, then peered around it, my eyes following the rows of feathers along its neck. Then my foot caught in a root.

My hands caught my fall. But when I looked down at the dirt, my hair was rising. At first, I thought it was from fear, but then the static ran along my arms like I could reach out and shock someone if I touched them. My head snapped up at the dragon, with horror shooting up my spine, but he didn't look like a dragon anymore. Instead, there was a young man, around the same age as me, his eyes alight with terror as he tried to back away from me.

One hand rested on the hilt of his sword, and his other hung strangely at his side. His face was slim, with high cheekbones and long silver hair that looked like his feathers. He stood only a few inches taller than me, continuing to back up like I was the scariest thing he had seen in his entire life. Broken and hissing like an injured kitten.

"Are you hurt?" I stood and advanced toward him. His gray eyes shined brightly in the sunlight, and despite his fear, he didn't show any sign of crying. I certainly would have been crying if I were in his position.

"Stay away." He tried to pull the sword out of its scabbard, but it was belted on the opposite side of his injured arm. He lost his grip, and the sword clapped as it fell back in.

"Stop, stop," I said, "you're going to hurt yourself worse."

He held an arm straight out in front of him, his fingers spread as he spoke a language I had never heard before. It wasn't Matsic, but it also didn't sound like any of the other common languages I'd sometimes hear from travelers in town.

"My name is Maryan Evrouin." I held up my hands. "What is yours?"

The dragon stopped moving away as I set down my basket, sat on the ground, and pulled my handkerchief from it. I held it out to him.

"Here." I waved for him to come closer. "You have dirt all over your face."

He stared at me, his eyes wide as he searched for a way to distance himself from me. The dragon stopped chanting, lowering his hand. His skin was fair and smooth, with pinkish lips and a slim, pointed nose. With his mouth hung open, he panted quietly, his hand moving to brace his injured arm.

"Listesh, Finder of Hope." He cringed yet took a step toward me. I did my best to smile like I would at a child in the clinic who didn't want me to put alcohol on a deep cut.

"Listesh, that is an unusual name for this area." I waved for him to get closer, but he didn't move. "I'm not going to hurt you. Did you fall?"

"How do I know you won't hurt me?" He took another step back.

I sighed and stood up, setting my hands on my hips to look as unthreatening as I could. "I just want to help. Your arm looks like it's out of the socket."

"It will be fine." Listesh didn't move away that time, but he didn't offer any additional information.

"It will not be fine," I said. "I can put it into a sling for you."

He looked at his arm as I shifted on my feet. I set the handkerchief down and held my hands up where he could see them.

"My uncle is a doctor." Removing my scarf from around my neck, I approached him slowly, and while he leaned back, he didn't step away. When I first put my hands on his arm, I narrated what I was doing, as I had seen Onas do with every patient. He had told me once that it made people feel better to know what he was doing.

Listesh winced and squeezed his eyes shut. When I asked him if something was okay, he nodded or said yes. He looked away from me while I fashioned the sling, though I had a feeling he turned away to avoid my gaze as well.

After finishing, I looked up at him. "My uncle can put your arm back in the socket."

"Can he come here?" Listesh asked.

"It will take far too long for me to go get him and bring him back here. We should go to him."

Listesh shook his head quickly and then cringed from the pain. "If I have to go into town, I do not need help. I will find a way to put it back on my own."

"Stop being so stubborn. You'll make it worse if you try to do it yourself." I stood a little taller, leaning into his space.

"I can do it myself." He tilted back and bit his lip. Then he considered his arm again. "I think."

"No, you can't." Determined to be a good doctor like my uncle, I decided a good doctor would do anything they could for patients, so I knelt in front of Listesh. I set my shoulder against his stomach, gently wrapped an arm around his waist, and managed to pick him up over my shoulder.

"Ow! What are you doing? You're going to drop me!" Listesh's sword shifted and knocked against my arm as I walked. He wasn't very heavy. "Stop, this is humiliating! Put me down."

"What is worse? Being carried by me or losing an arm?" I asked.

Listesh's voice caught in his throat, his good hand gripping my shoulder. "Could I really lose my arm from this?"

"Yes." I didn't know if it was true, but it seemed as though I would not convince him to come with me otherwise. I kept walking toward the village, each step making Listesh groan or whimper, depending on exactly how it made his arm move.

"All right, all right, just put me down. Every step you take hurts." He kicked his legs, and I shifted, nearly tipping over as he moved. I held on, barely managing to keep him on my shoulders, and through some bickering and yelling about pain, Listesh landed back on his feet. He huffed, straightening out his clothes, and then willingly followed me back to the clinic.

As soon as we arrived, Listesh recounted the story of my picking him up to Onas. My dear uncle, much to Listesh's displeasure, only laughed and fondly agreed it sounded like something I would do. Onas didn't ask Listesh how he injured himself or what he was doing in the woods, simply examining him to ensure it was only a dislocated shoulder. He pushed Listesh's arm back into the socket, despite some screaming and crying from Listesh, which then left me to look after him.

"Is it supposed to hurt still?" Listesh's whole demeanor had subdued, for he let me gently slip his arm into a sling.

"It will continue to hurt for a while, yes," I replied. Listesh studied his arm as if he were mourning a loss.

"I do not know if I will be able to fly again." Listesh's voice, quiet and tired, left me heartbroken. He didn't even seem to notice me staring. I squeezed his good arm, and he finally looked up at me. Tears were in his eyes, his cheeks rubbed raw from the way he'd pawed at them while Onas realigned his shoulder. He looked pathetic in a way, but I knew what it was like to lose a part of oneself permanently. I loved my uncle Onas, but I missed my parents often.

"Let it heal in full before you turn back," I said. "Once it has healed, we can see if there is a way to rehabilitate and strengthen your wing until you can fly again."

"I have nowhere to stay," Listesh said.

"Stay here. The clinic is always open to those who are injured."

He didn't like the idea. Listesh looked especially on edge, his fingers fidgeting with the leg of his trousers. I added, "Think about it."

To my surprise, Listesh stayed. He was useful around the clinic, strong even though he only had one arm, and a quick learner. He even knew some basic healing magic. Listesh told people he was a mage who trained in the Capitol, that he had magic all his life and carried a sword only for his own protection.

During our time alone, he told me he was a Silver dragon, raised with his twin sister by a rather coddling mother. She had taught him basic magic, but his father had taught both him and his sister to fight. Together, they taught them to fly and raised them to gather their own knowledge, which was how Listesh had learned more complex magics. He was always careful in the village to perform nothing more complicated than healing, except when it was only me.

Listesh liked the wildflowers, too, and I told him all about losing my parents and Onas taking me in. He enjoyed hearing about my childhood, and he talked a lot about his twin sister. I didn't realize it at first, but it hadn't been long before Listesh looked at me like I was the whole world. It was Onas who told me, Onas who gave his late wife's ring to Listesh and suggested he give it to me. He was happy Listesh and I had grown together in the year or so since he'd been there.

We got married in the fall, and while Listesh still couldn't fly, he told me he was happy there with me. By our third spring together, I was with child, and Asith was with us by the fall. Our home was always warm, and our love for each other was only growing. I would watch Listesh cradle Asith in his arms by the fire each night, kissing his small face and singing songs in Endethi, the language of dragons. He held us both like we were the light of his life, and I never saw him as happy as the days we spent in the small home Onas helped us buy, holding our son and speaking to him softly in a language I hardly knew.

But we grew complacent, and we never worried about our safety or someone discovering Listesh's secret. We were still carrying Asith everywhere when it happened. I'm still not sure exactly how, but all I know is that someone must have learned Listesh was a dragon. The town was small and distrustful of dragons; they told the stories of the way the dragons betrayed the rebellion against the king all those years ago regularly. There was no way for us to be safe once the people knew.

We went into the woods to gather mushrooms and flowers and sold them for a bit of extra money for Asith's education. Onas had suggested a few times to leave, the four of us, to find a place where Listesh and Asith would be safer. We considered it, but we also thought my uncle's anxiety was getting the better of him. When we got to the clinic where we had left Asith with my uncle, we found Onas frantic already. He had heard, and since we were home, the town was coming.

"The three of you must leave, now." Onas had Asith bundled in a tight sling and tied it over my shoulder before I even had the chance to ask. "They know, they know about Listesh, and now they know about Asith too."

"What?" Listesh took a bag from Onas, who set his hands on Listesh's shoulder once he had handed off his sword as well.

"Protect them please," he said. "Now, go."

Onas forced us through the back door of the clinic just as the sound of shouting and pounding on the front door reached our ears. I tried to turn back, but Onas shut the door and told me to go. I could hear the glass windows shattering, the din of people I had grown up with yelling as they forced their way into my uncle's clinic. Listesh pulled me into the woods, carrying only the small bag of things Onas had packed, and I looked back at my childhood home, begging for Listesh to stay long enough to see if Onas had followed us.

The light from the fire appeared before the smoke, and we were too far from him to know if Onas had made it out somehow, if he had escaped from the hoard of people. I fell to my knees as the smoke rose in the distance, fearing the worst for Onas. Listesh took Asith from me, allowing me to sit on the ground and grieve in the comfort of the woods. We could only stay for a few minutes, but I sat and sobbed into Listesh's shoulder.

When I got up, we headed into the woods with only Asith and each other. We walked for days until we found a road distant from my hometown and followed it. Listesh was on edge, his hand on his sword when he wasn't holding Asith. He cast magic for a simple shelter that would only allow the three of us inside. He kept the two of us so close, I thought he might have developed a paranoia about all humans, save for me. I couldn't blame him, and I knew, in some ways, he blamed himself for what had happened.

We started talking as we walked to distract Listesh, and as the days went on, he calmed down. We had little money, traveling across the country as far as we could go. It felt as if we could not get far enough away from the town that had chased us out. Listesh heard rumors of a town near the Southern border that consisted of primarily elves and half-elves. He and Asith would blend in more easily, for their pointed ears and silver hair would be more common there. We decided to go there, and while we had nothing, most people struggled to turn away two young parents and a baby looking for a place to spend only a night or two. Listesh took a few odd jobs and whispered each night to Asith in Endethi whenever we slept in the woods in the shelter of his magic. He didn't dare speak it in town.

I had never even realized my hometown held such old views about dragons. I knew the stories, that people claimed dragons had attacked humans during the war, that they'd sided with the kingdom rather than the people. No one even knew if that was true, I had never seen any proof of it, and the only dragon I had ever known was Listesh.

But some humans never let go of what they had been told and they passed it on to their children, and their children grew to fear and hate dragons. They heard of the attacks by the Blues and Greens, and there was enough hatred that they wouldn't want a dragon living among them. So much so that they would attack an innocent doctor over taking in an injured dragon and treating him like the person he was. Even I began to hate other humans as we walked toward a town where we might have to hide, anyway.

Eventually, we drew near South Cairn. A place where it wasn't likely for people to question us too much. A place where people didn't wonder why Listesh and Asith had silvery hair and could use magic. We could hunker down and build a new life.

Just before we arrived, Listesh recognized something. The shape of a distant mountain grabbed his attention. Even from the ground, he recognized it. He knew his sister was there and that his family probably worried for him. They wouldn't have known what happened to him, and it hurt him.

I convinced him to go. It would be fine, and he would be back soon. I would be all right with Asith, and we could find them a place to live in South Cairn. He could join us as soon as his family knew he was alive and well. They didn't even know that he was married or that they had a grandson and a nephew.

Listesh was hesitant, but he held Asith on a rock, gently bobbing Asith in his arms, and kissed Asith's face as he slept. He cradled him tight and whispered to him in Endethi for a long time. I gave Listesh his space, letting him say goodbye to Asith before he returned Asith to my arms and kissed me.

"I will be back." Listesh hugged me, Asith between us. "Soon. I promise."

Listesh went down a different road, and I carried Asith to South Cairn, where we were welcomed.

We arrived in early spring, just as it had been when I first met Listesh. A tailor who needed an apprentice offered me her home, and it wasn't long before Asith was walking and talking. Asith called the woman, Zena, his grandmother, and I trained to be a tailor.

I told her my husband would be returning soon. I would look out of the front window of Zena's small home as Zena taught Asith new words. He could speak Matsic, but none of the Endethi his father had spoken to him stuck. It made my stomach knot, but I knew better than to tell Asith. He didn't need to know the horrors; he didn't need to know I was waiting for his father to return.

Even as he grew taller, as he became self-sufficient, as Zena passed away, as I became known in the town as a tailor and dressmaker, as Asith started school, Listesh stayed on my mind. I never heard what happened to Onas, and I never knew what happened to Listesh.

CHAPTER 10

Year 573 with Vitiope
16th of Kasdiel

Asith could hear his own heartbeat, and his mouth hung open. His mother was wiping tears from her cheeks, the wedding ring shining in the flickering lantern light. He couldn't see anything else, his arms and hands stiff as he gripped the cup of tea between his palms.

She brought her tea to her lips before clearing her throat, her voice shaking as she spoke. "Sorry, I know this is a lot to take in."

"Mama, I'm so sorry," he stuttered. Asith's throat was thick as he forced himself to speak. He had thought his father was an elf from the northern part of the country, for plenty of people up there had hair and ears like his, but he never expected to be so incorrect. Asith had wool between his ears, the fibers turning and trying to spin, but they kept breaking off before it became yarn. "I wish you had told me sooner. That must have been hard to keep all of that to yourself."

His mother's face softened, and she chuckled, pressing a hand to her forehead. "I should have known you would be worried about me first. I thought you would be angry with me for not telling you that you were dragonborn sooner."

Asith shook his head and took his mother's hand again. "No, I'm surprised. But after that, after what happened to you, to Onas, I trust that you only did it to protect me."

His mother didn't speak, tears running down her face. She took a few deep breaths and nodded at Asith before looking at Dradevai. Asith had accidentally tuned Dradevai out at some point. Dradevai was staring at the table, quiet and dead-eyed, gripping the amber necklace in their palm.

"Dradevai." His mother spoke first, gentle and careful as she moved toward the catatonic dragon. Dradevai shook their head, starting to come back to reality after getting lost in their head. "Are you okay?"

Asith stood, picked up the carafe of cream, and poured some into a pot on the stove. He then took the chocolate from the shelf and shaved it as he had seen Dradevai do in the past.

"I am fine." Dradevai's voice came out small. His mother didn't seem to believe them. She ran a loving hand over the back of their head, something she had done to Asith before.

"It is okay if you want to talk," she said, "or if you don't."

Dradevai looked at her, rubbed their eyes gently, and nodded. Their eyes found the cup that Asith set on the table in front of them. It wasn't nearly as dark in color as when Dradevai made it, probably because he hadn't used enough chocolate, but he hadn't really made it before. Dradevai cupped their hands around it and pulled it close.

They didn't look at Asith as he shifted his weight back and forth. Asith didn't know what to say or if he should say anything at all. He wrapped his arms around his middle, looking toward the door, and he realized if he walked his mother home, he could get out of the house.

"I'm going to walk my mother home." Asith turned to Dradevai. "Do you want to stay here?"

They nodded and kept their eyes on the chocolate drink. Asith exchanged a look with his mother, and she gave Dradevai's shoulder a good squeeze and stood up.

"I will see you tomorrow, Dradevai," she said.

Dradevai smiled, with a struggle, it seemed. They glanced up at Asith's mother with a furrowed brow and a tight-lipped smile, which was enough to make Asith's worries settle a bit. Dradevai might be upset, but they didn't seem to hold anything against either of them.

"Goodnight, Maryan." Dradevai waved at her slightly as they left.

The night air cleared Asith's mind enough that he could release some tension and relax. His mother let him have a quiet moment, then she turned to him.

"Are you okay? How are you feeling about your father?"

"I'm still in shock, I think." Asith rubbed his forearm with his thumb. "I know you found that journal I left behind."

His mother nodded. "I wasn't angry about it. I can't blame you for wanting to know."

Things grew quiet between them. Asith had expected more, but he wasn't sure why. His mother had never really gotten angry with him for asking about his father. His mother's fingers found her wedding ring and rubbed it. She worried her lip, and Asith was reminded just how much she had given for him, for his father.

"Mama," Asith said, "where do you think he is?"

His mother's lips opened gently, and she looked down at her ring again. She slipped it off and offered it to Asith. "When we got married, your father added an enchantment to our rings. If either of us is wearing it and rubbing it, the other will feel it. Sometimes, I can still feel someone running their fingers over the other ring."

"Then you think he might be out there?" Asith ran his fingers over the ring, carefully slipping it onto the end of his pointer finger, since it wouldn't go down much further.

His mother took a deep breath, and her eyes swam over the sea of small houses. "I don't know. I feel the rubbing less and less often. Like whoever is on the other end is fading."

They stopped in front of his mother's home, and she took the ring back and slid it onto her finger. If his father was on the other end, Asith needed to find him soon, or he might never have the chance to know him.

Asith hugged his mother, letting her settle into his shoulder. He had been taller than her since before he left for the Capitol, but in that moment, she was especially small in his arms.

"Will Dradevai be okay?" His mother's voice was low. "Do you think that story was too much for them?"

"It could be that, but I have a feeling that talking about my father's family might be what's bothering them," Asith said.

"You know…" She stopped Asith before he could walk away. "You and Dradevai, I am glad that the two of you met. Even if the circumstances made me worry." His mother smiled fondly, staring at the ground as a sweet, nostalgic look came over her face.

"What do you mean?" he asked.

"The two of you remind me of us." She looked up at him, her smile firmer even though her eyes still appeared a little sad. "I think you will be good for each other. Just pay attention to them, Asith."

Asith nodded. His mother had told him that before, to pay attention to another person. It was when he had been in his first relationship with Elin, the son of the town's blacksmith. She had always told him the most important thing in any relationship was listening to the other person and paying close attention to them. He was beginning to wonder what his mother thought of his relationship with Dradevai, but as he stood in front of her, his anxieties bubbled to the surface.

"I'm worried, Mama. They know so little. I don't want to overwhelm them."

She pressed her hand to his cheek and chuckled. "Are you sure you're not afraid of being overwhelmed by them?"

Asith froze, staring at his mother as her smile grew a little more. He opened and closed his mouth, trying to form words. But his thoughts were becoming wool needing to be spun into yarn again, and the fibers kept breaking before they could.

"I don't know," Asith said.

His mother wrapped her shawl around her shoulders a bit tighter. "You are a very considerate boy; you always have been," she said. "Just pay attention to Dradevai. I think you will start to see what I mean about them being good for you."

Asith frowned but eventually nodded. His mother finally said good-night and pulled him down to kiss his forehead. He confirmed she was inside and that her door was locked before strolling back to his home, to Dradevai. His mother may have been right, but he still had that guilty feeling low in his stomach.

When he opened the door to his home, Dradevai was sitting at the table near the stove, rubbing their face to try to hide they had been crying.

Asith shouldn't have left. The tingle of guilt slid up his back, and he became overwhelmed by the need to fix it even if he had no idea how. Asith didn't say a word, walking over to Dradevai and setting a hand on their shoulder. While Dradevai's expression did not differ much from before, they turned in the chair and faced Asith to wrap their arms around his middle.

"Do you want to talk?" Asith asked.

Dradevai pulled back, their facial features trembling as they started to cry again. "Why was I born alone? I don't understand. I thought that all dragons experienced this, but your father, he had a family, parents, a sister. He was raised."

"I thought that might be what you were thinking about." Asith pulled up a chair and rubbed Dradevai's shoulder while they cried. Once Dradevai started to calm down, Asith carefully ran his fingers down the leather cord and touched the amber carving at the end. "I have been wondering what this is. You were holding on to it earlier."

"It was." Dradevai sniffled and wiped at their face. "I found it, when I was born. It was there in the nest of sand and rocks I had been left in. I have had it ever since."

Asith turned it over in his fingers, looking at the etching on the back. "It was left there for you?"

Dradevai shrugged and carefully took it from Asith's fingers so that they could take it off. They studied it for a moment before they handed it to him.

"Couldn't this mean that the ones who left it were your parent?" he asked. Asith couldn't quite understand why, but something about the symbols made him think it might be an enchantment. "Where is the spell book?"

"It could have been, but then why would they leave me all alone?" Dradevai looked worried, their eyes on the table. "It is on the bookshelf."

Asith set the necklace on the table. He had seen a spell once to determine if an object was magic, and as he flipped through the pages, he thought it might be useful.

"I don't know why they would have left you alone." Asith placed the book in front of both of them and read over the instructions for the spell. "But you could ask the same of my mother. Why did she not tell me I was dragonborn?"

"That was to protect you." Dradevai frowned, their words emphatic and confident, quick to defend Asith's mother. It only took them another moment to realize what Asith was getting at, their voice growing quiet. "I see what you mean."

Asith held up the necklace. "This might be a key to finding them. This looks like an enchantment, right?"

"It does." Dradevai looked the necklace over. "It might be a way to find them, but Asith, what about your father? Don't you want to find him?"

He froze, then looked back at Dradevai. Asith had been afraid to say the next words in front of his mother, but there, looking at Dradevai, who looked back at him like they very much cared , he broke.

"What if…" Asith tried to swallow his fear. "What if I do try to find him, only to discover that he never came back because he no longer loves my mother, or that he wants to forget he had a son at all?"

Dradevai's eyes grew angry for a moment, but Asith could tell it was not an anger directed at him. Then they furrowed their brow, and their eyes glowed brightly like when they cast a spell. Dradevai took a deep breath that caused their shoulders to rise and fall, the glow fading as they calmed down.

"I don't think Maryan would have told you about him at all if she thought he had left the two of you on purpose." Dradevai ground their teeth, the muscle on top of the bone flexing as they did.

"You are probably right." Asith clicked his teeth and set Dradevai's necklace on the book. "Maybe if we can find one dragon, any dragon, we can find the parents we are both missing."

Dradevai observed the amber necklace as if it might move on its own.

"I guess I cannot repeat my worry about them rejecting me, considering I just reassured you about your father."

Asith couldn't help the way he laughed; it was soft and sort of broken but still a laugh. He rested his hands on either side of the book. "We will figure this out, even if we find out things we otherwise might not have wanted to know."

"You are right, but do you really think this is the place to start?" Dradevai asked, and Asith began the incantation for the spell, the necklace glowing. The enchantment was some sort of illusion, for it didn't really tell Asith anything. He frowned at the necklace, willing it to speak so it could tell them more.

"This was not very helpful." He picked up the necklace and offered it back to Dradevai. "There is not a spell in here that can tell us of previous owners, is there?"

"I don't believe so, but it is maybe something we can create." They sighed and put the necklace over their head before setting their chin in their hand. "I don't know what else we can really do. Rove the country until we find another dragon?"

"I don't think we have that kind of time," Asith mumbled.

"What do you mean?" Dradevai sat up, their whole attention on Asith again.

Asith ran his hands through his hair and covered his ears for a moment as he tried to choose his words. He didn't want Dradevai to panic, so he had to be careful.

"My mother's ring is enchanted, so she can feel it when my father rubs his ring." Asith looked at Dradevai. "But she said she feels it less often, as if my father is fading."

Dradevai rubbed their cheek, eyes scanning the room. "Then you're right; we have to hurry."

Asith pursed his lips, nodding at Dradevai gravely. He tapped his fingers on the table, taking a moment to think before he closed the spell book. "There is a library in the Capitol at the Maeria Spire that might have information about finding dragons."

"A library?" Dradevai paused. "What is the Maeria Spire?"

"It is the academy for learning magic in the Capitol. In the library in the Stonegarde Guild's headquarters, where I learned to fight dragons, we could get books there that came from the Maeria Spire."

Dradevai perked up. "Do you think we could get a spell book there? Something that might have what we need?"

"I never tried to rent a book about magic that way, but it might be worth a shot. Otherwise, only students are allowed in the Maeria Spire library." Asith got up and set the spell book back on the little bookshelf near his chair. He wasn't sure how safe it would really be to bring Dradevai into the Capitol, which was swimming with dragon knights and people who probably hated Blues and Greens. They wouldn't see Dradevai as any different. But Asith couldn't think of any other plan. It was scarier to imagine taking them into Stonegarde, where the dragon knights were trained.

"Well," Dradevai said, "it is a place to start. Why do you look unhappy about it?"

"You are a dragon. Taking you with me into Stonegarde could be dangerous."

Dradevai frowned, then they stood up and said a short chant, sweeping their hand over their chest. In a rush of magic, they looked completely different. Their hair was short, cropped near their head, with pale skin not unlike Asith's and deep green eyes. He took in their soft features and auburn hair, finding them sort of odd since he knew that was Dradevai despite looking nothing like themself. Although they looked specifically like a man, which seemed intentional, Asith still found them attractive.

"I have been working on this spell," Dradevai said. "Do you think it will be enough?"

"Maybe." There were areas of the city where they used enchantments to effectively remove spells that changed one's appearance, so they would need to be careful. "We will need to find a way to disguise your horns without magic as well. Just in case."

"We could do a hood like we did before?" Dradevai suggested. "Maybe something to secure it to my horns, so it won't blow off."

"That," Asith said, "could work rather well. I could sew small pockets into the hood of a cloak for you."

Dradevai's anxiety from earlier completely gave way to excitement. They both spent the rest of the night trying to form a solid plan. They could easily get into the Capitol under the guise of trade if they had goods, and the Stonegarde would let Asith in because of his status as a dragon knight. As they planned, each of them seemed more convinced their parents might be out there. And they might want to see Asith and Dradevai again.

CHAPTER 11

17th of Kasdiel

Asith's mother was confused when they appeared at her house the next morning in search of a cloak and clothes his mother had made. They needed to bring them to the Capitol and help determining how much food they would need for travel, since Asith had never traveled the whole way alone. Normally, he would meet a regiment of dragon knights along the way. He also asked about water, though there were rivers they could stop at without going far out of the way. Dradevai was concerned about how well eggs would last in the warmth of the valley, but Asith and his mother quickly convinced them they would last fine.

They told his mother that Dradevai wanted to try attending the Maeria Spire, so she offered to sew the hood for Dradevai since she could do a better job at disguising them. Asith created the fib in case his father turned out to be for the worst. His mother didn't need to suffer that if he could prevent it. Though, he realized that was exactly why his mother only just told him he was dragonborn, but it was still the right decision. It had been the right decision when she'd done it as well, after all.

Though, every time Asith caught her looking down at her ring, Asith wondered if he should reassure her they'd find his father in time, that he would be okay. He couldn't, though. As much as he didn't want to believe it, there was the possibility his father really had left them behind.

Dradevai had the cloak on by midday, slipping their horns into small pockets that his mother had added to the inside in just the right place. It settled on their head in a way that when they tied their hair back into a ponytail, the hood stood higher. His mother still looked concerned, so she added thin metal combs into the hood she normally used on veils.

Over the following two days, Asith and Dradevai scrambled to gather everything they needed before they could leave. Dradevai learned the ins and outs of daily interactions with others, while Asith helped his mother prepare the uniforms and tunics to take into the Capitol. They didn't really need it, for Asith was a dragon knight, and he could argue they were entering to go to Stonegarde. But he wanted to make sure they didn't question Dradevai going with him. If they were simply there to help him sell belts and armor fittings, the guards on the wall wouldn't spare a second glance at Dradevai and potentially notice their horns.

Asith was embroidering the crest of the Republic of Cairn onto a soldier's tunic. He had done it a thousand times before, so he barely had to look while he did it anymore. "When we get to the walls, let me do the talking, and please don't judge me for anything I say."

Dradevai looked up from their book. "Why would I judge you for what you say?"

"I don't want to draw any attention to you." Asith stopped embroidering and looked at them. "And to do so, I might have to lie or say something underhanded."

"Asith, I…" They paused, their face illuminated by the soft light of the late evening sun. The reddish hue made them glow and exaggerated all the warm tones of their skin and the almost-orange honey color in their eyes. "I wouldn't judge you for lying to protect me. But I feel like if you have to keep lying about me, will I ever really be able to go in public by myself?"

"I don't know." Asith's mouth was dry. "I know that's not a good answer, but I don't want to lie to you."

Dradevai frowned, their eyes scanning his face, and they sighed. They scrunched up their nose, then brushed their bangs out of their face. "Thank you for not lying."

"Of course, Vai," Asith said. It was daunting that he was responsible for Dradevai's safety. He wanted to protect them, so he would do everything he could.

When they set out, they had a small cart and two horses borrowed from Corym in exchange for Dradevai eliminating several deer and a rather ornery wild boar that had threatened a few young kids playing along the forest edge. Dradevai said they wouldn't have to eat again for a few weeks after getting to eat so much. Though, they felt slightly bad because the deer had clearly never been hunted by anything like them. Asith assured them that so long as they died as quickly and painlessly as possible, it was really okay.

"What is the Capitol like?" Dradevai asked, their hood down since the road was empty. Several days of travel had gone by quickly. They were still on a noncentral road, meaning it would eventually lead into a wide trade road that led to the Capitol. The central roads were a series of spokes that lead straight from the Capitol walls all the way to the very edges of the country. Before the Republic had been established, the Capitol had been a town called North Cairn, which sat along the very edge of the country in the Northern mountains. All that was left was the old castle with its high walls, and according to rumor, no one was living there at all.

"It is a large city," Asith said. "Very different from South Cairn. There are a lot of people. Most of them are dragon knights and mages from the Stonegarde, but also a lot of hold workers. My friend Delri is probably still there."

"There are lots of dragon knights?" Dradevai shifted to look over the front of the cart where Asith was. They had sat amongst their various goods so that they could stretch their legs for a while.

"It's where they're trained, so yes. We'll have to be careful about whom we speak to while we're there."

"Do you think any of them will know about me kidnapping you?" Dradevai asked. They toyed with the edge of their vest, moving their fingers over it until they reached the amber necklace and pressed that into their palm.

Asith shook his head. "No. Even if the Stonegarde found out, they would quickly cover up that a Sterling had been spotted. They'd make sure everyone thought it was nothing more than a rumor."

Dradevai frowned, their eyes narrowing. They rubbed the back of their head and then sat up. Their mouth opened, but they stopped, shaking their head slightly.

"What about your friend that you mentioned?" Dradevai toyed with a splinter. "Is she safe for us to speak to?"

Asith paused, unsure how to answer that. Delri was also a dragon knight, and while Asith loved her dearly, he wasn't sure how she would react to finding out Dradevai was a dragon. She might be accepting because she trusted Asith, but she could just as easily turn them in to the Stonegarde.

"I don't know." Asith looked out at the road. "I would like to think she is."

"What city were we in that day we left my hoard? It was smaller than South Cairn." Dradevai's voice changed in tone. They were trying to bring up Asith's mood, if he had to guess. They would do that sometimes, trying to make him feel better by changing the subject.

"We were in Windgate that day." Asith had found out when he'd sent the letter to his mother from there. She had received it about two days before they left for the Capitol. "That city is in the far west part of the country next to the mountains."

"There are mountains near every part of the country." Dradevai frowned and set their arms on the side of the cart, looking up at Asith.

"This is a valley you're in."

Asith chuckled, feeling a little better thanks to the distraction. "I know, but my point was that your hoard is somewhere in the Western mountains. Northwest, to be specific."

"My hoard would be slightly east of that town, then, since we flew southeast to get there."

Asith glanced back at them and smiled. "Where have you been besides that part of the country?" He had been curious since Dradevai had the chocolate and claimed they had gotten it from somewhere far away.

"I have been to the West. As you go past the Western mountains, there is a sea and lots of small islands where the air is so thick that it feels like you're breathing in water."

"Really?" Asith looked back at Dradevai, their smile growing as they nodded. They sat up on their knees, leaning so that they could hold on to the back of the driving seat.

"Yes, it didn't suit me. It was far too humid and made me constantly feel sticky even when it was cold." Dradevai shivered and stuck their tongue out like a child who'd been given a bitter vegetable. "I was hoping I might find people who didn't know what I was, but they seemed just as scared of me as anyone here. So, I returned."

"Did you stop in any of the towns along the Western coast?" Asith glanced at their glinting eyes. They were clearly excited to be telling Asith things he didn't know, given Asith had been doing so much explaining in the last week.

"Yes." Dradevai's lips jutted slightly. "It was a city entirely of furred people with pointed ears on the tops of their heads. But they wanted to treat me like a god. They gave me all this jewelry and tried to trap me in a temple. It made me really uncomfortable."

Asith's eyebrows raised up into his hair. "Wait, so someone has tried to keep you against your will, and you didn't like it?"

"No!" Dradevai sat up and then froze. "Well, I guess sort of. I liked that they didn't seem to fear me the way others did at first, but then I realized they feared me in a different way and that they kept trying to put these lead bracelets on me that would prevent me from doing magic."

While Asith wanted to continue to point out the irony in that situation, talking about it rattled Dradevai enough that he let it be. "You were able to get away; that's what matters."

"Yes, yes." Dradevai sighed and rested their head in their hand again. "But it was that experience that made me think I should take you home."

"Really?" Asith looked back at the road, listening to Dradevai's heavy sigh.

"Yes." Dradevai's voice grew small. "I had told myself it was different, being part of my hoard would be different, but I realized that those people were trying to collect me in a way. And the fact that I had let myself do the same to someone else made me question the decision. I'm sorry."

Asith set his hand on Dradevai's head, partially because it was all he could think to do. Dradevai looked up, their honey eyes appearing guilty and almost sad. It was a small gesture, but he remembered his mother telling him to pay attention to Dradevai again.

"It's okay, Dradevai," he said, Dradevai leaning into his touch. "I know that I tease you about it, but you were going to do the right thing on your own and that's what matters. I'm not mad at you for what happened now."

Dradevai's eyes turned away in a bashful movement that Asith realized they only did with him. They settled lower in the cart as if they were trying to hunker down and hide entirely.

"Yes, but I have caused you so much trouble." Dradevai frowned, their head resting on their hands. "You wound up taking care of me because you happened to be there when those hunters showed up."

Asith's mouth fell open. He had tried his hardest to put the hunters out of his mind as much as possible. The memory made Asith smell the blood again. He focused on Dradevai to get his mind off it. Dradevai's shoulders were hunched up to their ears, as if the guilt had settled into their skin when he was not looking. As usual, his mother had been right about more than he realized; she was good at making sure he figured it out on his own.

"I was going to ask you to come back with me regardless of what happened with"—Asith hesitated—"with those hunters."

Asith moved his hand so he could see Dradevai better. Looking at their face made the visions of the hunters dissipate somewhat. He tried not to close his eyes.

"Really? Why?" Dradevai's nose scrunched, and their brow pressed down over their eyes. They really didn't seem to have an educated guess even. Asith looked back at the road, for he didn't want to be making direct eye contact. His anxiety about the smell of blood was replaced by his stomach flipping. He hoped he wouldn't have to talk about the hunters anymore.

"I could have just let you take me home, but you looked so lonely." Asith watched the back of one of the horse's heads, its ears flickering. "It seemed better to just give you a home where you wouldn't be so alone."

"Oh." Dradevai's voice had gotten small in a way that Asith did not recognize, and when he spared them a glance, they looked contemplative. They didn't say anything more. Instead, they turned into themself, sitting back down in the cart, keeping their thoughts private. It made Asith's nerves worsen, but it was a nice distraction from other subject matters.

He focused on steering, their cart puttering along at a pace Asith set rather purposefully. It kept them comfortably between the faster groups and the slower groups, so people had less time to study them. Dradevai slipped their hood on when they saw other carts, sitting low with the belts and armor fittings, and read a book. It wasn't the spell book; after going back and forth, they had decided it was better to leave that behind before they'd left. But Dradevai had bought several new books, tearing through them rather quickly.

They hadn't been passed by another cart in a long while when Dradevai shut their book and leaned against the side of the cart, just behind Asith's back. They sighed as if they might be exhausted, and the silence indicated they had fallen asleep. The quiet had settled into Asith. When he was small, his mother would sometimes take him into the Capitol to sell things with her, and he would always start off rather talkative, only to eventually settle down and sleep, as Dradevai seemed to do.

"Asith." Dradevai's voice startled him. He had thought they were still asleep, or maybe they hadn't slept at all. "You said you were going to invite me to return to South Cairn with you regardless of what happened with the hunters, but I have been wondering about something."

"What is it?" He glanced at Dradevai quickly and found they were staring at the cover of their book.

"Why did you kiss me that night, then?" Dradevai's eyes turned up to him, wide and curious and innocent in a way that made Asith feel as if they were doing it on purpose. His face grew hot, so he snapped his attention back to the horses and the road. Their ear flicking was not very distracting.

Asith opened his mouth to speak, glimpsing at Dradevai, but couldn't catch if their expression had changed at all.

"I..." he said, "you were acting as if you wouldn't listen to me if I didn't do something to get your attention."

"So, you only did it so that I would listen?" Dradevai asked. When Asith glanced again, they seemed to have deflated, and Asith could understand why. He wouldn't have liked feeling as though he'd been manipulated, either.

"N-no," Asith stammered. "No, that is not the only reason I did it."

Dradevai's lips pouted, and they tilted their head. "I don't understand. It feels like you have avoided the whole thing since we got to South Cairn."

"Well, I…" Asith realized the hole he'd dug himself, and at that point, he didn't want Dradevai to think he'd manipulated them. He didn't really have enough time to think of a good way to dodge the conversation without hurting Dradevai in the process, so he sucked it up and hoped he could explain as little as possible. "When we got back, I knew a lot of things were new for you. I felt like adding on to that was maybe a bad idea."

"A bad idea?" Dradevai seemed too focused on those words, misunderstanding what Asith meant. His shoulders fell, and one of his hands let go of the reins.

"I meant I didn't want to overwhelm you more than you already were, because you were trying to figure out how to be around people." Asith looked away from Dradevai, his face growing hot. "Do we have to talk about this?"

"Yes, we have to talk about it." Dradevai's brow knitted. "You can't keep running away from these things. Was kissing me a mistake or not?"

Asith's stomach fell to his feet. He had never been good at dealing with that sort of thing, and with Dradevai, it took so much more clarity in his explanations that he got embarrassed and flustered. He was so stupid.

"It wasn't a mistake! I just wanted you to feel safe." Asith's voice cracked, and he tightened his grip on the reins. "And I didn't want you to think you had to date me to be welcome in South Cairn or in my home."

He spared a glance at Dradevai, and it seemed like they understood what he meant that time, which he thanked the gods for, because he would not have been able to say any of that a second time. Asith never wanted to talk about his feelings again, in fact.

However, Dradevai stayed quiet long enough to make Asith uncomfortable, and when he couldn't bear it anymore, he returned his gaze to the horses. It was about then that Dradevai's arms snaked around his middle tightly, their palms flattening on his ribs and their head planting firmly between Asith's shoulder blades.

"I am glad that you were trying to be considerate of me and not that you thought you had made a mistake." They said it simply, and it made heat snake up Asith's body. Dradevai tended to be direct, and that made his throat dry. Even as they pulled away, Asith was abashed, and his whole body had probably turned red. "Come on, though, it is my turn to drive the cart."

"Huh? Do you know how?" Asith's brain came out of the fog just long enough for him to fall right back into it as Dradevai climbed onto the seat next to him. They had their hood up, and it seemed as if they were using it to hide their face.

"It can't be that hard. Just make sure the horses don't stop or go off the road, yes?" Dradevai looked at Asith briefly, the smile on their face cavalier and hiding something that Asith sort of hoped was an equally embarrassing feeling to what he was experiencing. "Besides, if I drive, I can see in the dark, and we can travel farther today."

"Well, you aren't wrong." Asith handed the reins over to Dradevai, who appeared triumphant. Asith welcomed his free time, sitting in the back of the cart and trying to avoid any thoughts about the conversation they'd just had. Though, when he climbed in among the leather and other goods, he wasn't very surprised to find that what Dradevai had been reading so intently seemed to be the third book in a series of romance novels. It would at least explain why they'd been thinking about the kiss so much.

Asith tucked the book away, the sun warming his skin despite it still being late autumn. He closed his eyes, his hand resting gently on the grip of his sword. It took him a long time to fall asleep, his thoughts racing about the blood of the dragon hunters and every wrong thing he'd said during his conversation with Dradevai, but eventually, he did sleep.

> *Blood rolled down the blade of Asith's sword toward his hands. He tried to pull away, let the sword drop to the ground, but he was paralyzed.*
>
> *His foot was far enough forward that blood was dripping off the sword and onto his boot. Dread filled him. He wanted nothing more than to pull away from the sword, his hands hot and tense as they squeezed around the hilt. The blood drew closer and closer, to where Asith was holding his breath until his lungs burned, in hopes that would slow the blood down somehow or he'd pass out before it touched him.*
>
> *Then he heard a noise that made his stomach retch. He felt the slick, watery blood as it poured over his blade and onto his hands. It flowed over his fingers and seeped into his skin, and fresh tears hit his hands, which made the blood look translucent and wet even after it dried.*

"Asith."

He sprung awake, cold sweat running down his back as his hand tightened around the grip of his sword. Asith panted, and to his surprise, tears were on his face. He wiped his eyes with the back of his hand and found Dradevai looking down at him with worry from the seat of the cart. The sky had gone dark, and they were pulled over on the side of the road again.

"Are you okay?" Dradevai looked frantic, their hand on one of Asith's shoulders.

"Yes." Asith shook his head. "Just a bad dream. Sorry."

"It's okay." Dradevai furrowed their brow, setting a warm hand on Asith's hand, which still grasped his sword. He finally loosened it. "What was it about?"

"Nothing in particular." Asith looked up at Dradevai, and they frowned deeply at him.

"You have been having these dreams a lot lately." Dradevai had been sharing a bed with him, so he shouldn't have really been surprised they had noticed. "Are you sure that it isn't something specific?"

Asith's mouth fell open, and he made a largely involuntary noise, since he didn't want to lie to Dradevai outright and he also didn't want to talk about it directly. He worried Dradevai would think it was their fault he was having these dreams, which, in reality, Asith brought upon himself. He likely could have let go that man he killed.

"I have been having a recurring nightmare." The worry in Dradevai's face broke him a bit. He didn't want them to worry, the same way he didn't want his mother to worry. "It is about that man I killed in your hoard. I promise, I am fine. I think it just bothered me more than I thought it would."

Dradevai's face softened, their worry still there, but they sat back, giving Asith the space to get himself up.

"You were only protecting us," Dradevai said.

Asith shifted to get out of the cart. "Yes, but I have never killed another person before. I am sure it will fade. You are right. I was only protecting us."

Dradevai nodded, their hands cupping each of their elbows. Asith was surprised their nightly camp was set up already, except for the fire. He stepped down from the cart and approached the horses, but Dradevai had already given them something to eat.

"I was trying to give you some more time to sleep," Dradevai said, "since you keep waking up so early."

Asith nodded at Dradevai, who hopped off the cart. "Thank you."

Dradevai smiled, stopping next to him to gently run their hand down his arm, then went to light the fire. Asith took a deep breath, slipped the sword from his belt, and set it inside the tent. He didn't really need to have it on him, and it might be making their situation worse.

They cooked some food together, Asith's eyes on the fire as he sat on a rock with his plate in hand. He had never realized the licking flames of a fire looked like a stream of blood. In the places where it was red, he could only see blood.

"Asith?" Dradevai's voice was gentle. "Are you okay? You aren't eating."

Asith's breath left him, and his frame shook slightly. He was so tired that he hadn't realized he had been sleeping little. His head shook on its own, and his hand came up to press over his eyes as if it would stop him from seeing the blood anymore.

A weight pressed on his arm first, heavier than expected, as Dradevai shifted to settle into Asith's shoulder. One arm slid around his neck so that Asith could turn and press into their chest. He embraced the gentle affection. They ran their fingers over his hair and held him tight.

"Cry," they mumbled, "it might help."

Asith broke and sobbed into Dradevai's chest, his tears warm and soaking the tunic he'd made for them. Dradevai wanted to take care of him the same way he tried to take care of them.

CHAPTER 12

24th of Kasdiel

They made quick work of leaving in the morning, gathering supplies, and getting into the cart. Dradevai gave each of the horses an apple at the discovery they would eat from their hand. They seemed to like any and all animals they met, especially any that were more like pets than wild ones. They tended to look at the wild ones as if they might be a good meal.

As Dradevai cared for the horses, Asith's thoughts from the night before escaped. After he had cried until he couldn't anymore, Dradevai managed to get him to eat and distracted him with a conversation about rabbits, of all things, then they simply pressed close to Asith when they went to bed. Dradevai had been curled up on Asith's chest when he woke. The weight of their body leaving when they got up still felt like an absence. His skin ached for the contact again, but they had to keep moving; they didn't have all day to use Dradevai's warmth to heal his dreams.

When they left the campsite, Dradevai was in the driver's seat next to Asith, with their hood up. It was quiet, and the day was a bit warmer than it had been previously. He'd left his sword off his belt, figuring it would be easier to get through the gate if he was not actively armed. The guards would understand if he was carrying it for protection on the road, but in the Capitol, a weapon wasn't needed.

They could see the Capitol in the distance, the rolling hills leading up to its walls. It had been built on the highest part of the plane, so the very landscape seemed to rise to meet it. An unnatural stone wall shot straight up from the grass, which sparkled in the light of the second sun.

"The walls make it look like a box," Dradevai said, their elbows on their knees and their face in their hands.

Asith chuckled, tilting his head at the shape. "I guess it does look a bit like a box. It sort of feels like being inside one."

Dradevai froze, and they went from looking bored to startled. "There is not a roof on it, is there?"

"No," he answered, and Dradevai's entire body relaxed. Asith thought about the hole at the top of their hoard. He wanted to soothe their fears if he could, but Asith didn't really know how. All he could do was assure Dradevai they could fly away if needed.

"Good." Dradevai looked up at Asith and wiped away the sweat pooling on their temples.

"You can probably take the cloak off for a while if you lie down in the cart," Asith said.

Dradevai's lips pulled into a pout, and they set their chin back in their hand. "I really need to find a better way to hide my horns." Dradevai climbed into the back of the cart. Then they slipped the cloak off and lay against a pile of clothes they'd been using as a pillow.

"This is the safest way for now," Asith said.

Dradevai nodded. "I know."

They lumbered along from there. When dusk approached, Dradevai wanted to keep driving, but Asith reminded them he needed to see at least a bit to help make camp. It got them to stop for the night, even if an hour later than usual.

Once they'd eaten, Asith found himself promptly in the tent. He wanted more sleep; he hadn't gotten enough the night before and any sleep he'd gotten lately hadn't been restful, regardless. His bones seemed to knock and creak as he lay on the soft pad and pulled a blanket over his chest.

When he woke, Dradevai was fast asleep on his chest again, and for the first time in a few days, he'd only woken long after the first sun had risen. Sometime in the night, he'd pulled Dradevai closer though, his hand resting on the back of their head between their horns, and Dradevai had wrapped their legs around one of his own. It sort of hurt, being trapped between Dradevai's legs, but the night was still better than the ones he hadn't slept at all.

"Vai." He nudged Dradevai's shoulder, and they mumbled unintelligibly and pulled Asith tighter. "Vai."

Dradevai's eyes opened in slits first, then promptly closed again. Asith kept talking to them, poking them awake until they shifted and rolled away from him.

"You still can't go back to sleep," Asith said. He stretched his leg, and Dradevai grumbled at him again. Asith sighed and leaned close to their ear. "If you do not get up, I'm going to come back and throw water on you."

Dradevai shot up, pressing their hands to their ear and neck. "Don't you dare!"

"Then get up." Asith laughed, shuffling to move out of the tent. They didn't have much travel left; they'd be in the Capitol by sundown if they left quickly enough.

"Mean." Dradevai rubbed their neck gently. The way they seemed to hide behind their bangs and pout caught Asith's attention. He'd only seen that expression once before, and it was after he'd kissed them.

"What are you looking at?" Dradevai's brow furrowed, a scowl coming across their face.

"I was making sure you didn't go back to sleep." Asith ducked out of the tent. "I'm going to start getting the horses ready."

"I'll be there soon." Dradevai sighed.

Asith drank some water and splashed it on his face, wondering whether Dradevai had been blushing in the tent. It was hard to tell sometimes, for their skin was darker than Asith's. As he stood with his hand pressed to his face, his stomach flipped like it had when Dradevai asked about the kiss, and he forced himself to move again.

"Do you want me to start a fire for breakfast?" Dradevai stood in front of the little ring they'd made the night before, rubbing their eyes.

"Yes," Asith said, "if you do, I can fry a few eggs for you."

Dradevai smiled. "That sounds good. Why are we up so early? The second sun hasn't even risen."

"If we get going quickly enough, we can make it to the Capitol before the second sun is down." He hooked the feed bags in front of each of the horses and patted them on the head. "Then I can show you a bit more of it."

"Show it to me? I thought we were just trying to go to the library?" They followed Asith as he packed up the remaining feed.

"It will be closed when we get there. I thought you might like to see how humans there tend to live. Especially if you might want to go to the Maeria Spire at some point." He set a pan on the edge of the fire ring and let it heat before putting a few links of sausage into it. After he cracked the eggs into the pan, Dradevai took the shells from him. Asith suspected they had been burying them each time they did that, but as he turned back, Dradevai was eating one of the shells.

"I would like to, if you don't mind showing me. How long did you live there?" Dradevai stuck the other half of the eggshell into their mouth and crunched. Asith cringed; he could almost feel eggshells scraping against his gums and piercing his tongue.

"You know, you don't have to eat those," Asith said and smiled. "But no, I wouldn't mind showing you. I lived there for about eight years.

We might be able to see if you can sufficiently hide yourself while in the school."

Dradevai hummed softly as Asith slid their eggs out onto a corn husk so that they could hold them easier. They shifted slightly, moving the eggs so they could slurp them up while they were still hot.

"It seems wasteful not to eat the shells." Dradevai sat with their legs crossed and pulled an entire egg into their mouth. "I don't know if I would want to go to school."

"Egg shells are good for the soil, so it's not a waste. Why would you not want to go to school?"

Asith was wary of their sudden change of opinion; they'd been so excited about the idea before. They squirmed in their seat before rolling the mat they'd been sleeping on and tying a leather cord around it. Dradevai opened their mouth and then closed it. For once, it seemed like they weren't sure why they had said it.

"I have told you before that dragons are born knowing," Dradevai said. "Well, it's like, when you first told me about it, it sounded like something I'd enjoy. But the more I think about doing it, the more I feel my stomach unsettle."

"Are you sure you're not just feeling anxious about the idea for some reason?" Asith slipped his eggs onto a corn husk, setting the pan aside carefully so that it could cool.

"Anxious..." Dradevai retracted, gripping the bed roll in their arms. They ate their third egg and pressed their lips together. "Is that something that can be felt outside of a romantic situation?"

Asith shoveled a piece of sausage into his mouth, trying to register what Dradevai had just asked. Asith had noticed they would understand words but in one context, or they thought they were only meant to be used in one way. Usually, they had only seen it in a book once or twice and just didn't know.

"It can. I was very anxious when I left South Cairn to go to school in the Capitol."

"Why?" Dradevai looked the way they always did when they were trying to understand something new. Their expression was slightly befuddled but curious. Asith rather liked when they looked like that.

"I had never left home before without my mother. I hadn't ever lived anywhere else, and I knew I was going to meet a lot of new people that might not like me." Asith shrugged and took a deep breath, trying to think of a better way to explain it. "It was scary. The idea that I might not like it and not have a good way to get back home if I didn't. Is that what you're feeling?"

Dradevai considered his words, carefully folding the corn husk. "That sounds sort of how I'm feeling. I'm not sure I would want to be away from you, and I don't have to hide in South Cairn."

It would make sense if Dradevai wanted to stick with him, for they knew him the best. It did not differ from the way Asith did not want to leave his mother. He couldn't help the way it made his stomach churn, something like excitement and guilt.

"That sounds like anxiety," he said. "Sometimes, that feeling is a sign you shouldn't do something, like trying to jump over a gap you don't know if you can clear. Other times, it means that you should try to do it, anyway."

"That sounds complicated. I liked my explanation better." Dradevai scattered the fire with a stick.

Asith chuckled. "Not doing things that make you anxious might seem like the right answer, but if I hadn't done them, I wouldn't have met you." He shrugged. "Including walking out to that field the day you appeared in South Cairn."

"You were anxious?" Dradevai looked up at him.

Asith scoffed. "Of course. You are a lot bigger than me. I was worried you would try to step on me even if I was being polite."

Dradevai laughed without making eye contact. "Sorry. You didn't look scared."

"Well, fear and anxiety are a little bit different. It's more like worry. I was worried that you would hurt me, but I was confident I could reason with you." He stopped, thinking it over again. "Though, I don't know why I felt I could trust you more than I would have trusted a Blue or Green."

"I have been sort of wondering about them, Blues and Greens. I hadn't known of them before meeting you."

"You have only met a Copper, right? So that's not surprising." Asith went back to loading the tent onto the cart, checking the feed bags, and taking them away from the horses.

"Yes, but I was born knowing of the other dragons. I knew I was a Bronze, and that there are Silvers, Golds, Pewters, and Coppers. But I did not know of the Blues and Greens."

Asith got up on the cart as Dradevai finished putting the tent in the back. The dragons he had fought all had wings and scales, but they had been scales with no feathers on top. None of them had horns, just spikes or spines, and nearly all of them were a head taller than Dradevai's and weighed more. Their feet had always been large and clawed, with narrow talons like an owl's, and their tongues stuck out and lashed when they hissed. Blues would sometimes blow fire from their mouths, but it smelled thickly of burning oil, like a fire started by knocking over a lantern. Dradevai's fire smelled like wood burning in a well-kept fireplace, crackling and popping like a log that hadn't been left to dry long enough.

"Now that I think about it," Asith said, "you don't particularly look like any of the dragons I fought."

"Really?" Dradevai climbed onto the cart and said a spell that made their horns disappear.

"Yes, and for that matter, none of them ever spoke." Dradevai nudged the horses to move. Asith didn't particularly have the heart to push the horses too hard.

"What made you speak to me, then?" Dradevai asked.

"Well, Sterling dragons have a reputation from the war for being…" Asith's thoughts stalled. He had never noticed that very little about the story made sense. "Well, for being reasonable. But I don't know if anything I learned at the Stonegarde is actually true, now that I'm thinking about it."

"The war? Your mother mentioned that too." Dradevai crossed their arms. "Can you tell me about it?"

"I can tell you what we learn in primary school, but I don't know a lot of the historical details." Asith narrowed his eyes at the road, trying to remember the details from when he was in school as a child.

"That's all right. Please?" Dradevai made a gesture that Asith should go on, so he took a deep breath and tried to remember the story.

He summarized the details as best he could, thinking of the way history books always did it. When the people of the Kingdom of Ewehar became tired of the king living lavishly while they had nothing to eat, they went to the Golden Queen of the Dragons, begging for her help. She was hesitant at first but made a deal that if they would never hunt dragons again, then her mages and armies would help them fight the king.

The people agreed, and the people and dragons started to overtake the king's armies, but after a large and bloody battle, the queen disappeared. Her body was never found, and the dragons accused the people of stealing her so that they could harvest her blood and feathers for their mages. The dragons eventually turned their backs on the people, siding with the king's armies and helping them fight. At first, their allegiance caused the people to lose battles, but a woman who fought alongside the dragons figured out better ways to fight them. Soon, the people's army had scattered the armies of the king and the dragons, pushing them back into the castle.

However, when they arrived, there was nothing but a note of surrender. The king, his family, and any remaining dragons had disappeared.

"What happened to the woman who led the army?" Dradevai asked. "And why would the dragons turn against the people based on rumors? Does anyone even know if the people really did harvest the queen's body?" Dradevai's lips deepened into a frown.

"The woman who led the army established the Stonegarde where I trained. She told people she knew dragons would be returning, and they did several years later." Asith scratched his head and nudged the horses so that they wouldn't go off the road. "We have no idea what happened to the queen or why the dragons believed that the humans had harvested her. Considering what my mother told us, it could be that the queen left on her own for some reason."

"That could be true." Dradevai seemed rather introspective, their head in their hand. "That's why your family was run out of town, wasn't it? Because the people still see the dragons as traitors to the people and friends of the monarch?"

"Yes." Asith swallowed, his stomach turning. He had been trying not to think about it until that point, but he let the understanding wash over him. "I believe that is what happened."

"Something…" Dradevai mumbled. "The story has a hole. Why would the dragons ally with the monarch because their queen disappeared? Wouldn't they have simply abandoned the people instead? And where did the king go? It doesn't really make a lot of sense. It's like it's half the story."

"I agree. It doesn't make a lot of sense." Asith noticed their intense expression. "Are you okay?"

Dradevai nodded. "Yes. Sorry. I am just thinking too much about it."

"It's okay. It's a lot to think about." Asith sighed and rubbed the side of his head, looking up at the walls of the Capitol.

The cart bumped over stones while they watched the road in front of them. More and more people appeared, so Dradevai pulled up their hood while they neared the Southern gate of the Capitol. The massive doors stretched up into the sky the same way the wall did.

The Capitol was roughly shaped in a hexagon, the towering walls filled with small windows just large enough for armies to shoot arrows from. Farmlands surrounded it, but leading up to the wall, fifty or so feet of wet grass acted as a barrier if the farms were ever set ablaze. A river slipped out from under the wall to their left, running from a large lake in the North to the oceans in the South. It not only provided the city with fresh water but also offered quick passage if people needed to evacuate.

Guards walked along the top of the wall, their helmets carrying the distinct horns of a dragon. The walls of the Capitol were always a coveted post among the dragon knights, mostly because it was so rare for a dragon to make its way so deep into the country. Most politicians insisted their children received that post. Asith had always disliked that politicians' children received priority in Stonegarde assignments; that meant some dragon knights among the ranks never saw combat and never understood the struggles the rest of them dealt with. It just seemed unfair.

"Wow." Dradevai sat up, holding their hood down on their head to look up at the top of the wall. "I think that's taller than me, nose to tail."

Asith laughed, trying to imagine it. "It might be. I wonder if we could find a way to measure it."

"I can just turn back right now." Dradevai's mischievous look on their face scared Asith.

"That is a bad idea," Asith said.

"Well, I could always just fly away and sneak back to you looking like this." Dradevai seemed confident in their plan, and Asith couldn't stop them if they decided to try it. They stared at him with a beaming smile on their face that quickly dropped into a look of worry. "Oh no, you look really panicked. I'm just kidding."

Asith gasped, breathing for the first time in a few moments. "Don't scare me like that."

"Don't get so worked up about everything I say!" Dradevai laughed, their shoulders shaking as the sweet sound filled Asith up. He rolled his eyes and turned his gaze away. As Dradevai continued to giggle, Asith huffed, not dignifying Dradevai with a response as their cart approached the people waiting for inspection at the gates of the city.

There were merchants from Gelermand, Caleah, and even from Nala, which was on the other side of the Western mountains. A few of the travelers on foot appeared to be from Syuty, their delicate grayish-lavender skin mostly covered in dark fabrics of green, purple, and black. He had only ever seen a few elves of that ancestry, and when he did, they were typically powerful mages visiting the Maeria Spire. Unsurprisingly, there was no sign of any person being from Wacot, and even if someone was, they were probably not flaunting it. Guards wandered among the groups, examining the people as carefully as they examined the items with them.

A woman from Nala, with a bright auburn mane surrounding her well-trimmed face, looked up at Asith and smiled. She walked alongside another woman, each of them having thick blonde fur covering her entire body and gently curved ears on top of her head. Heavy shawls covered their shoulders, for they weren't used to the cold like the denizens of Cairn. Asith waved, which prompted Dradevai to do the same, and the two of them waved back. One had a heavy bag over her shoulder that was filled with stone fruits Asith had only ever seen in the Capitol, and as she turned back to her companion, the two giggled, speaking to each other in a language Asith did not understand. It reminded him of visiting the Capitol with his mother, when all the different people he had never seen before would come there to sell their wares.

It soothed his mind until a group of guards walked up to the side of the cart and examined its contents. He straightened up, and so did Dradevai, noticing the change in Asith's energy. The guards didn't pay them much mind, just looking over the cargo before carrying on.

"There will be more of that," Asith said once the guards were far enough away. "Did you think of a way to change the way you look?"

"No." Dradevai shook their head and pulled their hood up more. "I'm not sure if it's a good idea to use magic for this."

"Are you sure? You have that spell to look different. Could you use that?"

Dradevai pursed their lips, hesitant still. "I guess now would be a better time to test it than in the city."

They ran their hand over their chest, and unlike the time they had shown Asith back at his house, their disguise only made them look like they did not have horns. Otherwise, they still appeared like Dradevai always did.

"You are going to have to teach me that trick," Asith said. Dradevai popped up and got back onto the bench with him.

"I can show you tonight if you'd like." They set their hand around their horn, tugging on it gently to show that it was still there. "It's only an illusion."

"It's still rather clever." Asith reached out and poked Dradevai's horn.

"The magic isn't very strong," Dradevai said. "This could be taken out with a very simple magic ward. That's why I was worried about doing it. I tried to make it more subtle."

"I know it will work. You are a great mage, Vai. I trust in your ability to do magic."

Dradevai fiddled with their necklace, smiling. "I hope you're right."

"I haven't even seen that in the spell book yet." He wanted to change the subject to help ease Dradevai's nerves. "Is it more advanced than what you were teaching me?"

"I created it on my own. There are a few pieces of other spells in it."

"I didn't know you could make your own spells." Asith's eyes widened. Dradevai grew sheepish, and he couldn't help the way he smiled at them. It seemed to make them more modest, but Asith sort of liked that about them.

"It's something I've done from time to time," they said. "It's a lot of work, but it seemed necessary for what we'd be doing."

Asith nodded. "I trust it even more now."

Dradevai grinned, then they settled onto the bench on the front of the cart. Regular caravans pulled past them, getting into a separate line that moved much more quickly.

Asith's breathing had sped up, his eyes scanning the crowd of people and guards. Anyone around them causing trouble would make the guards more aware. He had once seen them pull a merchant from their cart and toss the whole thing until they pulled up a hidden compartment with weapons inside. The man was immediately arrested and sent for trial, but after that, the guards triple-searched everyone coming through, even the company of dragon knights he was with at the time. He chewed his lip, hoping that something like that did not happen again.

When he and Dradevai finally got to the front of the line, the guards swiftly asked them to remain seated and searched the back of the cart. Another stood in front of Asith, looking up at him with a hand on their sword.

"Nice to see you today. What are you bringing into the city?" The guard didn't wholly pay attention to Asith, looking at Dradevai instead. Asith spared them a glance and saw the spell they had used to hide their horns had worn off, and the very bases of them appeared behind their bangs.

"Some uniforms and armor fittings. Running an errand for my mother. She's a tailor in South Cairn," Asith said, his back stiff as a board as he tried to focus on the guard again. He didn't need to give him a reason to look too closely at Dradevai. "I have a sword with me. It is registered with the Stonegarde, if you would like to check the sheath."

"Ah, a dragon knight, are you?" The guard smiled, their attention turning back to Asith. This was part of the reason he had brought the sword; it gave him an excuse to bring it up. Everyone loved a dragon knight.

Dradevai twitched next to him, and out of the corner of his eye, he saw them cast a spell, hiding it in the movement of pressing their hand to the back of their hair under their hood. The guard's eyes darted toward Dradevai briefly as they rubbed the back of their neck.

"I was, yes," Asith began. "I'm certainly not retired, but my mother needed me. You know how that is." Asith's stomach turned, but his voice became confident in a way he could only call obnoxious.

"I know very well. Either way, thank you for your service." The guard folded their arms over their chest as one guard who had checked their cart moved to their side. They had a quick conversation, and the guard interrogating them looked back up at Asith. "And the books you have?"

"Those are ours. They will be leaving with us. They helped pass the time during travel."

The guard nodded and trained their eyes on Dradevai again. "Do you mind if I ask you to take your hood down?"

A chill ran over Asith's arms, spreading along his ribs until it settled directly into the center of his chest. Dradevai had to have noticed their spell had worn off, but the guards would see if they recast it. Asith's mind spiraled into a flurry of lies he could tell, but none of them came out. Instead, he simply watched as Dradevai reached for their hood with a flick of their wrist, the spell rolling off them like they had flicked sweat from their fingertips. With it came no sound or visual, so Asith had no idea how they had done it.

Dradevai lowered their hood and smiled. Their horns hidden by their spell, they waved. "Sorry, trying to keep the sun off of my skin."

"No trouble." The guard looked transfixed, though, their eyes on Dradevai as they leaned forward. Asith recognized that look, and it took him everything not to grow immediately defensive of Dradevai. It was not worth potentially angering the guards. The guard cleared their throat and puffed out their chest when the third came back to his side. They finished with their inspection and waved Asith and Dradevai on.

As soon as they moved past the guards, Asith's face fell into a scowl, his eyes down on his hands. Dradevai let out a rough breath and relaxed against the back of the bench, flipping their hood back up.

"That was close," Dradevai said. "You distracted them just long enough for me to find a way to cast the spell."

Asith didn't respond, too focused on his own thoughts about the guard. Adrenaline made his blood pump through his arms and legs.

"Why do you look angry?" Dradevai turned to Asith, their eyes big and curious.

Asith took a deep breath, setting the reins in his lap in an attempt to rub the look off his face. "I didn't like how that made me feel."

"Telling him that you were a dragon knight?" Dradevai asked. "Or that my spell almost didn't work? Or when the guard looked at me like I was a piece of meat?"

"All of it." Asith grunted.

"I didn't like it either." Dradevai sighed and folded their arms, holding onto their elbows. They leaned forward and looked ahead of them. "But we made it inside. That's what's important. Well, I made it inside. I don't think it was a question for you."

Asith sighed and picked up the reins again. He guided the cart through the narrow street as Dradevai looked up at him with bright eyes. They smiled, more genuinely than they smiled at the guard. He had to admit, it made him feel better.

"You're right." He smiled back at Dradevai. "Now we just have to get you into the Stonegarde without anyone noticing."

Dradevai nodded, sitting up straight and looking around as people buzzed around them. They spotted the two Nalan women again, so they waved. The women waved back. "We can do this," Dradevai said.

They headed into the city behind a line of other carts carrying other goods. As he settled into the uneasy feeling of what they had to do there in the Capitol, he turned the cart toward the center of the city. While he and Dradevai could handle a lot, he feared that this might be more than either of them could deal with. It was one thing to bring Dradevai into the city, for they didn't look much different from a human when their horns were hidden, but to bring a dragon into the Stonegarde still worried him. There were typically anywhere between fifty and seventy-five dragon knights and more than a hundred knights in training. One wrong move and Dradevai would certainly be noticed.

Dradevai turned to look at Asith, the smile on their face bright as they asked questions about the city. Asith couldn't help but smile. When Dradevai looked back at the buildings, Asith watched them take everything in, enjoying Dradevai's excitement for a moment and reminding himself of why they were doing this.

CHAPTER 13

25th of Kasdiel

The city opened up to them, the buildings made of wood and sandy-colored stone rising from the ground in circular rings. The population of the Capitol rarely grew; usually, the people who lived there learned a trade and returned to wherever they had come from or to whichever town offered them the most money to be there.

Asith actually liked coming back. He hadn't been to the Capitol since he had left Stonegarde to return to his mother, and while he loved South Cairn, the Capitol was the home of his later teens and early twenties. Nostalgia took him easily, the same way it had when he first returned to South Cairn at his mother's request. He smiled fondly at the streets, most of which were simple dirt or the occasional cobblestone, save for the inn district which had sleek slate streets, the stone held in place with magic. It catered to guests from all over the country, inns of various levels of comfort and cost scattered all along the same street. Foreign merchants were bustling around the area as well, some finely dressed and others more modest.

They headed straight for the hold office to drop off the uniforms and fittings before it closed. Dradevai stuck close to him inside the office, which wasn't really an office so much as a promenade with a roof over it. Asith had done this a few times with his mother as a child, so he took the paper that the hold worker offered him, grabbed his sword, and swept up the books. He handed those off to Dradevai and let the cart go with the hold workers. Their tent, food, and cooking utensils got marked as personal by a worker.

Hundreds of uniformed workers bustled around them, taking carts from their owners and sending them off to the right. Each owner walked away with a paper that marked them as the owner of that cart. Dradevai looked confused, and they grabbed onto the sleeve of Asith's tunic.

"You're fine." Asith leaned into Dradevai, who was watching the crowds nervously. He pulled them closer and took their hand so that he wouldn't lose them. Dradevai only relaxed slightly as they made their way up to the tables.

Some hold workers sat behind broad desks while others directed cart owners to the proper tables based on the goods they'd brought. They followed the instructions of an angry-looking man, who wasn't much taller than Dradevai's waist, to a table with an older woman sitting behind it. Her table was stacked with inventory registries and various writing utensils, as well as a couple inkwells. She smiled a lot, took the paper from Asith, and quickly marked items off based on the sheet she received from one of the other workers.

Her customer-service smile made Asith think she was actually very tired, or maybe just that she desperately wanted to be anywhere else at the moment. She had dark black hair and russet skin, the red undertones making her warm and approachable. She directed them to gather their personal items from the cart, and Asith gave her a ledger of what needed to stay with it, like their camping gear.

Asith led Dradevai toward the exit, letting the cart and horses stay behind. They headed toward the inn district, Dradevai keeping close as they looked back at the office. Eventually, they asked why they were leaving the horses behind as the workers took the horses from the cart and guided them toward a stable. He explained they were going to board the horses and take care of them. Dradevai looked almost a bit embarrassed they didn't figure that out, but Asith could see how it would be confusing without context.

"Asith!" A voice rose over the crowd. Asith stopped to turn back as Delri shoved herself out of a group of hold workers and strode toward them. Dradevai stopped a step after he did, looking back at him first before staring at Delri.

"Your hair makes you really obvious in a crowd," Delri said. "I never thought about how useful that was until now."

She attempted to ruffle his hair, and Asith brushed her hand away. He couldn't help but smile. Delri had joined the Stonegarde at the same time as him, and they had grown close quickly. Her hair was much longer, pulled back in a sleek ponytail, and her eyes were as dark and lively as ever.

Honestly, with everything that had happened over the last few months, Delri's excited smile was like a breath of fresh air for Asith. She still stood with the strength of a dragon knight, her sturdy figure in impeccable shape from the years she'd spent training to fight, much like Asith's used to look. Delri had obviously kept up with the practice, whereas Asith hadn't as much. The scars on her hands, face, and body looked about the same as when he'd last seen her, which he regarded as a good thing.

Though, it only occurred to him as he smiled and said hello that she might be making Dradevai uncomfortable. "It's been a long time," Asith said. "I thought you'd gone back to Martivin?"

"Ah, well…" Delri smiled in a way unusual for her, somber almost. "Remember that woman I told you about? I went back to try to be with her, but it… it didn't work out. So I came back here and got a job working in the hold."

"Oh, I'm sorry." Asith hadn't meant to bring up bad memories, but Delri smiled widely and shook her head.

"Don't worry, I'm okay." She waved a hand and then looked at Dradevai. "It's nice to meet you. I'm Delri. I'm sorry, when I saw Asith, I didn't realize he was with someone."

Dradevai slowly took Delri's extended hand, their eyes on her gloves. "It's all right. My name is Dradevai. It's nice to meet you."

Their eyes darted to Asith as they stepped back from shaking Delri's hand. They looked jittery, forcing a smile as they stood next to Asith.

"That's an uncommon name. I like it." Dradevai grew sheepish and thanked her, which earned them a small chuckle from Delri. "What are you doing here? Just making a drop-off for your mother?"

"No, we're staying for a little bit," Asith said. "Dradevai is considering attending the Maeria Spire."

It was the fastest lie Asith could think of. He just hoped it didn't bother Dradevai. It made the most sense in the moment, since Delri knew for a fact Asith had retired from the dragon knights. She quirked an eyebrow at him, like she had picked up on his lie, but Dradevai nodded.

"Asith was kind enough to let me travel with him. I'm from South Cairn as well," they said.

Delri nodded, looking at each of them slowly. Delri had been to South Cairn often enough she knew the people there well, so she easily caught on to their lie. But there was nothing Asith could do, for he couldn't talk about the truth in the open. He was just glad Dradevai had tried to support the lie even if it made it harder to believe.

"Well, I hope your visit goes well," Delri said slowly, as if she were still thinking. "If you have a moment while you're here, we should catch up. I have officially surpassed your kill count, you know."

Delri beamed with pride, her grin growing as it always used to, but Asith couldn't bring himself to match it. He laughed slightly, nodding as he stumbled over his thoughts about how he should be acting. Delri and he would rib each other all the time over kill counts and trainees, but at that moment, the thought of either made him nauseous.

He didn't recover fast enough, for Delri's grin faltered. Her eyes stuck on Dradevai, whose face had scrunched into a mix of disgust and anger.

"Sorry, uh…" Delri looked at her feet. "I'm not a dragon knight anymore, though, but I have some embarrassing stories about Kosor you might like to hear."

Asith shook his head slightly. "No, it's okay. Catching up sounds fun. Sorry, we have been traveling for a long time, and we're tired."

"Yes." Dradevai sounded like they might snap a pen in half if they were holding one. Delri's eyes swam over Asith and Dradevai, and she wrapped her arms around her middle.

"Yeah," Delri said. "I've missed you, Asith."

Asith's throat burned; he didn't like hurting Delri's feelings. "I missed you too, Delri."

Delri held a gentle curve to her lips as she let go of her elbows.

"I have to get back to work." Her eyes scanned Dradevai from top to bottom, and then she smiled. "It was nice meeting you. Good luck at the Maeria Spire."

Dradevai blinked, and then they cast their eyes down and away from Delri, nodding.

"Thank you." They sounded more sincere that time and waved as Delri headed back into the crowd. Once she was far enough away, Dradevai turned to Asith.

"Sorry," they said, "I just, to hear her boast like that, it…"

Asith shook his head and led Dradevai away from the crowd of people at the hold. "No, it's okay. I probably should have warned you about Delri having been a dragon knight with me."

"She seemed to know you really well," Dradevai added.

Asith smiled a little bit. "Ah, well. She's my best friend." Before he went on, he took a moment to choose his words carefully. He didn't want Dradevai to find out about their history from someone else. "And she and I had a physical relationship for a little while."

Dradevai looked surprised. "Did she leave you for the woman she was talking about?"

"No." Asith chuckled. "No, I knew about that woman before she and I were even together. We were both looking for something temporary. Sometimes when you are losing friends as often as we were, it's something you need."

"Losing friends?" Dradevai froze. "Oh, to the dragons."

Asith nodded solemnly.

Dradevai smiled, sympathetic. "Well, she was nice even though I was sort of rude to her." They toyed with their necklace, frowning. "I'm not sure if I would trust her with knowing about me."

"That's okay. I wasn't going to tell her about that. In fact, I wouldn't tell anyone that without your permission."

"Okay. Thank you."

"Come on, let's find a room to stay in."

Asith adjusted the bag on his shoulder, shifting awkwardly to get the other strap over his arm. Backpacks were sort of difficult when his shoulder didn't always want to work correctly.

They found an inn that looked moderate in price, by Asith's guess. Dradevai had looked at every big fancy inn with wide, interested eyes, and while they definitely had money to pay for it, Asith didn't want them to spend all their gold immediately. They weren't difficult to convince, either, since the less Dradevai spent on a room, the more they could spend on books.

The man at the counter wore a pair of narrow glasses and his hair swept over his face in an odd way, but he smiled at Asith and Dradevai. After a bit of talking, he asked, "One bed, or two for you?"

To which Dradevai promptly said, "One."

Asith felt his ears heat up, and as the man looked at him for confirmation, he shook his head. "Two, please."

"But——" Dradevai closed their mouth when Asith made a small gesture with his hand and paid the man at the counter of the inn. He took the key and nudged Dradevai up the stairs as they tried to ask why he wanted two beds.

Asith closed the door to their room behind him, sighing softly. "Because the room is bigger if you get two beds."

"Oh," Dradevai said, "then why'd you blush?"

"Never mind."

Asith's ears were still hot as he set his pack down on the small table. Each bed had a small curtain on its side for privacy. Dradevai took a few quick strides toward Asith, who fixated on taking items out of his pack. They leaned over to look up at him.

"Why are you being cagey about it now?" Dradevai hummed. "We don't have to share a bed if you don't want to."

Asith took a deep breath and slipped his sword from his belt. He only spared Dradevai a glance as he set it on the table. "We can share a bed; I don't mind. I just got flustered because usually only couples take a room with one bed."

"Couples?" Dradevai looked confused, and then their face reddened. "Oh, like a romantic couple."

"Yes." Asith pulled his wallet from his bag and moved a few pieces of gold into various pockets. "What did you want to do tonight? We won't be able to get into the Stonegarde library until tomorrow."

Dradevai snapped out of their embarrassment so quickly, it was unfair. Asith always stayed flustered for hours. "Can we do anything toward finding that spell tonight?"

"There's not much we can do this late in the day. Most fronts are closed." Asith shook his head and then frowned. "We did just get into the city. I know we're in a hurry, but maybe we should take it easy for the night."

"Are you sure?" Dradevai looked at Asith carefully, their eyes narrowed. "I know you're worried about your father's safety."

Asith sighed. "I am, but we have no leads to help us look into it tonight."

"Maybe we should get something to eat and find Delri," Dradevai said. They set their jaw, looking uncomfortable at their own suggestion, but their eyes were sharp. "It might be good to know more about what's going on here and at Stonegarde before we go running into this. She might be able to tell us."

Asith blinked and nodded slowly. "That's a really good idea."

"Really?" Dradevai looked rather proud of themself, their chest puffing up and their back straightening as the pompous demeanor Asith had known so well came back for the first time in a while. "Well, then we should do that. Do you know how we can find her?"

"It's been a bit since we've been in the city together, but I might know a few places she could be." Asith looked outside. "But she could also just go home right after work, and I don't know where she's staying."

"You need to eat tonight, anyway," Dradevai asserted.

"I do, you're right. It wouldn't hurt to go somewhere for food that Delri might also go to." Asith rubbed the back of his head, trying to see if his hair was a disaster or if he could get away without washing it.

"Then it's settled. We're going." Dradevai picked up their entire wallet and tied it to their belt.

Asith's shoulders dropped. "Okay, but I wouldn't suggest carrying your whole wallet on you." Asith tucked his wallet back into his pack once he'd retrieved a few coins from it. "There are a lot of pickpockets here. It's better only to carry a little and spread it out."

Dradevai untied their wallet. "Spread it out?"

Asith nodded. "Several different pockets. You're only going to need a few gold and some silver for tonight."

"Thank you." Dradevai smiled, dispersing their coins and tucking their wallet back into their pack. "You're always looking out for me." The way Dradevai smiled made his stomach light, but he tried to ignore it. "Of course."

After confirming the door was locked behind them, Asith led Dradevai back into the street. The inn district was livelier now, people bustling around in nice clothes or goofing off in small groups. Dradevai instinctively got closer to Asith, watching the people move about the slate road. The lamps illuminated, throwing a soft yellow glow from whatever magic they used to keep them lit. They made their way through the crowd and toward the hold office first, trying to see if they could find Delri there again, but she'd already left.

Asith headed toward Stonegarde next, the streets far less crowded in that area. They found the pubs where many dragon knights spent their downtime. "You might want to disguise yourself completely."

"Even if we're meeting Delri?" Dradevai asked.

Asith considered that, chewing on the inside of his cheek. "Good point. Maybe just use the magic to hide your horns."

Their hood was already up, and their horns were peeking out a little. They cast the spell, their fingers crossing their chest again. Dradevai would keep their hood up, and Asith hoped people would assume Dradevai was simply not from Cairn. Though it wasn't very cold out, many foreign visitors were not used to the cold in Cairn and bundled up.

The crowd was mostly people with tan skin and round faces, but there was the occasional person from the eastern part of the country with lighter skin and a square face. His mother was originally from the base of the Eastern mountains, and as such, she had the same red hair as many of the people there, with pale skin. All kinds of people wearing uniforms from the Stonegarde wandered through the crowd. Most of them bore a crest on their left shoulder and carried a shield with a pair of blue wings wrapped around it. Some had the well-trimmed tunics of a knight, with heavy leather belts across their middle, while others wore the sleek suits reserved for mages. The mages wore lighter belts, but they had thick harnesses going over their right shoulders that held small pockets for the materials to cast spells.

Asith and Dradevai received looks. Dradevai didn't quite seem to notice, too focused on people-watching. Some looked at Asith as if they might recognize him, so he hoped he wouldn't be running into anyone undesirable.

Of course, as he had that thought, he heard someone over the crowd in front of a pub he always avoided when he lived there. "Ay, s'that white-haired asshole."

"Are they talking about you?" Dradevai tried to look into the crowd, but Asith grabbed their hand and pulled them past the pub. The last thing he needed was to start a fight with Kosor, who Asith was fairly certain was in the crowd. That would be his guess based on being called "that white-haired asshole" and the sound of his voice.

"Yes." Asith kept his eyes ahead of them, navigating through the crowd, but Kosor bounded behind him. Definitely Kosor, given that a hand the size of his head came down on his shoulder and squeezed him.

"What's this? Finally replaced Delri with someone as puny and ugly as you?"

Kosor's hulking figure loomed over Asith now, thick black hair and chiseled jawline the same as Asith remembered it. After so many years, Asith really thought he would have let his grudge go. Asith's hand tightened around Dradevai's, unsure if he should let them go or keep them close.

"If they're hiding in a hood, they must be particularly disgusting to look at. How badly did you do after she left you?"

Kosor, clearly still angry Delri never returned his advances, reached out for Dradevai's hood, and something in Asith snapped. He spun on his heels and took a cheap shot at Kosor's stomach. Kosor coughed, grunted something Asith didn't understand, and then raised his hand to throw a punch at him. The fight had already started to draw a crowd, for most dragon knights loved good hand-to-hand or something they could place a bet on.

"Hey." Dradevai's voice rose over the crowd, their hand now clutching Kosor's thick outstretched wrist. They still had all the strength of a dragon in their human form, which seemed to bear down on Kosor's wrist. Asith had never seen that look on their face before. Their eyes looked deadly, and Asith thought they might breathe fire straight into Kosor's face. "Do not touch him."

Kosor, who looked shaken to his core, tried to save face, struggling to take his arm back from Dradevai, but they tightened their grip and pulled him in closer. "F-fuck, are you really letting this little thing defend you?"

"That's what you get for trying to bring them into your petty insults." Asith nudged Dradevai. "He's not worth our time."

Dradevai frowned, letting go of Kosor's arm before they flicked their wrist and said a few arcane words. The cigarette behind Kosor's ear lit, which made Kosor jump and try to bat it away. Asith pulled Dradevai away, looking back as Kosor stomped out the cigarette and spoke with several other dragon knights, some of whom Asith remembered. Kosor wasn't about to give up, so he kept Dradevai moving.

"Who was that?" Dradevai's said lowly. Their fingers were linked together, and they pressed closer to Asith.

"Kosor," Asith said, noting the stares of people. "He's a few years older than me. Used to work together sometimes, hates me because Delri never paid attention to him."

"What do you have to do with Delri not wanting him?" Dradevai's feet were quick next to Asith's.

"Nothing, he's just stupid and angry." Asith's eyes scanned the crowd. Usually, if there was a fight, Delri would come out to see what was going on.

"That did not seem like just stupid and angry." Dradevai looked over their shoulder, trusting Asith to lead them through the crowd.

"He was always angry that Delri liked me but hated him," Asith said with a groan. "Even when Delri and I were only friends, he would get upset that she didn't want to hang out with him."

"He sounds like a jerk. Also, I think they're following us."

"He is, and I'm not surprised he's following us. We kind of made a fool of him back there." Asith pulled Dradevai into a tighter crowd of people to blend in better.

Dradevai swung around to look at Asith again, beaming and grinning. "We did make him look like a fool. I'm proud of it."

Asith couldn't help but snort and laugh, which made Dradevai's grin grow. Then he spotted Delri heading directly for them. "Ah, perfect."

"Did Kosor just try to attack you?" She still had her hold uniform on, but she had taken off the leather gloves with the emblem on them, making her one of the few people in the area not wearing the crest of the Stonegarde.

"He tried to insult us, and then Asith hit him." Dradevai let go of Asith's hand to cross their arms, closing off to Delri.

"Well…" She looked back at Kosor, who was pointedly not following them anymore. "He won't come after you if you stay with me. Come on."

"Thank you," Asith said.

As she led them toward the Stonegarde, Dradevai stayed close to him, eyeing the people around them.

"I can't believe he's still holding that grudge! What a child." Delri pressed her hands to her face and shook her head like she was trying to rid herself of the thought. "I'm sorry he tried to go after you because of me again."

"It's okay," Asith said. "It was sort of worth it to see Dradevai nearly light him on fire."

Dradevai scowled and shifted to walk between Asith and Delri.

"I almost actually lit him on fire," they said.

Delri knew Dradevai was a mage, so Asith didn't try to cover up the comment.

"You should have." Delri threw her head back and laughed. "I'm going to report him to Stonegarde again. I don't care how good a fighter he is. He shouldn't have weapons."

They approached a nearby pub with large tables outside of it, surrounded by a lively crowd of hold workers drinking after their workday. They took one of the open tables, and Delri promptly ordered mead for the three of them.

"Were you looking for me, then?" Delri asked.

"Yes, I had a feeling you'd be somewhere around there." Asith took the tankard from the server and sipped on it quickly. Dradevai sniffed at theirs curiously, which earned them a strange look from Delri they didn't notice.

"Well, I can't be angry because you were right." Delri rolled her eyes and took a long drink from the tankard. "Did you need something?"

"Nothing in particular." Asith glanced at Dradevai, who sipped at the mead and seemed more satisfied with it than with the ale. "We didn't have much to do tonight, so we thought we'd find you."

Delri smiled, then gave Asith a knowing look. "You're here for more than just the Maeria Spire, aren't you?"

Asith and Dradevai glanced at each other. He wasn't sure it was a good idea to be completely honest with her, and he could tell Dradevai didn't like the idea, either. They shrugged their shoulders at Delri, who waited for an explanation. Then he realized there was one way they could talk about the subject without giving her all the information.

"I'm looking for my father," Asith said. "Dradevai agreed to help me."

Delri's eyes narrowed, her lips pressing into a hard line. "Really?"

Asith nodded and set his tankard down. Dradevai straightened up and rested their arms on the table.

"We think we might be able to get a spell from the Maeria Spire library to help find him." Dradevai spoke slowly, hesitant to share the information.

Delri looked back at them and nodded.

"So you are only trying to get into the Maeria Spire library?" She looked between them, and when they both confirmed it with a nod, she hummed.

Asith perked up. "Since you work at the hold, is it possible for you to help us get to the Maeria Spire through the holds? It's connected, isn't it?"

"Well, it's not entirely legal," Delri said slowly, "but if you get desperate, I can maybe get the two of you in there."

Dradevai's tone elevated. "Really?"

"Yes. It would put my job at risk, but—"

"Delri, I don't want you to lose your job for us."

Delri looked between them again, and she shook her head. "No, it's okay. I can always go back to Martivin if something happened. It's just…"

"You're worried about sneaking in?" Asith asked.

Delri furrowed her brow. "No, I think we could do that easily enough." She sipped on her tankard and then set her chin in her hand. "But there's been rumors about that part of the hold lately."

"Rumors?" Dradevai looked entranced, and Delri smiled, turning her attention to them.

"Hold workers have been saying that it's haunted." She reveled in the wide-eyed reaction she got from Dradevai, though she probably didn't believe any of what she was saying. "There's a voice coming from the walls. It moans and calls out sadly, begging for someone to come help them."

"W-what does it call out for?" Dradevai looked pale already, and Asith had to admit their conversation was a bit humorous. He hoped Delri didn't scare Dradevai too badly.

Delri lowered her voice, making herself sound as creepy as she could. "It says, 'My child, I can feel my child. Please, help me get to them.'" Then she let out a laugh and leaned back from Dradevai. "But I'm sure it's just a rumor. The holds are dark, and they echo. They're probably just hearing someone a few halls away."

Dradevai visibly swallowed. "Right."

"Don't let her get you worked up," Asith said. "She likes to tell ghost stories."

"No, I swear!" She set her hands down on the table. "Well, I mean, I'm sure it's not true, but people are talking about it."

"There has to be some explanation," Asith argued, though Dradevai still didn't look convinced. He could always reassure them later.

"Either way, I can take you there." Delri nudged Dradevai with her elbow. "And you can get your spell."

Dradevai smiled as they sipped on their tankard of mead. "Thank you."

Delri then spent at least fifteen minutes telling Dradevai every embarrassing story she had of Asith, which certainly made Dradevai less afraid of the ghost, much to Asith's shame. He didn't mind particularly, and to his surprise, she never once brought up any of their time fighting dragons. She didn't tell any stories of being in the field or that she now had more kills than Asith or that each of them had more than double Kosor's recorded kills, though he boasted more. It must have been because of their reaction earlier.

When they each had finished their tankards, Delri offered to walk back with them to the inn district to ensure Kosor didn't bother them again. Delri wrapped her arm around Dradevai's shoulders, and at first, Dradevai looked like they might recoil. But Delri said something that made them stop. Their shoulders shook with laughter instead, the two of them continuing to joke around about whatever it was.

Delri had to lean down quite a bit to be on the same level as Dradevai, for Dradevai was more than a head shorter. It was nice, for a moment, to only think about something trivial. He could feel the mead in his head more than he had expected. He swayed a little as he walked, trying not to look too closely at the magic lanterns that lit the streets or he might lose his balance and fall over. Delri whispered something to Dradevai that had them both giggling. More particularly, whatever it was made Dradevai blush and look back at him, just briefly. Delri then stood up straight, her arm still loose on Dradevai's shoulders. She shot a devious look at Asith, and all he could do was wither.

They stopped just beyond the inn district, the people milling about more loudly from drinking, some holding a stumble to their step. Delri hugged each of them and told them not to start any more fights before leaving.

"I'm starting to like her more," Dradevai said. Asith chuckled, watching them sway slightly and offering them his hand. Dradevai took it and leaned into Asith's arm with a smile, their eyes fluttering closed for a moment.

"I'm glad the two of you are becoming friends." Asith liked Dradevai clinging to him like this. His limbs buzzed, and his chest inflated like a balloon. The alcohol had made him feel that way, and it was part of the reason Dradevai clung to him more freely. But for a moment, he let himself enjoy it.

"What was Delri whispering to you?" Asith wanted to know why Dradevai had been blushing. Dradevai's smile grew a sly edge.

"Nothing." Dradevai tugged on Asith's arm gently. "Come on. Let's go inside."

Asith pouted, but he let Dradevai lead him into the inn and to their room. He didn't ask about it again, stumbling a bit as he tried to get his boots off. Dradevai grabbed his arm so that he didn't fall over. Their horns were out in the open again, Asith instinctively reached out to run his fingers over one.

"Asith?" Dradevai looked up at him, still holding his arm.

"S-sorry. I was thinking I hadn't seen them in a while."

Dradevai chuckled. "It's only been a few hours."

"That's a lot longer than I have ever gone without seeing your horns before."

Dradevai leaned toward Asith and examined his face and eyes.

"Are you drunk?"

Asith laughed and nodded. "Maybe a little. I never did eat."

Dradevai's mouth fell open. "You're right. I'm sorry, I completely forgot."

"It's okay," Asith said. "I can eat in the morning."

Dradevai sighed and set a hand on their hip, toeing their shoes off without moving away from him. "Asith."

"Yeah?"

"You're still holding onto my horn." Dradevai's voice had a light tone. Asith promptly released his hand, moving it onto their shoulder.

"Sorry," Asith said. Dradevai giggled and told him it was okay again, then moved away to change their clothes.

CHAPTER 14

26th of Kasdiel

His arms reached into the unfamiliar sheets for Dradevai's warmth, but he couldn't find them. Asith's head hurt, and as he opened his eyes, his heart rate increased.

If they had gone off on their own, they easily could have been noticed. His brain fed him an image of Kosor bearing down on Dradevai, pulling their hood off to reveal their horns, and a shiver ran down his chest and stomach. It was like he had to wake up a second time, though he was certain he had been awake a moment ago, too, but it allowed him to put the image of Kosor seeing Dradevai's horns out of his mind.

He sat up in bed. It was still dim in their room, the first sun not quite up yet and the window in their little room open to the street below.

Dradevai stood near it, looking out into the street with their hands on the windowsill. Their whole body glowed gold in the light from the streetlamps, skin glittering as their shoulders rose and fell, their breathing quick. They'd pulled their hair out of the braid, their face turned away from Asith, and ran trembling fingers over the wooden frame.

Asith wanted to stare at them for hours, but something about the way they worried their hand on the window frame concerned him.

"Vai, are you okay?" he said gently. Dradevai spun around, which made their hair shine in the lamplight. But what caught Asith's attention more than anything were the tears running down Dradevai's cheeks. He stood up before he'd even thought to do it and took a few steps toward Dradevai. "Vai…"

"Sorry, did I wake you?" Dradevai wiped at their face, but when Asith reached out for them, they let him set a hand on their cheek, and carefully move the hair that had stuck to their face.

Asith shook his head. "You didn't wake me, no. What were you doing?"

"I…" Dradevai paused when Asith smoothed their hair back on their head. "It's going to sound silly, but I heard that voice. The one that Delri talked about, and it felt so real, Asith. It called out to me."

Asith nodded and found the handkerchief his mother had given him years ago still in his pocket. He used it to dry off Dradevai's face. They leaned into his touch, their eyes watery and their shoulders shuddering.

"And it sounded so sad." Tears spilled over their eyes, and they pressed the heel of their hand to their face as they hiccupped. Asith offered them the handkerchief, and they took it.

"What did it say to you?" Asith asked. Dradevai swallowed and looked up at him.

"It begged me to come to it." Dradevai folded their arms, holding their elbows as they stared absently at Asith's chest. That was the most shaken Asith had ever seen Dradevai, and while it scared him, he couldn't help the swell in his chest as the urge to protect them overtook any worries he'd had about taking advantage of them.

"Did it tell you why?" Asith drew Dradevai into him and placed his arms around his shoulders, letting them wrap their arms around his middle. As they pressed closer, their trembles slowed. He carefully picked up their hair with one hand, brushing it back so that he didn't accidentally pull it. Asith hadn't thought about how long it would be unbraided.

"No." Dradevai shook their head. "It begged me to come to it and release it."

Asith frowned, looking out the window as the light coming from it grew brighter. The first sun had peeked just barely over the horizon.

"Let's try to get more sleep," Asith said. "If the voice comes back to you, wake me up."

Dradevai nodded and pressed their face directly into the center of Asith's chest. "You don't think I was just imagining things?"

"Well, you could be," Asith said, "but if you are this shaken up, it doesn't matter if it was a dream or not."

Dradevai considered that and then nodded slightly. "I am sorry for making you worry."

"It's okay." Asith combed his fingers through Dradevai's hair so it wasn't knotted. He couldn't braid it the way Dradevai could, but he could at least pull it out of their face. "Here, give me the tie for your hair."

Dradevai handed it to him and leaned into his hands as Asith gathered their hair. He was as gentle as he could be, scooping up locks and running his fingers through them.

"What if it was real?" Dradevai asked. "What does that mean?"

"I don't know." Asith paused, trying to think of a better answer. "Do you think it was real?"

Dradevai was quiet, then said, "I think it might have been."

Asith contemplated that, wrapping the tie around the ponytail he'd made.

"Do you want to investigate it?" he asked.

The question made Dradevai's shoulders stiffen. They shook their head, which loosened some of the strands of hair.

"No, no," Dradevai said. "We need to find your father. He's not safe; he could be dying. Let's focus on him first."

Asith frowned, smoothing down Dradevai's hair again. "I don't want you to give up just to find my father, Vai."

"No, I… We have a concrete plan to help your father right now," Dradevai said. "This voice, it could lead us nowhere, or investigating in the hold too much could get us in trouble. It's not worth the risk."

"All right." Asith secured the tie. "But if you change your mind, please just tell me. We're going to find your parents too."

"I will."

They pulled away just enough to lead Asith back to the bed, their eyes tired as they crawled into it ahead of Asith. He pulled the curtain across, closing them in so they wouldn't be woken by the first sun in twenty or so minutes.

"Thank you." Dradevai set their head against Asith's shoulder and their hands curled around his tunic. Asith nodded, adjusting their ponytail so that it lay comfortably before settling his head back on the pillow.

Dradevai fell back asleep fast, their form relaxing next to Asith. He stayed awake a while, watching them sleep and making sure they didn't wake up again. Eventually, he fell back asleep as well, and when he woke, Dradevai was still pressed close to his side.

"Good morning." Their voice sounded hoarse as they shifted to look at Asith.

"Morning." Asith's mouth was desperate for water. His head hurt, but it got better when he shifted, like his sinuses were realigning.

"Do we have water?" Dradevai asked.

They sat up, their hair falling over their shoulders like a river of black, and Asith remembered how beautiful and gold their skin had looked while they had stood by the window. His eyes followed the line of their neck down to their chest before he caught himself.

"We do." He got up and found their waterskin. He gave it to Dradevai, who drank about half in one sitting. They offered it up, their fingers brushing Asith's as they handed it over. His stomach jumped at their touch, then Asith sipped on the water, trying to avoid thoughts about Dradevai's skin.

"I liked the mead, but my mouth is so dry now." Dradevai braided their hair, their hands working quickly so that it was out of their face again. Asith nodded and rubbed some water on his face.

"It's probably because it's sweeter." Asith searched for clean clothes and scooped them up. "I'm going to the bath. I'll be right back, or I can meet you downstairs."

"Okay." Dradevai looked down at their clothes. "I should maybe get more things to wear before these get too dirty."

Asith chuckled as he left the room. "We can get you some today." He closed the door behind him and made his way down the hall to the small bath.

When he returned to the room, Dradevai wasn't there, so Asith set down his things and pulled on his boots. When he met Dradevai downstairs, they didn't seem nervous, for they sat comfortably at a table near the wall, a tankard in front of them as they read a book. Asith sat across the table and set the empty waterskin in front of him.

"More mead?" Asith joked.

Dradevai's face fell into a frown. "No, water." Dradevai closed their book and looked at the waterskin. "What's the plan for today?"

Asith took a deep breath and looked out at the people waiting for their food. "I am tempted to take Delri up on her offer, but I don't want to get her in trouble trying to help us."

"Should we try the Stonegarde first, then?" Dradevai glanced at the approaching server. They each ordered breakfast, and Asith got more water. He waited for the server to be well away before responding.

"I think we should." He studied Dradevai. "Have you been okay? Since last night?"

Dradevai nodded. "I haven't heard the voice since. Maybe I just had a vivid dream after all."

"Maybe." Asith smiled. "If it happens again, just let me know. Maybe going down there will help it out. Even if we don't go to the Maeria Spire."

"If it keeps happening. Is it possible for us to go to a bookstore today as well? Since we're here?"

"Was there something you were looking for in particular?" Asith wasn't sure if they really had time to wander through the marketplace. The server came from behind him and set down their food and Asith's water before taking the waterskin from them.

Dradevai grew sheepish. "There are two more novels in the series I've been reading, but the store in South Cairn said they won't have them for a few more months."

Asith chuckled. "How many books are even in that series?"

"Six total. I want to know the ending."

Asith could not imagine reading six romance novels, but he liked the determined look on Dradevai's face. He noted that they'd like something like that and kept it to himself.

"All right, so long as we're quick we can go," Asith said, "but I think you should also get something to read after you finish the series. At the rate you read, you'll be done with those two books before we leave the Capitol."

"That's not a bad idea." Dradevai looked as if they hadn't thought about that. "Oh, I was also thinking I should buy some fabric to bring back to Maryan."

"What makes you say that?" Asith had never heard them express wanting to buy anything other than books. In fact, that was the first time they'd mentioned buying something for someone other than themself.

"I want to buy her something as an apology," Dradevai said, "and as a thank you."

Asith smiled. "All right."

They paid their tab and headed toward the marketplace. It was easy to find, for lots of people always crowded the area that led to the market. The dirt road was lined with stalls, each with a colorful awning hanging over it. They were built into the open first floor of the buildings, above which had homes and housing for those who worked in the district. Many of the stalls featured flags from foreign countries above them, for the traders had come to sell items from their native countries.

Some fabric vendors were from Nala, their soft fur adorned with the finest fabrics, and dwarves from Hruktar sold unique clothing fasteners and delicate jewelry made of intricately twisted metal wire. A group of Syuty mages showed off small devices that could do simple magic, as well as some small toys and other incredibly useful tools for all sorts of projects. There were trinkets and spices and baubles that glittered in the light of the suns. People moved about and stopped at food stalls featuring grilled meats and confections of all sorts.

Asith paused in front of a booth being run by two older gilliedhu men and a much younger one wrapped tightly in quilted jackets with finely made leather gloves on their hands. Each had mahogany patches of wood-like skin across their necks and jawlines, ending at their short pointed ears. Their booth was rather plain, but they had very fine leather goods, belts, armor, pouches, and more.

Dradevai was still looking over the market with interest, patiently waiting for Asith to finish speaking with the leather workers. "Where should we go first?" they asked.

"Well, fabric will be hard to carry, so we should get that last." Asith scanned the stalls. "So let's start with small things."

"Like books?"

Asith laughed. "Yes, just don't buy too many. They get heavy fast." There was no use in Asith saying anything negative about it, for Dradevai had already taken off toward the nearest stall full of books. Asith might have to prevent them from going to every single stall with books, but that might not be possible.

He just let Dradevai enjoy themselves. They picked up four or five newer books. While they didn't have a lot of time to find his father, he wanted Dradevai to experience life in the market because he didn't know when they could come back.

Asith wandered into the history section, a thought occurring to him. Eroan, the mage who had traveled with their troupe of dragon knights, had told them once he'd found magic books in a shop by complete accident. The story quickly became all Asith could think about, his curiosity thoroughly piqued.

He glanced over his shoulder, casting the spell he'd learned to detect the arcane, and examined the books until, to his surprise, one of the history books glowed. He picked it up and flipped it open as the glow settled down. Illusion magic. It buzzed against his fingers as he read the first page.

It appeared to be a normal history of the Maeria Spire, but the writing glowed along the edges. In fact, the illuminated letters settled over the original black lettering. He closed the book and found Dradevai, who had already purchased a stack of books that the stall owner had wrapped up for them.

"What are you getting?" Dradevai followed Asith up to the owner, a pleasant portly man with a slight point to his ears. The man smiled, as if he had no idea Asith had just picked up a book with magic writing in it.

Asith waited until they were out of the stall and tucking the books away to explain himself. He didn't want to give away he'd bought a magic book for just a few silver.

"It has writing in it," Asith said, and when Dradevai looked like they might walk away from the conversation entirely, he elaborated, "I mean, it's magic. It has writing in it that's over the normal letters."

Dradevai hummed. "What do you think it is?"

Asith shook his head and shrugged. The buzz of the magic through the paper started to fade.

"Well, maybe it will be useful." Dradevai nudged Asith's arm. "That was clever, though, casting that spell in the bookstore. I wouldn't have thought to do that."

"Thank you."

They had to stop to get more food and buy a few practical items like canvas bags. Then they reached a shop that had all sorts of sweets, which Dradevai took an interest in. Asith tried to prevent them from getting too much, but they didn't really want to listen.

Asith stopped in a small booth while Dradevai was still buying candies, picking up a bracelet like the one Dradevai used to wear all the time back in their hoard. They had mentioned missing the weight of having something on their wrist, and while that one wasn't gold, it was just as heavy. It had thin spindles of shining silver with a few orange stones that matched the necklace Dradevai always wore. It was wrapped in a cuff, meeting in the middle with a shape that appeared somewhat like a wing.

He bought it and tucked it away so that Dradevai wouldn't see it before they walked back to the inn. When they met back up, Dradevai seemed to be in high spirits, feeding Asith candy and easily carrying a basket full of food, books, and a few other items they'd picked up. Finally, they bought some nice fabric for his mother, which was a bit difficult to carry, but Asith was so proud of Dradevai for wanting to get her a gift that he didn't care.

After they finished dinner at the inn and made their way toward the Stonegarde, Dradevai asked, "Do you think I should disguise myself more for this?"

"That might be a good idea."

Their bronze skin and golden eyes appeared a bit more unusual than the dark eyes and range of cool brown and tan skin of most people in Cairn. Although, by all arguments, Asith stuck out far more than Dradevai did, with his pale skin and light eyes. Most probably mistook him for having ancestry from the elves who lived in the far Northern mountains. Knowing he'd had draconic blood the whole time made Asith feel like he stood out more even though he didn't look any different from before.

They slid into an alleyway where Dradevai promptly turned into a young woman. They could be Delri's sister. Asith raised an eyebrow at Dradevai, who crossed their arms easily and stuck their nose up in the air.

"Don't look at me like that. I had to pull inspiration from somewhere." Dradevai turned around the corner, glancing back at Asith. "Are you coming?"

Asith rolled his eyes, following Dradevai. "Yes."

They walked up to the Stonegarde, where Asith pulled a small medallion from his pocket and showed it to the guard. The guard had her eyes on Dradevai for a moment but let them through when Asith explained they were only going to the library. Dradevai kept close to him, their eyes scanning the people and halls with care and attention.

"Is it strange to say I expected it to be more sinister in here?" Dradevai said lowly, examining the entrance to the dormitories where a few people waved at Asith, who waved back.

"What do you mean?" Asith asked. He could see why they might feel uncomfortable there, with all the dragon knights milling about. Asith was only comfortable because the halls of the Stonegarde were familiar. He had lived there for a long time, after all. But if he thought too much about being dragonborn, he got nervous.

"I thought there would be stuffed dragon corpses and trophies of battles here and dragon torture devices. But it's just people walking around in armor and training with weapons and barracks."

"Oh." Asith paused, wondering what sorts of books besides romance Dradevai had been reading. Though, he could see why their fear might have caused their imagination to act up.

Before he could comment, the library opened up in front of them, the warm wooden walls lined with shelves of books with leather or wooden bindings. Most of them had a nice reddish or brown color, natural to the materials used to make them. Asith hadn't spent a lot of time there but knew many books had information on dragons and the ways they killed humans. Another group contained a slim history of their origins, but most of that had to be untrue.

"I'm going to look around." Dradevai looked like they might break with so many books around them.

"Maybe we should stay together," Asith said.

Dradevai shook their head, relaxing slightly. "No, I'll be fine, I promise." Dradevai stepped toward a stack of books. "Plus, it's probably better if no one gets a good look at me."

Asith couldn't really argue with that, so he nodded. "Just be careful not to draw attention to yourself."

Dradevai zipped off into the stacks and stacks of books, touching them all carefully. Asith worried separating was a mistake, but he tried to put it out of mind to focus on finding what they needed. He walked toward the attendant's desk, pausing when he realized Eroan, his troupe's mage, was standing behind it.

"Asith, it's good to see you. I hope you're enjoying your retirement." Eroan smiled, bright and gentle as always. "Can I help you with something?"

"Yes, uh…" Asith briefly forgot what he was doing. Eroan had saved his life many times over, so his brain was briefly distracted. "I was actually hoping to see if I could borrow a few books from the Maeria Spire library."

Eroan perked up. "Of course. There's a catalog of the ones we can get on that table there. It will take us about three days to get any that you want."

"Three days?" Asith's eyes widened. They didn't really have that kind of time. Eroan gestured toward a table with a catalogue book, then curiously looked Asith over.

"Are you not staying in town that long?" Eroan tilted his head.

"No, I was hoping it would be faster than that." Asith rubbed the back of his head a little. He wasn't sure what he was going to do. Maybe they would have to ask Delri for help getting into the holds.

"Well…" Eroan leaned toward Asith just slightly, lowering his voice. "I can get the books you want from the Maeria Spire library for you today."

Asith blushed. Eroan had always flirted with him, and while it never went anywhere while he was with the knights, Asith used to always flirt back. Asith assumed Eroan would have forgotten all about his interest in Asith by then since it was just a fun distraction from what was going on, not unlike the relationship he had with Delri.

"Maybe," Asith said. "Uh, let me see if they have what I'm looking for first."

"Of course, just write down their numbers and bring them to me." Eroan straightened up, winking at Asith before he returned to his usual soft smile. When Asith turned around after thanking him, he caught Dradevai studying them. Dradevai quickly tried to act demure.

Asith ignored it, going to the catalog book to search for anything that seemed relevant. He poured over the list for a while and flipped through the categories in hopes of finding a "spells" or "arcane" section. There didn't seem to be any, and his stomach sank. He turned back to the corresponding letters hoping to discover a hidden section, but that didn't exist, either. For good measure, he went to the rituals section, only to find it was mostly about old holidays rarely celebrated anymore or ways to worship gods like Viteus or Sula.

"Not finding what you were looking for?" Eroan swooped by the table with a stack of books in hand. His eyes were bright and shiny, an excitement in his posture.

"No," Asith said, closing the catalog. "I was looking for something on magic."

Eroan hummed. "The Maeria Spire won't let their magic books out to just anyone. You'd have to be a student. What were you looking for?"

"I have discovered I can weave enchantments into textiles. I was hoping to find something to help me hone the ability." Asith moved, catching the way Eroan's eyes followed him. The skin on the back of his neck crawled, someone was watching them closely, and he was sure it was Dradevai.

"Well, I have access to their library as a student there." The smile Eroan flashed made Asith flustered; Eroan was good looking, he had to admit. "If you wanted, I could pick something up for you, and letting you borrow it could be our secret."

"Ah, no need, it wasn't very important." Asith shook his head, and Eroan's smile faltered slightly.

"It's no trouble," Eroan said, not giving it up. "After all, I go there a few times a week. We could meet here after I am done working."

Asith shook his head again, wishing Eroan would leave it alone. Years ago, he might have gladly accepted the offer, Eroan was handsome, and after all, he could get what he needed if he agreed. But he had a feeling, based on the way Dradevai was staring, that it might hurt their feelings.

He waved. "Really, it is—"

"Asith?" Dradevai was at his side, still looking like Delri's younger sibling, and they smiled sweetly at him. "I don't think they have the book I was looking for. What about you?"

"Ah…" Eroan backed off entirely with a cordial smile. "I have to put these books away. Let me know if you need anything more."

Dradevai linked their arm with Asith's as Eroan walked away. It was a relief to be out of that situation, and he probably would have hurt Eroan's feelings.

"Thank you," Asith said.

"You seemed stuck. It's no trouble." Dradevai chewed on their lip. They probably had questions, but they didn't ask them. Instead, they gestured toward the back of the library. "Delri is back there."

"Really?" Asith looked where they pointed, and without thinking, he walked back there. Something weird was going on with Delri, and he wanted to know what it was. Dradevai led him to where Delri was reading a book near a bookshelf. She noticed them first, then her eyes met Asith's.

"Dradevai?" Delri looked at them carefully. Dradevai didn't seem worried about looking a lot like Delri. "That's a neat trick. You look like you could be my younger sibling like this."

Asith should have expected Delri to find that cute somehow. Delri pinched Dradevai's cheek, much to their chagrin. They didn't seem to understand the gesture, pouting as they rubbed their face and Delri giggled.

"What are you doing here?" Asith asked with a frown. He interrupted Delri's explanation of the cheek-pinching to Dradevai.

"Oh, I was reading about Sterling dragons." Delri closed the book and slid it back onto the shelf.

"Why?" Dradevai asked.

"Just a bit of research for a class I'm supposed to teach here in a few weeks." Delri crossed her arms, hunching her shoulders.

"You're teaching classes here?" Asith tilted his head.

"Sometimes." Delri shifted on her feet and looked at the two of them, adding, "What are you guys doing here?"

Dradevai looked at Asith with a frown. "We were looking for books from the Maeria Spire."

"Oh. Did you find what you needed?"

Dradevai's shoulders dropped. "No, coming here was a little useless."

"Well." Delri rubbed the back of her neck. "I could still maybe help you get into the Maeria Spire. If you wanted."

Dradevai and Asith exchanged a mildly guilty look, and to Asith's surprise, Dradevai picked up explaining. "We thought we would at least check here first. We were worried about getting you into trouble."

"That's okay." Delri smiled. "I am not offended. I might actually need a bit of a trade."

"Do you need help with something?" Asith asked.

Delri nodded, her eyes watching Eroan like she was making sure he couldn't hear them.

"I can explain later." She looked back at Asith and Dradevai. "But I can help."

"We want to try," Dradevai said with such confidence that Asith agreed without thinking about it. Delri nodded and gestured for them to follow her out of the library. Asith paused before he followed, looking at the title of the book she'd been reading. He wanted to see if she'd been telling the truth. When he saw The Metallic Dragons, he wasn't sure if it was better or worse that they were trading Delri a favor.

CHAPTER 15

27th of Kasdiel

When they left the Stonegarde, Delri took them into a back alley quickly, her eyes scanning the area before planning anything. They worked out that they should try to sneak into the hold the next day. Asith didn't really want to wait, but Delri thought it would be easier to hide in the daytime crowds. After they agreed on a plan, Delri left for a shift in the holds, so Asith suggested they go back to the inn for the day since it was already early evening.

They ate dinner and went up into their room to regroup a bit. Dradevai lay on the bed with one of their books for a while. Asith couldn't help but notice their exhaustion, probably because they didn't sleep much the night before, but he didn't mention it.

Dradevai rubbed their hand nervously over their left wrist, something they had developed since they hadn't been wearing much jewelry any-more. Asith reached for his pack and pulled out the folded package with the bracelet.

He got Dradevai's attention and held it out to them. "Here, I got this for you."

"What is it?" Dradevai asked, setting their book down on the bed. They leaned forward, took the package from Asith's hand, and started to peel it open.

Asith chuckled. "Just open it."

Dradevai smiled, rolling their eyes as they pulled open the package, and paused. They looked up at Asith with surprise, then examined the bracelet.

"Why did you buy me this?" Dradevai's brow furrowed, their mouth hanging open as they turned the bracelet over in their fingers.

"You said you missed having one to wear, and you were rubbing your wrist a lot."

Dradevai slipped the bracelet on. Their lips turned up, and they ran careful fingers over the silver details around the gems, a softness to their expression Asith hadn't seen before. It was enough to make Asith turn his eyes down to the table, his stomach turning nervously for a second. He swallowed the feeling.

"Thank you." Dradevai got up to walk around the table and bent over to dig out one of the books. "I actually bought something for you as well."

"Really?"

Dradevai slid a wrapped book and a smaller box across to Asith. "Yes, really."

Dradevai sat back down and set their head in their hand with a smile. Asith pulled the paper, and it was a leather-bound book, dyed greenish with fine blank pages. The second package was an inkwell and a pen.

"A journal?" Asith turned the empty book over in his hands, and Dradevai laughed easily.

"So you can start recording your own spells." Dradevai shifted in their seat. "I feel like you're close to developing your own."

Asith blinked at them. "My own?"

"Of course." Dradevai nodded. "Many of the spells in that book I developed on my own, and you've certainly at least caught up to me."

"I don't know if I've caught up." Asith laughed slightly and studied the book again. "But I appreciate that you think I've gotten better at it."

Dradevai chuckled. "I think you have caught up more than you realize."

They picked up a novel they had bought and headed into bed, leaving Asith to stare at the journal. Then he opened the inkwell and wrote his name on the back of the front cover, leaving that to dry while he unpacked the last of their things. He caught Dradevai holding their arm out and smiling at the bracelet.

Heat rose to his cheeks again, so he took a long drink from the waterskin and tucked away the gifts from Dradevai, making sure the pen wouldn't snap there.

"Will you be ready to leave right away in the morning?" Asith looked at the small army of books Dradevai had amassed since they'd arrived.

They picked their head up, catching Asith's glance. "I should probably do something with all the books." Dradevai got up and gathered them, and to Asith's surprise, they tugged their spell book from their bag.

"I thought we agreed you shouldn't bring that with you," Asith said.

A defiant look grew on their face. "You agreed that I shouldn't bring it." Dradevai opened the book and flipped through the pages. "I didn't feel comfortable leaving it behind. It's too important to me."

Asith frowned. "What if they'd taken it at the wall?"

"I hid it. Here, look."

They opened their bag and picked up one of the other books to drop it in. As soon as the book hit the bottom of the bag, it disappeared. They even held the bag open to show him it really looked empty.

"All right, all right." Asith let it go even if he still thought they should have listened to him. Instead, Dradevai found the spell they were looking for, and for the first time, Asith noticed the way the handwriting in the book changed. The spells in the back half of the book appeared to all be in Dradevai's handwriting, and as he thought about the few spells he'd learned so far, he realized a lot of them had been originals Dradevai had created. He wondered if one of their parents had left it for them as a way to make sure they could learn magic.

He didn't have time to ask about that, though, because Dradevai flipped back to an original spell in the book and slapped it on the table. Then they picked up a bag they'd gotten from the fabric seller and found a metal rod in their pack next. Dradevai spent about half an hour heating it with fire blown directly from their lips and burning a pattern into the inside of the bag. Once they'd done that, they set their hands down on it and chanted.

After finishing, Dradevai slipped both bolts of fabric and all their books into the bag, which had barely held the fabric originally. Dradevai closed their spell book and looked at Asith, grinning.

"Do you want me to teach you that?" They looked self-righteous, so Asith frowned at them and shook his head.

"No, you can just do it for me whenever I need it." He picked up his pack and set it in front of Dradevai. "Right?"

At a loss for words, they frowned, then huffed and set their head in their hand. "I probably deserved that." They tapped their fingers on the table, watching the window. Asith set his bag out of the way, giving Dradevai a moment to see if they could work through whatever was making them anxious.

"You okay?"

"Yeah, I…" Dradevai sat up. "I was thinking about maybe trying to stay awake."

Asith thought about the night before, and he set a hand on Dradevai's shoulder. "I can hold on to you again tonight. If that's what you need."

Dradevai looked up at him and then frowned, their eyes narrowing. "You're so confusing." They got up and slipped their shoes off before crawling into the bed fully clothed and flopping into the pillows.

"What do you mean?" Asith blew out the candles and followed them into bed. Dradevai turned over the moment Asith cuddled closer.

"You kissed me and then pulled away completely. Then you started to treat me like I was made of glass the moment something scared me. I'm an adult, Asith, I know what sex is, and I know how to ask for support when I need it."

"I…" Asith started, but Dradevai pressed against him. He snapped his mouth shut.

"We're alone in a bed together. What do you actually want to be doing with me right now?"

"W-well…" Asith's head was spinning, his voice coming out quiet despite his best efforts. "Right now, I'd probably try to get out of bed because you're flustering me."

Dradevai paused. "I—okay." They pulled away from Asith slightly.

"I wish you wouldn't keep doing this. It doesn't feel very good."

When they pulled away completely, Asith wrapped his arms around himself. "You're right, what I did probably didn't make a lot of sense and I don't really have an explanation for it."

"I guess… I'm sorry, I think I misunderstood." Dradevai's eyes slid away from Asith's face, their usual brightness fading, and Asith needed to fix it. He wanted to fix it. They only seemed to wither further, glancing down in the darkness. In the faint light from the window, Asith saw tears well up in their eyes.

"No, Vai." He cupped Dradevai's face, feeling the warmth that constantly radiated from their skin. "I'm sorry. I just wanted to take care of you. I know you're not weak, but I wanted to be there for you."

Dradevai looked up at him like they might say something, but Asith cut them off. "I promise, I promise you didn't misunderstand." He didn't want Dradevai to think he didn't want them around or that he didn't love them. Even if he was far too scared to admit that.

They stared at him. The way their eyes bore into his face made Asith's skin crawl. His eyes darted to their lips, he wanted to kiss them, to make them feel better, but he worried they would be upset by that. He leaned closer, feeling Dradevai stiffen ever so slightly, but Asith shifted to kiss their hair gently.

"I'm sorry," he repeated. "I'll try to be better."

"Okay." Dradevai nodded. "Okay, I believe you. Don't worry."

Asith relaxed and kissed their hair again. They settled against the bed, pulling Asith's hands away from their face to press into his chest, nearly smacking their horns into his chin. But Asith didn't really mind, setting his head on top of Dradevai's, just holding them.

"You don't have to be so afraid, you know," Dradevai said. Asith nodded, closing his eyes as Dradevai cupped his face with warm hands.

"I will protect you, too, the way that you've been looking out for me."

Asith smiled. "Thank you, Dradevai."

Dradevai nodded, their horns nearly hitting Asith's chin again, but Asith dodged them. He set a hand on the back of their head to keep them from doing it again, and they seemed content to fall asleep there, anyway. Asith took a while to settle, the edges of sleep coming to him slowly as something far away reached his ears.

It wasn't very clear, nor did it unsettle him, but a faint voice said, "Take care of them."

He fell asleep to the sound of Dradevai's soft breathing and woke to the bed shifting. They looked nice in the morning light as they pulled on their boots and slipped their hood over their horns. When they walked into the hallway, Asith thought about the way he'd often follow their form with his eyes in their hoard. He missed that feeling, the security of being high up in the mountains and sleeping on Dradevai's feet, only to spend the rest of the day learning magic or sewing.

At the same time, a new energy grew in him, swelling his chest with a vigor he had never experienced. In that moment, he wanted nothing more than to follow Dradevai through the world, watching as they moved from place to place with their brightness always surrounding them. That same light led Asith to believe they were good even when they had been trying to proclaim him as part of their hoard. Asith was being pulled in by their light more than ever, and as Dradevai came back through the doorway, a comfortable touch of warmth followed them.

"What?" Dradevai frowned, not coming back to the bed but rather beginning to pack up their things. "We have to leave early, remember?"

Asith smiled, somehow finding confidence for once, and stood up. "I know. It was nothing."

He stopped Dradevai and slipped their hood off to gently slide his hand over the back of their hair. Dradevai stared up at him with wide eyes, but they pressed their mouth into a hard line.

"I just like watching you," Asith said. He took his hand off Dradevai and pulled on his boots, not feeling particularly like he should keep eye contact with Dradevai. So, he laced his boots and gathered his pack before looking at them again. When he did, Dradevai somehow seemed to shine even brighter, their eyes back to their glowing honey color and their form buzzing with excitement.

"Ready?" they asked with a grin, their hands in their hair as they untied and re-braided it.

Asith nodded, and they headed out to meet Delri outside the hold office. They found her quickly, and Delri led them a bit farther away into an alley, where she instructed Dradevai to leave their physical appearance as it was but to match their clothes to Delri's uniform. Dradevai nodded and cast the spell, and for a flicker of a moment, Dradevai's horns appeared. Asith's eyes snapped to Delri, but luckily, she was looking in the other direction.

His panic subsided, and he followed the two of them to a hold entrance with no attendant next to it. They moved through the door into a small room that stored piles of hold uniforms, many of which looked old and worn. They found some that Asith could pull over his clothes, and they set out into the dimly lit tunnels of the hold.

Delri knew exactly where they were going, but with the weight of the ground above them, the low ceilings, and the knowledge that they weren't supposed to be there, Asith became uneasy. It didn't seem to bother Dradevai, though, and he reminded himself that Delri wouldn't get lost even if the long, winding corridors sometimes looked the same.

The hold was a place out of a legend to Asith, everyone knew it was there, but unless you lived in the Capitol or worked in the hold, citizens rarely went into the tunnels. Occasionally, they'd come across a room where the door was open, people bustling around and organizing food and other goods. Delri led them straight past the workers, checking for people following them as they went. Asith almost wished he had his sword on him, but it was for the better he didn't.

They moved away from the areas where food stores were fewer and farther between, fewer people were around, and the halls were lit a bit better. More torches meant more heat, which seemed to be why the other halls weren't as bright. Then they worked their way past soldiers and guards, their uniforms heavier with more armor than the regular hold workers.

"Their armor doesn't look like yours did," Dradevai whispered as they turned away from a group carrying weapons and pieces of armor. Delri glanced back at them to be sure they had made the turn. She picked up a torch before entering the next hallway, confirming no one would see them slip through the intersection.

"That is because the soldiers wear plate armor made of metal," Asith answered. "Fighting dragons requires you to wear armor that won't melt in the heat of their fire."

His armor was made from the scales of a Green dragon he took down himself, and his helmet was carved from the dragon's skull. He didn't need to go into this detail with Dradevai, for they already looked shaken. But what surprised him was that Delri shivered at Asith's response. Delri would proudly wear armor made from a Blue dragon alongside Asith. Something had changed in her. He hadn't figured out exactly what it was, but for her to stop boasting about being a knight and start researching Sterling dragons was odd. He wondered if she'd figured out Vai, but if she had, he didn't understand why she hadn't said anything about it.

"This way." Delri's voice was low as she waved them down a darkened hallway. Her torch was the only light guiding them down the abandoned tunnel. "These tunnels are here for emergency evacuation, in case the city ever needed to move into the underground shelter."

"So, they connect to the Maeria Spire?" Dradevai asked.

Delri nodded, looking down a hallway before passing it. "The Maeria Spire has some storage down here, But it's my understanding that they don't use it much."

"How did you know about this area?" Asith peered down the same dark hallway. Something about that area made him more uncomfortable than the maze of hallways from earlier.

"Since I was from the Stonegarde, I'm allowed to work in some of the areas where they store magical items." Delri checked another hallway, that time turning down it. "Not many have clearance like that, even after being with the hold for a while."

"Clearance?" Dradevai asked. "Like only certain people are allowed over here? If there are only spell components, they should be normal objects."

Delri nodded. "I thought the same thing when I was first brought down here, but they have rooms full of potions or obscure objects. I couldn't tell what they did."

Dradevai hummed softly, studying a heavy wooden door as they passed by. Their brow furrowed, and they took a deep breath.

"What else is close to this area?" Dradevai asked.

"There is a commerce area nearby. So butchers, merchants who are renting a booth here, lots of foreign spices."

"Why?" Asith asked Dradevai.

They shook their head. "Just curious."

Asith couldn't help but feel like it wasn't just the smell of a butcher that did it. Delri led them to a small staircase, which then led to a trap door labeled LIBRARY.

"Only one of us should go in. My suggestion would be Dradevai. Remember the clothes that Eroan wore?"

Dradevai scowled. "Yes."

Delri chuckled. "He was wearing a uniform from the Maeria Spire. Can you recast the spell and do what you did before? To make that uniform?"

"Yes." Dradevai frowned and stood back, hiding a bit in the darkness. Then they took a deep breath and recast the spell. Asith tried to distract Delri, but this time, her eyes landed on Dradevai's shape. Their horns weren't easy to catch, though, not without knowing what to look for, so she simply tilted her head slightly.

"Is this right?" Dradevai stepped back into the light wearing the clothes Eroan had been wearing. Delri agreed and then helped Dradevai quickly slip into the hatch door, leaving them alone in the library.

Asith stared at the door, knowing that it could take some time, but the fluttering in his stomach and chest was hard to ignore. Something was off. Not because of the dark tunnels, but something about that part of the hold made his bones quiver. He worried it was an enchantment to trap intruders.

"Dradevai doesn't seem to like Eroan much." Delri had an expectant look on her face. "Didn't he always have a crush on you?"

"I don't know." Asith tried to brush Delri off. "It's not like it was something I paid attention to."

Delri smiled and chuckled softly. "Well, it seems like Dradevai certainly paid attention to it."

"I think they were just worried about getting the books." Asith caught the sly look on her face. She didn't seem to believe his attempt to further brush this conversation off.

"I think they were more concerned with the way that Eroan looked at you. I saw them watching the two of you when I walked into the library."

"Oh." Asith closed his mouth, fearing further discussion about it, especially since his face was growing warm under Delri's careful eye. She knew him rather well, after all, and his skin crawled like when his mother used to tease him about the crushes he'd get on classmates as a child. Delri smacked his arm and grinned more.

"Don't clam up on me." She laughed as he stared at the hatch door. "You are lucky. Dradevai cares about you a lot, obviously."

Asith didn't have the chance to respond, which he would have been thankful for if they were not interrupted by a chilling voice that filled the hallway. It moaned like the winds through a dying forest, somber and sweet and desperate to bring some life back into the trees. A shiver traveled down Asith's spine, his eyes darting in every direction. It only said a few words.

"My child." Its tone was yearning. "Please, my child."

Delri's mouth hung open, and as she turned back to Asith, she realized it wasn't his voice "Please tell me that was Dradevai somehow."

Asith shook his head. He crossed his arms and looked in the direction it might have been coming from. "That sounded—"

"Please!" The voice shook him again. It prickled the back of his neck, his hair standing on end. "My child, bring them to me please, my child."

The voice wallowed with sobs that made Asith feel an immense need to run toward it. He resisted the urge, looking at the hatch door and praying Dradevai returned soon. Delri stood closer to him, the loud sobs echoing before they slowly grew quiet.

"I…" She clicked her mouth shut. "The rumors."

"I know." Asith thought about what Dradevai had said the night before, the voice that had called to them.

When the voice completely faded, Dradevai opened the hatch door, slipped through, and pulled the books along with them. They only had three, but they were large and looked difficult to maneuver all together.

"I was able to find something," Dradevai said. They looked over their uneasy expressions, frowning as they turned. When they stepped into the hallway, the books screamed, and then so did the hallway.

The area lit up quickly, magical orbs appearing on all sides of the hall. The books yelled in a scratchy voice, "We are not to be removed without being checked out!"

Dradevai's eyes were huge, staring at the books in their arms, while Delri and Asith nearly jumped out of their skins. As Asith realized the books were not coming with them, Dradevai quickly threw one open, poring over the pages and flipping until they found what they wanted. Tearing a few pages of the book out, they dropped the rest of them and led Delri and Asith to the bottom of the stairs.

When they hit the last stair, a bright flash emitted from the placard that labeled the door, and the pages of the book Dradevai had torn out turned to ashes. They looked at their hands, confused, and then looked up at Asith, a look of panic coming over them.

"There's something blocking magic here." They touched the vest Asith had made them.

"How do you know?" Asith asked.

"The enchantment on the vest stopped working." Dradevai tried to cast a spell, moving their hands and saying the words, only to come up with nothing.

That was when the voice started again, wailing and sobbing inconsolably, "My child! My child, please, hear me!"

It stopped Dradevai dead in their tracks, their eyes staring off in the direction it had come from. Asith then noticed the spell disguising Dradevai had dropped as well. He grabbed Dradevai's wrist and tried pulling them away from the voice.

"Vai, we have to go."

Dradevai turned back, tears in their eyes as the voice wailed again.

"Vai, please."

Dradevai nodded, still looking dazed as Asith led them along after Delri. She guided them down a hallway that had been empty previously but was alive with people pouring out of the rooms and trying to determine where the alarm was coming from. She pressed Asith and Dradevai back, then pushed them in the opposite direction. Her brow furrowed at Dradevai, just briefly, but she continued to nudge them along.

They ran past the stairs where the books were burning in a pile of blue flames, and Delri pulled them down a hallway with no one in it. That one was still unlit, Asith couldn't really tell why, but he was thankful for the darkness. They stopped at a crossway, and Delri carefully peered around the corner.

She turned back to them, pressed a finger to her lips, and then mouthed, When I say go. Dradevai looked confused, so Asith tightened his grip on their hand. Another glass-shattering wail rattled down the halls, that time shaking the stones and releasing dust from the ceiling. Dradevai's panic started all over again, their hand gripping Asith's painfully.

When Delri signaled for them to follow, Asith tugged Dradevai along; he'd carry them if he had to, for he wasn't about to get them thrown in jail. Every time they crossed a lit hallway into a dark one, Asith saw guards walking in the other direction. From what he could tell, they were heading toward the library.

Then they reached a dead end.

Delri stopped cold. But she thought fast, pushing them back and tucking them tightly into a door frame. They stood as still as possible, watching a group of guards march down the hallway a few feet away.

After a few minutes of standing there with only their breathing, Delri leaned out. "There's a door that leads out, but there are guards. There aren't usually guards."

She looked panicked, like she'd been expecting to just walk right out. Then again, they had just walked back in; none of them had anticipated being cornered.

"Are you sure?" Asith's voice came out louder than he expected, the panic tightening his throat and making it difficult to control his volume. Dradevai's eyes were glassy, and their posture was off kilter.

But then they shook their head hard and stood tall as they murmured a chant. A flame burst between their fingers. They said, "Delri, come here. Drop the torch."

Delri looked confused but allowed Dradevai to grab her shoulder. They grabbed Asith's hand, too, and leaned around the corner for a quick look, then pressed in close to Delri and Asith.

The spell that slipped from Dradevai's lips had a lot of arcane words that Asith recognized, and they all dissipated like a puff of smoke. The movement made him lightheaded, his whole body floating almost as if he were in water or in a cloud. The three of them landed outside the door to the hold. As soon as Asith registered where they were, he dragged Dradevai and Delri toward the nearest alleyway.

He ran down a narrower passage, and they slipped between two buildings where it was dark. It was unlikely anyone would see them. Then Asith and Delri stacked up a few spare crates to further hide them.

When Asith turned to Dradevai, their spell had dropped. He gestured nervously to his own head. "Horns."

Dradevai's eyes widened, and they recast the spell. But Delri was already staring at Dradevai, her mouth hanging open, and she reached out to where Dradevai's horns were. She grabbed one although she couldn't see it.

"Delri." Asith turned to her quickly. "We can answer all of your questions, but we need to go somewhere safer first."

Delri didn't pay him any mind, studying Dradevai more carefully than she ever had before. "Dradevai, are you a dragon?"

Dradevai stared at Delri but conceded by nodding slowly. Delri's eyes lit up, only for a moment, and then all her intensity from earlier came back. She let go of Dradevai's horn and turned to Asith. "Where can we go?"

"Back to the inn?" Dradevai suggested. Asith wondered how he became the decision-maker in that situation.

"Let's go back to the inn," Asith confirmed. Although nobody was looking at them, they still didn't doddle, making their way straight into the inn and up to their room.

When they got there, Dradevai sat down with a small noise of frustration and wiped the ash off their hands. "That went terribly."

"It did," Delri agreed. "Sorry."

"It's all right," Asith said, drinking some water and settling in a chair. He looked at Delri. "Do you want to explain your reaction in the alleyway?"

Dradevai perked up, looking between the two of them. Delri shifted, then sat on the unused bed. She took a deep breath.

"Remember the reaction that Dradevai had when I started talking about being a dragon knight?" Delri asked. They both nodded. "Well, it wasn't the first time someone reacted to me like that, and I started thinking about a book I had read at the Stonegarde about Sterling dragons assuming human forms."

"Do you think you've met another dragon?" Dradevai's said. "Another Sterling dragon?"

Delri pressed her finger to her lips, and Asith remembered how she shivered at the mention of their armor earlier.

She nodded. "I don't know for sure, but I want to find out. That's why I asked for a favor when I saw you at the library. I thought maybe you two could help me somehow."

Dradevai leaned back in their chair. Asith took a few moments for his brain to catch up, but he eventually nodded.

"Yes, yes, we'll help," Asith said. He looked at Dradevai. "We probably need to explain what's going on here as well."

Dradevai looked guilty but then threw on their intense confidence, which Asith thought might be a way of overcompensating.

"We can tell each other our stories," Dradevai declared.

"We can, once we're far out of the Capitol," Delri said. "Also, we will need to go to Martivin."

"Martivin?" Dradevai tilted their head.

"My hometown. The two of you came here from South Cairn, yes?"

"Yes," Dradevai said.

"Then we should be able to travel easily." Delri crossed her arms, smiling. "It might be good for us to not be in town for a little bit."

"You are probably right." Asith looked at the wall, thinking about how they'd almost gotten caught. "When do you want to leave?"

"As soon as possible." Delri looked at her uniform. "I need to tell someone that I won't be working in the hold anymore and gather my things."

"Are you sure?" Asith asked. "Will you be able to find work if you leave?"

Delri smiled. "I will be okay, I promise."

"Okay." Asith didn't entirely believe her, but he could speak to her about it more once they were traveling. "Go do that now. We can meet you outside the hold office."

Delri agreed, assuring again that she would explain once they were out of the Capitol, and then she left the inn. Asith and Dradevai gathered their things quickly, but at one point, Dradevai stopped Asith, touching the vest Asith had made.

"Asith," they said, "I should tell you something."

Asith furrowed his brow, worried about them. "What's wrong?"

"I…" They frowned. "The enchantment on the vest. It's gone completely."

"Oh." Asith blinked. "That's okay. I can try to fix it if you'd like. I'm not sure how I would."

Dradevai sighed softly. "I'm sad it's gone, but it's okay. We have more important things to worry about. I'm just, I'm sorry I let that happen."

"That wasn't your fault," Asith said. Dradevai looked hesitant still, so Asith set a hand on their shoulder, squeezing it a bit. "I promise, I'm not upset with you over it, and you shouldn't be upset with yourself for it."

Dradevai nodded slightly. "I guess you're right."

They returned to gathering their things, though they still seemed a bit down. But Dradevai shouldered their bags and followed Asith out of the room. Asith led them downstairs to pay the innkeeper and then out onto the street. Their illusion restored, they put their hood up, but they still looked somewhat nervous about exposing themself on the busy street.

"Do you think that they'll find us?" Dradevai looked over their shoulder at the soldiers milling around. There were more than usual, but Asith shook his head slightly.

"I don't think so." Asith wanted to be confident for Dradevai; they needed the support.

"What makes you so sure they won't know? And that voice? It—that was terrifying."

"No one saw us. And we didn't take anything, so they have no evidence."

"Okay." Dradevai took a deep breath and looked up at Asith. "I trust you."

Asith set his hand on Dradevai's shoulder, trying to ease their mind. That voice in the hold scared Asith, too. Asith hoped it was just that their hearing was much better than his and Dradevai could somehow hear it from the inn, or it really was a dream. Asith didn't want to think about what it might mean if it was calling out to Dradevai specifically, but from the sounds of things, it had been calling out to other people too.

As the people on the streets walked by, Asith tried to see if any-one was looking at them too carefully, but no one seemed to pay them mind beyond an occasional glance. But all the chatter was surrounding the break-in. Since word had already spread, leaving was the right idea. Asith's mind started to tunnel-vision as he focused on getting Dradevai to the hold and then out of the city. Asith would do anything he needed to protect Dradevai.

CHAPTER 16

28th of Kasdiel

"I don't see why we can't just fly." Dradevai huffed, crossing their arms. The argument had started as soon as Asith explained they needed to go around a mountain. "It's not even that far, and you brought your goggles."

"We don't have goggles for Delri," Asith said, "and what would we do with the horses?"

Dradevai considered that. "It wouldn't be that far. I could carry the horses."

"They'd die of shock once you got up too high. Plus, I didn't even mention the cart. We'll need that, and what if someone sees us?" Asith shifted in his seat, and a shiver shot down his spine. The thought of someone finding out Dradevai was a dragon and rallying a group of people to hunt them down scared him.

"No one—" Dradevai closed their mouth when they looked up at Asith again. "Maybe you're right. We should just take the cart."

Asith relaxed. "Thank you. Do you think that the dragon Delri is looking for lives up in the mountains somewhere?"

"Maybe." Dradevai crossed their arms, looking at their feet as they walked. "It depends on their color. Copper and Iron dragons don't tend to have feathers, so they'll live in places that are warmer."

"You don't all have feathers?" Asith asked.

Dradevai shook their head. "Copper and Iron dragons don't always have them, Bronze dragons almost always do, and so do Silvers, and Golds always have feathers. And like I said, I know nothing of Blue or Green dragons."

They cut off their conversation once they were close to the hold office. Asith picked up their cart and the horses, leaving Dradevai outside to wait for Delri. The horses showed up looking well fed, sniffing at Asith in recognition. He made quick work of hitching the cart to them and leading the horses out to Dradevai, who stood next to Delri. They were whispering about something, each of them smiling.

"We're going to share the tent," Dradevai said to Asith, starting off toward the exit. "Delri doesn't have one."

"I will be fine by the fire," Delri said. Dradevai pouted, but she didn't seem bothered. "I have a bedroll. I have slept in worse places."

"We can share the tent," Asith answered. He had a feeling Dradevai wasn't about to let it go. "Delri can sleep outside if she wants to, though."

Dradevai scrunched up their face, giving him a quick glare before they looked back at Delri. "You will get cold, even by a fire. You should just share with us."

Delri laughed. "You really are determined."

"You'll die!" Dradevai crossed their arms.

"It is not as cold down here in the valley as it is in the mountains," Asith said. "This is not like when I was at your home."

Dradevai huffed. "It still gets cold at night here."

"I promise, if it is too cold, I will sleep in the tent with the two of you," Delri said. Dradevai seemed satisfied with that answer, and Delri smiled.

They made it out of the Capitol easily, without any guards checking their cart or asking what they were doing, and as they got onto the cart just outside the walls, Dradevai slipped their hood up and dropped the illusion on their horns.

"How are you able to sustain that magic for so long?" Delri asked, facing Dradevai in the cart. They had a lot more room back there since they had dropped all the uniforms and armor fittings at the hold office.

"What do you mean?" Dradevai had a book in their hands already, getting ready to speed through one of the romance novels they had bought.

"The magic users at the Maeria Spire can usually only maintain things like that for an hour or so." Delri glanced at Asith, and he nodded because he did remember that. He hadn't thought about it, but Asith never struggled with holding a spell for a long time, either, though he had trouble getting them right in the first place.

"I guess I am just able to." Dradevai frowned, clearly thinking about it a little harder. "It does sometimes tire me out. Especially doing the illusions for a long time to hide my horns."

"Were you just doing that the whole time?" Delri looked horrified by the prospect, and Asith was starting to feel like he'd just gotten used to it.

Dradevai shook their head and flipped their hood up. "I had this too." They beamed with pride under their hood, holding the sides as they grinned at Delri.

He was sure that Delri responded and they kept talking, but Asith lost track of the conversation, focused on the road. It would take a good while to get to Martivin, and then they would need to find the dragon Delri might have seen. If she was wrong and it wasn't a dragon she had met, they'd have no leads to find his father. The thought of the taps on the ring fading into nothing as his mother waited for them made his stomach hurt.

Eventually, Dradevai climbed onto the bench next to Asith, taking their hood off to reveal their horns. They shifted in their seat and looked back at the walls of the Capitol behind them. It was still visible in the distance, but they were getting far enough away that fewer people were on the road.

"Why is it so warm here? I feel like it was never this warm in my hoard." Dradevai grumbled, frowning when their hair fell. They pulled it out of the braid and tied it up instead.

"Because your hoard is high enough in the mountains, one would need climbing gear to get there," Asith said, "at least a human would."

"You haven't spoken in a half-hour, and the first thing you say is cheeky." Dradevai crossed their arms and stuck their nose in the air, their usual goofy, haughty demeanor returning. Sweat gathered along their hairline and the back of their neck, so they cast the illusion back on their horns, slipping the hood off their shoulders and huffing as they dropped into the cart behind them.

"We're going back into the mountains, though, right? Will it be cooler there?" Dradevai asked.

"I don't really know." Asith glanced back at the cart to find that Delri had been listening to their entire conversation. "How warm is Martivin this time of year?"

"It's a little cooler in Martivin than in the valley, but it won't be as cold as on top of a mountain." Delri paused and looked up at them. "Are you warm?"

"Yes." Dradevai somehow made one word sound like the most dramatic response that could have come out of their mouth. Delri laughed, though, shifting to sit up and face them.

"Is it because you're covered in feathers? Sorry, is it safe enough to speak about this openly yet?"

Dradevai turned back and thought about it. Asith furrowed his brow, too, thinking about it more than needed, but he turned back, checking that the Capitol was well behind them. They were far from any other carts or travelers, so he looked at Delri.

"It's probably safe to speak about this now." Asith looked at Dradevai. "I always just assumed you were so warm because you could breathe fire."

Dradevai frowned, looking over their arms. "I only have feathers when I am in my normal form."

Delri laughed. "You both look like I fed you a lemon. Also, you are just magically a human, right?"

"No, I am still a dragon." Dradevai turned back to Delri, dropping the illusion on their horns and tapping one of them gently. "See?"

"Wait, what?" Asith questioned. "But you look human."

Dradevai furrowed their brow. "No, I look like a dragon. You heard Maryan's story; dragons just look like this."

"Maryan? Your mother?" Delri interjected.

Asith was going to respond to Dradevai, but he stopped, looking back at Delri. "We should tell each other our stories now. We're far enough from potential eavesdroppers."

"Yes, I'd like to know about the dragon you think you saw." Dradevai turned back to Delri, setting their hands on the back of the little bench in the front of the cart.

"Wait, but start here, what's going on with Maryan?" Delri looked worried, so Asith decided they could go first.

"It's not so much my mother as it is my father," Asith said. "He was a dragon."

Delri crossed her legs. "Really?"

"I guess she met him in the woods after he injured himself. He couldn't fly anymore and wound up staying." Asith glanced back at her, for the horses mostly knew what they were doing, but he was still wary of letting them go for too long without watching.

"Maryan tells that story much better," Dradevai said, turning to Delri. "She told us that he went to find the rest of his family, and she hasn't seen him since."

"Oh, so was he Silver, then?" Delri eyed Asith's hair in a way that made Dradevai laugh.

"Yes," he said, "he went missing when I was very small still."

"We're trying to find him now," Dradevai added.

"Do you think something bad has happened to him?" Delri looked worried again. "Poor Maryan, I never knew she was missing her husband."

"She thinks he's still out there somewhere." Dradevai held up one of their pointer fingers. "Her ring is enchanted, so they both feel when the other plays with it. An enchantment like that only works for the person it was made for, so if she can still feel him, then he had to be on the other end."

"Really?" Asith turned to Dradevai. "I didn't know that."

"Oh, I'm sorry. One of the books I had you read explains it, but an enchantment made for a personal item like that is usually bound to the owner."

"That's great, though," Delri said. "Your father still has the ring, then."

Asith scanned his brain, trying to remember if he'd read something like that. Maybe he hadn't gotten to that book yet before the hunters showed up. After all, Dradevai had given him a lot of books, and Asith did not read nearly as fast as they did. He had thought Dradevai's confidence about that had been naivety, but Asith was obviously wrong. If the enchantment was really bound to his father, then he had to be alive and out there somewhere. While his father might still no longer be interested in them, at least Asith knew it was most likely him wearing the ring.

Delri looked between them briefly. She didn't seem to entirely understand Asith's reaction, but she gave him a moment to collect himself before asking more questions.

"So then, how did the two of you meet?" Delri asked. She must have thought Dradevai would somehow be involved in his situation. In reality, they were just the catalyst for his mother telling him about it.

"Well..." Dradevai looked decidedly embarrassed.

Asith cut in, "Dradevai showed up in South Cairn, and when I arrived to try to ask them to leave, they picked me up and took me back to their hoard."

Asith smiled at Dradevai who tried to stammer out some kind of explanation for their behavior. Delri laughed, holding her stomach as she curled in on herself.

"Wait, so the rumors that a dragon knight got picked up by a dragon were true?" Delri wiped tears off her face with the heel of her hand. Dradevai still looked embarrassed, but they were laughing a little too. "Everyone in the Capitol decided that was just a rumor."

"I'm not surprised; no one really saw it happen," Asith said. The Stonegarde was always quick to cover up rumors of dragon knights doing anything stupid, and they were especially quick to dispel talks of anything but a Blue or Green dragon having been spotted. It was on official record that dragons like Dradevai and his father were basically extinct or likely not a threat.

"Well, I am glad you didn't eat my best friend, Dradevai." Delri was still giggling.

"I wouldn't have! Dragons don't eat people!" Dradevai looked distressed, as if they thought Delri might have believed they would eat someone.

"She is only kidding, don't worry." Asith glanced at the road, leading the horses to turn toward the mountains, toward Martivin.

"Yes, only kidding. Though, I can't believe after all our training, you were stupid enough to approach a Sterling on your own."

"What else was I going to do? It sounds like you approached a dragon on your own, too."

"Well, my situation was a little different from yours." She shifted in her spot, looking ashamed. "There was a girl I knew from home whom I was in love with. I only ever saw her hunting for mushrooms deep in the woods, so I assumed she was from the town on the other side of the forest."

"But she was a dragon?" Dradevai asked.

"I don't know. When I went home a little over a year ago, not sure if I was going to stay in Martivin or go back to the Stonegarde, I ran into her. Wanting to impress her, I mentioned that I had become a dragon knight and tried to talk about my record."

"Did she know what it meant?" Asith turned back to Delri. He could already see where her story was going before she even nodded.

"She did." Delri rubbed her forearm. "She got upset; she looked so disgusted with me. She had never looked at me like that before."

"Oh no." Dradevai's voice sounded small. "I'm sorry, Delri."

"It's okay." Delri looked somber. "She ran off into the woods before I could try to explain myself. I didn't understand, but I started to suspect she might have been a Sterling dragon. When I met you, Dradevai, you had the same reaction, and then I saw your horns. They confirmed it."

Delri shook her head, her eyes welling with tears. She shrugged and then continued, "I just wanted to explain and apologize."

Dradevai looked between them both and then added, "I think once she knows you were protecting people, her opinion might change."

"Maybe." Delri sighed. "I wouldn't blame her if she didn't."

Dradevai looked like they were going to say more, but they stopped. Delri wasn't easy to rouse from sadness, and Asith had a feeling they could see it in her face. Instead, they climbed back into the cart to sit across from her. They looked thoughtful, and after a long span of silence, Asith stopped the cart.

The sun was setting, and they needed to set up camp. They managed to convince Delri to share the tent, since Dradevai seemed so worried about her being cold. What Asith didn't expect was getting stuck between the two of them, sweating so much he couldn't sleep.

Delri took the cart the next day after they determined Asith had gotten very little sleep, so he spent most of the day napping in the cart. By the time he woke up, they had gone much farther than he expected; Delri accounted for the speed with a shortcut.

Travel to the foothills went quickly, the rolling landscape covered in sweet-smelling grass going by quickly. Dradevai read, sometimes tucked up against Asith's side. The mountains rose around them, the heavy rocks scattered about like they'd fallen from the high cliffs above.

Asith sort of liked it, the cool gray rocks as opposed to the reddish ones in the mountains near Dradevai's hoard. Everything there was cooler in color, greens, blues, soft purples, and varied grays that reminded Asith of the fabrics his mother kept. She usually had a pile of cool-toned wool around for making winter gear like cloaks and the occasional wool underlayers.

As they made their way up the road, Asith kept his eyes out on the mountaintops. He looked for any signs of wings or birds that looked a bit too big for how far away they were. He didn't really think he'd see a dragon but couldn't seem to stop doing it, his eyes drawn to the edges of the rocks to find a cavern entrance like Dradevai's. Asith thought again of his father's fading touches to the ring. It really was his father on the other end, and Asith needed to find him before it was too late.

When they started their descent into the valley that held Martivin, Asith's eyes caught on something in the distance, the curve of feathered wings too large to only be a bird. He watched the shape soar over the tip of a mountain, turning ever so slightly before flying behind a ridge sitting between Martivin and the town over. Even if that wasn't the girl Delri was looking for, another dragon was nearby. His toes and fingers tingled, his chest rising as if he had become weightless. There was still a chance that could help him find his father.

"Welcome to Martivin!" Delri yelled. She spread her arms out wide as they passed by the small village office painted with blue and purple wildflowers. Dradevai laughed, excited to take in the new place. Dradevai and Delri acted just as much old friends as Delri and Asith. In fact, they'd taken to teasing Asith together, especially if his hair was a mess when he'd first woken up. Delri also liked to quietly point out whenever Dradevai made him blush, which only made it worse. Thankfully, she made it a point to do that if she was certain only Asith would hear.

They rolled into town shortly after Asith had seen the shape of the dragon in the sky. He had told Dradevai and Delri right away, and there was a renewed sense of excitement.

Asith's body was light, and he didn't feel at all like he'd been sleeping in a tent on a rock with only a feathered bedroll under him. They had spent the final days of the trip creating a million plans for finding the dragon he had seen that probably wouldn't work the way they wanted to, but it made Asith feel better. Dradevai wanted to move as quickly as he did, and Delri was willing to follow their timeline.

Martivin looked the same as the last time Asith had been there, and that comforted him the same way getting into South Cairn after a long trip always would. The houses and inns were built into the mountainsides of the valley, spreading up onto the hills along the main road. All the markets and little shops Martivin was known for were nestled directly on the central road that wound through the valley and on to the pass that would eventually reach the Zotia Coast.

When Delri had first brought him to Martivin after they'd been stationed at a nearby outpost for almost a year, Asith had talked with her about one day following the road and leaving for the Zotia Coast. It had been a dream of Delri's, her mother had grown up there, and sometimes, when things were really bad, she talked about retiring there. Asith promised he'd help her get there, and when he was alone, he imagined taking his mother there so that she could retire too. It was funny what ideas he had while daydreaming.

The little buildings looked dreamlike as well, painted white with hand-painted blue flowers decorating the sides and the trim around the doors. Many also had tree leaves painted along the edges, the heavy wooden beams cutting the murals in places, but that made the flowers more vibrant. The people of Martivin were very proud of their delicate craft, claiming it couldn't be seen anywhere else in the world. Asith agreed, and the structures were prettier than the plain wooden buildings of South Cairn. Up in the mountains, they had more things to grind into paint than in the valley, so it wasn't really South Cairn's fault. Martivin also had more money in the town because of the tourism and silver mines.

Dradevai had been amazed by the trees along the mountain road, touching as many of them as they could. Their thin white trunks with dark splotches intrigued them. Dradevai hopped out of the cart, walking right up to the paintings on the buildings. A woman chopping wood nearby waved at them, for the locals were used to that sort of admiration.

Dradevai climbed back into the cart. "This looks so different."

"It's very different from South Cairn and the Capitol," Delri said. "It's because Martivin was originally part of the kingdom to the West, but they joined the people of Cairn in the revolt against their king. The Zotia coast really couldn't argue with us since they were across the mountains."

"Really?" Dradevai looked earnestly impressed, so Delri excitedly recounted the town's history.

"Not to interrupt," Asith said, looking back at Delri, "but where are we staying?"

Delri thought it over. "We should stay at an inn."

"Wouldn't it be better to stay in the woods? Since you said you would see her in the forest?" Dradevai suggested.

"I've only ever seen her there during the day." Delri folded her arms. "And we've been traveling. It will be nice to have a bed for a night."

"Which inn should I go to?" Asith asked. He knew some inns could be rather expensive.

"Go to the Firelight. They won't mention me to my parents."

"If you're worried about being recognized, I might be able to change your appearance," Dradevai said.

Asith and Delri turned to them. "Could you?" Delri asked, amazed and excited. She probably wanted it more for fun than anything, which she confirmed when she added, "Could you make me look just like Asith?"

Dradevai laughed. "I could do that, but it would be confusing, wouldn't it?"

Delri pouted. "True, but it would be funny."

"Do you really not want your parents to know you're here that badly?" Asith asked softly. While Delri had never been as close with her parents as he was with his mother, she usually went out of her way to visit them.

"I would prefer if they didn't. There's been some stuff going on. We can talk about it later." Delri waved him off with a smile, so Asith dropped it.

He turned the cart down the road toward the many inns that made Martivin a famous spot to vacation. That, and the view of the mountains.

"Did you want me to change the way you look, then?" Dradevai asked.

"No, thank you, though, Dradevai."

Dradevai handed over their hood to Delri, and she pulled it up around her face. Asith focused on reading the names of the inns as he drove, trying not to accidentally hit any of the people on the road.

The Firelight Inn was small and smelled thickly of warm charcoal, reminding Asith of the smell that came off Dradevai's fire. The door had been painted a vibrant red color that faded into orange and then yellow at the top, with a shock of blue and purple wildflowers surrounding it. They were more simply painted than others, less realistic, but he could still tell they were the wildflowers that would grow on the hills in the spring. A thick layer of soft snow had settled along the pitched roof and near the foundation, gathered in odd shapes where the wind had blown it in. It had come down the night before; they were grateful they could cling to Dradevai for warmth in the tent.

When they entered, only a few people were sitting at the tables, with one dwarven man sitting behind the counter and speaking to a guest in a chipper tone. When his eyes fell on Delri, he lit up like a candle and hopped off whatever he'd been standing on to come around the counter and hug her.

"This is Asith and Dradevai. They are friends of mine from South Cairn." Delri turned back to them. "This is Char."

"Char?" Dradevai asked. "Like burn?"

"That's right," Char said, setting his hands on his hips. He was shorter than Dradevai but certainly rock solid as many of the dwarves in the town were. They came from mining families, much the same way Delri did. "What are ya sneakin' in here for, Del? Your parents angry at ya again?"

Delri laughed. "No, but I don't want them to know that I'm here."

"Well, I'll keep your secret." He made a hand gesture and a gruff noise. While Asith wanted to ask how many times she'd asked for that before, he knew he should wait until they were alone to ask. "Do you all want one room or two? How long are ya stayin'?"

"Just one for the three of us. Do you mind storing the cart?" Delri looked back at Asith and Dradevai. "Not sure how long we'll be here."

"Okay, just settle up with me before ya leave. I'll take the cart around and feed the horses." Char walked back around the counter, getting up on a stool to offer Delri a key he'd gotten from underneath it. "Don't be a stranger now, come down and talk sometime."

Delri nodded. "Of course."

She took the key and led Asith and Dradevai up to the room. When they closed the door, the first thing out of Dradevai's mouth happened to be, "So how do we get the other dragon to speak to Delri?"

"I don't think she'll talk to me," Delri said. She took her hair out of her ponytail and smoothed it down.

"Who would she talk to?" Dradevai asked, and when Asith and Delri turned back to look at them, they panicked. "Wait, me? But I've only ever seen one other dragon."

"It's not like she'll know that," Asith offered, but Dradevai did not look convinced at all. "You talked to me just fine. And you hadn't spoken to many humans then."

"I guess that's true…" Dradevai's face turned into a nervous pout, all their pomp leaving in one fell swoop. Asith didn't understand entirely why Dradevai was so nervous. They had put themself in positions where they had to speak to people alone before, so it must have had something to do with speaking to another dragon on their own. He didn't know how to fix it, either, so he just tried to reassure them.

"You'll have the advantage of just looking like an ally to her. If it helps, I'll be there with you. She might assume I'm also a dragon if I look like my father."

"Do you look like your father?" Dradevai asked.

"I don't know, but my mother said I did?" Asith really would have no idea. After all, he had never seen his father.

"That's not particularly reassuring," they said, "but what if we just gave you horns?"

"Well, she didn't have horns when I saw her," Delri countered, sitting on the bed now.

"She might be hiding them the way Dradevai does." Asith gestured at Dradevai. "So it might be a good plan for us to look noticeably dragon-ish."

"Noticeably dragon-ish?" Dradevai raised their eyebrows, arms crossed. They looked very small, which worried Asith.

"You know what I mean." Asith set his hand on Dradevai's shoulder. "The point is, we're in this together."

"Yes, we are." Delri set her hand on Dradevai's other shoulder. "Realistically, depending on what that spell can do, I could always be there too. Though, you'd probably have to change me quite a bit."

"Well…" Dradevai looked lost to thought, the anxiety still lining their face. When they looked back up at Asith, they seemed calmer. "If I could teach the spell to Asith, he could maybe give himself horns, and then I could turn you into someone else."

"That could work. Do you think you could learn the spell?" Delri asked Asith. Anxiety made his ribs flutter.

"I can try? I have never done that type of magic." Asith took a deep breath; something like that would be far more complicated than lighting a fire or determining whether an object was magical. Dradevai spun toward him, perking up as they slid out of their anxiety and into the confidence they had whenever they taught Asith.

"You have your own book now, so it should be easier for you to learn something new." Dradevai ran a hand over their hair, smoothing it down before finding their bag. They pulled their spell book out and set it on the table as Delri sat in a chair.

"Do you mind if I watch? I don't think I can do any magic, but I'm interested to see how this works."

Dradevai told her that was fine, and Delri smiled. Then they dragged Asith into the seat next to them.

Dradevai started by having Asith transcribe the spell into his own spell book, carefully copying the ruins and going over how the spell was supposed to work. The more they spoke with each other, the less daunting a task it seemed. But it was quickly late, Delri giving up on watching the whole process and falling into her bed with a sigh. She made a few comments about how cold the tent had been and how much warmer it was inside the inn. Asith's eyes were falling shut by the time Dradevai suggested they should pick it up in the morning.

They set their hand on Asith's arm to get him to stop writing. "This might not be something you can learn by tomorrow," Dradevai said gently, trying to urge Asith out of the seat.

"I'm going to stay up a while longer," Asith said. "You go to bed. I want to have this by tomorrow."

Dradevai sighed. "All right. Try to get some sleep, okay?"

"I will, I promise." Asith turned back to his books and heard Dradevai crawl into bed. As the lantern light lowered, Asith started a new transcription of the spell, trying to follow it from the very beginning. He listened to the light breathing of Delri and Dradevai, who were sleeping peacefully by then.

He finished the new transcription and tried again, the cool night air hitting him as he drew his thumb over his chest as Dradevai had always done. A sudden wind came from his feet. The runes connected with his chant, moving around him in a figure eight before they disappeared. He scrambled to pick up the little hand mirror they'd been using during their practice, and when he drew the lantern close, Asith saw two tall silvery horns atop his head that curved away from his face.

He moved his hand through them, the illusion wobbling like he had touched still water for a moment, then went back to normal. Asith grinned, looking at the horns a bit more before he let the spell drop. His stomach fluttered as he set the mirror back down, a smile still on his face.

CHAPTER 17

12th of Zepha

Dradevai wandered around the room in the morning, pulling things from their bag and laying them out on the table. Asith sat up, wishing he could sleep more, but they were making too much noise. His head hurt slightly, so he reached for his water. Delri was still sleeping soundly, so he whispered.

"Are you looking for something?" Asith rubbed his eyes with the heels of his hands.

"No." Dradevai was placing everything they'd taken out on top of their spell book. "But I had a thought this morning, that I have a spell to prevent other spellcasters from trying to find us."

"Do you think we need to worry about that?"

Dradevai took off the bracelet Asith had given them back in the Capitol and set it in the middle of the arrangement on their book. They frowned at the series of small objects they'd gathered.

"I think we do." Dradevai looked up at Asith. "I can't really describe why, but I—"

"You don't need to explain. I trust you." Asith sat next to them, looking over the spell they'd laid out. It was complex and had layers Asith had never seen before. Dradevai smiled, though.

"Do you have something I can enchant?" Dradevai nudged the bracelet. "It has to be something you'll always keep close to you."

Asith looked at the silver spindles and orange gems shimmering in the morning light. He smiled, pleased by the thought that Dradevai would always be wearing it. His stomach fluttered.

"I'll have to get something from Delri, too," Dradevai said.

Delri stirred at the sound of her name, rolling over onto her back and mumbling quietly, but it sounded like she just asked them to be quieter. Asith dropped his voice to a whisper. He had experienced the wrath of waking her before she wanted to be awake, so he didn't want to deal with that.

"I don't wear jewelry." Asith tried to think of anything he wore daily or always had with him. "Beyond my sewing kit, I don't think I carry anything constantly. Even the goggles you made me stay in my pack if we're not flying."

"Those already have an enchantment on them, so they won't work." Dradevai frowned, thinking it over. "Can I see your pack?"

Asith nodded, bringing them his backpack. Dradevai quickly poked through it, opening each of the pockets, and then withdrew a long bronze feather. Dradevai blinked at it.

"Is this one of my feathers?"

Asith had swept it up sometime when they lived in Dradevai's hoard, he realized. He, for whatever reason, had grabbed it, kept it, made sure it came back with them, and then transferred it to his pack when they left for the Capitol.

"Have you been keeping this on you this whole time?"

"In case I needed it if I fell while we were flying," he lied. Asith didn't have any other explanation for what he'd done.

Dradevai looked between him and the feather. "This feather wouldn't work for that spell. You need down feathers for that."

Asith couldn't tell if Dradevai was concerned Asith had picked up the wrong kind of feather or if they could see straight through his lie. Either way, his face was heating up, so he cleared his throat and avoided eye contact with Dradevai.

"Well, why don't you use that?" Asith said. "It's all we have, and I have some leather cord I can use to tie it to me somehow. Can I help?"

Dradevai pressed their lips together, looking at the feather, but didn't speak whatever was on their mind. That surprised Asith; normally when he lied, they had something to say about it, but that was a different lie than he usually told. Maybe they felt that was more harmless somehow.

"I think I have everything I need for now. Thank you, though," Dradevai finally said.

Asith nodded, and they set the feather aside to activate the spell they had already set up, their eyes glowing as the bracelet imbued with magic energy. Dradevai's voice quickly rose enough to wake Delri, though. While at a normal speaking volume, their chanting was loud enough for her to sit up in bed. She watched with wide eyes, the bracelet levitating and spinning at a pace that made it blur.

Then it dropped back to the book with a dull thud as it shimmered against the pages. After a few seconds, the glowing stopped. The bracelet looked perfectly normal again.

"Well, that was something to wake up to." Delri rubbed her face and tugged at her long black hair until it was all the way back. "What's with the magic so early in the morning?"

"They're making wards," Asith explained, "in case the Maeria Spire comes after us."

"What?" Delri looked completely awake now. "You mean like wards to prevent them from finding us magically?"

"Yes." Dradevai slipped the bracelet back on and set the feather Asith in the same spot where the bracelet had been. "Do you have anything you always wear? Something you never take off, even at night?"

Delri worried her lip. "I guess I do have this."

She slipped off a leather necklace from her neck, a small piece of raw silver ore dangling at the end. Asith remembered when her mother had sent it to her in their first year of training at the Stonegarde to alleviate Delri's homesickness.

"That will work well." Dradevai reached out to take the necklace and then set it aside so that they could focus on the feather.

"Delri," Asith said, tuning out Dradevai's chanting, "why didn't you want to go home to your parents?"

Delri pressed her lips together, and she wrapped her arms around her knees. "Well, they've been putting pressure on me to get married and move back here. I just didn't want to deal with it."

"Wait, who were they trying to marry you to?" There wasn't really anyone in town that was, well, if he were being honest, worthy of Delri. But Asith might just be defensive of her. Even if they were never romantically involved, he didn't like the idea of his friend being pushed into a marriage with someone who didn't live up to her as a person.

"Anyone they could really," Delri said in an annoyed tone. "Including a girl who had just finished her apprenticeship. That was after they'd presented so many men to me that I told them I would leave if they suggested another. I moved back to the Capitol permanently after that."

Asith put the pieces together. Perhaps that was the reason she was so determined to find the dragon she had fallen for as a teen. It would at least take some of the pressure off for her to be with anyone. His shoulders fell, for he was feeling oddly empathetic. Even though his mother had never pressured him to be with anyone, he had been forced to work with plenty of knights at the Stonegarde whom he didn't particularly like. Asith didn't exactly like the feeling of having no other options then, and Delri was only being offered the option to settle or find someone she really loved.

Meanwhile, Dradevai was watching the feather spin a few final times before settling back on the book. "They presented people to you?"

Dradevai looked rather upset about that information, their nose scrunching up like a rabbit's. Asith's stomach became unsettled, so he reached out and took the feather from Dradevai, then pulled out a piece of leather from his sewing kit to wrap around the base of the feather.

"Yes, that's not uncommon here in Martivin." Delri stood, rifling through her bag. "They suggested I talk to Asith first, though, so at least they somewhat tried to suggest I marry a friend."

"Oh." Dradevai grimaced and then furrowed their brow. "That sounds… uncomfortable."

Delri nodded and watched Dradevai as they set up for the final spell and started to chant again. Asith could feel the discomfort rolling off them, their shoulders tense as they spoke. When Dradevai finished the enchantment on her necklace, Delri smiled, remarking it looked even shinier than before.

She slipped the necklace over her head. "So, what is the plan?"

"I think we should go to the spot where you've seen her the most," Asith said, finishing his stitches to make the feather a necklace. "Maybe we could use a spell to draw her attention? Or Dradevai, you could fly in the area so she would know there's another dragon around."

"Flying might draw less attention from humans." Dradevai rubbed their jaw. "If we're far enough away, they'll just think I'm a large bird."

"I think that might be our best option, then," Asith said.

Delri nodded. "And we will try to appear to be dragons ourselves?"

"I'm not sure I'll be able to change both of your appearances," Dradevai said, "especially not if I'm also flying around."

"That's okay." Asith sat up, smiling. "I have that part covered."

"You have it covered?" Dradevai tilted their head, their eyebrows rising.

Instead of answering, Asith chanted and dragged the tip of his thumb across his chest, casting the spell Dradevai had tried to teach him the night before. The same sudden wind came from his feet, and a crackle of static made his hair rise slightly before two horns appeared on the top of his head again.

A wide grin crawled across Dradevai's face, their arms falling to their sides. They stared, a radiant glow coming over their entire body, starting with their eyes. Dradevai threw themself into Asith's arms, surprising him, but he managed not to fall backward.

"You did it!" When they pulled away, they had their hands on Asith's shoulders. "I'm so proud of you."

Delri had a bright smile on her face. Asith's skin tingled, and a warmth spread down his shoulders and back from where Dradevai's hands still held him.

"Thank you." Asith rubbed his head. He couldn't stop smiling, though. Dradevai was proud of him.

"Then we just need to get Dradevai ready to speak to another dragon on the way." Delri's eyes flitted up to the ceiling. "Who knows, maybe this will be the first time she's seen another in her life as well."

Dradevai frowned, pulling away from Asith. "I hope that is not the case."

"Is that not common?" Delri asked.

"I…" Dradevai looked worried. "I don't know. Asith's father, he had parents and a sister, according to what Maryan told us."

Delri nodded. "Then, maybe my dragon does as well."

"I don't know if I would feel better or worse knowing that she also grew up alone," Dradevai said, as if it were an admission of guilt.

Asith set his hand on their shoulder again. "It's okay." He let go of Dradevai once they were looking at him, their eyes gathering tears. "That kind of thing is normal. Wondering if you would rather know everyone hurt like you or if you should feel comfort that they don't."

Dradevai wiped their eyes with the heel of their hand and nodded again. They didn't say anything else, instead taking a deep breath and getting ready to leave.

Delri led the three of them out to the woods just north of Martivin. They walked down a dirt path until Delri took a sharp turn onto an old hunting trail. The early morning dew made the moss a vivid green color that South Cairn never saw. Though, South Cairn didn't have much in the way of forests, either.

As they hiked up the trail, they followed a ridge that descended into a small thicket of trees, the tops of which were visible for a short moment when they walked over a rock. Delri had told them the best place might be a low gulley she often met the dragon in while picking mushrooms.

The canopy blocked out most of the sun, a few beams hitting mushrooms and making them look as if fairies could live inside. While Asith had never quite believed in fairies, he had to admit that seeing things like that up close made him wonder. After all, he hadn't believed dragons could talk.

"Wow." Dradevai stopped at a small break in the trees. "The mountains here are so green."

"This mountain range and the forest extends all the way to the Zotia coast," Asith said, stopping behind Dradevai and looking out at the sprawling mountains that were covered in pine and birch. The forests were dotted with groups of thin trees that held blazing green leaves, all of which seemed to be awake in the light of the mid-morning sun.

"Zotia is the next country over, yes?" Dradevai looked back at Asith, starting to follow Delri again. "Is there water on the other side of these mountains?"

"Lake Zotia is where the country gets its name from." Delri stopped at a fork in the path. They were far enough behind her that they might get separated if she went on without checking. "It's very pretty, I was there once as a child."

"You were?" Asith asked. Delri had never spoken about that before.

"My mother brought me there once." Delri started down the path that descended into the trees. "For my grandfather's funeral."

Dradevai looked back at Asith, a sudden curiosity on their face. "Have you never left the country?"

"I have not," Asith said. "My mother and I couldn't really afford travel."

Dradevai looked completely confused as to why that would make a difference, but then their eyes glazed over in a way Asith had never seen. They mumbled, "Right, you don't have wings."

Asith and Delri laughed, and after a moment, so did Dradevai, their shoulders shaking and their eyes bright. They looked better than they had since the three of them had arrived in Martivin, and Asith felt like they might all be okay after everything was done.

"You know," Delri said, "on the Zotia coast, they worship a goddess called Phela. My grandfather worshipped her, and apparently so did my mother before she moved here."

"Really?" Dradevai asked. "Why did she stop worshipping her?"

Asith's chest hardened.

Delri smiled softly as she turned back to Dradevai. "It's illegal to worship Phela in Cairn, so my mother chose to cut ties with her faith."

"It can be illegal to worship a god?" Dradevai stopped in their tracks. "I've read about Phela, it's not like her teachings are harmful."

Delri looked wistful, her eyes turning up to the trees. "Phela was a goddess worshipped mostly by the dragons. That's all my mother would tell me."

Dradevai frowned and set their hands on the straps of their pack. "The more I learn about this country, the more I'm confused about whether I should like it."

Delri laughed. "You know Dradevai, I had the same thought when I realized the girl I loved was a dragon."

Dradevai paused, not having a response to her statement. They looked back at Asith, a look of realization on their face.

Asith's stomach churned as he wondered how many of the dragons he'd killed could think and talk like Dradevai. Even if they were attacking sometimes, they might have just been scared or hungry.

He fell into his thoughts entirely as they descended into a clearing. Their footfalls startled a rabbit into the path ahead of him. Asith stared at it, the long ears turning before the rabbit's head turned directly toward him. Asith's hair stood on end, a floating feeling in his limbs as he watched the rabbit hop down a narrow path that diverted away from the clearing.

"Hey," Asith said, "I think we should go this way."

Delri turned around. "Really? Why?"

The rabbit peeked just above the leaves of a bush to look at him again, like it was waiting for him. Its brown fur had the slightest bit of water gathered on it.

"I just have a feeling," Asith responded.

"We should follow it, then." Dradevai joined Asith at the fork of the road, and Delri trailed after them. She eyed the path carefully, pulling a knife from her belt to carve a notch in a tree. Once she had, Asith followed the rabbit, watching its white tail bouncing over the plants and roots until they were in a darkened gulley, where the rabbit ducked into a burrow.

The trees in the small valley looked like they had been shaped by logging, but so long ago, there was little evidence of the stumps left behind. Instead, smooth-topped mushrooms and white wildflowers dotted the soft green moss.

Dradevai's eyes had gone huge, their mouth hanging open as they approached flowers that glowed in the low light of the canopy. Asith hadn't thought about that effect too closely, for there were forests leading up to the mountains Dradevai lived in, but not like that. A desert was on the other side of those mountains, and they were taller so their tips were snow-capped and rocky.

"Will you be able to fly out of here, Vai?" Asith asked. Dradevai was already picking flowers, smiling.

"I should be able to." Dradevai set their pack next to Delri and set the flowers on top.

"Should we just wait here while you fly?" Delri looked up at Dradevai, pulling her knife from her belt again.

Dradevai nodded. "I'm going to hunt a bit before I go into the sky. It's been a bit since I've eaten a deer or two."

"That sounds good to me." Delri pulled a hard sausage from her pack and cut it up.

Dradevai transformed and flew off into the forest, their wings stretched out until they dove through the pine trees. Delri watched them closely, her knife halfway through the sausage.

"They're so big!" Delri sat up, trying to catch the occasional sight of Dradevai's wings among the trees. "They're so small when they're a person."

"Well, they are a Bronze dragon." Asith pulled the book he'd bought in the Capitol from his bag and cast the spell to see the hidden writing.

"I guess you're right." Delri returned to cutting pieces of sausage for them both.

"I'm going to disguise us now." Asith put a piece of sausage into his mouth and chewed it quickly.

Delri frowned, her eyes soft as she looked at the ground. "You should make me look like Dradevai, like their sister."

Asith chuckled. "Okay, I think they'll like that."

Delri smiled, and Asith began the chant for the spell, skimming the tip of his thumb from one of Delri's shoulders to the other before he drew it over his chest. As they sat shoulder to shoulder, Asith made himself look how he sort of imagined his father might appear, based on how his mother described him. White horns on top of his head, and slightly opalescent skin.

He gave Delri horns that curved around her ears like Dradevai's back horns when they were in their larger form. Her shoulders were slighter, and her dark hair had a bluish undertone to it. Her brown eyes turned lighter, a similar honey color to Dradevai's, while her skin stayed the same tone, and her nose became sloped like Dradevai's. Delri's clothes looked like Dradevai's as well, the embroidery appearing on velvet that wasn't really there. He liked creating clothing that way, visualizing it and it just appearing. It would probably be useful for him later.

When he finished, Delri looked nothing like herself, and Asith looked more dragonborn than he felt.

"How do I look? What do I look like now?" Delri asked as she rummaged through her bag.

"You look like you could be Dradevai's older sister."

She pulled out a small hand mirror. "That's a lovely and detailed description, Asith. Whenever did you learn to be such a wordsmith?" Delri held the mirror up, her eyes growing wide. "Oh, wow, that's weird." Delri turned the mirror away as Asith laughed.

"It is strange," Asith said.

They settled into eating together, the two of them sharing bread, cheese, and sausage. Dradevai was gone for the better part of an hour, eventually emerging from the trees in their small form. They stretched their arms, chuckling as they walked around the mushrooms and flowers to join Asith and Delri.

"You look so cute." Dradevai pinched Delri's cheeks gently, and she laughed and tried to pull away.

"I thought you'd like it," she said. "How'd it go?"

"I did my best." Dradevai sat with them. "I can always do that again in an hour or so if we think we need it."

Asith nodded, his eyes scanning the area for movement in the trees. If he had been wrong about following that rabbit, he might have set their whole plan behind. Asith chewed on his thumbnail, then a phantom tap hit his ring finger, making him look down at it.

The rabbit burst out of its burrow and ran full speed along the edge of the clearing before disappearing into the foliage. Asith's breathing stopped, until a shift in the trees near the burrow caught his attention. He followed the movement with his eyes, trying to figure out if it was leaves moving in the wind. But then he saw eyes looking back at him, soft and nervous.

Asith reached over to Delri, nudging her because he couldn't reach Dradevai, while keeping his eyes on what seemed to be a girl. Her eyes flicked to Dradevai, and she retreated into the bushes as if she might run away.

"Wait." Asith jumped to his feet. "Wait, please, will you speak with us?"

Delri looked startled as Asith ran across the clearing. Dradevai followed him without hesitation. Though, in hindsight, that might have not been the best approach, for the girl flinched like a deer who'd heard an arrow connect with a tree. Her pale skin didn't blend in with the bushes though, so she was easy to spot, but she vanished in a second.

"How did she do that?" Dradevai asked.

"Did that look like her? I didn't just try to talk to a fae creature, did I?" Asith asked Delri, and she nodded.

"That was her." Delri's brow furrowed, her hands running through her hair. She got to her feet and looked around the gulley. "Did you see where she went?"

"She disappeared," Dradevai said, turning back to Delri. As they did, Asith's eyes registered movement. The leaves shifted unnaturally like someone was moving past them, but he still couldn't see her.

"Are you still there?" Asith asked as the bush shifted. "Please, my friend here is a dragon. We just want to talk."

After a tense pause, the leaves stopped moving. He wasn't sure there was much else he could say. He wasn't exactly good at words, though.

"Please?" Asith's tongue stuck to his teeth, eyes stinging from tears. "My father is in danger. We need help."

That seemed to be the right thing to say, because as suddenly as she had disappeared, the girl was there again. Well, Asith should say woman, for she looked older than him. Her reddish hair hung around her shoulders, and her eyes were a vibrant green that looked like a tarnished metal roof. Her face held fear still, but she receded from the tree line.

"Who told you about me?" she asked.

"A girl in town," Dradevai said. "She said she was worried after the last time she'd seen you."

The woman looked skeptical, and her mouth pulled into a frown.

"The dragon knight? How do I know she didn't send you to kill me?" The woman's voice shook slightly, betraying the confidence of her stance.

"She didn't," Delri said. "She sent three people, not a legion of dragon knights. We would surely die if we tried to kill you."

"And I am a dragon," Dradevai added. "She said I might be able to check on you for her."

"You said you are a dragon, but of what den?" The woman focused on Dradevai, her eyes narrowing. "You have not given me a name, nor any reason to believe you are what you say you are."

"Den?" Dradevai looked confused. "My name is Dradevai, my distinction is Freer of Wings. I do not have a den."

The woman's face twisted. "Do not have a den? No dragon is without a den these days. Not since the war."

"You saw me flying, didn't you? That was me in the sky."

"That easily could have been done with an illusion."

Dradevai looked at Asith and then turned back to the woman before they changed into the large Bronze dragon Asith had originally met. The woman nearly fell backward, pressing herself against a tree and staring at Dradevai like she had never seen her own kind.

"I don't have any other way to prove this," Dradevai said, "but I assure you, I am what I say I am."

"Y-You're..." The woman stepped through the bushes, finally entering the clearing. "Four horns! And you're so big!"

Dradevai looked at themself. "I have always had four horns."

"Yes, but that is very rare in a Bronze, a Silver, or a Gold less so." The woman slowly approached Dradevai with less fear etched on her face. "But I guess that does prove you to be a dragon. A human wouldn't know of a four-horned dragon."

"It does?" Dradevai turned back into their smaller form, their fore-horns remaining, which seemed to also catch the woman's attention. "What?"

"You say you do not have a den, but you're within your first century." The woman leaned in, then took a step back. "At least, I'm guessing based on the size of your horns compared to the rest of you."

"I do not know what a den is. I have been on my own."

"Then these two are…?" She looked at Asith and Delri, who was standing a ways back from the three of them.

"My friends," Dradevai answered. She first walked toward Asith, but as she looked at Delri on her way, something caught her eye.

The woman backed up from Asith. "Why is there an illusion on them?"

"Uh…" Dradevai probably hadn't anticipated the woman seeing through the illusion. "Well, you see-"

"You're that dragon knight woman again. I can see it now." The woman growled at Delri, low and guttural, a sound that didn't match her body now that she was on the defensive. She backed up more, her arms stretching out. In a burst of what Asith could only describe as a shadow, she switched into her draconic form. "I don't know what tricks you're trying to pull, but I will not fall for it."

"No, please, I'm sorry." Delri dropped to her knees. "I'm sorry! I didn't know, I never meant to-"

"Do not apologize to me. You have been killing our kind." Like lightning, her claw was coming down on Delri. Dradevai dropped their illusion, and as his friend was folded under the paw of the dragon, he realized there was nothing he could do.

So, he drew his sword, running toward the largest dragon he'd ever tried to fight, and he didn't even have his axe. He didn't know what else to do, fighting was his only option, but he didn't want to fight with that dragon—that woman. She was just another person, like Dradevai, Asith, and Delri. He didn't want to hurt her.

Delri cried. They'd both taken injuries as dragon knights that had made them cry, but the noise she made in that moment was far worse. A sorrow was behind it that Asith had never heard before. As he ran for the dragon, he feared the worst. Asith didn't want to fight because the dragon could hurt Delri more. When he raised his sword, ready to cut her claw, he realized there wasn't any blood.

Asith's sword fell to his side. Delri was surrounded by a soft reddish-brown glow shaped like an egg. He could tell it was Dradevai's doing, their energy radiating off it. The dragon couldn't seem to get past the barrier, and Delri appeared to only be crying out of sheer sorrow and guilt.

"They haven't! Please listen!" Dradevai's voice sounded pinched, like they were struggling to speak.

"You are young, but how can you be so naïve, little one?" The dragon turned its head to Dradevai. It had a similar sleek shape to Dradevai's, feathers forming behind her eyes, and her horns curved in two spirals like an old ram's.

"I am not." Dradevai's voice gained strength that differed from their usual bravado. They stood taller, their head up and their eyes fierce like they had been when Kosor tried to hit Asith. "The dragons they speak of are Blue and Green, and they attack villages in Cairn. They do not attack or hunt Sterlings like us."

"I…" Delri's voice was meek and cracked between a sob and a hiccup. "I promise, I have only defended towns from Blues and Greens."

There was a tense pause, the dragon's eyes still on Dradevai. Her feathers rippled in the wind.

"I'm dragonborn," Asith said, "and even I was a dragon knight. Blues and Greens attack all the time."

The dragon's head turned toward Asith, her eyes narrowing. They looked like glass marbles, the green intermixed with bright copper flecks. As she took Asith in, he stood up a little taller, sheathing his sword.

"Please," he said, "I'm begging. I just need to find my father before it's too late."

The dragon slowly backed down, her claw coming up from the barrier and settling in the moss. Then she turned back into her smaller form.

"Is that true?" The woman was a few feet from Delri, her red hair fluttering in a sudden breeze. Dradevai dropped the spell they'd used to protect Delri, their arms falling to their side as they took a few deep breaths.

"Yes. I have only ever killed Blues and Greens. I didn't, I didn't know they were like people. I'm sorry, to humans, a dragon knight is like being a hero. I was only trying to impress you."

Delri was sobbing, so Asith closed the distance. He helped her to her feet, and her illusion had dropped, which meant his own disguise was gone as well. There was just Delri, her shoulders folded in and her face broken as her voice cracked quietly.

"We spent so many days together. I just wanted you to see me for more than just the girl you spoke to in the woods. I never knew being a dragon knight was something so shameful."

"And they did attack," Asith added, unsure how to feel about the dragon while Delri was still sobbing from guilt and maybe even terror. On top of that, his own guilt was swelling in his stomach, putting him on the verge of sickness. All he could see was the last dragon he killed, their stomach cut open like the hunter he'd killed in Dradevai's hoard. "They'd burn down entire villages, pick people up, and carry them to their deaths. We were only ever defending ourselves."

Asith wasn't sure if he was trying to convince the dragon or himself. The woman crossed her arms, her shoulders hunched as she grimaced. Her eyes moved away from Delri and Asith, like she couldn't look at them anymore.

"Let's just talk." Dradevai approached the woman. "We need help finding another dragon, and you're the only hope we have at this point."

Her eyes scanned Dradevai slowly, then she looked back at Asith and Delri. She bit her lip, and when she opened her mouth, she'd broken the skin.

"All right," she said, "talk."

"I'm sorry," Delri said. The woman's shoulders dropped, and she rubbed her temples.

"I know you are," the woman snapped. "I meant explain what help you need."

Delri twitched, her lips pressing into a line and wobbling slightly, but she nodded and gripped Asith a bit harder. Asith resisted the urge to yell at the woman for treating Delri poorly, but he needed her information.

"I think my father is dying. He's a Silver dragon named Listesh. We were hoping that maybe you'd have a way of finding him."

The woman gripped her biceps, a perpetual frown on her lips. She looked at Dradevai again, as if wanting some form of confirmation.

"We're looking for a spell." Dradevai stood between the woman and Asith and Delri. "Or an idea of where we can look for him."

"My name is Pystra. I don't feel comfortable talking here where I have no control over the situation."

"We'll go wherever you feel most comfortable." Delri sounded horrid. "I'm Delri. This is Asith."

Delri was still holding on to Asith like he was the only thing keeping her standing. She hiccupped and wiped at her face, which was usually a sign she'd recover soon. It made Asith feel better that Pystra looked at her, her expression slightly ashamed.

"Please, they need help," Delri said.

Pystra took a step closer. "Come to my home. We won't risk other humans running across us."

Delri sniffled and nodded, using the heel of her hand to wipe the tears away from her eyes. She let go of Asith, looking back at Dradevai, and then she straightened herself.

"How do we get there?" Dradevai asked.

"I can take us," Pystra said. "We need to be holding hands."

"Let's go." Delri looked at Asith. "It's your only chance. Take it."

Asith looked at her and nodded, reaching out and squeezing her hand lightly. He wanted her to know he could see her, that he saw what she was doing for him. Delri was putting Asith first.

Dradevai looked decidedly disturbed, mostly by the way Delri was acting, from what Asith could gather. They also seemed momentarily wary of holding hands with Pystra, but Delri nodded at them. Dradevai then took Asith's hand and Delri's other.

Pystra didn't seem to notice Dradevai's skittishness, or if she did, it didn't show on her face. She simply took Asith's hand and spoke a language Asith didn't know but could understand. All the vowels slotted into place in his head, and even as she spoke more quickly, he recognized the words of the incantation, though none of the sentences seemed to make sense.

The rush of air that came after Pystra finished speaking knocked Asith over, his feet going straight out from under him, but he held his grip on Dradevai's hand. When he hit the ground, his elbow slammed into the rock floor.

"Ow, shit." Asith let go of Dradevai and rolled over to cradle his arm. Luckily, it wasn't the arm he wrote with, but the pain radiated up into his shoulder.

"Sorry!" Pystra pulled her hands toward her chest and grimaced. "I probably should have warned you better. That can be a rather rough transition."

"It's fine." Asith gritted his teeth. "What are we going to talk about?"

"I think we should start with Blues and Greens." Dradevai approached Asith, kneeled to help Asith sit up, and then set their hand on his elbow.

They said a short incantation, and Asith realized the language Dradevai used for magic was the same one Pystra had spoken. He hadn't even noticed Dradevai wasn't speaking Matsic. "Better?"

"Yes." Asith moved his arm back and forth a few times, feeling it bend. It was sore but, by his guess, not broken. "Thank you."

Dradevai helped him up, and he saw the countless shelves absolutely covered in books to the point that stacks were piled high next to the shelves, sometimes as tall as the table, which had open books sitting on them. Pystra waved her hand, and the open books all promptly closed. He couldn't blame her for not wanting them to see. So, he directed his attention to the books that sat in small piles near potted plants. Some kind of magic sunlight hung among the blooms, but the points of sunlight didn't burn his eyes. In fact, they also seemed to light the small cave, about half the size of the one Dradevai had lived in, but Pystra's was much smaller. Though, Pystra had a human-sized bed rather than a large pile of pillows to stretch out on in her larger form. It explained why Pystra took up much less space.

"Blues and Greens," Pystra said, "yes, I think that's a good place to start, and with that comes an apology."

Pystra looked at Delri, her small grimace wavering slightly. Delri didn't meet the gaze. Instead of trying to get Delri's attention, Pystra flicked her wrist, and a book floated off one shelf and into her hands.

"I've done some research on Blues and Greens. As far as I can tell, they evolved to look somewhat like Sterling dragons, but they're more like giant mimic flies. They've only existed a few hundred years."

Pystra flipped through the book and encouraged them all to sit. She settled in a chair next to Delri, tapping on the table three times to make tea appear in front of all four of them as well as a platter of fine pastries, the likes of which Asith had only ever seen in the Capitol. "Please, feel free."

"So…" Delri paid no mind to the sweets, but she looked at Dradevai as they reached for one like a curious child. "We were never killing dragons at all."

"You were not," Pystra said. "When you said dragon knight, I assumed you were part of the groups of hunters I have seen that roam the mountains looking for Sterlings like us."

"I never knew that dragon hunters were capturing Sterlings, and not Blues and Greens," Delri said. She furrowed her brow and set her jaw.

"I didn't even know the hunters existed until they attacked Dradevai."

Asith wrapped his hands around his tea, feeling the heat on the cup. He could tell they'd teleported high into the mountains, but it wasn't as cold as where Dradevai lived. The blend smelled like one his mother often made, which was comforting.

"My father went out with a dragon hunting party once," Delri said. "He came back and said he'd decided that hunting wasn't for him. He'd been so shaken. He didn't even take the money he'd been promised."

Pystra and Dradevai both looked at Delri with a fair amount of revulsion, but Dradevai simply looked back at the pastry in their hand and set it on the small plate under their teacup.

"I think I have lost my appetite," Dradevai said. They sipped on their tea instead.

Pystra frowned and looked at Delri. "He probably didn't realize we aren't like Blues and Greens. When he found out, he didn't have the stomach for it."

"This explains why he reacted the way he did," Delri said shakily. "When I'd told him about seeing you in the woods, he told me to never tell anyone. He must have known somehow."

"Your father at least sounds like a good man." Pystra sighed. "I take measures to protect myself, I try to only teleport from here, and I keep myself hidden from the villages even if I get fairly close sometimes."

Dradevai picked their head up. "I used to fly away from my hoard all the time."

"Your hoard?" Pystra chuckled. "You know, I haven't heard anyone call it that in a long time."

"You wouldn't call this your hoard?" Dradevai tilted their head. "You only ever call it your home?"

Pystra sighed again. "Most of us have not had a true hoard since the war. Now, we mostly live in dens with other dragons for security. That, or we have a home like this, too small to be a hoard but closed off and safe. There are some who live in a city high in the mountains too."

"A city?" Dradevai sat up, fascinated yet confused. "Are the dens typically a family, then?"

"Yes. I lost my parents and my partner in the war. So I lived in a den for a while with a family I had grown up with. I eventually came here so I could gather books and study the Blues and Greens more easily."

"I'm so sorry," Dradevai said. "I didn't even know there were other dragons out there for a long time."

"It's been long enough that it doesn't burn quite the way it did. Jyrdenth, my partner, he chose to fight in the war. I didn't." Pystra shook her head. "So you raised yourself? What did you do when you thought it was time to find your parents?"

"I never hit a point where I thought I should find my parents." Dradevai considered it for a moment longer. "I just knew I was alone. I thought that's what it was like for us all. I do want to find them now, though, after we find Asith's father."

Asith turned to Dradevai and smiled. They hadn't expressed anything about finding their own parents in a while. It made him feel better that it was still on their mind; he wanted to help them in return after they found his father.

"I'm sorry." Pystra frowned. "Usually, dragons leave their eggs near their hoard, and about a year after we hatch, we know to return to our parents. That's how it was for me and most others I knew before the war when we still had hoards."

"I don't really know why I was alone." Dradevai shook their head. "But I'm hoping after we find Asith's father, we can try to find my parents too."

"Maybe someone made sure you would never try to find your parents for a reason," Asith said.

"That could be," Pystra said, "but it would take a lot of magic to erase a dragon's instinct. It would need to be another dragon doing it."

"Maybe my parents chose this for me." Dradevai looked between them, tears gathering in their eyes but not spilling over yet. When they looked back down at their tea, Asith's hand twitched to reach out for them, but he couldn't bring himself to with Delri and Pystra staring at the two of them.

"They might have had a good reason," Asith whispered. "It might have been to keep you safe. Just like my mother never telling me that my father was a dragon."

"Asith's right." Delri leaned toward Dradevai. "Parents do lots of things that don't make sense to their kids, but they're just trying to help."

Dradevai looked at Delri and said, "Like how your parents tried to arrange a marriage for you?"

"Yes." Delri nodded, chuckling as she rolled her eyes. "They never meant anything wrong by it."

Asith smiled. He hoped if Delri could laugh about it, then she was getting over the hurt of her parents trying to marry her off. It also helped knowing maybe they were trying to help her, rather than thinking she was doing something wrong by being unmarried.

Dradevai nodded and wiped at their face. Honestly, the whole day had taken more out of Asith than expected. So, he pushed past the anxiety and set his hand on Dradevai's forearm. It was enough to earn a soft smile from Dradevai.

"You said you're both looking for your family, yes?" Pystra said to Asith. "Your father is missing?"

Asith nodded. "I'm hoping to find him."

"Why are you looking for him?" Pystra rubbed her hands together. "I'd like to understand."

"Well, I…" Asith's eyes swam over the room, focusing on no single plant or book yet studying them all individually somehow. "I want to know him. My mother always spoke so well about him, and I know she misses him."

Pystra's expression stayed stony, her frame silhouetted by the magical sunlight behind her. She didn't say anything, waiting for Asith to say more. Asith searched his brain for an answer, but he didn't really know how to articulate all his thoughts. Looking for his father was something he wanted to do, but trying to explain why was beyond words.

Dradevai squeezed his hand, pressing their palms together more. Asith turned back to Pystra in hopes that keeping eye contact would make his intentions clearer.

"Because then I would know why he left me." Asith forced the words out even though he hadn't fully thought them through. His voice shook, his fingers trembling. "I thought if I could find him, I could understand myself better."

"Do you have to keep pressing them like this?" Delri asked sharply. "I understand you are angry and distrustful of me, but they didn't do anything."

Pystra's eyes darted toward her, her shoulders relaxing slightly, and she crossed her arms on the table.

"I am just trying to understand."

"To understand or to test?" Delri set her jaw, her eyes alight with the strength she was known for as a knight. "All while Asith's father slowly fades somewhere we don't know about. We are trying to save someone here, and you knew me for years. Why are you so skeptical of us?"

Pystra raised her voice. "Plenty of people have come to dragons saying they need help, only to bring them directly to a hunter's trap"—she gestured to Asith—"including other dragonborn, so I apologize if I am cautious."

Delri bared her teeth and began to speak, but Asith held up his hand. Delri crossed her arms, chewing on the inside of her lip as she leaned back in her chair.

"I understand your caution," Asith said. He swallowed a lump in his throat, locking eyes with Pystra. "I saw the traps that hunters use; I killed one of them with my bare hand. I am looking for my father because I am worried that hunters are the reason he never came back."

Pystra's eyes were focused wholly on Asith as she picked up her tea. She looked at Delri again, sighing softly and shaking her head.

"How did you all know where to look for me? I was actually trying to avoid you all when I went to that gulley even though I had seen Dradevai flying."

Delri and Dradevai turned to Asith, their eyes wide. Asith shook his head slightly, his jaw falling open as he blinked rapidly. He didn't really have an explanation for that, either, so the truth was the best choice.

"A rabbit crossed my path and then ran down the trail to the gulley." Asith rubbed the back of his head. "It seemed like it wanted me to follow."

Pystra's mouth fell open, a ragged laugh coming from her. Her chest heaved, her cheeks beginning to shine as she shook with laughter.

"The three of you are unreal." She pressed a hand to her forehead, still laughing, but more controlled. Asith looked at Delri, who was raising a brow, and he shrugged because he didn't understand, either.

"Can I ask you something, Pystra?" Dradevai's voice sounded small in comparison to the laughter. Pystra nodded, clearing her throat and setting her arms at her sides.

"Are you capable of doing the spell we're talking about?" Dradevai fiddled with the pastry they had rejected earlier, picking it apart.

"I might be able to cast it." Pystra stood up and walked over to one of the taller stacks of books. She removed books until she found the one she wanted. "I have a spell that can locate a family member, but I'll need some of Asith's blood to do it."

"His blood?" Dradevai sounded disgusted. Asith just nodded, looking at Dradevai.

She added, "The other thing is, Dradevai might actually be more advanced than me."

She flicked her wrist, and a book floated into her fingertips like a sheet of parchment on the wind.

"I may be older, but I could never cast a shield as strong as the one Dradevai cast earlier." Pystra opened the book, setting it down in front of them. "This is the spell; you should read it." Pystra then tapped her nails on the table. "Delri, may I speak with you alone?"

Delri looked confused but popped up from her seat. "Yes of course."

She followed Pystra deeper into the cave, and then Pystra said a quick incantation that created a wall between them and the table where he and Dradevai sat.

Dradevai turned to Asith. "She used a silencing spell too." They looked at the book. "Are you sure you want to give her your blood? That kind of magic could be very dangerous for you."

"How else are we even going to start to try to find my father?" Asith lowered his voice, facing Dradevai.

"Asith, if the spell backfires, it could damage your mind." Dradevai fiddled with their necklace, their leg bobbing up and down. "Imagine hitting your head so hard that you can't remember yourself anymore. And those sorts of spells can be traced easily. It could lead right back to you."

Asith removed their hand from their necklace so that he could hold both of their hands in his. Dradevai looked at him, their lips pressed into a hard line.

"I don't know what else we can do," Asith said, "and I don't know how much time we have."

"If you're okay with doing it, then let's do it. But I want to be the one to cast the spell."

"Okay. I trust you, Dradevai. I have a good feeling about this."

"I do too." Dradevai nodded.

Asith smiled, and they pulled their hands from his, shifting forward to hug him. Their arms were tight around his neck, and they carefully set one knee on his chair to put their weight on him. Asith panicked, but his brain caught up and he remembered they were alone. So he wrapped his arms around Dradevai's middle and sunk into the feeling. Dradevai settled their nose against his hair and took a few deep breaths, so Asith followed their lead, finding himself much more centered than before.

"Also," Asith said, "thank you for protecting Delri today."

He gave their hand a squeeze, and color rose to Dradevai's cheeks. Asith still rather liked the way they looked when they got bashful. Dradevai smiled, rubbing the side of their neck gently, and they separated.

Pystra walked around the makeshift divider, smoothing down her dress, with Delri close behind her. Both looked a bit disheveled in a way Asith certainly recognized, so he hoped they had worked something out.

Dradevai said, "We want to try the spell."

"I'm willing to use my blood for it," Asith added. "But Dradevai would like to be the one to cast it."

Pystra nodded, approaching the table. "I can assist Dradevai."

Dradevai sat up with the book in hand and asked if they could remove sigils from it. Pystra sat next to them, following along as they discussed ideas and changes they could make to the spell so that it couldn't track Asith easily.

Delri flopped into the chair next to Asith, looking more herself as she smiled at him. Her shoulders had relaxed, and her arms remained uncrossed as she listened to the conversation between Dradevai and Pystra. Asith smiled back, then turned his attention back to Dradevai's concerns, trying to help where he could. Delri said nothing, simply nodding if someone asked her to bring something over. Eventually, she started to take notes on everything she was responsible for during the ritual.

After that, they spent a good amount of time setting up the room, drawing a chalk outline on the floor, save for a few key pieces, and gathering a pile of feather ashes in the center of the circle. It was well into the evening before they were done, the four of them checking their work by the light of Pystra's sunlight orbs two or three times before any of them suggested stopping for the night.

CHAPTER 18

13th of Zepha

Pystra laid out thick blankets, piling them up for Asith and Dradevai to sleep on. They had worked themselves ragged, all of them dragging their feet as they readied for bed. Dradevai kept grumbling about sleeping as a dragon but not having enough room, so Asith had to assure them he'd find a way for them to sleep in their larger form soon. Once Pystra heard them voicing their complaint, she stopped making the temporary bed.

"If you'd like, you could sleep in my storage room? It might be large enough."

"Storage room?" Dradevai spun around, looking for signs of a door.

"Sorry, over here." Pystra waved for them to follow. A stack faded out of existence, revealing a large stone archway that led into a much larger cavern. Inside, a collection of bookshelves was packed with books, a system of stone shelves holding various foods, herbs, and other miscellaneous items. It wasn't huge, about the same size as her home, but everything was pressed against the walls, meaning the middle was open.

Pystra walked directly to the stone shelves, turning away from them as she picked up a jar with a greenish ball inside it. Asith couldn't see clearly what it was, but she examined it before she put it back and picked up a different jar with a similar ball inside.

Dradevai turned into a dragon, spinning gracefully before they settled in a semi-circle on the ground. They smiled, their tail wrapping around their paws.

"This is perfect," Dradevai said, "thank you."

"Oh, wait." Pystra turned around with the jar in hand, pulling the ball from it. "Stand for a moment and pick up your feet when this gets close."

Dradevai stood, and Pystra threw the ball at their feet. It grew, spreading and reaching the walls of the room. As it drew close to Asith, he picked up his feet, and a thick layer of moss grew on top of the stone floor. Asith stepped on it, and Dradevai did the same.

"Oh, this is even better." Dradevai rested on it, their tongue just barely sticking out like a cat's sometimes did. Pystra chuckled, walking to the archway to cast a spell that stopped the moss from growing into her home. She carried the blankets and pillows to Asith, handing them off as Asith thanked her.

Asith walked over the moss, setting the blanket on it near Dradevai, but they picked their head up to look at him. They nudged their nose against him gently, their soft feathers tickling his face as he dodged their horns.

"Sleep with me tonight," Dradevai mumbled. "Please."

"Of course." Asith cupped their face, then hugged them gently. After a moment, Dradevai pulled away and shifted so that Asith could climb onto their paws. Their feathers were soft and downy, which gave Asith a good base to sleep on, especially once a pillow was under his head. Dradevai pulled the blanket over for him, tucked their head in, and closed their wings around them.

Asith settled onto Dradevai's warm paws, snuggling into the pillow. Dradevai's head was near his feet, their tail coiled around their paws carefully, and their eyes were on Asith.

"Comfortable?" Dradevai asked.

"Very." Asith smiled at Dradevai and set a hand on their head to rub the soft feathers there. "Thank you."

Dradevai hummed when Asith touched them. He'd never pet their feathers before, and he wasn't sure what possessed him to do it. Asith curled into his blanket, and Dradevai closed their eyes. Eventually, he closed his eyes, too, thankful Dradevai didn't say anything more.

A rush of cool air woke Asith as Dradevai opened their wings. Dradevai nuzzled their nose against Asith as he ran his hands through his hair. Once he had crawled off Dradevai's paws, they turned back into their smaller form, yawning. Asith rubbed his eyes and contemplated trying to sleep just on the moss a while longer, though he could hear Pystra shifting around in the next room. Dradevai had made a surprisingly good bed but it wasn't a position he was used to sleeping in, so he was just a little sore. He got up and walked over the moss to join Pystra.

"So long as there's no magic blocking him from being found, it should work." Pystra spoke confidently, as she had the night before when they discussed the ritual.

"It could backfire." Dradevai was helping Pystra make tea. "I don't want Asith to get hurt."

They looked over their shoulder at Asith, their eyes settling on him. Asith smiled, trying to be a comforting presence even if only half-awake. Pystra offered him tea when he sat at the table.

"I won't let it come back on Asith," Pystra said. "If that happens, I'll redirect it."

Dradevai nodded. "Okay."

Asith sipped on his tea without milk, though he didn't mind having it that way. Dradevai politely declined the tea; they still hadn't found a reason to drink it when it was so bitter.

"Should I wake Delri?" Pystra asked as she set a cup of tea on the table for herself.

"Honestly, I wouldn't recommend it," Asith said. "She once slapped me for waking her up too early."

Dradevai laughed. "Wait, really?"

"Yes," Asith replied. Pystra giggled. Somehow, though, the look on her face was still fond. "She had asked me to wake her, too, but she did apologize after."

"Asith." Delri looked like a hair monster at the moment, tangled from rubbing her face into the pillows, sticking out at odd angles. "This is not a story anyone needs to hear."

"I was only trying to keep Pystra from getting hit," Asith said. Pystra and Dradevai were both laughing, and while Delri looked flustered, she also didn't look humiliated. So, that was decent payback for every joke Delri had made with Dradevai at his expense.

"To be honest, normally, I would sleep in too." Pystra set her head in her hand, then took a sip of her tea. "But we have important magic to do today."

A crooked smile grew on Delri's face. "See, you two are just up far too early all the time."

"I like to wake up with the suns," Dradevai asserted. Delri and Pystra both looked at them incredulously. "So, should we start?"

"I think we should," Pystra said. She encouraged them to all eat a little something, bringing out a tin of honey-flavored tea cookies. Delri and Asith took out some of their food to share as well to round out the meal.

They moved to stand over the chalk outline, Dradevai carefully placing Asith in the exact location he needed to be, while Pystra helped Delri line up components in the order she would need to bring them to Dradevai. Once they were ready, Dradevai instructed Pystra to kneel next to the chalk circle and handed Asith a silver dagger before walking to their spot. They nodded at Pystra then, and they both imbued the spell with their magic.

Dradevai chanted the incantation in the same strange language Asith seemed to half-understand, and Pystra chanted a spell of her own.

Asith gripped the knife, ready for the moment Delri handed over a small bowl of water to Dradevai, which would start the most complex part of the ritual. The last ingredient was Asith's blood, and while he didn't quite understand how they would get it from him when he was about five feet away, he listened to them.

As Dradevai lit a bundle of incense and drew runes in the air Asith recognized but couldn't quite place, their eyes glowed, boring into Asith. Even as they continued to write, they focused on him fully, their hand going out to Delri for the bowl of water. They dropped the ashes into it, and Asith drew the knife across his thumb, leaving a cut large enough to bleed.

The blood dripped down his finger but only for a moment before a droplet gathered in a bubble in the air and drifted into the water where Dradevai had put out the incense. Everything lit up, the chalk a glowing wall of light that blocked Asith's view of Dradevai. He could only hear them chanting, the melodic sound of whatever language they were speaking.

His vision started to go dark. Pystra had warned him the night before that the ritual might be intense, and at that moment, he wished he'd asked more questions about it. He looked at his hand in time to notice it was no longer bleeding, and his vision blurred and blackened until it opened back up in another cave, that one vast.

The cold hit his arms, his tunic far too thin for the air coiling around him. Then he realized he was floating just outside a row of cages. He heard noises, some like voices but many more like the sounds a deer made after one would sink an arrow into its chest. A group of men dragged a chained griffon from its cage, the eagle head whipping back and forth as it squawked like a turkey going to slaughter. Asith cringed when a man in armor activated a spell on the chains and the collar burned white.

Next to the men pulling the griffon was a stately figure, with a long mantle on his shoulders that nearly touched the ground. His arms were tucked behind his back as he watched the griffon. The man wore the colors of Cairn, red and gold with white underneath. He didn't say anything, simply waiting like he was in a line at the bakery. Asith tried to remember why he seemed familiar but couldn't put his finger on it.

"Hurry up, we have orders to fulfill." The man's fine robes shifted as he spoke. He raised his hands, speaking a chant full of vile-sounding runes, and directed them at the fighting creature. The griffon stopped moving, a pained noise coming from deep within its chest as it grew still.

"Get it on a roller and onto the table," the man said. "We need a pound of feathers and one of its eyes."

The griffon's eyes darted around like it was still aware. His stomach shivered, for he finally registered what he had said, identifying the existing bald spots on the griffon's wings and back.

A voice came through the darkness that was soft and dry, like the person speaking desperately needed water. "Who's there?"

Asith tried to find the source of the voice until he realized, the cage just in front of him had something in it. Not something, someone. A person.

They sat up and turned their face to Asith. He was gaunt, with sunken cheeks. His hair was matted, a dull white color, but what struck Asith was his eyes—silver and large as his mother had described.

"You're scrying." He sounded hurt. "I can see you, just barely. If you can hear me, please, I have people to return to."

"Dad?" Asith asked.

The person stared up at him, their silvery eyes locked on Asith yet looking past him at the same time. Asith took in the bronze bars on the cage, the floor a hard clay tile that had been cut into hexagons. A number was on the cage, obscured slightly by the edges of his vision.

"Please come." The voice sounded like he had eaten gravel, and as he shifted into the light, a chain rattled. As quickly as the noise came, magic flared up the length of the chain wrapped around his ankle. He screamed and rolled around, and Asith's chest ached. However, the magic going off provided him with more light. The numbers on the cage read 10037, and another cage was next to it, with only a small gap between them. The man curled into a ball on the ground, sobbing, the rags he wore barely hanging onto his small frame.

"I'm coming," Asith said. "I promise."

His father's face pinched as he forced himself to rotate onto his back. Then Asith's vision blurred, revealing the outside of the cave with two guards standing in front of it. Then the forest in the mountains. Asith tried to hold on a bit longer, but the vision was unraveling like a piece of fabric. Asith raised his hand, a chant leaving his lips before he even thought about how it might affect the ritual. It moved like a thread through the edges of the magical window, forcing it to stop for one moment as he looked down on the forest. His heart pounded in his chest, and his eyes scrambled over the forest, looking for something, anything.

His spell was slipping. It was as if he had tried to close a seam with a basting stitch and unwaxed thread. Asith tried to fight it, but it snapped and his vision pulled away again. However, something he recognized came into view.

A high tower with a blue roof stuck out against the trees. It belonged to a small dragon knight base he'd spent some time in when he'd first finished training. The tower had been built before the country had chosen red for its flag and guards, and while it matched the blue and green armor dragon knights wore, the Stonegarde never changed the color to match the flag.

Someone picked up Asith's hands first, their fingers holding them carefully. The warm sensation of Dradevai's healing magic flooded his veins. He coughed, his throat dry and his body stiff, but his muscles relaxed quickly.

"You're awake!" Dradevai pressed their hands against Asith's chest, probably harder than they meant to, but still, Asith couldn't help the sudden pang of frustration as he coughed harder.

He grunted in pain, moving away from Dradevai so that he could try to sit up. "What happened?"

"You passed out." Dradevai looked apprehensive, their hands drawing back slowly. They put one hand on his shoulder to keep him still. "Don't move too quickly, okay?"

"Okay." Asith took their advice, relaxing against the stone floor and running a hand over his face. Pystra and Delri were behind Dradevai, staring worriedly down at him as Pystra's small home came into focus.

All Asith could think about was how the chain had lit up and the sound of his father's scream. A pit the size of the entire valley of Cairn was in his stomach. His father had people to get back to, people like Asith and his mother or someone else. He couldn't help but fear his father was in prison for a reason, though he wasn't sure how that would have happened if he'd left South Cairn toward the mountains as Asith's mother had said.

His brain turned over ideas, consumed by thoughts of what had been done to the many people and creatures being held in the facility. A knot formed in his stomach, and he thought he might throw up. The more he thought about it, the more he feared that would have been Dradevai's fate had he not stopped the hunters from capturing them. That meant those being held in those cages were innocent.

"How do you feel?" Dradevai asked, and that time, Asith reached out for their hand. They helped pull him into a sitting position. He was woozy but otherwise fine.

"I'll be okay, Vai, promise." Asith squeezed their hand and looked at all three of them. He collected himself, pushing down the fear. "It worked, though."

"It did?" Pystra looked excited. "I was so worried we put you through all that for nothing."

"I thought the chances of it failing were low?" Dradevai looked at Pystra with a good deal of concern.

"They were, but his passing out was unusual. I thought it was a sign that we had failed for sure."

"I think I passed out because I cast a spell inside the ritual." Asith rubbed his head, a lingering headache traveling along the crown of his head.

"Asith." Dradevai's voice popped like steam bursting from a flaming log. Their nostrils flared. "That could have caused the spell to backfire."

"I'm sorry," Asith said. "I hadn't seen anything that would give me a location. I didn't know where here was. I needed to do something; I needed to see a little more."

Dradevai's brow furrowed, and they shook their head, a deep frown on their lips. They bared their teeth at the ground and took a deep breath through their teeth. Then they set their hands on their thighs.

"It's okay." Dradevai's voice came out pinched. "What matters is that you're okay."

Asith looked down, pulling his knees to his chest and wrapping an arm around them. He set one hand on top of Dradevai's, trying to calm them down. They deflated, their hand moving to lace their fingers with his.

"I saw the Brittlebell Outpost." Asith looked up at Delri, knowing she would be familiar with it. He let go of his knees and pushed himself to his feet. Dradevai grabbed his arm to steady him.

"Really?" Delri followed Asith over to the table, Pystra running to grab a book off one of her shelves. "What else did you see?"

Asith recounted everything he'd seen as Pystra brought over a large book. It was an atlas of sorts, the pages expanding out into maps that were only slightly out of date. Luckily, Brittlebell was an old city, so it was still on the map even though High Cairn wasn't.

"So, you think the person in chains was your father?" Dradevai was sitting over the map, huffing softly when Asith pointed Brittlebell out. They sounded somewhat frustrated, probably because of the distance between Pystra's den and Brittlebell.

"I think it was," Asith said, "but I'm not really sure."

"That is how scrying works, unfortunately," Pystra said. "Though if they could see you, they must be a fairly powerful caster themselves." Pystra sighed, folding her arms. She mumbled to herself, calculating the exact distance between her home and Brittlebell. "I know of a way to teleport to places I haven't been to, but we could appear two hundred feet above the arrival location. Or much worse, two hundred feet underground."

"We could also fly," Dradevai said, dragging their finger over the map. "If we go around the mountains like this, we might not be seen."

"That's a long flight, even for a dragon your size." Pystra pointed to a valley in the mountains north of the country. "There's a city here that you could stop in."

"A city? That deep in the mountains?" Delri looked up at Pystra.

She nodded slowly. "That's where the Graveyard Trees are, from what I'm told. Only dragons are allowed in."

Asith looked the map over, already seeing Pystra was probably right. The valley she had pointed to was only a two-week walk from South Cairn, and his mother had said his father recognized the mountains.

"It's a city of dragons?" Dradevai looked entirely intrigued, and they turned to Asith. "We will find your father first, but after?"

"Yes, we can go after. And I think we should have Pystra teleport us if she can. My father didn't look good."

"You're right, your father needs us if he's being held in a cage," Dradevai said. "It's worth the risk to have Pystra teleport us."

"Okay," Asith said. "We will need a way to break that chain though. It looked like it was magic."

"We'll find a way." Dradevai's eyes were sharp and determined.

"I can teach you a spell for that," Pystra said, then turned toward Dradevai. "It will have to be you, though; it's going to be rather advanced."

Dradevai nodded. "I can learn it. Anything to get Asith's father out."

"Thank you." Asith turned his hand over and squeezed Dradevai's, their soft palm pressing against his as they smiled.

Then it was time to prepare again, and suddenly, Asith wished he had brought his axe. At least he had his father's sword.

CHAPTER 19

Pystra held an atlas in her hands and paced back and forth. She was muttering coordinates from the map, but Asith didn't know enough about reading maps to understand them.

"This is going to be even rougher than when we teleported here." Pystra chewed on her thumb, looking directly at Asith.

Asith blushed. "I'll make sure to land on my butt if I fall this time."

It was the best answer he could give, and Pystra seemed satisfied with it. They had spent the last several hours teaching Pystra about Brittlebell, trying to make sure the teleportation spell would work properly. The more she knew, the less likely they'd end up buried underground.

Pystra looked at Delri. "Are you sure you want to go?"

They had been bickering on and off about Delri going since they had decided to teleport. Pystra thought it was an unnecessary risk since Delri was just going to go right back home with Pystra.

"My staying doesn't increase your odds of doing it correctly, so I'm going." Delri snatched the book from Pystra's hands. "We don't know what you'll be teleporting into, so you might need my help."

Pystra sighed, nodding and giving up on the fight. She did ask Asith to hold on to Delri in case they were in the sky when they arrived and he could cast a spell to slow her fall.

Once Pystra was ready, she gathered them in the center of the room, the four of them forming a ring as they took each other's hands. When Pystra started the incantation, Asith braced himself for the rush of air and the feeling of the ground shifting underneath him.

They didn't land hundreds of feet below the ground, thankfully, but they did appear about fifty feet above it. Asith reacted quickly, gripping Delri's hand like a vice as he squeezed the feather in his other hand. Dradevai had already let go, turning into their larger form and flying away from them.

"Asith?" Delri's voice cracked. Asith tried not to look at the ground, but he had a feeling they were approaching it rather rapidly. He spoke the chant, the magic making his skin tingle like static gathering in his hair.

The spell went off, stopping Asith midair while he clung to Delri, who was dangling. They were only ten or so feet off the ground. Asith panted. He hadn't done the spell completely right. Blood pumped past his ears, buzzing across his entire body. They drifted to the ground, Delri touching the grass first and pulling Asith down like a balloon on a string.

"Sorry." Asith landed. "I don't know why it didn't work on you too."

Delri shook her head. "It's okay. You did your job. You kept us safe."

Asith smiled and thanked her. Dradevai gently set Pystra on the ground near them. She was still in her smaller form, looking slightly dizzy as she sat on the ground. Delri ran to her side as Dradevai turned back into a human, their lips pursed.

"I'm okay, I'm okay," Pystra said. "Thank you, Dradevai."

"What happened?" Delri rubbed Pystra's shoulder carefully.

Pystra laughed. "I think I've just done a bit too much today. Everything was spinning the moment we arrived."

Delri helped her up once she was feeling a little better. They all took stock of their things, which were scattered about the field they had landed in. Asith's bag had stayed on his back thankfully, meaning his sewing supplies weren't among the knee-high grass.

Once they had gathered all their things, Dradevai was talking about the city of dragons to Pystra. They waved him over to discuss the city, but Asith wanted to start toward the outpost. Delri had confirmed she briefly spotted it in the distance to the north, so they would need to walk a bit still before they could even start looking for that cave or Asith's father.

"Thank you," Asith said to Pystra, "for bringing us here."

To his surprise, Pystra softened. Her shoulders relaxed, and she toyed with a ring on her right hand as she looked at the ground.

"You know," Pystra said, "I'm glad the three of you found me. It's been a long time since I've interacted with someone other than another dragon."

Asith scanned her face. Her eyes held a somber edge, and the slightness of her smile looked like rain on a day when one wanted to go outside. He furrowed his brow, rubbing his left shoulder gently.

"You mentioned a dragonborn leading a dragon to hunters." Asith stopped rubbing his shoulder, his hand lingering there. "Were you the dragon in that case?"

Pystra nodded, her eyes downcast still. Asith took her in, thinking of the Blues and Greens who had broken his body and killed his friends. He looked at Dradevai, who was watching as they spoke to Delri, a little smile on their face.

"The two of you restored a lot of hope I once had." Pystra's voice brought him out of his thoughts.

"Hope for what?" Asith asked.

"Hope that I wouldn't have to keep hiding." Pystra crossed her arms, smiling. "That the humans and dragons would eventually amend what happened between them."

Her hair fluttered, the copper curls shifting like grass in the wind. Pystra's eyes were on Delri now, her fingers reaching up to brush her hair from her face. Her shoulders were back, her free hand gripping her skirt, the suns hitting her straight on and making her entire being shadowless.

"We just need to make sure the people know Blues and Greens are different," Asith said, "that you all are different."

Pystra considered that. "Maybe that's something I could do."

"Delri can help." Asith looked between them. "I'm sure she'd like to continue to get to know you better."

Pystra smiled, giggling until she snorted, her hand coming up to cover her mouth. Asith laughed with her, grabbing Delri and Dradevai's attention again.

Delri tilted her head at Asith, a smile on her face, but he shook his head. She didn't need an explanation, and he didn't need to embarrass Pystra.

As Delri approached him, he realized his anxiety was better. Asith was still nervous to leave but willing to hug Delri tightly. She held on to him, their temples pressed together the way they used to in their armor after the last dragon had gone down.

"You better come back." Her voice wavered. "I don't know if I can go on without my best friend."

Asith buried his face in her neck, his grip on her tightening. "I promise, I will."

Delri sniffled, and she took a deep breath. When she stepped away, she kept her hands on his shoulders, gripping him like she would her glaive. She cleared her throat and swallowed.

"If you do not," Delri said, "I will find you, and I will kill you again myself."

Asith laughed, and Delri did too. They said things like that to each other before they'd get into a fight.

"I know." Asith nodded. "I know you will."

"Good." Delri squeezed his shoulders and let go. "Keep Dradevai safe too. Look out for each other."

"We will."

Dradevai nodded at him. They had been talking to Pystra, but they must have heard their name.

Delri turned to hug Dradevai next, picking them up off their feet, which made them laugh. They exchanged a few quiet words that Asith couldn't hear, but he had a feeling they were somewhat similar to what Delri had told Asith.

Asith's throat tightened as Pystra said goodbye to Dradevai. It made him happy to see them talking so freely with another dragon, since they wanted kinship like that. And he was pulling them away from it. But Dradevai wanted to come and they wouldn't have left Asith alone, yet it still made Asith's chest ache.

When she'd finished speaking with Dradevai, Pystra took a step toward Asith. She crossed her arms, a sternness to her posture as she said, "Take care of them."

Asith nodded, the breath leaving him. He didn't know what else to say, but the way Pystra set her jaw and leaned into his space made him take a step back.

"Good." Pystra walked back to Delri, telling her they should go.

Asith didn't expect tears to well in his eyes when Delri and Pystra stepped away from them, holding hands as Pystra began the teleportation spell. Asith let them roll down his cheeks. Delri waved as his stomach burned. He wouldn't ask her to put herself in the middle of whatever he and Dradevai were about to do, but he didn't want her to leave. There was safety in her dark eyes and deep voice, and Asith had to resist the urge to beg her to stay.

Dradevai took his hand, lacing their fingers with his and squeezing their palms together. Asith swallowed, looking at Dradevai, who also had tears in their eyes.

"Ready?" Their voice wobbled.

"Ready."

CHAPTER 20

Asith woke to the sound of Dradevai shifting next to him in the darkness, their first night alone in the woods in a long time. They'd spent the rest of the day finding the Brittlebell Outpost, so they were no closer to finding his father. As they lay on the soft moss ground they had found with only the light of a full moon peeking from the front of their tent, Dradevai settled on the bedroll, stretching their legs out as they moved their hair out from under their shoulder. Asith looked at the bare side of their neck, the moonlight making it glow slightly silver.

Asith sat up, looking down at Dradevai, and smoothed his thumb over Dradevai's neck. Their skin was soft and warm, bumps raising along it.

"Asith?" Dradevai's eyes turned up, luminous and bright in the dim light of the tent. "Are you okay?"

Asith dipped his head, sliding his thumb just out of the way so that he could kiss the skin of Dradevai's neck. They tasted sweet, no shock of salt or bitter edge. Dradevai's pulse raced under his lips, their breathing quick as he trailed kisses up to their jaw.

He couldn't entirely see in the dark, moving by touch, and he found Dradevai's lips. Dradevai met the kiss equally, pressing up into Asith's lips even though he'd sort of missed, catching the corner of their mouth instead.

Asith's hands found their way to Dradevai's waist, pulling them in closer. It was awkward as they both grabbed for each other in the dark. Dradevai's tongue found his own, and then he settled between their legs, their thighs resting on either side of his waist.

He didn't know quite how it happened. Usually, there was a lot of talking before, too much talking, too many specifics, or like Delri, a quiet conversation about just needing someone in the barracks of a dragon knight outpost. With Dradevai, it was entirely different. They followed his movements without words, simply touching Asith's body and guiding his hands to their soft skin.

He tugged off Dradevai's clothes, and they started to do the same to Asith. Dradevai's skin was so warm, something Asith hadn't noticed until he had his hands on the smallest spot of their waist, just feeling their heat on his palms and calloused fingers.

"Is this okay?" he asked, dipping his hands between Dradevai's legs and running his fingers over the soft hair there. Dradevai set their hands on Asith's shoulders, a soft gasp leaving their lips. Asith wanted to hear more of their voice.

"Yes." They shivered under Asith's touch, so he gently took their shoulder in his hand and pushed them down. His fingers slipped inside Dradevai's soft, wet folds, which earned him a moan, and something crept into Asith's stomach, familiar but different from anything he'd experienced.

He kissed their skin, running his tongue along their neck, just to feel the way they shivered underneath him. Dradevai's eyes fluttered closed, their back arching into every touch of Asith's fingers. The only time they made a sound of protest was when Asith paused, their brow furrowed, but they didn't get a question out because Asith curled his fingers and kissed their folds.

Their hand gripped Asith's hair and pulled slightly. Asith hummed, enjoying the way Dradevai reacted. He flattened his other hand on their stomach to help keep them still, feeling their thighs press against the sides of his head.

Dradevai squirmed under each tiny movement Asith made, a sudden, extreme admiration hitting him. It glowed in his chest, the feeling of lightness and joy coming from making Dradevai feel good, making them grab his shoulder and beg for more. It also came from the way they clung to his shoulders, wrapped their legs around his waist, and begged him to stay close. Every little thing Dradevai did made Asith feel like his chest was going to burst with such intense want and need to connect with them that he could really only call the feeling love.

Asith held Dradevai close after, his nose buried in their soft hair as he basked in their warmth. Dradevai had their arm slung over Asith's chest, their fingers in his hair and nails running along his scalp. Their legs were wrapped around one of his, their skin smoothing along his own and making his stomach curl.

He woke, that time in the early morning sun with Dradevai draped over his chest. Asith had undone their hair, so it cascaded over their shoulders in soft waves formed by the way they always braided it back. He ran his fingers through it, feeling the warmth of Dradevai's skin and watching their relaxed, sleeping face.

They'd be awake soon, he was sure, for even if they'd been up late, Dradevai always woke shortly after the morning sun. Asith reveled in the calm, examining their dark eyebrows, sloped nose, and pouty lips. He loved them so dearly, the way their nose would scrunch up when they got frustrated or the wrinkle that formed in their forehead when they were far too confident for their own good. Asith loved Dradevai, and somehow, he hadn't even noticed it. It hadn't taken any explanation, they just returned his touch and revealed it to Asith before he'd even known himself, and he couldn't say he minded.

He never wanted to shy away from that feeling again, his fingers smoothing down Dradevai's hair as he let the tingle in his chest travel over his whole body. Asith let himself float with Dradevai in his arms.

"Good morning," Dradevai mumbled against his chest, their breath tickling Asith's skin. "My hair is too warm."

"Morning." Asith picked up some of their hair, feeling the sweat on their neck. "If you sit up, I'll braid it for you."

Dradevai nodded, adjusting to a sitting position so that Asith could sit up behind them. He then realized he only wore the feather around his neck, and Dradevai still wore only the bracelet Asith had given them in the Capitol. They needed the two magic wards to protect themselves, even when they were at their most alone.

He found the tie Dradevai had been using in their hair, put it between his teeth, and pulled all of Dradevai's hair back. It had gotten long enough in the front that they no longer had bangs. When he finished, he leaned forward to place a kiss on the back of Dradevai's head.

Dradevai giggled, leaning back into him for a moment before they pulled on their clothes. The two of them ate breakfast, sitting near the small fire they'd made and watching their water heat up.

When they got on their way, their tent safely in Asith's pack, they followed the map Pystra had given them. They scanned the area in long sweeps where the mountain just started to get rocky, looking for caves and listening for the sound of any wailing. It felt like they did that for weeks, but in reality, it had only been a few days. They were taking their time to peer into every crevice so that they didn't miss anything.

Asith's body was light and heavy all at once, the gravity of his father's situation weighing him down, but Dradevai's confidence and soothing words made his bones feel hollow like a bird's. When they didn't find the cave after the first day, Dradevai had Asith lay his head in their lap in the tent before bed, petting his hair and talking about their plan to fix everything in the morning.

By the second day, Asith had chewed off all his nails as they'd walked along a barren ridge. The trees seemed to laugh at him with every rustle, his thoughts lost to the worst possibilities. He tried to make dinner, but Dradevai had to take over. After, they settled themself between his legs, sitting by the fire as they leaned into his chest.

"Have you ever heard the story of the two bakers?" Dradevai asked. Asith wrapped his arms around their middle, feeling their warmth as he shook his head.

"I don't think I have."

"It was in a book in my hoard when I hatched." Dradevai looked up at the sky. "I read it over and over, but it starts with two bakers, each opening a new bakery in a small town."

Asith settled back against the tree he'd been sitting against, letting Dradevai lean on him more. Their weight made his breathing easier, and for a little while, he could forget about the way he shook all the time.

"One made lots of bread every day. You could always get a loaf when you stopped there, but the other made just a few, taking his time to make each one perfect." Dradevai's voice bounced, their eyes on the dwindling flames of their fire. "At first, everyone favored the baker who made lots of bread, happy to always have it when they needed it."

Asith furrowed his brow, thinking about the taste of bread. It had been a long while since he'd had any, and though his appetite had been mostly gone, his stomach rumbled at the thought. Dradevai pulled a piece of jerky from their pack and offered it to Asith. He took it and chewed on it as they continued.

"But, after a while, the people of the town found out their bread sometimes was underbaked or burnt. And as they did, they started going to the other baker, buying his perfect loaves and savoring each one that was so good, they wanted to eat every last piece."

Dradevai turned to Asith, smiling. "So, people would go to the slow baker's first each day, trying to get one of his few loaves, and when they couldn't, they would buy bread from the other baker."

"I don't think I would go back to buying burnt bread," Asith said.

Dradevai nodded, shifting to take one of Asith's hands between both of theirs. "That is exactly what happened. People stopped going to the baker who worked fast and made many loaves, choosing to buy no bread at all if they could not get one of the few perfect loaves. Eventually, the fast baker went out of business."

Asith hummed, resting his head on Dradevai's shoulder. "That's it? That's the whole story?"

"Yes." Dradevai shrugged. "The fast baker became a farmer, and the slow one had a very successful bakery that he passed on to his son."

Asith picked his head up and brushed his hair from his face. They kissed his forehead, tucking his hair behind his ear.

"I feel like you're trying to tell me something with that story." Asith leaned into Dradevai's hand. They chuckled softly.

"I thought that maybe it would make you feel better," Dradevai said, "or at least distract you for a moment."

Asith smiled. "Thank you."

"Of course." Dradevai cupped his cheek. "Your hair is getting long. I like it."

Asith hugged them tighter. Eventually, they scattered the fire and curled up in the tent together.

On the third day, Asith woke with the first sun and picked up his sword. He stood in the small space they had cleared the night before, walking himself through the forms as he had at Dradevai's hoard. He moved around the fire carefully, and when he finished, he found Dradevai staring at him from the door of the tent, with their head in their hands.

They left shortly after, following a hunting path that led to a nearby road. Asith kept his eyes on the rocks in the distance, listening for the sound of voices or armor clanking. Though he didn't hear anything, his eyes caught the movement of an animal along the rocks. A rabbit poked its head up above a boulder before they hopped atop it. It was eating a plant that had grown in a small patch of dirt gathered on the boulder. After that, he found he was keeping up better as they continued their search.

It was on the fourth day they found the hunters. Approaching a clearing, Asith noticed a collection of men with a covered wagon and realized what he'd thought was a clearing was actually a road. Dradevai smacked Asith's arm at the sight of them, hard enough that Asith almost said something and gave them away, but Dradevai pulled him down into the bushes. Dradevai led him along the road, managing to follow the group without being noticed, practically crawling through the bushes and among the trees as the hunters walked and talked amongst themselves.

Asith wasn't very good at walking quietly, keeping his pack from making noises, or stepping over sticks, but he did his best. That was a skill he would have to work on; otherwise, his anxiety was going to get the better of him anytime he had to keep out of sight. Dradevai moved like a skilled hunter, putting their feet down in the exact right place or always noticing when someone might be looking in their direction.

Occasionally, Dradevai would turn back and look at Asith or stop him if they thought he might be making too much noise. At one point, the bushes thinned, so they had to set their packs down to be quieter. They ducked lower and kept their eyes on the men for any sign that they might notice either of them.

Asith set his foot directly on a dry stick, feeling the snap and hearing the noise echo through the trees. He ducked into the bushes and held his breath, biting his lip. Dradevai was nowhere in sight, so Asith squeezed his eyes shut, hoping for the best.

"What was that?" one of the men asked. Another grunted like he didn't care, but Asith could hear the footfalls of another approaching him.

"I don't see anything." The voice sounded like it was directly above Asith, but he couldn't say if that was true. He opened his eyes but couldn't really see anything, so he just closed them again.

"Probably just a deer or something," the first man said. They started to walk again, and the sound of the wagon wheels rolling joined their footsteps.

Dradevai was suddenly at his side. They pressed a finger to their lips and led him to a spot where they could see better. Asith tried to follow their footsteps exactly, hoping that would prevent another situation with a stick.

As the men approached the cave, they were met by the same man in red, gold, and white Asith had seen while the griffon was dragged out of its cage. Since Asith could see him better in the clear light of day, he realized it was Chancellor Heskel Ashe from the Maeria Spire. He had spoken at the Stonegarde while Asith was there because he trained the mages who fought with them.

"I hope you brought me what I ordered this time." Heskel's voice was low, with a rumble to it from years of smoking tobacco "We are behind on orders."

One hunter grunted some form of agreement and lifted the cloth covering a cage, another pulling it from the back to remove it completely. Inside, a creature with the head of and wings of an owl and the body of a lion gnashed its beak and tried to chomp down on the bars. It screeched, Dradevai covering their ears as it made noises of distress and desperation.

"It's a little small, but it looks young." Heskel approached the cage, studying the creature carefully. Another man in simpler yet similar robes joined him with a pencil and a notepad, writing notes as Heskel mumbled, "Very well, bring it in."

The scribe waved, and several people walked out of the cave and took the caged creature inside. Heskel followed the wagon, leaving the scribe to hand over a bag of coins to the hunters.

Asith ground his teeth, for the hunters would have done that to Dradevai, what they probably did to his father. His pulse pounded in his temples, and he bit down on his lip hard enough to taste blood. He wanted to stop them; he wanted to stop all of them. He no longer cared about his relationship with the imprisoned; Asith wanted to free every creature inside the cave.

The hunters lingered by the entrance, passing around coins and talking about which tavern they'd go to in town. Then the wagon was returned to them, and they started down the road again. Asith's stomach rolled; he was looking at the cave he'd seen in his vision.

"I want to see something. I'll be right back." Dradevai disappeared before Asith could say a word to stop them, their form turning completely invisible. Asith clamped his mouth shut, resisting his urge to call out to Dradevai since it would give them both away. He hoped they didn't do something foolhardy.

Dradevai reappeared at his other side about five minutes later, startling him, but he managed to keep his voice down. They took his hand, pulling him all the way back to where they'd left their packs so that they could speak more freely.

"Don't do that again," Asith said.

"Sorry," Dradevai said earnestly, "but there are a lot of cages in there. And that man in the robes was talking about harvesting a creature."

"He what?" Asith's jaw dropped open. "We have to go in there, right now."

"We can't go in without a plan." Dradevai set their hand on Asith's shoulder. "What do we do if your father isn't there?"

"Vai, he said harvest. We can't wait." Asith looked back toward the cave. "He's in there; I know he is. We can create a diversion and sneak inside."

Dradevai's nose wrinkled in thought, and their fingers carefully toyed with their hair.

"Can you turn us invisible?" Asith asked. "Or should I disguise myself?"

Dradevai paused, then said, "I can only turn myself invisible, so disguise yourself. I'll be close. You just won't be able to see me."

"Okay, we'll look for my father first, but I want to release them all if I can."

"Me too." Dradevai set their jaw. "And what if the guards resist?"

Asith's throat went dry, he hadn't thought about it too clearly, but the guards were probably just doing their jobs. "Let's try not to kill them, just subdue them."

"I can do that. I might be able to just scare them away."

"That's a good idea. But how do we get the chain off him?"

"I might be able to do something." Dradevai pursed their lips and shook their head. "I wish I'd had more time to study something for that."

"It's okay, you'll find a way." Asith smiled and picked up his sword. "I can defend you while you do that."

"Last time you hurt someone with that," Dradevai said with a frown, examining the sword, "you hated yourself for weeks afterwards."

"I know, but I would do what I did that night again to protect you. I don't think I'll regret anything I do to save my father, either."

Dradevai studied him and then leaned in to press a kiss on Asith's lips. "Okay."

Asith brushed their front strands from their forehead, cupping their cheek in his hand. Dradevai placed their hand on Asith's and pressed their forehead against his. They stayed quiet for a few moments.

"Asith..." Dradevai's voice wavered, their fingers trembling. "Do you think they have dragons caged under the hold?"

Blood drained from Asith's face, hitting his feet and making him unsure of his balance. A ringing in his ears became the wails of the voice that had called for them in the holds.

"Dradevai, I am so sorry." Asith pulled away from them, his eyes peeled wide to the point that they were getting dry. "I'm so sorry I told you to ignore it."

Dradevai shook their head and swallowed, rubbing the bracelet on their wrist. "It's not your fault. I only just realized."

"We'll go back for them." Asith picked up Dradevai's hand. "I promise, we'll release them all."

Dradevai smiled and nodded, taking a deep breath before they rummaged through their bag for spell components. Asith inspected his armor, trying to decide if wearing it was worth it. He had a feeling he would need it, but he had to be quiet as he moved. He chewed his lip, eventually pulling on his scale mail, and tied his gambeson over it. Tying his grieves to his legs, he hoped it would all be enough to protect him in a fight.

They stalked through the trees back to the mouth of the cave. Two guards were posted at the front, who they needed to distract so that Asith could run in unnoticed. Dradevai explained they needed to separate, which made Asith shake, but then they would follow him inside. He trusted them, but as they crept along the bushes, his armor scraped and clacked, making his pulse jump each time.

"Are you scared?" Dradevai asked. The sun had started to set, the red and orange hues painted on Dradevai's skin. It was enough to draw Asith's attention away from the way his arms seemed to vibrate rather than shake.

"A little," Asith said.

"Me too." Dradevai looked up at Asith. "This is what they would have done to me."

That thought made Asith's hands clench the sword much harder, making him feel justified about killing that hunter all those weeks ago.

"It is," Asith said.

"There are probably more dragons than just your father in those cages." Dradevai's eyes were cast down at the ground and their jaw set like they were grinding their teeth.

Asith nodded. "There probably are."

Dradevai shifted their pouch of spell components at their side as if readying a weapon. "I know it isn't right, but just that thought makes me want to get rid of all of them."

Their mouth turned down, and they scrubbed their hands over their face. Dradevai hid in their hands, their entire form trembling.

Asith's hands stopped shaking, his focus entirely on Dradevai. Had he done this to them? Asith had brought them into the human world, and they were talking about freely killing people. When Dradevai picked their head up and met Asith's eyes, they were near tears. Their voice sounded sure at first, though Asith could see they were wrestling with the fact they'd thought it at all.

"I used to think the same thing about the dragons," Asith said. "The Blues and Greens, I mean. They would kill one of my friends, and I would want them all gone."

Dradevai swallowed, their voice wobbling. "They killed your friends?"

"There were five of us on my team." Asith could still remember their first deployment together, overeager and ready to prove themselves. "Delri and I are the only two left."

"So, this is a normal feeling?" Tears were running down their face. Asith nodded, and they took a deep breath. "We're not going to try to kill them."

"No," Asith said, "just subdue them. I promise."

Dradevai nodded. "Okay."

They took a shaky breath, wrapping themselves in a hug, so Asith carefully draped his arms around their shoulders. It was awkward with his armor on, but he pulled them close and let Dradevai lean into him.

When they pulled away, they leaned up and kissed him. "I'm going to split with you here. I'll meet you inside."

Asith swallowed the lump in his throat and kissed them again. They parted ways, and Dradevai slipped into the bushes on their way to the far side of the cavern entrance. Asith took a deep breath and started toward the tree line. He crouched among the bushes and crawled part of the way there.

The wait was long, like hours, though it was only a few minutes. He watched the two guards standing at the cavern, keeping his breathing slow. Asith had been the fastest runner in his troupe, so if he could outrun a Green flying directly at him, Asith could run the sixty or so feet into the cavern.

A loud pop sounded off like a firework, the noise echoing throughout the trees and rattling the birds. The guards looked at each other with confused expressions before three more bangs rang through the air. They turned toward it, looking in the opposite direction of Asith as he chanted. He disguised himself as a guard, his eyes locked on the two at the entrance as they moved toward the noise.

That was Asith's opportunity. The wind kicked up as he sprinted for the cave, holding his sword at his side so that it wouldn't knock on his armor. The rustling grasses concealed his footsteps as two more pops rang out.

"Go, I'll stay here." A guard gestured at the other, trying to get him to walk toward the woods further. The second guard groaned but started toward the trees. Asith was more than halfway to the cavern as the guards parted ways, completely in the open. His breathing shortened, his chest aching as the panic took him. The guard looked directly at him, his face twisting as Asith held up a hand like he was calling to the guard.

"Did you hear that?" Asith stumbled over his words. "I need to speak with Chancellor Ashe immediately."

"On what business?" The guard tried to get between Asith and the cavern, but Asith barreled forward. Another pop went off in the distance, and the second guard who had gone toward the trees yelped.

"Classified, I was sent by the Stonegarde." Asith gestured at the emblem on his gambeson. The guard scanned the trees where the other had entered the forest, which allowed Asith to side-step him. He ran for the cavern entrance, only about ten feet from it when the guard yelled back at Asith. Asith didn't hear what he said, wholly focused on getting inside, and put his head down as he slipped into the entrance.

He panted softly, swallowing air in hopes of calming down faster. He had to look like he blended in, and being calm was the best way to do that. Meanwhile, he examined the cages carefully; he hadn't gotten a good look at them when they'd been scrying on his father. Haunting beams of metal with runes carved around them loomed in the low light of whatever magic they had in the lanterns. In the scrying spell, everything had been fuzzy and warped slightly, as though he'd been looking at it through a lens of some sort. In that moment, the cave ahead of him looked unfamiliar since everything was sharp and detailed.

"Asith." He heard Dradevai's voice as he felt a touch on his arm. Asith jumped, but Dradevai, still invisible, pressed a hand to his mouth to stifle him. "Sorry."

"It's okay," Asith said.

They moved further down the corridor in hopes of getting away from the guards at the entrance.

"Does anything look familiar?" Dradevai whispered, wrapping a finger around one of Asith's. He resisted the urge to take their hand, wanting to feel grounded, but it would look strange.

"Sort of." Asith's eyes scanned the cages and caught the numbers near the top. The nearest cage read 10013. "We can follow the cage numbers. We're looking for 10037."

Asith was thankful he'd left his leather boots on rather than pulling on his scale boots. They were quieter as he pulled Dradevai along the rows of cages. After they'd gone to the far end, the cave curved into the mountain, the walls lined with cages along the corner. Asith couldn't imagine that being natural. Though it was dank like a cave should be, someone had made this cave for those cages.

Guards passed them every so often, each of them nodding at Asith, so he just nodded back. None of them seemed to find him suspicious, which meant that either the guards from the entrance hadn't gotten back or they had decided not to say anything. He had a feeling it was most likely the former, which meant they needed to move quickly.

Asith worried the guards all wore uniforms of the legion, which also patrolled the Capitol. Though, if Heskel Ashe was here, the facility was probably being run by Cairn or the Maeria Spire. Asith wasn't sure which, but it stuck in his mind as he walked along the cages.

Asith pulled Dradevai around another corner, and to his surprise, the cave started to look familiar. He heard a chain rattling against the stone, and the person he had seen previously shifted on the floor. They lay on their stomach, their head on one of their narrow arms. Asith's stomach churned, for he could see in the person's face they'd only been fed enough to keep them alive.

He stopped and tapped Dradevai on the shoulder before walking directly up to the cage. The person had white hair, similar to Asith's, but it looked damaged and dirty. Their skin was the same pale color Asith's was. When the person shifted slightly, picking their head up and revealing a ring on their left hand, Asith gasped. The more Asith looked him over, the more he knew that was his father. He was gaunt, dirty, and desperately trying to move closer.

"I see you," he whispered, "the invisible one."

Dradevai dropped the invisibility spell and began working on the spell to release the magic on the chain. Asith drew his sword, standing at their back.

"Pherrosh?" his father asked.

"We're here to help," Dradevai mumbled. "Is there anyone else we need to let out?"

They chanted, and Asith heard them draw on the cage with a piece of chalk. Asith backed up, eyes trained on the far corner where the guards had been emerging from as they made their rounds. It seemed like they walked the caves in circles in a single direction. If they were lucky, they might avoid them entirely.

"Everything." His father sounded tired. "There's a way, a switch."

"We can do that." Asith turned toward him. "You first."

Dradevai's chanting sped up, which, from what Asith could tell, meant they were about halfway through. Two guards came around the corner, so Asith, in a flash of panic, tried to stand like he was guarding Dradevai.

"There are people coming." Asith looked down at Dradevai, and they nodded without looking away from their work. Asith looked back at the guards, and they were pointing at them. Asith waved and nodded in their direction, hoping it would put them at ease, but the guards shouted at them, then sprinted at Asith and Dradevai.

Asith surveyed the area, spotting a caged creature he couldn't identify that had large talons and a beak but its body didn't quite look like a bird. Asith ran for it, and it screeched when he got close. No spell circle surrounded the cage like his father's, so it was his best bet on creating a distraction.

Asith placed the pommel of his sword against the lock that held the chain on the cage and cast a heating spell until he could break the lock away. Once it broke, he tugged on the door hard, worried that it was held shut with magic, but the door swung open and Asith ducked out of the way of what he could see was a griffon. But it was oversized and seemed off in ways, missing feathers or entire claws on its back legs. Luckily, he had chosen the right cage, because the griffon flew past him and headed toward the guards.

More guards were coming from the other side, but the griffon swooped down onto the two closest guards.

"No, no!"

Asith turned to see Dradevai's chalk explode in their hand, causing them to whip their hand back and shake it. The spell's glow faded, and the shimmering orange light that came with Dradevai's magic disappeared with the wind.

"Vai, cover me." Asith ran back toward his father's cage, his sword raised above his head. Dradevai stood, getting out of Asith's way as they turned their attention toward the guards not occupied by the griffon. They pulled some sand from their pouch and chanted, and a gust of wind burst from their fingers.

The sand swept through the cave, whipping through the air and knocking the guards backward. Asith then brought his sword down on the lock of his father's cage. The lock shuddered but didn't break, so Asith hit it again and again, his hands buzzing from the vibration. On the final hit, Asith nearly fell into his swing, and the lock broke away, with the door swinging inward.

He stumbled into the cage, his father's eyes wide as Asith dropped to his knees and examined the spell circle on the ground. Asith wouldn't be able to remove the spell if Dradevai couldn't, but he might be able to destroy it. Reading the runes as quickly as he could, he found something vital and rubbed the lines. They were painted on, so he searched his pockets and pulled out his mother's thimble. He didn't want to, but he slipped it onto his finger and pressed it into the ground where the rune was drawn and scratched the paint away.

The circle glowed and then crackled, the magic destabilizing until it popped like a bubble. His mother's thimble was destroyed. But his father was already beginning to look less weak. He was still thin, but his skin held a vibrancy that hadn't been there before. It was as if the spell had been making him sluggish.

Asith barely had a chance to take it in, though, because one guard was barking at the other to not leave him with the griffon. He swiveled his head toward the sound, and the guard was running for Dradevai, who was focused on their wind spell. He looked back at his father, the chain still around his ankle.

"Vai!" Asith yelled.

"Go," his father ordered. "I can get this off myself."

Asith took his word for it, so he grabbed his sword again and sheathed it. He ran full speed at the guard who was drawing their sword. His shoulder connected with the pauldron on the guard's shoulder, and pain radiated up Asith's arm. But that bumped the guard away from Dradevai, and Dradevai fell, too, their spell wavering and then fading completely as they lost their focus.

"Sorry." Asith got on his feet.

Dradevai shook their head. "Keep them busy. I'll clear us a path." Dradevai ran toward the two guards covered in sand trying to collect themselves.

Asith drew his sword as the guard jumped up. When he approached Asith, he noticed the guard's dark purple skin peeking out of their helmet and their yellow eyes. They took the first swing and managed to throw Asith back. They were a little bit stronger with a sword than Asith was since he had never fought like that for real. The Stonegarde had them train in hand-to-hand of course, but they fought dragons primarily.

Asith knocked the guard's sword to the side and thrust, trying not to hit anything vital. He was only trying to stall. Their swords clashed against each other, but that time, when they threw Asith's sword to the side, Asith followed with a swift kick to their chest. It was enough to send them stumbling back, but they were still on their feet.

Lucky for him, the griffon smacked the guard he'd been fighting with its wing, and Asith caught a glimpse of the other guard lying on the ground in the distance, unmoving with their helmet on the floor.

He turned to the guard he'd been fighting again, but they weren't looking at Asith anymore. Two more guards came around the corner on the other side of the griffon.

The guard on the ground got up, and they were covered in blood, the griffon's talons having done a number on them. Asith jumped back as the wounded guard took an upward swing at Asith, straining against the gashes the talons had left in their torso. He caught the blade on his grieves like he would deflect a dragon's teeth. The bloody guard yelled, swinging their sword rashly.

Asith remembered a spell that Dradevai had taught him back when he first started learning. He hadn't tried it yet, but it would bring forth a wave of fire. It wasn't really hot enough to hurt anything, but he thought it might startle the guard as it hit them.

He cast it, and blood spattered the ground as the guard recoiled, though the flames passed over them without so much as singing their hair. Asith had made the wrong choice in letting the wounded guard get so close, now it was easier for them to box him in. The guard who had been trying to subdue the griffon realized this too, and now they were running to join the fray with Asith. The griffon had flown off from what Asith could tell, probably deciding that it wasn't worth it.

Two more guards were also running toward them, and a third set was rounding the corner. Asith felt like a caged animal suddenly, looking behind him to find Dradevai, but the wounded guard swung his sword at Asith. They grazed Asith's arm, his gambeson tearing open as he tried to step backward, and he tried to think of a spell that could help him.

However, the chain on his father shattered like glass, grabbing all their attention. His father turned into a sleek dragon, smaller than Dradevai but still intimidating in size, and hopped toward him and the group of guards.

His father's foot landed next to him, knocking the guard away and hiding Asith under his chest as he swung his tail into the group of guards behind them. The hairs on Asith's head stood on end, and he smelled sulfur in the air. He looked up to see his father's mouth glowing, then he ducked on instinct. Lightning coming from his father's mouth lit the entire room with a bright flash, hitting the guards in the distance. They writhed and dropped like rocks, smoking slightly.

The remaining guards turned tail, and frankly, Asith didn't really blame them. But he was fearful they would come back, so he tried to find Dradevai. As he stepped away from his father's leg, his form shrunk back to his gaunt, smaller shape. His hair was at his shoulders, he wore rags that looked like they were once fine clothes, and he doubled over into Asith.

"That maybe wasn't the best idea." His father swayed, even as Asith wrapped an arm around him, pulling one of his father's arms over his head to support him.

"Are you okay? Can you walk?" Asith could feel his father's ribs under his hands, but at least his father was standing. Even if he was holding onto Asith, he could move, and his eyes were sharp as he looked down the hallway.

"A little." He shifted more weight onto Asith. "We need to release the rest."

"How do we do that?" Dradevai appeared on his father's other side. The guards near them had been wrapped up in stone. They were both trying to wrestle themselves out of the boxes that only left their heads free, but the stone held fast.

"There's a switch in the middle of the next hall, before it opens up into the testing area." His father glanced between them. "Who are the two of you?"

"We can explain later." Asith started in the direction his father had directed them. "We need to move fast if the switch is deeper in the cave."

"Right." His father's voice was low and confused still, and as they rounded the corner, another group of guards was securing chains on the griffon. Asith held up a hand, following his gut instinct to keep the guards away.

"Look the other way." When they did so, Asith chanted quickly, which created a light that emanated from the griffon's chest. It grew bright enough to blind, Asith amplifying the spell he'd use for reading in the dark with another spell Dradevai had taught him, stitching them together like two pieces of fabric. The guards yelled, and they lost hold of the griffon. It to flew away as the guards stumbled.

More guards spotted them as they approached another turn in the cave. His father hobbled ahead toward some mechanical device covered in runes on one wall. Asith let him go, understanding they would need to keep the guards at bay, and Dradevai transformed into their large Bronze form.

Asith marveled at them as their chest expanded. They stood over Asith protectively, the same way his father had. Then, as they breathed in, the guards faltered. The flames licked at Dradevai's nose, their elegant face covered in what looked to be soot, and fire cascaded across the entire area in front of them.

They barely missed the guards, the flames curling against the stone and rising again, which started some small fires with the half-dead foliage growing on the cave floor. They must have done it on purpose. Once they realized they hadn't been hit though, the guards began to advance towards them.

"Don't you dare." Their chest expanded again, and the guards reeled back. Asith turned toward the way they came, seeing a few guards rounding that corner. Dradevai didn't need to breathe any more fire, though, because his father grabbed a switch and threw it down.

A spark flew out, and a magical static fell over the area like a piece of fabric floating slowly onto a table. Then, all at once, it reversed, a wave drawing back toward the control panel his father had been adjusting. Asith nearly fell backward when a weight hit his chest, and the panel sizzled and exploded, sending a flurry of sparks raining down on the floor. The whole system backfired, and a surge lit up the cages and burst them open, some of the doors flying free from their hinges.

Asith's ears rang as creatures of all shapes and sizes swarmed the guards. Dire wolves, harpies, and hippogriffs were either escaping or attacking the guards. Dradevai turned small again as Asith's father returned to his side.

"Let's go," Asith said, getting his arm around his father again, and that time, his father threw an arm around Asith's shoulders, nodding.

"I've wanted to do that for so long." His father genuinely looked alive, the light in his eyes returning as he hobbled alongside Asith and Dradevai.

"Is the front the only exit?" Dradevai asked, leading them away from the angry creatures and desperate guards. Some guards, upon seeing them, tried to pursue them, but the creatures got in their way. Another dragon, copper in color, was spitting acid on anything that tried to stop it from flying away. Asith didn't see a single Blue or Green, though.

"I don't know. They knocked me out whenever they moved me." His father was keeping step better; the adrenaline must have done him some good.

"Then that's our only option," Dradevai said.

They found the first cave where they'd entered, and Dradevai chanted more loudly, which seemed to keep eyes off them. They only stopped when they reached the entrance they had first come through, but a pile of stones covered it entirely.

"How did that happen?" Asith asked. They should have heard something as loud as rocks falling over the entrance, but there were so many creatures screeching and braying and bleating.

"Shit." His father turned around, looking over the mess of creatures and guards.

"I can deal with this." Dradevai stood taller. "Keep them off me."

They stepped toward the stone and took a deep breath. They made a wide motion with their arms, then hit the wall with both their hands, and the rock began to move to the side. A tunnel formed all the way to the other side, and Dradevai expanded it so that they could fit through.

"Go ahead of me." Dradevai looked at Asith and his father.

"Thank you." Asith's father moved past Dradevai, smiling.

"Asith," Dradevai said, "follow him."

"I can't leave you here" Asith stood at the opening of the tunnel.

"Go, I'll follow as soon as I can," Dradevai snapped. "He needs your help, and I can't leave this place like this. There were other dragons. I have to make sure they get out."

"Vai…" Asith's limbs were shaking.

Their fists tightening and arms shaking, they stepped toward Asith, with eyes still locked on his. "I have to." Dradevai grabbed Asith's arm and pushed him toward the tunnel. "Go. If I can't find you, I'll meet you back in South Cairn."

Asith stopped Dradevai, grabbing their shoulders to press a kiss on their lips because it was all he could do. Kissing them had worked to get them to follow before. It might not work that time, but he was desperate.

The look on Dradevai's face when Asith pulled away said it all, though. Dradevai wasn't going to leave without the other dragons. They would die trying to get them to safety. Just as Asith would do for Dradevai or Delri.

"I'll wait until sunrise where we left our packs and then leave if you haven't come back." Asith couldn't hesitate much longer. He had to let Dradevai go, and he needed to help get his father to safety.

Dradevai hiccupped, tears streaming down their face, and they swallowed, shaking off whatever fear they still had.

"Go, please, you're making me want to change my mind."

CHAPTER 21

Asith ran down the tunnel, unable to look back because he knew he'd go after Dradevai if he did. Their crying face was burned into his brain, the feeling of their soft lips still lingering on his own.

After he got out of the tunnel, his father spun to face him. No guards were in sight, and it was quiet compared to the commotion of the cavern. Asith took a breath of the fresh air as the wind rustled through the trees and chilled his skin.

When he looked at his father, he was surprised to find himself nearly looking in a mirror. His mother was right. His father had the same sloping jawline and slight point to his chin, his cheekbones high but more exaggerated by how thin he currently was. He even had the same shape to his eyes and hairline, the only difference being that Asith had his mother's green eyes.

"Where's our third?" he asked.

"They're going to try to help the other dragons." Asith looked back at the tunnel. "We need to go."

His father looked at him like he might ask if Asith was sure, but he spared Asith that question. He nodded. "Let's go."

Asith led his father into the darkened woods, still no sign of guards, but the occasional flying creature escaped into the night sky. He helped his father walk until they were about the same distance from where he and Dradevai had started. He poked around carefully, looking for the marks on the trees they had left. It was difficult in the dark, but Asith eventually found their backpacks and supplies in some bushes.

His father was panting, so Asith set him down near a tree and pulled open Dradevai's spell book. He had once seen a way to make a tent that would be hard to see.

He set the book down, going through the ritual until they formed a small dome overhead, which also lit up the small area. While they could see out, no one could see them. They would only see the tent.

"Who are you?" His father shifted, observing the tent and then Asith closely in the light.

Asith offered him a waterskin, which he gladly took and drank his weight's worth, which wasn't much. His father was thin, so horribly thin.

"Your name is Listesh, right?" Asith asked. He didn't know how else to get into this.

His father nodded, still drinking, but he looked confused.

"My name is Asith Evrouin. My mother's name is Maryan. How much do you remember?"

His father dropped the waterskin, splashing Asith and the ground with water. He scooped it up and closed it, then examined Asith carefully.

"That…" His father looked skeptical, his eyes darting over Asith's crouched form and landing on the sword at his side. "It couldn't have been that long. I couldn't have been there for that many years."

Asith took a deep breath. He couldn't really think and didn't even know where to begin.

"I'm sorry." Asith's stomach lurched as his father's face screwed up in horror and tears streamed down his face, cleaning his dirty skin as he began to sob.

"Asith, you were this big when I saw you last." He held up shaking hands to show the size of an infant.

Asith closed his eyes; he couldn't watch his father go through that.

"Look at you, your mother raised you so well. It's nice to meet you." His father's voice shook around a sob. "Asith, it's nice to meet you again."

"It's nice to finally meet you too." Asith's voice sounded more hoarse than his father's, all his feelings caught in his throat.

Asith opened his eyes, and his father was clutching his ring finger, petting the spot where a ring would sit. Then, after a moment, a ring just like the one his mother always wore faded into existence around the spot he was rubbing. His father sobbed, his jaw clenched in a way that looked painful. Asith didn't know what to do.

"They took your whole life from me." His father seemed to be thinking out loud. "And Maryan, she must think I left her."

"They didn't take my whole life from you. I'm still here." He thought of Dradevai as he reached out and set his hand on his father's shoulder. "Don't worry about Mama. She'll understand."

He didn't feel comfortable speaking for his mother even if he was sure she missed his father. She wouldn't still be wearing the ring if she didn't.

"You're right. You're right. I'm sorry." His father hiccupped and nodded as he wiped at his face.

"None of this is your fault." Asith frowned.

"I know." His father looked up at him. "That's the worst part."

Asith looked away, and then some strange form of relief washed over his body. His skin tingled, hands shaking as he tried to avoid crying.

"I know it's not much to offer," Asith said, "but knowing that you had wanted to come back to us makes this easier for me."

His father studied him and then nodded. "All I ever wanted was to get back to the two of you."

Asith felt tears trickle down his face, so he wiped them away. The momentary relief was nice, but Dradevai hadn't turned up yet. It hadn't been very long, but he really hoped they would turn around as soon as they helped the dragons out.

"Your friend," his father started, "is he—"

"They." It came out of Asith's mouth on instinct.

His father nodded. "Are they a Gold?"

Asith shook his head. "No, a Bronze."

His father examined his face, some confusion in his eyes, and said, "They're young."

"They are. They're a little bit younger than me, I think."

"Their first century," his father mumbled, glancing at his hands in his lap. "So we haven't been wiped out, then."

"I don't think so. When we used the scrying spell to find you, a dragon named Pystra helped us do that."

"Good. Then the Graveyard Trees might still be there."

"You know of it?" Asith asked. His father nodded again.

"I grew up there." His father wrapped his arms around his knees, appearing small and frail. "That's where I was trying to go. My sister will be there. My parents are probably gone..."

Asith crossed his legs. They were going to be there longer than expected, so he should at least somewhat distract himself from waiting for Dradevai. "We wanted to go there next. Dradevai wanted to try to find any family they might have."

"They weren't raised there?" His father picked up the waterskin and drank more.

Asith shook his head, picking up his bag and pulling out the jerky to offer him some. "Do you think their parents might be there?"

His father took a deep breath, taking the jerky from Asith and looking at the ground. "They looked like someone I grew up with. I thought they were she when I first saw them."

"Do you think she could be their mother?" Asith leaned toward his father, the conversation consuming his mind. It was better than worrying over where Dradevai was.

"I think it might be possible. Before I met your mother, I had been with two friends." His father chewed on the jerky slowly. "However, we were being followed by hunters and got separated trying to get away."

Asith frowned at his hands, and a knot formed in his stomach. His limbs stiffened as the voice of the ghost crept into his head.

"It said, 'My child,'" Asith said. "It told me to take care of them."

"What?" His father stopped chewing.

"The voice under the Maeria Spire kept calling out to Dradevai. It kept begging for their child to come to them." Asith pressed his hands to his face. "And I made them leave her."

"Hey, hey." His father's eyes were wide, and he rubbed Asith's shoulder. "Asith, it's okay. If she's in another facility, we'll go get her."

Asith took a deep breath and nodded, but a sob shook his body. He wanted Dradevai back, and he needed to take them to the Capitol so that they could free their mother. They needed to go as soon as they could.

"The Graveyard Trees." Asith rubbed his eyes, then looked at his father. "Can you tell me about them?"

His father nodded and spoke. Asith did his best to listen to his stories, but it was hard. It got harder when an hour had passed, and he still couldn't even hear any evidence of someone coming to join them, even the sound of wings in the air.

To his credit, his father seemed to keep talking just to distract Asith in the moment, his voice soothing and slow in the odd light of the magic tent. It reminded him of when his mother would read to him at night, and he wondered if maybe that was something she learned to do from his father.

His voice only stopped when a distant explosion shook the forest. The sound of falling rocks that followed made Asith jump to his feet.

"Shit," Asith muttered.

His father was on his feet as well and looked at Asith for a moment before running back into the woods toward the cave.

"Come on. We can't leave them alone," his father called.

Asith followed, catching up to his father quickly, because even moving at his fastest, his father wasn't in great shape. Asith offered him his arm, letting his father lean on him and slowing their pace so that he could keep going.

They were nearing the break in the tree line when they saw swarms of guards chasing the escaped creatures disappearing into the forest. His father pulled him behind a tree as they panted.

Asith leaned around the tree carefully, listening to the commotion, and heard Heskel Ashe yelling. Then he walked down the road near them, close enough that Asith could see and hear him clearly.

"How did this happen?" His voice sounded hoarse.

The scribe Asith had seen earlier was close behind. "I-I don't know. Somebody reversed the power and caused a surge and it—"

Heskel spun around and backhanded the scribe, the man stumbling backward and falling. He looked up at Heskel with eyes wide and mouth hanging open. Blood was pouring down his cheek from a wound Heskel's rings had created.

"Shut up." Heskel growled. "My containment system was flawless. There is no way someone could have reversed the enchantment, understand?"

The scribe nodded, his hand pressed to the cut on his cheek.

"Good." Heskel straightened and adjusted his robes. "Now, we have to get as many of the creatures back as we can, especially the dragons. If we don't meet our quotas, the council will use it as an excuse to try to push me out again."

"Yes sir." The scribe got off the ground, his eyes darting away from Heskel and catching Asith's briefly. Asith tucked himself behind the tree again, looking at his father and pressing his finger to his lips.

"What are you looking at? Is something there?" Heskel's voice suddenly sounded so loud, so close. Asith pressed a hand over his mouth, trying to stand still.

"No, sir," the scribe lied smoothly.

Asith glanced at them again, but he stopped himself from moving around the tree in case Heskel was looking. His hand fell away as his brow furrowed, because he recognized the scribe's voice. He didn't understand, it didn't look like Eroan, but it only made sense that it was Eroan since he lied to protect him. His thoughts went entirely fuzzy then, getting that wool feeling in his head. Eroan was working with Heskel.

Out of the corner of his eye, Asith saw them storm down the road away from him and his father. He turned to his father then, his thoughts shifting to Dradevai.

"Who were those two, do you know?" Asith asked.

His father looked at them over Asith's shoulder. "That mage runs the facility. The other is his assistant, I think."

"What were they doing with all of you?" Asith leaned toward his father, lowering his voice. "Did the assistant ever hurt you?"

"They would harvest pieces of our bodies to sell for mages to use in their rituals and magic." His father shook his head. "No, he kept out of things, just there to take notes and track orders."

"Okay." Asith looked at the ground, scrunching up his nose. At least Eroan wasn't torturing his father, but he still didn't like that he had been there. "We need to find Dradevai."

He stepped around the tree, searching for any sign of Dradevai in the area. They would have had to come that way to return to their backpacks, but they could have easily gone around and double backed. With Heskel being so close, Asith sort of hoped they had chosen the latter.

His father nodded. "Is this the only way they could have come?"

Asith's stomach hit the ground like a rock as he caught the glint of something silvery in the moonlight. Asith scooped it up, his fingers sliding over the stones and taking in the silvery spindles. It had dented somewhat, as if it got damaged when it fell on the ground, and a few of the pieces of silver wire that made the shape of the wing had broken.

He looked around again, hoping to find Dradevai hidden among the trees and bushes. As Asith scanned the nearest path, he made eye contact, not with Dradevai, but with a guard who was searching the woods for the escaped creatures. His lungs tightened, and his eyes grew wide as the guard turned back to his group, shouting for them to help him grab Asith's father. Asith pulled his father back the way they came.

"I don't think that matters," Asith said. "Come on."

Asith tightened his grip on the bracelet and raced through the trees and bushes as fast as he could, but his father's panting made him slow down. Asith hoped Dradevai was at their meeting spot so that they could all go home together. But as they approached the little clearing, they were painfully alone, and he could still hear the guards who had started to follow.

His father bent over, resting his hands on his knees for support to catch his breath. Asith needed to get him out of there. If the guards came down on them, they'd be overwhelmed in a moment.

"We're going." He picked up his pack and then looped Dradevai's over one shoulder, leaving the rest of his armor behind.

"Are you sure?" His father stood fast in his spot; he didn't look like he wanted to leave Dradevai behind.

"Yes." Asith couldn't lose both of them, and he didn't want what

Dradevai had done for them to be in vain. "Dradevai is smart, and they can fly. We can't. We need to go."

His father looked back toward the guards and then nodded at Asith. "I'll follow you."

Asith cast the only spell he knew that might send Dradevai a message. A flame fired high in the air and exploded fifty or so feet above them. It was hopefully above the tree line; Asith could only throw it so far. It distracted the guards, though, sending them in the direction of the flames as he led his father back down the mountain.

"Here." His father reached forward and turned them invisible with a spell like the one Dradevai had used, but it flickered. Sometimes, they would be fully revealed, and other times, they'd be a hazy outline among the trees. It still helped, and Asith held onto him as they fled to the nearest town they could get to.

They slept in a magic tent his father created on the outskirts, somewhat hidden from the trail, and they took turns on watch. The following day, Asith led his father through the town, both in disguise, and stopped to buy more food. Asith had given his father the rest of the food he had, so he bought as much as he could.

When they left, they passed the dragon knight outpost Asith had seen while scrying. His father was walking better with more food in his stomach. And, since he was away from the spell that was weakening him, he felt well enough to hunt deer for his next meal.

After two days of heading toward South Cairn, they stopped for a day in the dense woods at the very north of Cairn so that his father could devour as much game as possible. At first, he could only catch small animals, like rabbits and mice with the occasional rat. They stayed an extra half day there, Asith letting his father have the morning to catch a couple deer before they continued. The following day, he looked even better, his magic more stable, a shine returning to his hair and skin. He became more talkative as well, telling Asith about his childhood in the Graveyard Trees.

"I found a yew tree." His father held the branch of a yew tree in one hand as he approached their small fire, his eyes bright. He took a knife near his pack and whittled the branch into a long, crooked staff. His father often assumed Asith knew more about magic than he did, but it didn't really bother Asith at all. It was nice that he wasn't inclined to talk down to him even if Asith was still a beginner.

"What are you going to do with it?" Asith tilted his head as his father removed the bark and added it to the fire.

"I can use it to make a wand." His father glanced at him. "We have yew in our ancestry."

"In our ancestry?" Asith did not follow, more so than usual.

His father nodded, gliding the knife over the piece of wood to shape it how he liked, then snapped off the jagged end to make a more intentional point.

"Many of our ancestors rooted as yew trees when they passed." His father smiled. "I am used to casting with a wand to focus my magic. If I have one, I can get us home faster."

Asith sat up. "Can I help?"

His father asked Asith to gather some ash from their fire and draw a circle on a piece of parchment. When he had finished carving the wand, he laid it on the paper and chanted as he sprinkled the ash over them. His eyes shined silver like polished metal, and a flash emanated from the wand when he finished. The ash adhered to the side of the wood, wrapping it in a hardened layer of white and gray. It was about the width of a broomstick but only about two feet long, with a shock of lightning running from one end to another in the ash.

"It's not perfect, but it should work." His father scooped the wand up, looking at Asith. "We could go tonight."

"Then let's go." Asith gathered their few things, his father scattering the fire. Once Asith had packed his bag, he slipped it over his shoulders and moved to pick up Dradevai's, but his father stopped him. He put it on, telling Asith he could carry it for a while.

His father stood next to the remnants of the fire, with his wand in his left hand, and steadied his breathing. He straightened his back and started a fast chant that didn't sound familiar to Asith at all. He moved the wand in a calculated sweep, creating a glowing blue circle, which made Asith's hair rise and filled the air with static. The circle sparked, and electricity ran along it as an image appeared in the center. It showed a collection of trees with a small boulder sitting near one side, the clearing full of the grasses of the southern part of Cairn.

"You through first." His father's arms shook, straining to keep the portal open. That magic was unlike anything Asith had ever seen, and as he stepped through the portal, it did not differ from stepping through a doorway. His father followed right after him, his arms dropping to his sides and the wand falling from his hand as the portal shut in the blink of an eye.

His father doubled over, so Asith offered his arms for support. He panted softly, not as badly as when Asith had first met him, but he looked tired. Wiping at the sweat on his brow, he thanked Asith softly and gathered himself.

"Where are we?" Asith asked.

His father looked at the boulder only about half his height, and he smiled. "The last place I saw you and your mother."

He looked around the little clearing and walked toward a nearby road. Asith followed, picking up his father's wand and keeping on his heels.

Asith recognized the road, for it was about half a day's walk from South Cairn. A small sign stood in the fork, the one pointing south, directing them home.

When they walked into South Cairn, the second sun was coming up behind them. If Dradevai wasn't there, Asith couldn't face his empty house just yet, so he led his father to his mother's instead.

He knocked. "Mama, it's me."

His mother swung the door open, and relief washed over her face as she wrapped her arms around Asith tightly. He hugged her, letting himself sink into his mother's warmth.

"Asith, there were people here—" his mother started, but the words died in her throat. Her eyes grew large and soft as she caught sight of his father. Her arms slipped from Asith's shoulder, and she stumbled into his father's arms.

They both cried, and Asith took a step back, letting them have their time. But he peered into his mother's house. There was no sign Dradevai was there, and he feared what he'd find inside his home.

"Asith." His mother reached out, pulling him into the hug with his father. "Asith, what is going on?"

"We found Dad," Asith said. "Dradevai and I went looking for him, and we found him."

Asith leaned into his parents, the tears hitting his cheeks. He wiped his face, letting them hold him. Then his mother looked up and past his head.

"Where is Dradevai?" she asked.

"I'm hoping at my house…" Asith turned in the direction of his home.

His mother nodded slowly, her hand going back to shut the door behind her. "Let's look now. There were people here looking for you both."

"Who?" Asith looked at his mother as she pushed Asith toward his house.

"They were from the Maeria Spire." She slowed her walk when she realized his father was not keeping up. "They said they were investigating a break-in. Asith, what did you and Dradevai do?"

Asith's stomach dropped to his feet, his hands trembling. They thought no one had seen them, and as each of his ribs rattled in his chest, Asith thought of Dradevai and Delri. If someone was after him, then they were after all three of them.

"It's okay." His father's voice was low. "Dradevai will be here, and we'll go to the Graveyard Trees together."

He couldn't feel his skin, his body numbing as he followed his mother. When they reached his home, his mother didn't hesitate to unlock and swing Asith's door open before stepping into the house quickly.

"Dradevai?" she called.

Asith knew there wouldn't be a response. He stepped into his small home as his mother spun around to face him. They were alone in the room until his father entered.

"We can't wait to leave," Asith said.

Tears were streaming down his cheeks as his mother spoke to him, but he didn't hear anything his mother was saying. The ground was falling from underneath him, his body collapsing in on itself finally after days of adrenaline keeping him going. Asith had hoped they were in South Cairn, but if they were, they would have told his mother or been at his house.

The tears turned into sobs, and he let himself fold into the ground as his mother and father tried to reach out to him.

24th of Zepha

The cold air whipped at his ears, his socks wet, and his hair had fro-zen over in places. Asith scanned the snowy ground, his eyes watering in the wind and cold because he'd given his mother his goggles. She wasn't used to being exposed to the elements, and they needed to keep moving or they'd be taken over by the snow on the clear ridge. Thankfully, they weren't above the tree line yet, which meant they were heading for a clus-ter of dense fir trees, their needles bending from the weight of the snow with deep wells at the base of their trunks.

"Right here." His father led them just off the path they'd been follow-ing, pointing as his hair whipped around like a bird attacking his head. He had used a portal to get them as near as he could, but his father hadn't traveled by foot near the Graveyard Trees often and it wasn't safe to open a portal inside of it because of the magic protecting it.

Asith helped his mother trudge through the snow, wishing they had stopped to buy better supplies for walking in the weather, but it was too late. He lifted her out of a bank and threw her over, his mother swearing at him to be gentler. It made his father laugh, which was the first time any of them really had since they'd arrived home.

"Don't you laugh at me." His mother growled, trying to pick herself up and dig her way out of the snow. His father stopped and smiled as he offered his hands to help pull her up.

Asith tripped and fell face-first into the bank. He groaned and crawled his way through the messy path his mother had made. His parents helped pull him to his feet, the powdery snow clinging to every part of his body, and where it didn't, it melted on his skin.

His father led him under an arch created by the fir trees, snow hanging off it heavily. The trees deadened the sound of the wind that howled along the ridge, and the scent of fresh pine lay over them like a blanket, remind-ing Asith of how Dradevai's hoard had smelled. While snow gathering on either side came up to Asith's waist, a clear path made of cobblestones cut straight through the trees and led farther up the ridge. When Asith stepped on them, heat seeped through his boots that warmed his soaking-wet socks.

"This road looks like it was made by Sula themself." His mother fell to her knees and sat back on her feet as she took a breath. Asith had to agree; if the god of travel had blessed any path, it was that one.

His father chuckled. "I guess Sula imparted their love for finely made roads upon the dragons."

Asith ran his mittens over his hair, trying to shake the ice away. His mother held up the goggles to him, so Asith took them and pressed the warmed leather to his face. He closed his eyes and tried to pretend they were Dradevai's soft hands instead. He let himself live in the fantasy, only opening his eyes when his mother stood up. Her pack rattled and clanked every time she moved, a collection of various pots and pans she refused to leave behind clattering against her rulers and curves for sewing. They had filled the seemingly endless bag Dradevai had made in the Capitol with the rest of her fabric, so she had no other place to put the cookware.

They walked up the cobblestone path, the trees providing some protection from the wind, but the air was still bitterly cold. Asith took his scarf off and tried to shake the water off it before he gave up and carried it. It probably wouldn't dry until he could hang it by a fire.

The path wound around hills until it eventually became a switchback. It slowed their pace, the air thin enough to make it difficult to breathe, and the path was steep, but at least it was clear. His father didn't seem as bothered by the lack of air, so he took his mother's pack from her. They came around the final bend close to midday, though it didn't look like it because of the cloud cover and shade from the trees.

Asith's jaw fell, his eyes growing wide as he halted. The bend opened into a wide clearing, the snow blowing over it in soft folds, making it look like a blanket being thrown on a bed. Out of the snow rose a row of trees over fifteen feet wide each, with snow clinging to the reddish-brown bark. The trees climbed up into the sky and towered over the others in the area, seeming to become one farther up, but Asith wasn't sure if that was because he couldn't see it clearly.

His father had described that the large trees made up the walls, but silence overtook him as he absorbed the scene in front of him. He never could have pictured that in his mind without seeing it.

"Welcome to my home," his father said. Tears rolled down his cheeks, and his mother took his hand. "I always wanted to bring you both here."

Asith couldn't help but smile, looking at the large gate with some form of catwalk above it. Several bundled-up guards sat on it, looking down at Asith and his parents. When his father led them toward the gates, one turned into a small Iron dragon, their feathers a beautiful slate gray, and fluttered to the ground to meet them.

"Your business?" The dragon turned back into their smaller form, a heavy duster covering most of their body, with no clear sign of a uniform other than a broach pinned on their left shoulder.

"My name is Listesh, Finder of Hope." His father stood a little taller than the dragon. "This is my wife and son. We are fleeing Cairn for safety."

"Proof, please." The dragon adjusted their hat, short gray hair peeking beneath it. Asith's father transformed, and a flurry of static filled the air as he sat next to his mother. He wrapped his tail around her and Asith, his large paws hidden by the snow. He was still missing patches of feathers from the facility harvesting him.

The Iron dragon nodded and turned back to the gate, shouting up to the guards. They turned back into the slate gray dragon, only standing as tall as Asith before they fluttered back to their post. Massive planks of wood pressed together and simply floated over their heads as they walked under it. Asith took a deep breath and smelled the woods around them as he followed his father through a tunnel made of trees pressed close together.

As the path opened, Asith heard a bustling city. The city sprawled out before them, snow gently falling into the center of the large town built inside the ring of trees, with a rocky ridge on one side that had more trees atop it. A boardwalk wrapped around the city, rising high along the inner ring of trees, that was wide enough to host houses and buildings on it. Dragons fluttered about, flying among the bridges that connected the various levels of the walkway. People carried bundles of vegetables and toolboxes as they crossed swinging bridges, unbothered by the height. Some people on the ground stopped and looked at them, curiosity in their eyes. In fact, no one had fear on their faces, nor gave nervous side eyes or crossed their arms.

In the center of the ground level, a temple reached for the treetops, with a shimmering golden roof that came to a dramatic peak. Atop it was a statue of a woman with horns like a winding path rising above her head. Her arm extended high above her head and held a bell like one would hold a lantern. In her other hand, she held a rabbit, its ears sticking straight up as it stood on her forearm, its front feet on her palm.

Asith's throat grew thick, turning into a lump, as tears ran down his face. He mumbled, "Vai would have loved this."

"We'll find them," his father assured, setting a hand on Asith's shoulder.

"I promise, I will help you find them."

He hiccupped, a void forming in his chest as he rubbed his face. Asith needed to find Dradevai, he didn't know how he'd do it, but he needed to know they were safe. His mother stepped toward him, wiping the tears from his cheeks, and hushed him softly. As they huddled around him, a weight came down on Asith's shoulders that forced him toward the ground.

Asith looked up, trying to keep himself from bending like the branch of a tree under snow, and caught sight of the statue, the rabbit in the woman's hand looking down at him. He stared at it, feeling the weight lift itself from him, and he stood straight, collecting himself.

"They are half of my heart. I am bonded to them." Asith wasn't sure where the words were coming from. They bubbled up from his stomach and left his lips tingling because he had never said anything quite like them before.

"No matter where they are, I'll find them."

To be continued...

AUTHOR | GAME MASTER | YOUTUBER

Hi there! My name is Jess Galaxie and I write books, create videos, and all around enjoy being a nerd. During the day, I work as a content marketing manager for a large enterprise, and by night I write, play Dungeons & Dragons, make costumes, and much more. You may have seen me on either my Tik Tok or my Youtube channel, where I tend to talk about my passions and create movie-length video essays about characters I love.

Beyond my hobbies, I am a member of the LGBTQIA+ community, and care deeply about advocating for, and representing my community in my writing.

www.ingramcontent.com/pod-product-compliance
Lightning Source LLC
Chambersburg PA
CBHW020105310726
48970CB00002B/481